HIGH KING
BOOK 2

UNDER THE
DRAGON

S. M. DAVIES

Preface

In the first quarter of the 5th Century AD, the Romans abandoned Britain, leaving chaos and conflict behind them. The islands were threatened with invasion on all sides, but the Emperor Honorius told the Britons that they must look to their own defences, for there would be no help from Rome.

All kinds of people were competing for power – Romanised Britons, whose families had done well under the Empire; true Romans who had spent most or all of their lives in Britain, and regarded it as home; religious leaders, with powerful allies in the hierarchy of the Christian church in Europe; British warlords with personal wealth and private armies, who saw the demise of Roman power not as a disaster, but as an opportunity. None of these seemed able or willing to form a united front against their most immediate threat; the Picts, who were ravaging the North.

In the legendary accounts, Vortigern comes out of nowhere, a man of the West with no known antecedents. He must have been a man of rank, to hold the position he did; and yet he bears a Brythonic name, meaning 'high king', and gave Brythonic names to his sons, in an era when all men of noble birth were known by Latin names. In the first instalment of his story, *The West Rises*, he blazes a trail to power with the aid of his devoted companion and greatest ally, young warrior Kerin Brightspear.

This, the second part of Vortigern's story, begins the day after the assassination of King Constans by his own bodyguard. Now Vortigern is High King, at last fulfilling the promise of the name he adopted in his youth. He owes his triumph, at least in part, to Kerin. Knowing that the roots of Vortigern's power lie with the ordinary people of city and countryside, he has orchestrated an uprising so overwhelming that opponents were powerless to resist. Even Vortigern's detractors now accept that he is their best hope of raising a united force to confront the invaders in the North.

Under The Dragon tells the story of Vortigern's campaign against the Picts and what may have happened next. Although the episode is overlooked by history, it seems that he was able to raise an army large and cohesive enough to take on opponents so ferocious that the Romans never got the better of them. He may have found this simpler than the aftermath, attempting to control a kingdom riven by power struggles and fanatical religious disputes, even before these were spiced up by the arrival of Jute mercenaries and their enterprising leader, Hengist.

As in *The West Rises*, Vortigern's story is seen through the eyes of Kerin Brightspear, the young man now known as 'the King's Right Arm'.

Characters

Those marked * are recorded in history or legend

Cambria

* Vortigern, Lord of Cambria and the West,
King of all the Britons

* Vortimer, known as Rufus, his oldest son

* Katigern, his second son

* Paschent, his youngest son

* Sevira, his late wife, daughter of Roman emperor
*Magnus Maximus

Kerin Brightspear, Vortigern's companion and confidant

Lud, Vortigern's chief warrior

Macsen, Lud's oldest son

Custennin, Lud's second son

Elir, Lud's youngest son

Mora, Lud's wife

Bened, Lud's nephew

Cynfawr, Vortigern's bard

Gwyndaf, long-standing enemy of Vortigern

Derfyn, Leil and Cadfan, Gwyndaf's young warriors

Hefydd, warlord, Vortigern's ally

Hefin, Hefydd's younger brother

Branwen, Hefydd's daughter

Idris, young warrior, ally of Rufus

Cenydd, Vortigern's principal servant

Cheldric, Kerin's Saxon cook

Morvid, aged healer, now of Kerin's household

Marc, Morvid's grandson

Mabli, daughter of Vortigern's silversmith

Londinium

Severus Maximus, the praetor

Marcellus *magister*, his physician and soothsayer

Alberius, his acolyte

Graecus, his principal servant

Dimos, one of his scribes

Lucius Arrius, head of the praetorian guard, friend to Kerin

Petrus and Silvius, servants of Lucius's father

Publius Luca, commander of the city garrison, formerly of the Second Augustan Legion

Titus Luca, lawyer, his son

Gaia Fulvia, his wife

Larentia, his daughter

Cornelius, his principal servant

Gallus, wealthy merchant, friend of Vortigern

Horatius, Marcellus's assistant

Ashur, Alberius's stable boy

Glevum

* Eldof, Lord of Glevum

Varro, his chief warrior

Bertil Redknife, his kinsman and rival

Gael, Bertil's daughter

Morwen, Gael's servant

Balin, Bertil's chief warrior

Malan, elderly headman of a village in Eldof's territory

Flora, Malan's granddaughter

Berget, Malan's daughter

Edryd, blacksmith of Calleva, attached to Malan's company

Other warlords and their associates

* Gorlois of Kernow, Vortigern's loyal supporter

Gerdan, his younger brother

* Garagon of Kent

Brennius, Garagon's friend and warrior

Edlym, Garagon's uncle

Livia, Garagon's sister

The Jutes

* Hengist, leader of Vortigern's mercenaries
* Horsa, his brother
* Aelle, his nephew
* Rowenna, his daughter

Oswi the Horseman, a leading warrior

Priests and monks

Father Paulinus, abbot of Venta Belgarum,
ally of Rufus

Brother Padarn, of the same monastery,
man of the North

Father Iustig, abbot of Caerwenn,
near Vortigern's citadel

* Bishop Eldadus of Glevum, brother of Eldof

Father Septimus of Glevum, loyal friend of Gael

Father Giraldus of St Alban's chapel in Londinium

Caradog, Chief Druid of Henfelin, Vortigern's capital

Glossary of place names

Aquae Sulis - Bath

Armorica - Brittany

Blestium - Monmouth

Caerwynt - Winchester

Calleva (Atrebatum) - Silchester

Camulodunum - Colchester

Corinium - Cirencester

Durobrivae - Water Newton

Durovernum - Canterbury

Eburacum - York

Gallia - Gaul, France

Glevum - Gloucester

Glywysing* - The Glamorgans

Gwy - River Wye

Hafren - River Severn

Isca (Silurum) - Caerleon

Kernow - Cornwall

Leucarum - Llwchwr, Loughor

Moridunum - Caerfyrddin, Carmarthen

Vectis - Isle of Wight

Venta Belgarum - Winchester

Venta (Silurum) - Caerwent

*Glywysing was the name of the ancient Welsh kingdom which included all the Glamorgans; its boundaries changed over time, but it generally extended from the Tywi in the west to the Wye, or at times the Severn.

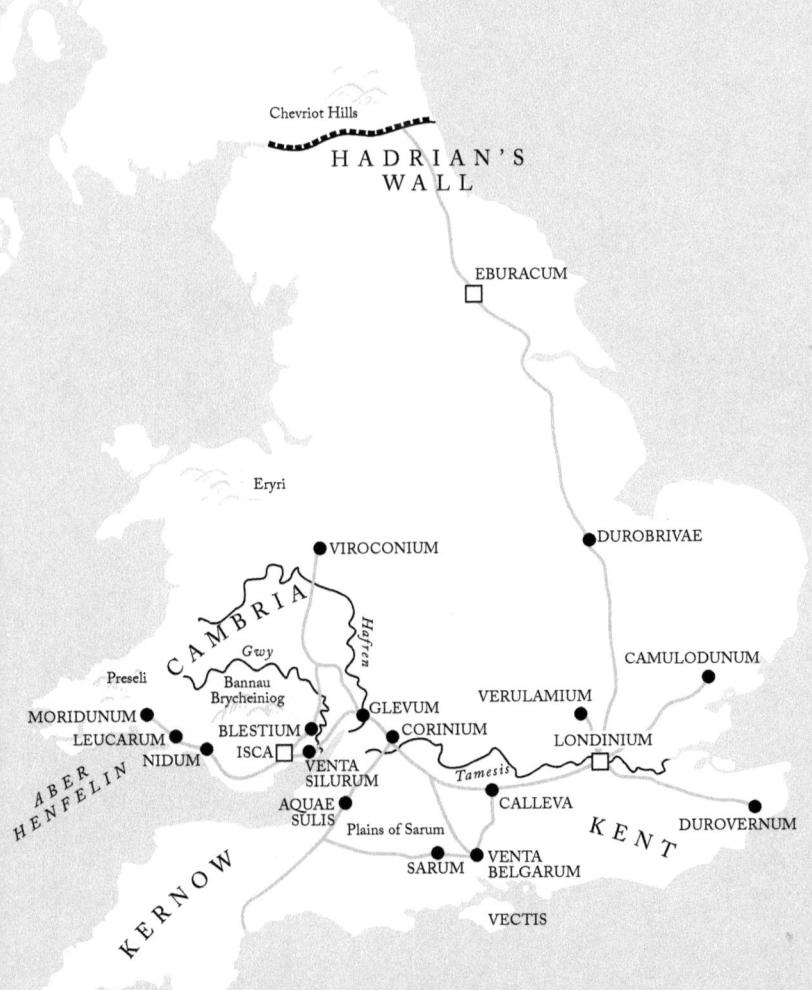

Chevriot Hills

HADRIAN'S
WALL

EBURACUM

Eryri

VIROCONIUM

DUROBRIVAE

CAMBRIA

Gwy

Hafren

CAMULODUNUM

Preseli

Bannau
Brycheiniog

GLEVUM

VERULAMIUM

MORIDUNUM

CORINIUM

LONDINIUM

LEUCARUM

BLESTIUM

NIDUM

ISCA

VENTA
SILURUM

Tamesis

DUROVERNUM

ABER
HENFELIN

AQUAE
SULIS

Plains of Sarum

CALLEVA

KENT

KERNOW

SARUM

VENTA
BELGARUM

VECTIS

To Isla and James

1

There was a beach like this a day's ride from Kerin's home. No cliffs; simply a vast expanse of sand and a fringe of dunes running away out of sight. Kerin couldn't get up. He felt as if he had a colossal weight pressing down upon him, immobilising his limbs and making it difficult to breathe. He remembered a time, an age ago, when Macsen and his little brothers had dug a hole on this beach and buried him up to his neck. He had never forgotten the feeling of utter helplessness. It was all in fun, of course; Macsen had come and dug him out long before the tide reached him. But Macsen was not coming this time, and the tide was rising.

Someone was hammering something close at hand. Kerin glanced around, trying to locate the sound, then felt something cold and wet running down his face. He blinked it away, and found that Lucius Arrius was sitting on him. For a moment he wondered what the head of the praetorian guard was doing on the beach, then he realised that he was lying fully-clothed on his bed in the praetor's house.

'I'm sorry,' said Lucius, who was holding a dripping rag. 'For squashing the breath out of you and for soaking you. I've been trying to wake you for a while. The king is asking to see you. He's still in the praetor's library.'

The king! For a brief moment, before his sleep-addled brain re-emerged into the present, Kerin's only thought was: the king cannot have asked for me. King Constans is dead.

I saw his butchered body, fingers missing, flesh hanging in gobbets from his naked arms and legs. I saw his head, hacked off with a dagger that looked like a fishmonger's knife. But then reality seeped in and he remembered the aftermath, and knew that his life had changed forever.

'You can't go like that,' Lucius said. 'I told the servants to bring water. You stink, and there's blood all over your tunic. I'll see you down in the courtyard when you're done.'

Kerin heaved himself out of bed, threw off his clothes and hurried naked into the bathhouse. His thoughts were still in disarray. He had now witnessed two coronations in six months, and neither had been remotely normal. Kings and emperors were supposed to come into their glory with a fanfare, congratulations and an orgy of feasting and strong drink. Nothing like that was happening here. The monks of St Alban had probably been awake all night, cleaning up after the only assassination their chapel had seen. It would have fallen to them, to deal with the bodies of victims and murderers; the king and his servant-lover preserved, the dead Picts piled outside in the street for the military to remove once they had dragged the survivors away.

Kerin plunged into the bathtub. The stench of blood and sweat rose as the hot water closed over his body. There was no time for luxury this morning. He climbed out, towelled himself dry and pulled on the clean clothes which the servants had laid out on his bed. They had placed a mirror on the side table; a hint, possibly. He barely recognised the young man who had left his home in Cambria less than ten months earlier. It felt more like ten years, and his face told the tale. Fine lines around the eyes, and probably around the mouth too, if they hadn't been obscured by a few days' growth. Usually he kept himself clean-shaven these days, like the lads of Roman descent, but there had barely been time to breathe, let alone for vanity. His thick brown hair straggled down to his shoulders like a damp dog's. He knew that he looked pale and drawn, and supposed that only time would cure him. He had not slept long enough, or deeply enough, to feel rested. Vortigern had probably not slept at all. The new king went straight from the chapel to Severus Maximus's library, and was still there, as a chill yellow dawn came up over the city and the empty streets resounded to the thud of carpenters' mallets. The scaffold in the square outside the curia was almost complete. Probably the captive Picts could hear the hammering too as they lay in their chains in the dungeon of the castra, waiting for the guards to come.

The praetor's courtyard was packed with men, some wearing the distinctive red and gold livery of the praetorian messengers. Others looked as if they might have been dragged in to make up the numbers. They were the ones with the air of purpose and the fit, fast-looking horses. Kerin threaded his way through the crowd. Many respectful nods greeted him. He knew what these men were waiting for. Royal decrees, authorising a tax to finance the protection of the seaways from Pictish attackers, were to be dispatched to the ordo of every significant town in the kingdom. The decrees had been prepared by the praetor's scribes before the assassination of King Constans, and had lain in the praetor's library for days on end, waiting for the king to stop dithering. Now they would go, bearing a brand-new seal which carried the inscription *Vurtigurnus Rex*; and even Kerin, with his smattering of Latin, had no difficulty in understanding what that meant.

No-one was taking any chances. Two beheaded monarchs were enough for any kingdom preparing to deal with an invasion. Kerin himself had ordered the guard on the library door. He had taken the first watch, accompanied by Gorlois of Kernow and a bunch of picked warriors. Now it was Publius Luca barring the entrance, heading a detachment of his city garrison who might have been selected for their size and ugliness.

'Go straight in,' said the commander. 'You're the only man I have leave to admit.'

Kerin went in and closed the door behind him. Vortigern was sitting at the polished table. It was littered with used pens and pots of ink. At one end was a stack of bound documents; the fleet tax decrees, which Kerin had seen last time he was in this room. Beside them lay fifty or more tubes of rolled papyrus, each bearing an inscription and closed with the king's seal. There were a few slimmer tubes, sealed and bound with fine black cord. Vortigern gave a hollow smile and pushed out the chair at his side. Large-eyed and drained of energy, he looked like a ghost of himself.

'Are you done here?' Kerin asked, as he sat down.

'Yes,' Vortigern said. 'In every sense.' There had been no time to sleep or eat, far less for a change of clothes. Above the faint scent of beeswax, Kerin could smell the dried blood of Constans and his killer, Bridei the Pict. Vortigern's shaggy black hair was crusted down one side with it. Kerin remembered watching the blood run over his hands and up his sleeves when he seized Constans's severed head from the point of Bridei's dagger.

'These are your responsibility now,' Vortigern said, waving towards the signed documents. 'The fleet tax decrees, as you know. The formal letters, requesting support for the campaign against the Picts in the North. And a few personal messages for good men who deserve them. Two of the praetor's servants are collecting the messengers' bags.

One of his scribes will sort the documents according to destination. After that, it's up to you to send the best men with the best horses on the worst journeys. You'll be the most hated man in the city by the time you're done.'

Kerin smiled. 'I can take it,' he said. Now that he had a purpose, it was easier to relegate the sight of Constans's mutilated body to a dark corner where he could ignore it for the time being. 'Go and sleep. We don't need another dead king. I'll ask Publius and his men to stand guard.'

'I'll wash the blood off first, I think.' Vortigern picked up a large key which was lying on the table and handed it to Kerin. 'Lock this room behind you. Then, when you're done with the documents, go to the praetor's apartments and remove the duplicate from the bunch he keeps over there. Nothing that happens in here is his business. If you can think of any other rooms that only you and I should be able to access, get the keys for those as well. I'm beyond thinking at the moment.'

'The wine cellar,' Kerin said. Vortigern grinned and cuffed him over the head, then went to allow himself to be escorted to his chambers. Kerin surveyed the piles of documents with a mixture of pride and apprehension. The king's right arm. It had taken him all of his twenty-five years to reach this point, but the shock had passed. The pride and elation which followed still warmed his heart, an unquenchable flame.

* * *

There were no arguments. A few long faces from the men who feared being dispatched to the North and the furthest tip of Kernow, but no opposition. Kerin had sorted men and horses into a column which snaked around the perimeter of the courtyard, the strongest at the front. Now he stood below the statue of Minerva with the praetor's scribe, who had the messengers' bags stacked behind him. Lucius had come along with a pair of his guards. They were keeping a watchful eye on proceedings, standing on the steps under the portico with spears in hand.

'Vinovia,' Kerin said to the first pair, dark, whip-thin brothers on powerful raw-boned bay mares. 'The largest for the head of the administration. The others for landowners to east and west.' One of the men leaned down and took the bag with a rueful smile. 'I picked the best for the longest journeys,' Kerin said. 'Take pride in it. Wait for replies. The king needs to know how things stand. These men are amongst the furthest north, so they'll have had the most trouble. They should be glad to know that there's an army on the way.' He took a saddlebag from another pile and handed it to the second brother. 'Enough food for a few days. They should provision you at Vinovia. If they refuse, tell them the king commanded it. Now, ride. God speed. We're depending on you.'

The messengers saluted and turned for the gateway. The scribe, a thin, fair-haired man of middle age, gave Kerin a guarded smile. 'That was more of a send-off than they usually get. As a rule it's just a bark and a kick in the backside.'

'Well, let's see what works best,' Kerin said, as the next pair edged forward. The time went surprisingly quickly. By midday, the courtyard was empty apart from a gang of slaves sweeping up piles of dung and dumping them into an ox cart.

'How long have you been with the praetor?' Kerin asked the scribe.

'Since I was a boy, lord,' said the other man. 'I was born in Antioch, but my father was a tutor to one of the patrician families, so we moved around with them. Judaea for a while, then Egypt. Eventually the head of the household took up a post here, so we all came too. My father had seen to my education, so I could write in Greek and Coptic as well as Latin. Severus Maximus offered me employment straight away. My name's Dimos, by the way. My father was a Roman citizen, but my mother was Greek, and she insisted on a Greek name. In the end my father caved in.' He raised an eyebrow. 'My mother was quite forceful.'

'Well then, Dimos, what do you get up to when you're not keeping records for the praetor? It can't take up all of your time, surely.'

'I teach some of the patricians' children,' Dimos said. 'Lucius Arrius over there was one of my first pupils. Quite sharp, but he couldn't concentrate. His sister Julia was a different pot of stew altogether. Not all the families bother to educate their daughters, but Marcus Arrius was quite enlightened in that respect. The older daughter, from his first marriage, can write as well as I can. I'm sure you'll have had a good teacher, as one of the king's household.'

'I did,' Kerin said, 'but I was like Lucius. I couldn't concentrate. Now I regret it. If could read, I wouldn't have needed a scribe to do it for me. So my next question, Dimos, is this. Do you think you could teach an ignorant warrior like me how to read? I'd pay you well, since it would probably be a painful process.'

Dimos smiled. It was a pleasant, open smile, completely devoid of irony or mockery. 'Why not? It would be an interesting challenge for both of us.'

Kerin tried to assess the scribe's age, but it was difficult. His features were fine and sharp, and in profile looked as if they might have been drawn by a fresco artist. His white belted tunic and sandals enhanced the impression. But there were deep lines on his forehead, etched by time or other things. Forty or thereabouts, Kerin speculated. Old enough to have a wife and children, but none had been mentioned as yet.

'Would you be free to leave if you wished?' he asked. 'I'd like to make some progress before I'm an old man too short-sighted to see the script.'

Dimos grinned. 'That'll come to me first. And yes, I'm free to leave; I have no dependants and I'm not under any legal obligation to the praetor. But it would be dishonourable to leave without giving notice.'

'Good,' Kerin said. 'That's as it should be.' The scribe's reply had pleased him. It would be no bad thing to employ a man who honoured his commitments. There would be no time for learning before the campaign in the North; but Kerin was confident that, when the king's army returned to Londinium, Dimos would be waiting for him with a pile of manuscripts and papyrus. His own part of the bargain would be to survive the months between.

2

Marcellus was at the table in his treatment room when Kerin arrived. He was poring over a small white dog which was sitting on the table, secured to one of the legs by a leather leash. It was a scene of incongruous domestic tranquillity, after the horrible bloodshed of the night before. A servant was hovering outside the door. The dog had a hole in its neck, probably inflicted by the canine tooth of something much larger. Kerin did not entirely succeed in suppressing a laugh. He had never supposed that Marcellus had more than one use for animals. The haruspex heard him come in, and looked up with an expression of acute embarrassment.

'It belongs to the wife of Severus Maximus,' he said. 'Please understand that I do not usually do this sort of thing, but the praetor's wife can be surprisingly forthright. And of course, she loves the dog far more than she loves the praetor, so there's little point in argument.'

Kerin smiled at the dog. It wagged its tail timidly and sniffed his hand. 'What happened to it?' he asked.

'It escaped from the garden and got into a fight with a mangy hound in the marketplace,' Marcellus said, reaching for a small glass bottle. 'It looks a gentle creature, but it isn't at all; it's a belligerent little beast. Now, would you please hold it for me while I dress its wound? It won't like it when I apply this tincture, I can promise you.'

Kerin planted one hand on the dog's shoulders and held

its muzzle gently with the other. The dog yelped as the thin, yellowish liquid dripped into the hole in its neck. Kerin tightened his grip. The dog scrabbled and squirmed, and a vicious snarling growl came from between its clamped jaws.

'You see?' Marcellus said, pressing a pad over the wound. 'I told you it was a nasty piece of work. I had less trouble with poor Tertius, I'm glad to say.'

'How is he?' Kerin asked.

'Uncomfortable, but he'll make a full recovery. I am less sure about Livius. He has lost a great deal of blood, and he has yet to wake.' Marcellus secured the pad with a strip of cloth. Kerin cautiously released the dog. It gave him a baleful look, as if it felt that its trust had been sadly misplaced.

'It is done, then,' Marcellus said, lifting the dog down from the table and handing its leash to the servant. Kerin waited until the sound of footsteps and skittering claws had faded away.

'Done? What do you mean by that, exactly?'

Marcellus looked up with a candid smile. 'I mean that Vortigern is king, as we both knew that he would be.'

'It wasn't *done*, exactly,' Kerin said uneasily. 'You can't think we had anything to do with killing Constans, surely.'

'No,' Marcellus said. 'We both know that the Picts killed Constans. But we also know, better than most men, that things like this are part of a larger design. So whilst it is manifestly true that Vortigern did not kill Constans, it is also true that he was, shall we say, a little careless in his choice of protectors for the king.' He looked up enquiringly. There was no point in argument.

'Who do you think let the Picts out of the guard room?' Kerin asked.

'I have no idea. But it must have been someone who had a clear understanding of what he was doing, besides having access to the appropriate key. Surely, very few men could have been in that position.'

'We may never know,' Kerin said.

'I'm sure we shall, sooner or later. But in any case, it should not be our first concern. Shall we go to see Tertius, or would you like to tell me about your powers of foresight? I realise that you have misgivings about them, of course.'

Kerin grimaced. He felt on edge, but had not realised that it was obvious. 'Let's see Tertius,' he said. 'I need to think before I talk about all that.'

'Marcellus *magister!*' a voice called. 'Livius wakes!'

'Come,' Marcellus said. 'Tertius must wait. If Livius has anything to say, you should hear it too.'

They hurried inside. The servant was bending over Livius, who was staring up at the lofty ceiling with vacant eyes.

'Thank you, Horatius,' Marcellus murmured. He stepped to the bedside and took one of Livius's limp hands. Horatius padded silently away and returned with two small earthenware jars, a bowl of water and a clean white cloth. Marcellus took one of the jars and added a few drops of its contents to the bowl, then he wrung the cloth out in the water and pressed it to Livius's brow. Kerin peered over Marcellus's shoulder. Livius's eyes flickered with recognition.

'I'm sorry, lord,' he whispered.

'There was nothing you could have done,' Kerin said.

'Livius Gaius, did you see who did this to you?' Marcellus asked.

'No,' Livius said weakly. 'I felt the knife, that's all. But Marcellus *magister*, that was afterwards. Someone knocked me silly, but I heard them talking as they dragged me behind the fountain. They spoke in a tongue I didn't know. Not Latin, not British. Nothing I've ever heard our slaves speaking. When my head cleared I started to get up, and then I felt the knife go in.'

11

Kerin's eyes met Marcellus's, and the look they exchanged held an equal measure of mystification. Marcellus took the second of the little jars which Horatius had brought, gently raised Livius's head and put the rim to his lips. Livius sipped, spluttered and sank back onto his pillow with a groan.

'Something for the fever,' Marcellus said. 'He'll sleep again now, please the gods. Sit with him, Horatius, and call me at once if you are worried.' He beckoned to Kerin, and they retreated to the garden. One of the resident doves flew up to Marcellus's shoulder and perched there, preening itself and cooing softly. 'He will live now, probably, as long as there is no poison of the blood,' Marcellus said. He looked up as Horatius closed the door. 'Well then, Kerin Brightspear, what did you make of that?'

'I'm as wise as you are,' Kerin said. 'Men who speak neither Latin nor British, nor any of the slaves' tongues? God knows. Was the weapon found?'

'No,' Marcellus said. 'From the size of the wound, I'd say it was something finer than the knives most warriors carry, but such knives are everywhere; every butcher and fishmonger has at least one in his workshop.'

'The Picts probably did it,' Kerin said. 'They all carry knives like that. But someone else clubbed Livius over the head. That's the real mystery. Who unlocked the guard room and let the Picts out?'

Marcellus threw his hands up. 'The gods know. In truth, I think it hardly matters. Constans is dead, the Picts are dead, and if you and I are honest with ourselves, we're glad on both counts.' He turned as another of his trainees came padding into the garden.

'Your pardon, Marcellus *magister*,' the lad said, 'but there's someone here for Lord Kerin. One of the monks, Brother Padarn.'

The haruspex raised his thin eyebrows. 'Show him in, then. We may as well get all the bad news over with.'

'He won't come in, master,' the lad said. 'He looks quite upset. Or angry. I'm not sure. Will you come out to him, lord? He's waiting in the courtyard.'

Marcellus patted Kerin's arm. 'Go,' he said. 'Padarn's a sensible fellow, and wouldn't have come for no reason. We have things to discuss, but they will keep until you have dealt with this.'

* * *

'I had to see you, Lord Kerin,' said Brother Padarn, shaking his head as if the prospect gave him no pleasure. He was pale and heavy-eyed, and looked as if he hadn't slept a wink. The courtyard was deserted and clean, though the stench of horse-dung and sweat still clung. They sat down below the statue of Minerva. 'That praetor Flavius has only gone and sent for Father Paulinus. Last night, before the body was even cold. How long will it take?'

'That depends,' Kerin said. 'If the messenger had a good horse and rode through the night, he should be there by now.'

'So Paulinus could be here soon.'

'It's possible. What will you do, now that you no longer have Constans to look after?'

'I'm staying,' Padarn said doggedly. 'I've still got my reasons for going north with you, if you want me to.'

'I do,' Kerin said. 'Now then. Have they buried Constans yet?'

'Not yet, lord.' Padarn sounded a little shocked.

'Do it, then,' Kerin said. 'Do it now, and do it quietly. Either that, or lose the body.'

'Lose the body?' Padarn said, appalled.

'I mean it,' Kerin said. 'The last thing we need is for Paulinus to get hold of a martyr. The next thing you know, he'll have buried Constans in some enormous tomb, and everyone will be making pilgrimages to his shrine.'

Padarn scratched his scarred crown. 'I hadn't thought of that. And I can see why you're not too bothered. You didn't even like him, did you.'

'Constans?' Kerin said. 'No, not much. That doesn't mean I wanted him killed like this. But you can't be a monk and a king. He had the choice, back in your monastery.'

'Well, I know that,' Padarn said. 'The trouble was, he'd had a sight of luxury at home, when he was a littl'un. The cloister wasn't his choice, and when he saw a way out, greed got the better of him.'

'You're probably right,' Kerin said, 'but you'd have to be even more stupid than Constans was, not to see the danger in it.'

'Oh, he knew there was danger in it, alright. He just couldn't see where the danger was coming from.' Padarn's knowing dark eyes held Kerin's, and he gave a little nod, as if to confirm that they both understood what that meant.

'Alright,' Kerin said. 'Come on. Let's do it. I'll come and help you.'

Kerin had been in the chapel of St Alban more than once, but never in this room; a tiny windowless box, as bare as a monk's cell except for a long trestle table brought from the refectory where the monks ate their frugal meals. On it lay the body of Constans. Now that he had been wrapped in a white shroud, it was not obvious that his head had been hacked off. Someone had gone to some trouble to position the body parts as naturally as possible; probably the provider of the embalming oils whose heavy scent filled the tiny space. Two candles burned at the head and foot of the bier, their flames wavering, starved of air. A second body, similarly enshrouded, was lying on the floor beside the table.

'Who's that?' Kerin murmured. It would be unseemly to raise his voice in here, he felt.

'Lupinus,' Padarn said softly. 'The two guardsmen's families came round and claimed the bodies, but no-one seemed to want this one. You'd think the praetor would have seen to it; the boy served him for long enough.'

They turned, hearing the quiet pad of footsteps. Father Giraldus came in, looked at the bodies and crossed himself.

'Father, Brother Padarn and I want to see to the burial,' Kerin said. 'I don't know if anyone has told you, but Father Paulinus has been sent for.'

The abbot closed his eyes and sighed. 'Who on earth did that? Don't we have enough to contend with?'

'Yes, we do,' Kerin said. 'And I'd like to get it done before Paulinus arrives, in case he has any ideas about claiming the body. It was Flavius, the praetor of Eburacum, who sent for him. He's not a bad man; I don't think he understood what he might be meddling with, that's all.'

'Indeed,' Giraldus said briskly. 'Well then, let's proceed. Burials aren't permitted within the walls unless you're a rich man and can afford a private mausoleum, but we do have a patch of consecrated ground not far from the western gate. We use it for the poor sick souls we can't save. I'll come with you to give a blessing, and we'll take two of the heftier brothers to help dig the grave.' He glanced at the shrouded body on the floor. 'And I suggest that we bury this young man with Brother Constans. They lay together in life often enough; they may as well lie together in death.'

Kerin smothered a laugh; it was the last thing he had

expected to hear from an abbot. 'Bless you, Father Giraldus. You're a man of the world.'

'It comes to you when you live in a midden like Londinium,' Giraldus said. 'Now, bring a cart – to the rear door, Brother Padarn, the one where the sick congregate. I'll meet you there shortly with the burial party.'

Kerin went straight to Severus Maximus's stables. No-one was likely to argue if he said that he wanted to borrow a cart. Lud's youngest son Elir was there as usual, tending the Cambrian horses.

'I need you to do something for me,' Kerin said. 'Get two of the praetor's horses out and harness them to one of those carts they use for the fodder. Then saddle a horse for yourself and bring everything out into the courtyard. Brother Padarn is waiting there for us. He'll drive the cart.'

'Where are we going?' Elir asked.

'I'll tell you when we're on the way. And I want you fully armed.' Kerin liked Elir and thought that he could probably trust his discretion, but there was no point in taking unnecessary risks. He went to the stall where his warhorse stood and slipped in beside her. She had heard him, of course, and greeted him with a soft nickering sound and a shove of the head. 'Patience,' Kerin said, slipping the bridle on. 'We have work to do. And no killing today, please. We've had enough of that for the time being.'

The guards on the city gate, members of the city garrison, saluted and moved aside to let the cart and its escort pass through. Kerin gave them a smile and a courteous nod.

'Well, that was painless,' Elir said, as they moved out onto the Roman road.

'Of course,' Kerin said. 'They're probably terrified of the

king's little finger. But all the same, I don't want you to tell anyone else what's in that cart.'

Elir glanced over his shoulder at the wagon, rumbling along with Brother Padarn and Father Giraldus sitting up at the front. Two well-built monks were squatting in the back alongside the cargo, which they had covered with a heavy brown sheet. 'What is it, then?' he asked.

'The bodies of Constans and Lupinus,' Kerin said, eyes on the road ahead.

'Oh!' Elir exclaimed. He recovered himself almost instantly and effected nonchalance. 'Why?' he asked, keeping his voice low. 'He was the king, after all. Shouldn't there be something – well, more official? More grand?'

'No,' Kerin said. 'By no means. Would it be a good idea if Rufus decided to challenge his father for the kingship?'

'Gods, no,' Elir said. 'But what has that got to do with burying Constans?'

'More than you think,' Kerin said. 'Father Paulinus is on his way here now. If he gets hold of Constans's body, he'll set up a huge memorial, and then you'll have hordes of people coming to pay their respects. Not good-hearted Christians like the men behind us. Mad bastards like Idris, who want to rid the kingdom of pagans like you, and murderers like Vortigern – that's what they'll say, believe me – and even of wise religious like Padarn and Giraldus. And they'll all put their shoulders behind Rufus, because he's the nearest thing they can see to a pure Christian leader, who would make a pure Christian king. So are you going to keep quiet about this, and help me bury these two nameless bodies in an unmarked grave that no-one can find?'

Elir swallowed hard. 'Yes,' he said. 'That's exactly what I'm going to do.'

'Here,' Padarn shouted as they approached the burial ground. 'Here on the left, behind the bushes.' Kerin drew rein and allowed the wagon to go first. He had ridden past this spot countless times without noticing that the tall, unkempt blackthorn and elder concealed rows of anonymous mounds. The perimeter was thick with coarse grass and weeds. The area simply looked like an extension of the waste ground beyond, which was uneven, overgrown and littered with broken wagons and hand carts left there to rot. Kerin and Elir dismounted, tied their horses to the elders and walked to the spot where Father Giraldus was standing, watching the three monks hacking a pit from the stony ground.

'You don't mark the graves, then,' Kerin said.

'It's impossible.' Giraldus cast an eye over the rows of sad mounds. 'Most of these poor souls came to us without a name. And for every one we bury, there are two more waiting at the back door of the chapel with their broken limbs or terrible ailments. If there were more hours in the day I'd care for this space, perhaps plant a few pretty trees and so forth, but usually I barely have time to tend to the living. I think God may forgive me, though. We did our best for them while they lived.'

'It's beyond praise, what you do,' Kerin said. 'Now, I know that you and Brother Padarn will be discreet, but can we rely on the other two brothers not to speak about this burial?'

'I can vouch for them,' Giraldus said. 'They're good men who didn't have much joy in their lives before they came to God. We've found a way to serve Him which depends on loving one's fellow men, not on some ascetic's ideas of purity. God preserve us all from the cruel faith that Paulinus preaches.'

The three monks had finished digging the grave. Kerin and Elir lifted the two shrouded bodies from the cart and lowered them down with the ropes which Padarn had brought. Giraldus said a brief prayer in Latin. Everyone crossed himself, even Elir, who didn't believe a word of it. The monks shovelled the earth back into the hole and made a mound over it. Padarn scattered it with a few stones, dug up some clumps of grass and planted them in the drying ground. The grave was already almost indistinguishable from all the others. It was a wretched end for a king, Kerin thought; but then, Constans had never been king in anything but name. Now he didn't even have a name to take with him into the otherworld. That was the pity of it; the real indignity.

Eryr heard the sound first. Kerin and Elir were watching the monks heading back towards the city in the praetor's cart, looking as if they'd just been cultivating some little vegetable patch. Kerin felt the mare stiffen under him. He heard the rumble in her throat, saw her ears flatten against her skull. His own hearing was better than most people's, but the mare's ears were keener still. He knew what all her little mannerisms presaged. Whoever was coming, she had divined that they posed a threat.

'On guard,' Kerin said, looking where the mare was looking. 'I don't know who's coming, but it's not a friend.' Elir eased his sword in its scabbard. Both men held their spears along their horses' necks, unobtrusive but ready for instant use. Kerin could hear the sound now; a group of men on good horses, making a fast pace over the cobbles. There were twenty of them, he saw, as they emerged from the muddle of carts and packhorses on the Roman road; the first few on matched white horses, all dressed identically in the white tunics, emblazoned with a blue cross, which he remembered from the previous night in the curia. The Sword of God.

Pale grey cloaks streamed behind them. They looked like a troop of guardsmen in the pay of some aristocratic master. Rufus was not with them, but Kerin would have recognised Idris anywhere, even in these unfamiliar clothes. They were followed by a bunch of youngsters on rough-and-ready ponies. Kerin saw Idris's eyes flick towards him as they drew level.

'Idris,' he said sharply. 'A word.' He had been in two minds, whether to accost the lad or simply have his troop followed; but there was no ignoring the contempt which those dark eyes held. Idris reined in.

'What?' he asked bluntly.

'What are you about?' Kerin asked. 'You and those men? And if you've got the nerve to tell me that it's none of my business, I'll put you on the road.' It was no idle threat. Kerin noted the way Idris checked the position of the spear lying along Eryr's neck. His skill with the weapon was so well-known, even men who had never met him talked about it.

'We're summoned by the Lord Vortimer,' Idris said. 'To a meeting of true Christians who deplore the rise of heresy and unbelief in this kingdom. We mean to lay our fears before God and pray for His guidance. Is that forbidden?'

'No,' Kerin said, remembering the last time Idris had asked him this question. 'Not in itself. But don't forget what I told you. Your first obligation is not to the Lord Vortimer. It's to his father.'

Idris gave a sly smile. 'Well, at least the Lord Vortimer knows who his father is.'

Kerin saw Elir's right hand tighten on his sword hilt, and laid a hand on his wrist. 'The Lord Vortimer is the king's son,' he said. 'But I am the king's right arm. Ask anyone.'

Idris grimaced. It was grudging, but Kerin knew that he had made his point.

'Alright there?' one of the white-clad men called.

'Yes,' Idris said, and gave Kerin a cocky little nod. 'You were wrong about obligation, anyway. My first obligation is to God.'

Kerin and Elir sat on their horses and watched the party jogging away down the road.

'I told you he was a prick,' Elir said. 'And now he's a god-fearing prick. Let me know if you need any more help. The thing about having older brothers like Macsen and Custennin is, no-one notices you very much. You can slip around doing stuff, because they're big red-haired war gods and you're a skinny little dark thing like your mother used to be.'

Kerin smothered a laugh. It was hard to remember that Elir's mother had ever been a skinny little dark thing. 'I'll let you know,' he said. 'But for now, just remember to keep your mouth shut.'

'Of course,' Elir said. 'Everyone calls me the horse handler. And that's what I've been doing out here. Training this new horse.'

'This ten-year-old new horse,' Kerin agreed, as they turned towards the city.

3

The seven bodies dangled in the cool wind, six hanging by the neck and one by the feet; Bridei, Kerin supposed, although the kites had done enough to make identity uncertain. A little knot of adults and children had gathered at the foot of the gallows, watching the large fork-tailed birds continue their leisurely feast. The doors of the curia were closed, and guarded as usual by two members of the city garrison. They recognised Kerin and saluted respectfully.

'Is the king here?' Kerin asked. It would be a while before it came naturally.

'Yes, sir,' the older guard said. 'I must ask your name, sir, if you don't mind. He was very insistent that no-one should go in except the Lord Kerin Brightspear.'

'That's me,' Kerin said. The guard coughed politely.

'He said you would be wearing a silver crucifix with a small silver ring on the chain, sir.' Kerin reached inside his tunic for the items. The guard smiled when he saw the ring, touched perhaps by its smallness and delicacy. 'A token from your wife, sir?'

'Er – yes,' Kerin said, because it seemed easier to agree than to explain. Once the words were out, he was surprised to realise how much he wished that they were true. I cannot pass Glevum without seeing her, he thought, as the guard opened the door for him; even if I find that she only gave me the ring out of thanks, for freeing her from Gadlyn. Not a breath of air disturbed the quietness within. Vortigern was sitting, alone and quite still, on the high dais from which Severus and Publius Luca had witnessed the accomplishment of his first impossible victory. Kerin climbed the steps and sat beside him on the stone bench. For a while neither spoke. There was a glow in Vortigern's eyes, the warm, fierce light of ambition achieved; and Kerin knew then, if he had ever doubted it, that this was where the road to Constans's monastery had always been destined to end.

'I thought I might find you here, lord,' he said. Vortigern looked round.

'None of this *Lord King* nonsense from you, then.'

Kerin pursed his lips. 'I can do it if you like.' Vortigern smiled and shook his head.

'No. There's some pleasure in hearing it from people who'd have spat on me this time last year, but I hope never to hear it from you.' He seemed himself again now; rested but alert. Like a wolf lying in front of the den, Macsen had once said. It looks at ease, but it isn't. It could have you in two paces if it wanted to. As always, Vortigern wore black; an ordinary cloak and breeches, and a simple woven tunic against which the golden clipeum gleamed. He had dispensed with the crown which Giraldus bestowed upon him in the Chapel of St Alban. In the end, Kerin supposed, he had no need for it. The West had answered to him for more than twenty years, and in all that time he had never dressed any more regally than his warriors. Perhaps he saw little reason to change, for the benefit of men he despised. 'We have hardly spoken since we left the chapel,' Vortigern said. 'What do you think of it all?'

'That we should waste no more time and get on with things,' Kerin said. 'You told me yourself that there's no profit in remorse.'

'Remorse? Is that what you think I should feel?'

'No,' Kerin said. 'However it happened, there'd be no point. Constans is dead now, and more people are glad than sorry. You may not be king by everyone's consent, but no man ever is. You have the blessing of most people who matter, and that's more than anyone thought possible. We're secure for now, I'm sure. But Padarn's brought some news. Flavius of Eburacum sent for Abbot Paulinus just after Constans was killed, and he's expected in the city at any moment.'

Vortigern stared up at the vaulted roof. 'The meddling idiot.'

'We've buried Constans,' Kerin said. 'It doesn't matter where. The fewer people who know the better. The most important thing was to get it done. We don't need a martyr's tomb for the faithful to visit.'

There was a knock at the outer door. A guard came in cautiously. Kerin ran down the steps to meet him.

'Publius Luca's outside, sir,' the man said quietly. 'I know the king told us to admit no-one, but Publius Luca's my commanding officer, sir, and it's rather difficult for me to refuse him.'

Kerin looked up. 'Publius Luca.' Vortigern nodded. 'Let him in,' Kerin said, 'but no-one else.' Vortigern came down the steps. The garrison commander looked as imperturbably calm as ever.

'The Abbot Paulinus is approaching the city gates, sir. He's in battle gear, and riding at the head of an armed troop. Do you want me to stop him entering the city, or shall we let him in and see what happens?'

'Let him in,' Vortigern sighed. 'I'll have to talk to him sooner or later. Just make sure that you take enough men to deal with whoever he's got with him.'

'It looks like the city garrison of Venta Belgarum, sir. To

be truthful, they'll probably take more notice of me than of the abbot, but I think it would be wise to avoid killing another cleric just now, don't you?'

Vortigern gave a wry smile. 'Just meet them and bring them to the square outside.' Publius Luca bowed and marched for the door. 'Publius!' Vortigern said sharply. 'Is my son with them?'

'I didn't see him, sir.'

'Well, so be it,' Vortigern said. He looked hard at Kerin as the outer door closed. 'What will Rufus do now, do you think?'

'I don't know, lord. A year ago I could probably have told you, but not any more.' It was on the tip of Kerin's tongue to say something about Idris and the pledge of faith which had got him thrown out of his father's house, but it couldn't be said now, when Paulinus was moments from the gate. Vortigern took off the clipeum and let it rotate slowly on the end of its chain.

'It's not every day that his father becomes king,' he said, watching the medallion as it spun and caught the light from the windows. 'He should be here to offer his congratulations, don't you think?'

'Yes, I do,' Kerin said. 'Unless, of course, he can't offer them; in which case he's better off where he is, for your sake as well as his own.'

Vortigern looked up. 'You know, you've grown years older in this place.' There was a commotion outside in the square. Men shouted, hooves rattled and above it all the sharp, high voice of Paulinus rose like a raptor's screech. 'Well,' Vortigern said, 'if that's the word of God, we're better off with the druids. Come on; let's get it over with.'

The Abbot Paulinus had dismounted and was standing with his soldiers just outside the tall outer gates, which the guards had taken care to lock. The little crowd below the gallows had grown fourfold, and was milling around the new arrivals, adding its communal voice to the racket. Paulinus was wearing a warrior's leather jerkin over his clerical robes and had a short-bladed legionary sword on his belt. He was ranting at Publius Luca, who was standing a short distance away with his arms folded, letting the tirade wash over him. The senior guardsman unlocked the gate with a look of deep misgiving. Paulinus heard the clank of the latch and spun round.

'You butcher!' he roared. 'What have you done to that poor innocent, you son of Satan?'

'Very little, really, Paulinus.' Vortigern indicated the gallows. 'There are your butchers.'

'It's the truth, abbot,' Publius Luca said, without a flicker. 'Is the king to be blamed, if the Picts betrayed him when he had spared their lives?'

'Oh yes,' Paulinus said, 'because only a simpleton or a black-hearted Judas could do what he has done, and whatever else may be said about this man, he isn't stupid.' His hand hovered over the hilt of his sword.

'Abbot, be careful what you say about the king.' Publius Luca had moved forward slightly, and could easily have deflected any blows aimed at Vortigern. His face had hardened into a ferocious iron mask, and Kerin saw at once that he would kill Paulinus on the spot if necessary. The abbot must have seen it too, because his hand fell back to his side and he took a deep steadying breath. His fists clenched, and the veins in his wrists stood out like ropes.

'What have you done with the body of Brother Constans?' he asked, between set teeth.

'Oh, someone buried him,' Vortigern said lightly. 'With his lover, Lupinus,' he added, with an alarming grin. Paulinus stared up at him in appalled silence. Vortigern placed his hands on the abbot's narrow shoulders and turned him towards the gallows. 'Now take a good look before you call me a black-hearted Judas. I killed Constans's murderer with my own hands, and at least half his fellows were dead before we fed them to the birds, unlike poor Tegid's brother.'

Paulinus twisted free. 'You killed my brother Maximian!' he howled impotently.

'No, I didn't,' Vortigern said. 'I'd be a liar if I said that I wasn't glad to be rid of him, because he caused me nothing but trouble, but I didn't kill him.'

Paulinus withdrew, his little grey eyes winter-cold. 'All this blood to make yourself king. How can it be worth it?'

'To make myself king?' Vortigern echoed him incredulously. 'If you think it's such a bed of goose-down, you should crawl out of your safe cloister and change places with me.'

'With you? A bloody murderer, cursed of God and despised by your own son? I'd burn in hell first, if I wasn't sure that I'd have you for company. Now, where is the grave? You may think it's good enough to throw Constans in a ditch like a dead dog, but I do not.'

'Hand on heart, I have no idea,' Vortigern said. 'And you needn't go harassing Giraldus at the chapel of St Alban. He didn't bury the bodies. Someone must have taken them during the night. The Sword of God, for all I know.'

'Ha,' Paulinus retorted. 'I would know about that. Believe me, I will find out, and when I do, that poor wretch will have the burial he deserves.'

'Father Paulinus,' Publius Luca said, mild as milk, 'I'd advise you not to go to the chapel of St Alban right now. You will find it guarded. For the sake of the city's peace, you understand. Go home, and take your men with you. Otherwise, I shall have to ask them to remove you. They'll obey me, I promise you.' He looked up at the leader of the abbot's bodyguard, who gave him a nod. With a growl of anger, Paulinus mounted up and rode for the city gates, followed by his garrison men. Vortigern watched them go. The crowd surged about him, eager for as little as a touch of the king's cloak. Publius Luca moved to his shoulder.

'We may as well leave him alone for now.'

'Yes,' Vortigern said, watching the riders out of sight. 'Have them followed, but no more. And then cut down those bodies and get rid of them. They've served their purpose.' He turned and walked quickly away. Kerin made to follow, but felt Publius Luca's restraining hand on his arm.

'Let him go,' he said. 'And come to me in two hours' time, at the garrison headquarters. There are things you should know.'

4

The streets and open spaces were still cold, but in Marcellus's sheltered garden it was mild enough to sit outside. The haruspex led the way to the stone bench beside his pool. A servant brought a tray with a dish of sweetmeats, a pair of small drinking bowls and a strange silver jug with a lid and a curved spout.

'An infusion of rosehips and mint, sweetened with honey,' Marcellus said, filling the two bowls with steaming, pale pink liquid. 'It refreshes mind and body.'

'We'd been playing with the dog all day,' Kerin said, without preamble. 'Lud's deerhound, Migwyn. But in my dream the dog was dead. Stretched out stiff as a board. I told Lud's wife, Mora. She told me to shut up and stop crying, then she took me outside and there was the dog with his tongue hanging out, ready to work. But two days later he was dead. The things that happened next, I didn't understand at all. Someone came to Lud's house for me – one of the servants, I think – and she took me to the chieftains' hall. There's a room there, Vortigern's library. It's completely private, no-one's allowed in there at all without an invitation. Vortigern's wife, Sevira, was sitting by the fire with her children. Rufus and his little brother. I'd never been anywhere so warm, so full of light. Sevira welcomed me in. She was expecting me, I'm sure of that. Vortigern came then; they were laughing about something, I've no idea what. But that was how it was. That was how it stayed. And then, a couple of years later, Sevira was dead. She died in childbirth. I missed her terribly, but apart from that, nothing changed for me. The servants looked after us. Vortigern changed, I think, but not towards us. Nothing changed until one day when I was around eleven years old. Lud took me to one side, the way men do when they've got something private to say. He asked me if I'd had any of those dreams lately. Marcellus *magister*, I swear I didn't know what he was talking about. I had no more dreams than the next young lad. But then Lud started ranting about the dream where his dog died. He told me – I think I can remember the exact words – that the only reason I was living in the chieftains' hall, and not in his store cupboard, was because of this dream. Because it proved that I was some sort of a prophet, and men like Vortigern needed prophets to smooth their way. I don't know if you can imagine how it feels, for a child to be told that his only value lies in something he can't do.'

Marcellus shook his head. Finding that Kerin's bowl was empty, he poured another measure of his soothing infusion. 'I understand now why you were so touchy when I speculated about this,' he said. 'It's irrelevant, of course. Vortigern has a quick mind, but even he cannot travel five years into the future and see that an abandoned baby is going to have a dream about a dead dog. Good. You can see the humour in that. And I suppose that, since Lud's little revelation, you've been beating your brains out to ensure that you don't end up living in the store cupboard again.'

'Yes,' Kerin said. 'I'm the best warrior I can be. And I'll never be a prophet – not in the way Lud meant it – but I've trained myself to notice things. To study what people do, and why. To see the things they hide. If I know what's coming next, it's because of that, not because I've had a dream. But I have to confess that sometimes I lie about it. When the other warriors ask me how on earth I knew that this or that was going to happen, I sometimes tell them that I dreamed it. All nonsense. I don't dream any more than they do. I just keep my eyes and ears open when they've got their noses in their tankards.'

Marcellus smiled. 'I wouldn't be so quick to dismiss it as nonsense. You still have your place in the chieftains' hall, and a rather more august one now. The king's right arm, indeed. Did that come from the king's own lips?'

'Yes,' Kerin said. 'And he was standing next to Gorlois of Kernow when he said it, so I'm sure the whole of Londinium knows by now.'

'And so it should,' Marcellus said. 'If you hadn't taken things in hand after the assassination, most of the city would be in smouldering ruins by now.'

'Probably,' Kerin said. 'But something will happen. Something will go wrong. So many things can't be fathomed yet. What Rufus will do. Whether the Saxons will be a real danger. And –' he hesitated – 'I hardly know how to put this, but what Vortigern will make of the kingship. Of course I have complete faith in him. But Father Giraldus said that it would be a crown of thorns. Vortigern's a battle commander at heart. He can't stand the sniping and plotting that goes on in places like this, and kings have to bear it, from what I've seen. What should I do now? Do you have an idea?'

Marcellus caressed a friendly dove which had alighted on his shoulder. 'You have the most important task in the kingdom, Kerin Brightspear.'

Kerin smiled. 'Hardly. No-one could have a more important task than the king.'

Marcellus set the dove down on the rim of the pool. 'You touched on this yourself just now, perhaps without understanding it completely. As I told you before, Vortigern is dangerous. To others, of course; but to himself, also. Severus Maximus and his acolytes, you see, are like my pretty friends here. Tame, biddable, happy within their comfortable walls. But put an eagle in a cage and he will beat his brains out upon the bars, even though they are made of gold. If I were you, I think I might suggest that the lords of the West go back to their homes, gather their forces and return in the spring, when there is work to do. You really don't need to dress it up as a dream; Vortigern is not a superstitious fool like Lud. Simply offer it as sound advice, from one man to another. Or from the right arm to the left, if you want to use the parlance of the day. He'll take it from you now, I can promise.'

Kerin got up, scattering doves. 'What would happen here, though?'

'Well, I expect that things would continue much as before,' Marcellus said. 'The governors will govern, the military will prepare, and the shipwrights will get to work. As we know, nothing worthwhile can be done until the roads open in the spring. So take your eagle home to Cambria and let him spread his wings for a while. And never forget that it's always easier to tell a man what he wants to hear. Even a mad fool who'll freeze himself to death on top of a statue to make people think he's indestructible.'

'It worked, though,' Kerin said, remembering as he spoke that Vortigern had said it first.

'Yes, it did,' Marcellus said, 'but someday he will do it once too often.'

Kerin suspected that the haruspex was right, but it was more than he could do to acknowledge it.

'He is not a god, you know,' Marcellus's voice followed him, as he walked away across the garden.

5

The young soldier saluted smartly, offered Kerin a polite greeting and invited him to enter the gloomy precincts of the castra. They crossed a wide, bare courtyard where twenty scruffy lads were being dressed down by a barking officer and passed through a low archway, the entrance to a warren of narrow, ill-lit passages.

'A moment, sir,' the legionary said courteously, and rapped smartly on a heavy iron-bound oak door. A voice responded, deadened by the thickness of the wood. Kerin was ushered in and the door closed behind him. To his surprise, there were two men seated at the scrubbed table in the centre of the stone-flagged room. The commander of the city garrison had with him a younger man, around thirty-five years of age. He was dressed in the customary white toga of the Roman gentleman, his jet-black hair a little longer than military regulations might have permitted. Kerin would have noticed the resemblance in a crowd of strangers. The two men stood up and shook Kerin's hand. As firm and uncompromising a pair of handshakes as he had come across.

'My son, Titus,' said Publius Luca. 'He resisted my attempts to turn him into a soldier, as you can see. Titus, Kerin Brightspear; the young man I said you should meet.'

They sat. On the wall opposite the door was an unexpected fresco, depicting a detachment of Roman cavalry charging some hapless barbarians. There was a lidded earthenware jug on the table which was emitting a gentle curl of steam. Three stout beakers of a similar clay stood on a tray beside it.

'A tisane prepared by the wife of Marcellus *magister*,' Publius Luca said, as he poured. 'An infusion of melissa sweetened with honey; good for the nerves, she informs me. As a family we're usually rather more partial to a good Italian wine, but perhaps not when I'm on duty.' He handed Kerin a beaker. His face remained serious, but the dark eyes held a glint of merriment.

'My father's a drunkard,' Titus Luca said amiably.

'And it's hereditary, unfortunately for you,' said his father. Everyone allowed themselves a friendly chuckle before the seriousness of their purpose reasserted itself.

'I'll let Titus explain,' Publius said. 'He brought the news to me a matter of moments before we met this afternoon. I couldn't give you half an account outside the curia.'

Kerin nodded his appreciation, wondering nonetheless why the commander had not chosen to speak directly to Vortigern.

'I heard this in the course of my work,' Titus Luca said. 'I'm a lawyer, practising here in Londinium, but I have associates throughout the Empire, and we help each other out when we can. I received a letter recently from a Julius Catulo, in Veronia – a small province in Gallia, as you may know. The governor is a mutual friend, and Julius is related by marriage to his former military commander. The case itself is quite unimportant, a property matter concerning the old general; but whilst I was there advising on it, we all dined together at the governor's residence, and I learned something which disturbed me.'

Kerin sipped the tisane, hoping that it was as calming as Marcellus's wife claimed, if the information could disturb a man as urbane and self-possessed as Titus Luca.

'Nothing much happens in Veronia, as a rule,' the lawyer said, 'but it is bisected by an important road, a section of the Via Agrippa, which passes through on its way to the coast. A few days before I arrived, the governor's troops had stopped a group of armed men heading west. They were wearing a livery the troop commander didn't recognise, so he asked them what their business was. A young man came forward; quite well-dressed, not in uniform. He addressed the troop commander in excellent Latin and introduced himself as Vortimer, the oldest son of the Lord Vortigern of Glywysing.'

'My God,' Kerin said. The shock was such that he felt a film of sweat form on his brow, as instantly as if some unseen hand had slapped him with a wet cloth.

'He told the commander that their intentions were entirely peaceful,' Titus Luca said. 'That they were simply passing through on their way to board a merchant ship bound for one of the Kentish ports.'

'Did he say what he was doing there?' Kerin asked, hoping that he sounded more composed than he felt. 'Did he say where they'd been?'

'No. The troop commander was a little uneasy about seeing him there, I'd guess. These days, the powers-that-be feel that Rome should address its domestic problems, and leave Britain to paddle its own boat. They wished each other well, and that was that. Except of course that it isn't, is it. I made a few enquiries of my own. I don't have any detail, but no-one in Veronia doubts that Vortimer was there to raise arms against his father.'

Kerin closed his eyes briefly as he wondered how on earth he was going to put it; or indeed, if he wished to share his news at all. 'Thank you.' He steadied himself. 'I can't say that the information was welcome, but it needed to be known.'

'It grieved me to bring it,' Titus Luca said. 'You'll make your own decision about what to do next, but as far as I'm concerned, it'll go no further.'

He got up with a nod to his father and went out into the dim passage. Kerin closed the door and sat down again. On his part at least, there was unfinished business. Publius Luca's grave smile acknowledged the fact. He poured two more cups of tisane and waited.

'I can see why you couldn't repeat that in a crowded square,' Kerin said. 'But why tell me, particularly?'

'Because Vortigern has more than enough to deal with,' Publius Luca said. 'Someone close to the centre needed to know, but it's my guess that whatever happened in Gallia will be kept quiet. If I were Rufus, if I may call him that, then I think I'd lie low and let my father deal with the Picts before showing my hand.'

Kerin found that the sweet fragrance of the tisane, so seductive when it first seeped from its jug, was beginning to make him feel sick. 'Do you really think he'll betray us, commander?'

'Probably,' Publius said dispassionately. 'I'm sorry to say it, because I do know how things stand between you. But I'd be less than a friend if I didn't speak my mind. I've seen emperors come and go. I know how it's done. There's hardly ever anything decent or honourable about it, and sometimes the most trusted men are the perpetrators.'

'Does anyone know about this, other than you and Titus?'

'No. Not here in Londinium, anyway. I'm sorry to lay this at your door, but there was no-one else with whom I could possibly share the information. And certainly no-one else who would have the first idea what to do with it.'

His eyes were troubled. Kerin thought of a green garden full of sociable doves, of bruised eagles, golden cages and a soothsayer's warning. There was a shadow moving beneath the surface which he needed to seize and hold up to the light.

'I have to ask you something, commander,' he said. 'Not connected with this matter at all, but I have to ask. How did you become acquainted with Vortigern? And what happened when he was growing up in Isca Silurum?'

There was a silence. Outside the window the courtyard gates creaked open. Men hailed each other jovially; some horses came in from the street. Kerin waited.

'You have no idea about this?' Publius Luca asked.

'It's never mentioned. Everyone knows that the family owned a grand house in Isca and had friends in high places. Lud says that Vortigern fell out with his father. I don't know if it's true. All I know is that he won't set foot in the place.'

'The father was well-placed in the administration,' Publius Luca said. 'And Vortigern came out of the womb loathing the Empire. Eventually the father had to choose between his son and his position.' There were footsteps and a sharp knock.

'Lucius Arrius of the praetorian guard, sir,' said the soldier who answered Publius Luca's summons. 'He said you sent for him.'

'Tell him I've been detained,' Publius said. 'Ask him to come back tomorrow morning. And if anyone else comes looking for me, they can come back tomorrow too.'

The soldier looked disconcerted. 'Yes, sir. Er – what if it's the praetor, or General Magnus Julius, sir?'

Publius Luca drew in his breath. 'Antonius, if it's the Emperor Honorius you can tell him to come back tomorrow.' The young soldier saluted hurriedly and went out. Publius locked the door and returned to the table. 'I was a young man when they sent for me. Just past my twenty-fifth birthday, stationed at Vindolanda, up on the Wall. The Second was based in Cambria, as you know, but there'd been a rebellion of mercenaries in the North, and my century was sent to reinforce the garrison. It suited me, as it happened, because my wife's father was highly placed in the administration up there. I was furious when a cavalryman arrived with orders for me to get down to Isca and take command of the second cohort. It was a promotion, so I should have been pleased, but my wife had just given birth to Titus's sister, and of course, they all had to stay behind with her family. My predecessor had died suddenly, they needed someone in a hurry –' he gave a wry chuckle. 'I cursed your countrymen all night as I rode south. In Isca, the first thing I did was go down to the mess room and have a jar of ale with the men. I soon found out that they all detested the garrison commander, Quintus Parvo, and that the worst bane of their life was a young lad who called himself the high king. "Parvo's got him locked up in the outhouse over there," one of them said. I was curious, so I went to have a look. He was lying on the floor in the corner, tied hand and foot. About fourteen years old, I suppose, beaten black and blue. I went closer and asked him who he was. I'd made a point of speaking in British, but he spat in my face and swore back at me in fluent Latin – something I wouldn't repeat, even to you. They used to laugh when he called himself the high king. I told them they shouldn't laugh too loudly; and then, of course, they laughed at me, too.'

He smiled fleetingly, as if touched by some vivid memory. Kerin understood now why Publius Luca had watched Vortigern take the kingship without breaking stride. There was little he hadn't foreseen years ago.

'The boys used to ride around creating havoc,' the commander said. 'Burning bridges, attacking baggage trains;

38

nothing was too much for them. Of course, we usually caught a few of them – never Vortigern, because he could outride anyone we had, but Quintus Parvo knew that if he locked up some of the lads, Vortigern would come back for them. It was like baiting a trap. As soon as we caught him, Parvo would let all the others go. He knew quite well that they'd spend all day throwing stones in the river if they had no-one to lead them. Then he'd lock Vortigern up, beat him senseless and dump him at his father's gate. It went on for years. I used to let him out now and again, when I had the chance. Parvo would have strung me up if he'd found out.'

There was a pause. Kerin thought about the miles he had travelled with Vortigern; the countless visits to towns and cities with their merchants' circles, leaders who needed cultivating, local disputes which demanded to be settled. Glevum and Corinium on this side of the river; every settlement of any size in Cambria, from Caerwent and Moridunum in the south to Segontium in the far north. But not Isca. Never, ever Isca. The men of Isca had always come to Henfelin, their questions and concerns settled from afar, in the hall of the chieftains.

'Things got worse as the lads became men,' Publius Luca said. 'They got tired of burning things and started killing people. A new provincial governor was sent to restore order; Marcus Decimus, he'd held office in Rome. A decent enough man. He was a cavalry commander in his younger days, and he'd had a horse shipped over from Parthia. A big black stallion, a cross between a racing mare and a battle chariot horse. It was a beastly animal, Decimus couldn't get near it. It killed one of its stable lads, so he kept it shut up on its own. Then one night, Vortigern and his crew came calling. They set fire to our stores and stole all the horses, including the Parthian. The next time I saw it, Vortigern was riding it straight at us. We were escorting Decimus to a meeting; twenty of us infantry and four cavalrymen. The Parthian flattened the cavalry commander's horse and kicked the man to pieces. The rest of us fought back, but Vortigern hadn't come to fight. They just wounded a couple of men and kidnapped Decimus. Parvo was livid. He saw it as a personal affront to his authority, which it was.'

'Did they kill Decimus?' Kerin asked.

'No. They locked him up somewhere; I've no idea where, even now. Parvo posted a reward for Vortigern; an obscene amount of money. For weeks nothing happened. Parvo started rounding up lads from the villages; ordinary, harmless children who'd never done anything to anyone. One day he had two little ones covered in honey and staked them out in the sun for the ants to eat. Someone told Vortigern. He sent Parvo a letter, promising to send Decimus back unharmed if Parvo released all his prisoners and stood down as garrison commander. Parvo burned the letter in front of the city gates. He was terrified, probably. He thought his own head would be on the block if he didn't get Decimus back in one piece. And then he had a stroke of luck. Some poor woman whose son was being tortured said she'd tell him where Vortigern was, if he let her boy go. Parvo gave his word. They dragged Vortigern back behind a horse, hanged the boy in front of him and locked him up. It went on for weeks. Vortigern wouldn't say where Decimus was; Parvo couldn't break him. In the end I couldn't watch it happen. I wrote to the imperial governor in Londinium, a man called Sextus Petronius. He came down to Isca himself with a few hundred troops. There were riots in all the towns by that time, and he was furious. He was angling for a consulship, and the last thing he needed was an insurrection in Cambria. It was over in days. Parvo was stripped of his command, Vortigern's people released Decimus and we freed all our prisoners. Vortigern was a hero, for what it was worth. And Decimus came back without a hair out of place. I was expecting him to jump on the first ship back to Italy, but he stayed and took up his post. There was no more trouble while he was there.'

Kerin sat quite still, staring at the fresco without seeing it and thinking about everything he had been told. The sun had come out, suffusing the pale grey stone with a soft brightness, but it lent him no warmth. He did not need warmth. Deep within him a savage anger glowed, incandescent, more potent than any he had known; and alongside it a feeling of wretched impotence, that all this should have happened far beyond his reach, years before a feckless thief grabbed a servant girl and forced him into life. He knew that what he had learned would inform everything he did from that moment forward. In a way which he could feel, but not begin to understand, he knew that he was a stronger man for hearing it.

'What became of Quintus Parvo?' he asked.

'Dead and buried years ago, no doubt,' Publius Luca said. 'He wasn't a youngster. Twenty years older than me, and not the healthiest of men. There were two sons, but they joined the Victrix to get away from their father, so I never met them.'

Kerin nodded an acknowledgement but did not trust himself to speak. Publius Luca, mistaking his silence for another kind of anger, gave him an anxious glance.

'Perhaps I should have kept quiet,' he said.

'No. It needed to be said.' Kerin paused, considering his options. 'If we went back to Cambria for the winter, what would happen? I know we can leave the military to you, but can Severus Maximus control the ordo, and the tax-collectors?'

'I'll make sure of it,' Publius Luca said. 'And I'll continue my preparations. We'll be bringing men in from the estates and the other garrisons soon. As for the cavalry, I want to involve your Lucius Arrius. That's why I summoned him. Can you vouch for him?'

'Without a second thought,' Kerin said. 'He's honest and brave, and completely dependable. The praetorian guard's a waste of his time.'

'Good. The answer I was hoping for. When will you leave?'

'Tomorrow, if I can manage it,' Kerin said. 'Eldof and the other lords must leave too, with their warriors. We'll gather here again in the spring, when it's time to march. You're probably the best man to explain it to the praetor, and please thank Marcellus for me. He's the one who advised me that we should leave. I can't share his beliefs, but I do believe in Marcellus *magister*.'

'He's a wise old bird, and a good judge of men's hearts,' Publius said. 'Go to Vortigern, then, and tell him that I'll meet you in the spring, with as many good men as I can raise. All in all, I'd like to believe that the Empire was a force for good in these islands, but some sins were committed in its name. I can't alter what's passed, but I'll help the king in any way I can. I owe him that much.'

'Thank you for telling me,' Kerin said. 'And for everything you did, and would have done, if it had been in your gift. I hope that Rufus is wrong, and that our God rewards such things.'

* * *

Kerin did not go straight to the curia. He needed time to cool his head. The knowledge that Rufus would go to Gallia without a word, driven by a force Kerin could barely understand; a lifetime's friendship, probably broken forever now and bleeding to death like Constans, on the floor of some cold chapel. But it was the other stuff which had poleaxed him. The things Publius Luca said about Isca; the things he didn't say, and God knew what they were, if the commander of a Roman legion found them unspeakable. Just along the river bank he found a deserted jetty and sat down on it, watching the slow lap of the rising tide. He thought of all that he had learned in the past hour, then of the miraculous confluence of luck and irrational pity which had saved his life, and knew that there was only one place he needed to be now.

The guards did not question him. Kerin let himself into the curia and barred the door behind him. Inside it was growing dark. It had taken time to find Eldof, Gorlois and Garagon, and tell them that the king had commanded them to take their warriors home. Elation broke out. Even Eldof shook Kerin's hand. Now it was time to break the news to the king. Vortigern was standing at the balustrade looking towards the western windows, where daylight was fading. Kerin sat on the edge of the table and waited, but in the end he realised that he would have to break the silence, if it were to be broken at all.

'Lord, there's something you should know,' he said. Vortigern looked round. In the strange twilight Kerin could barely discern his features, could only guess what nameless things lay behind those tormented eyes. 'I came down here to talk to you this afternoon, but then Paulinus turned up.'

Vortigern gave a hollow laugh. 'To talk? About a bloody murderer who's been betrayed by the son who despises him?'

'No, lord. About some tired warriors who should go

43

home to Cambria for a while, to renew themselves ready for the battle in the spring.'

'That's ridiculous,' Vortigern said.

'No. It makes sense. There should be a great feast in your hall, and everyone should come to pay tribute. It would be like raising a feast for the people who came to the curia. The warriors deserve a reward. Recognition. We should even invite Gwyndaf of Craig Goch.'

'Gwyndaf?' Vortigern scoffed. 'He'd starve to death before eating in my hall.'

'I doubt it,' Kerin said, wondering how on earth he was going to get out of this one. Gwyndaf's hatred of Vortigern was so well known that no-one even talked about it any more. It had become a commonplace in Cambria, like westerly winds and rainfall. 'We'd better go home and arrange it,' he said. The practicalities could wait. 'We could leave tomorrow, in fact. The weather's clear, and the horses are fresh. Why not?'

'Because I'm king now, you half-wit,' Vortigern said. 'There are things to settle.'

'Less than you think.' Kerin braced himself. 'I've told Eldof, Gorlois and Garagon to go home for the winter too. I told them you'd commanded it, of course. After that, there are only three men who matter; Severus Maximus, Publius Luca and Gallus. The first two already know what their responsibilities are, and as for Gallus – well, you could give him command of the war fleet, I suppose. He's a seafarer blood and bone, and he'd do a fine job. I could speak to him, but he's your friend, so it should probably come from you.' He hesitated, then found the courage of his convictions. 'Lord, I think you know I'm right. The choice wasn't mine to make, but please hear me. No man can be his own counsel all the time.'

Vortigern turned. 'No-one else would have had the nerve to do this.'

'I know,' Kerin said. 'That's why I had to do it, whatever the consequences.'

A moment of silence followed, and Kerin wondered what he had done; then Vortigern smiled. 'Very well. Find Lud and tell him. Then help him get the men together, and tell them not to get drunk tonight. We'll ride at dawn.'

6

The news began to spread as soon as Kerin summoned the praetor's servants and stable lads to the courtyard and told them to prepare horses, wagons and baggage animals for an early departure. By first light people were gathering in the street outside the gates.

'The city's humming,' said Dimos, arriving early for his day's work as usual. 'It's all they're talking about in the marketplace.'

'What are they saying, exactly?' Kerin asked.

'That the king's going home to gather his armies in the West, ready for the campaign in the spring,' said the scribe. 'But you'll still need my services afterwards, surely. Would you care to study writing as well as reading? They do go together naturally, you know. Most people are quite keen to be able to write their own name, if nothing else. I think it gives them a sense of permanence.'

Kerin felt mildly surprised. The thought had never occurred to him. Now he found that he rather liked the idea. 'Could you write my name?' he asked. 'I don't suppose anyone ever has. I'd like to see what it looks like.'

Dimos took off his leather satchel and drew out a sheet of papyrus, a quill and a phial of ink. He laid the papyrus on the step below Minerva's statue and knelt in front of it. 'Hmm. Kerin. It's – well, very British, isn't it.'

'So?' Kerin felt a little defensive. 'Vortigern is a British name, and the scribes don't seem to have any trouble with it. *Vurtigurnus Rex.* Even I can read that.'

'Yes, lord,' Dimos said serenely, 'but as you can see, they've latinised his name in order to be able to write it, and I shall have to do the same with yours. Kerinus, I suppose. With the emphasis on the second syllable. Ker*ee*nus, as it were.'

'Kerinus.' Kerin rolled it around his tongue. 'I suppose that'll do. What about my other name? Brightspear?'

'Oh, that's much simpler,' said Dimos, 'I can merely translate it. *Hasta* is the Latin word for a spear; it ends in 'a', so it's feminine, you might be surprised to know. Or perhaps not, given some of the women one comes up against. And there are a few words for bright, but I think I'd choose *clara*. *Hasta clara*, a shining spear. There you are. Kerinus Hastaclara.' Effortlessly, he wrote Kerin's new name on the sheet of papyrus and handed it over. 'It has a certain ring to it, lord. It'll look very well on the first page of your memoirs.'

* * *

The Cambrian warriors would precede the king as the army left Londinium. Lud would lead, of course; he was still chief warrior, whatever the rise in Kerin's stock. It was fitting for Macsen, as his oldest son, to ride beside him. Kerin fell in behind them, without the slightest sense of being displaced, and was joined by Macsen's brother, Custennin. Elir and their brawny cousin Bened moved up behind.

'The king's right arm isn't leading the charge, then,' Custennin said, with an arch little smile. Kerin was nettled, but tried not to make it obvious. The only way to rub along with Custennin was to avoid rising to his bait.

'Your father's the chief warrior,' he said easily. 'Who else would lead?'

'Someone with ideas above his station, perhaps?' Custennin suggested, in a tone just as mild and inoffensive. Kerin glanced over his shoulder and shrugged.

'I can't see anyone like that around here,' he said, as Lud signalled for the procession to come to attention. It was a long way from Londinium to Cambria, and he had begun to feel the weight of the trust Vortigern had placed in him. In a way he would once have found unthinkable, he was learning to see things on the king's behalf. To recognise the importance of friendly associations between men, which would need to become mighty bonds if they were to hold together in the North. To iron out petty disagreements before they deepened into poisonous, damaging rifts. And here was one of those, right in front of him now. He and Custennin had been having the same argument since they were children. Macsen's open, sunny disposition had never allowed him to resent Kerin's place in the chieftains' hall; it was all the same to him, if Vortigern had chosen to share his hearth with a foundling. But his brother's view was quite different. As the chief warrior's son, Custennin expected a degree of deference. More precisely, he expected to be esteemed above a man who only existed because some village girl up in the mountains had dropped her drawers for a randy horse thief. The argument was never about that, of course; it was always some triviality. Who could climb the highest, who could hold his breath the longest, who had the best horse. Now, Kerin knew, it had to stop. Custennin was one of the most valuable members of Vortigern's personal warband. He was a formidable warrior, fast on his feet and strong as a hemp cable. Technically Macsen was a more gifted swordsman, but Kerin always felt that Custennin had the edge because he didn't give a damn who he killed. Every commander needed at least one bastard like that in his warband. And so, instead of letting his irritation fester, he turned to the man riding alongside him and said, 'I could do with your help when we get home.' For a moment Custennin simply looked shocked; then he began to laugh.

'You need my help?' he crowed. 'What for? Too grand to wipe your own arse now, are you?'

Kerin breathed in and tried to remind himself what was at stake. 'We'll be on the march soon. When the year turns and the snow clears. As soon as we get home I want to start training the youngsters. I can beat anyone with the spear, but you'll be better at teaching swordcraft. Can you take charge of that, with Macsen?'

Custennin gave him a blank look. 'Yes,' he said. 'I suppose I can.'

'Thank you,' Kerin said, and left it there. There was no point in trying too hard. This would never be a friendship. Mutual tolerance would be enough, at least for now. Ahead of them the praetor's gates swung open.

'Farewell, lords!' a thin voice shouted. 'The gods speed your endeavours!' It was Severus Maximus, waving from the portico of his huge, pretentious house.

'I'll bet he's glad to see the back of us.' A voice at Kerin's side. Vortigern's eyes were alight; he looked eager and twitchy, like a wild creature anticipating release from a cage. Apart from the simple silver crown, there were to be no concessions to royal status. The same plain garments; the same plain black horse, with her functional, unadorned saddlery. But perhaps that was what the people wanted. That was what they loved.

Just visible outside the praetor's gates, the city garrison had assembled in ceremonial uniform. Publius Luca was in the front rank, with Gallus the merchant beside him. Lucius had marched the praetorian guard out to stand alongside.

Beyond them the crowd seethed; the ale-drinkers, carpenters, weavers and fishermen and all their fellow-citizens, dependants and hangers-on, the people who had brought this about. The fire which Kerin's spark had lit.

'Lord King!' a voice bellowed from the midst. 'Lord Kerin! We're heading back to the West with you, to raise men and forge weapons!' Old Malan, of course, on his bony black mule, with his granddaughter Flora perched behind him, one thin arm clasping her grandfather's waist while the other waved a threadbare blue scarf. A cry went up from the packed streets as Lud led the king's company out of the gates. High above the military men, Kerin spotted Marcellus, watching from the balcony of a patrician's fine house. Beside him was Dimos.

'*Vale!*' the scribe shouted, waving his arms. '*Vale, Kerine Hastaclara!*' Vortigern laughed out loud.

'What's that about?'

'Oh, that's Dimos,' Kerin said. 'The scribe who helped me with the tax decrees. He's going to teach me to read and write. If you hadn't sealed the decrees, anyone could have hoodwinked me. So learning to read is like learning Saxon from my cook Cheldric. Something which might benefit us one day. But perhaps not until after we fight the Picts.'

The people's chanting surged about them, as fervent as ever, but more muted than the roaring din outside the curia on the night of Vortigern's accession. This time, as the citizens of Londinium cheered and waved, they knew that the men they had taken to their hearts were leaving, and that the next time they saw them, they would be marching to war.

7

Nothing had changed. The church was precisely as Kerin remembered it; the buff-coloured stone warm in the afternoon sunlight, the door open, a candle burning within. The same two monks were working in the garden alongside, building a bonfire from prunings and dead vegetation. It was almost as if the scene had been frozen in time. But something else had altered, so profoundly that Kerin could barely believe what he was doing. For the first time in his life, he had lied to Vortigern; or at least, asked someone to lie for him. Elir had proved his good faith by keeping doggedly silent about Constans's burial. Now he was on his way to tell Vortigern that Kerin's horse was lame. Eryr, his best horse, his warhorse, his indispensable weapon in the battle to come, lame in front after her foot went down a hole you couldn't see. Only a fetlock strain, they happened all the time, rest and ice-cold water would cure it, but that would take a few days. How many days, Kerin was not sure. First of all he would have to find Bertil Redknife's daughter.

'Good day to you lord,' said the older of the two monks. 'The Father's round the back of the church, if you're looking for him.'

Father Septimus was standing behind a pile of stones with a mallet in one hand and a chisel in the other. 'Kerin Brightspear,' he said, putting the tools down. 'I rather feared that you might come back. Please don't take that amiss. It's very good to see you. But you must surely know that your life wouldn't be worth a corn husk, if Lord Bertil found you here.'

'Is he home yet?' Kerin asked.

'No. I'm told that he's with Lord Eldof's party, and not expected back for a week or so. Some of Bertil's household servants worship here, and they were on their knees yesterday, thanking God for allowing them a few more days' peace. Come now. These stones have spent eternity waiting for someone to split them, so they can wait a little longer.'

Kerin followed the abbot across the garden to the speech house; the place where he and Gael had shared their only brief moments of private conversation. The image of her burned so brightly in his mind that he almost expected her to materialise out of the darkness within. 'Father, you know why I've come,' he said, as Septimus closed the door.

'Of course. And I should tell you straight away that Gael is in good health. But she's not happy; oh no, not at all. You might care to know that she comes here to pray far more often than she used to. I might be wrong, but I doubt if she begs God to forgive her sins. I suspect she begs him to bring her a fine young warrior from Cambria, and the opportunity to commit one or two more.'

Kerin hardly knew where to look, but when he met Septimus's eyes, he found that they were twinkling with good humour. 'You haven't always been in holy orders, have you, Father,' he said, remembering the first time they met. The abbot's powerful shoulders and big, calloused hands had suggested a man used to hard physical work.

'Not at all,' Septimus said. 'I'm a stone mason by trade. There were too many mouths for my parents to feed when I was a lad, so I had to go and earn a crust. I came here to build walls, and never went away. I was thirty years old when

God called me to serve. Nothing dramatic, just a quiet little voice talking to me. I'd married young, but the plague got my wife, and I didn't want to go down that road again. So here I am. And here you are, thinking, why can't this stupid old monk be quiet and tell me where to find the girl.'

Kerin snorted with laughter. 'I'd never put it like that, Father,' he said. 'But I hope you can tell me. I've no idea where Bertil Redknife's citadel is.'

'I'll show you, but you should keep away,' Septimus said. 'Bertil has left a few men on guard. They're ordered to kill you on sight, according to the servants. And you won't find Gael there, anyway. She spends most of her time down in the valley where the old swineherd lived. Her father didn't get round to burning the house down, so she's tidied it up for herself. It'll all come to a halt when Bertil gets home, I'm sure, but for now that's where she stays. I'll fetch my mule and ride with you as far as the crossroads.'

Kerin recognised the place on sight, although he had been travelling in the opposite direction the last time he was here.

'That's the way I came with Gael,' he said, looking away to the left, where a well-worn path led steeply downhill beneath leafless oaks. 'The way to Morvid's valley.'

'It is,' Septimus said. 'If you stayed on this track, you'd soon find yourself on the Roman road to Glevum. It runs along past the beech woods at the other end of the valley. And that path to the right will take you straight to Bertil Redknife's citadel. Just a few minutes' ride on a horse like yours, so bear in mind that that works the other way round, too.'

'I will,' Kerin said. 'And thank you for helping me, Father. I hope it won't make trouble for you.'

'No more than I was in already,' the abbot said. 'Bertil's

never forgiven me for refusing to marry Gael to Gadlyn. I'm told that Eldof ordered him to leave me and the brothers alone; it might have gone worse for us otherwise. Once Bertil gets something in his gut, he won't let it go. So please, I know I'm preaching to the deaf, but don't stay too long down there.'

'I won't,' Kerin said. 'I'd never put Gael in danger.'

'You're already in it, lad,' Septimus said. 'You wouldn't have come back if you didn't love the girl, but there's no getting away from that. I can't see any way on earth that Bertil's going to give you his daughter without a fight, and I don't suppose you've even told Vortigern what you're up to, have you?'

'No,' Kerin confessed. 'I sent someone to tell him that my horse was lame. It was a good excuse, but I don't feel good for making it. I've never deceived Vortigern in my life. He deserves better, but you can guess what would happen, if I set off a bloodbath with Eldof's family. We need every man we can get to fight the Picts. I can't lay this on Vortigern's table when he's risked everything to take the crown and make it happen. But I couldn't come this close without seeing Gael, either. Look, she gave me this.' He held up the ring. 'I'm going to offer it back to her. If she takes it, my life will be simple. If she wants me to keep it, I'll have to find a way. God knows how.'

'You could do worse than ask Him,' Septimus said. 'I don't know if you're a God-fearing man. Most young warriors don't seem too bothered, unless they're zealots like Vortigern's son and his following.' The abbot's steady eyes met Kerin's. An unasked question hung in the air between them.

'I'm not one of them,' Kerin said. 'But I'm not above asking for God's help either. Perhaps you could ask on my behalf. I'm sure to need it, the way things are going.'

Septimus nodded. 'I will,' he said. 'And if you're minded to listen to advice, keep your counsel until you and Gael are sure about this. I'm not saying it's a passing fancy, that would be an insult, but you've hardly spent any time together, have you? So be sure before you whack the wasps' nest, that's all.' He held out his hand and Kerin shook it. 'Be off with you, then. If anything troubling happens, I'll send word.'

* * *

The valley seemed oddly quiet without Morvid's pigs rooting around on the wide river bank. There was a pony, though; a smart little grey one, in the pen where Morvid's sturdy brown pony had once stood. Kerin dismounted, hitched Eryr to the rail and approached the hut, treading cautiously. There was no reason to doubt a word of what Abbot Septimus said, but a year of danger and risk had made him wary. He was sure that the blanket screening the doorway was new. The old one was worn to shreds; he remembered the way the light filtered through it when he was lying on Morvid's bed, recovering from the wound Bertil's sword had inflicted. He drew the screen aside and went in. The interior of the hut was unrecognisable. A pillar candle, like the ones the monks placed on their altars, was burning on Morvid's rough table. Someone had swept the floor clean. The narrow bed, one of the most uncomfortable Kerin had ever had to lie on, now had a thick straw mattress. There were blankets, a pillow and a warm-looking tapestry bedspread. Kindling and dried moss, ready for lighting, lay on the hearth. Something in the far corner caught Kerin's eye. It was a stringed instrument, similar to the ones he had seen in Londinium. A lyre or some such; he had no idea about these things. He stood in the middle of the hut, astounded. In so short a time, and with such simple additions, this dank little hut had been transformed into more of a home than his own house had ever been. A sudden whinny came from the pen outside. He turned. The screen was drawn, and she was there, framed by the low afternoon light; carrying a wicker basket, wearing a brown woollen dress with a laced bodice, like the servants wore.

'How did you know?' she said, standing quite still.

'Father Septimus told me,' Kerin said. 'I didn't even know where your father's citadel was. He told me.' He waved a hand about. 'All this. I wouldn't have known the place. It's clean. And the bed. I spent a few days lying on it, when your father got me in the leg. It was like trying to sleep on a plank.'

'Believe me,' Gael said, 'even without the mattress, it was better than sharing a bed with Gadlyn.'

'For God's sake, why him?' Kerin asked. 'If your father wanted you married, couldn't he have found someone better? Younger? Morvid said Gadlyn was cruel to you. What father would do that?'

Gael put down her basket and sat down on the bed, inviting Kerin to sit too. He perched cautiously at the far end. 'My father cares very little for me, Kerin Brightspear,' she said. 'When I was younger he hated me, for surviving the plague; it killed my mother and brother, and he would sooner have had either of them. As I grew up, I suppose he saw that daughters have their uses. And so he cultivated Gadlyn, and made me marry him. Gadlyn had no heirs, but he had land and warriors and chests full of gold, and it must have been obvious that he wasn't long for this world.'

'Well, I shan't apologise for helping things along,' Kerin said. 'But surely your husband's possessions pass to you, not to your father?'

'I don't want anything of Gadlyn's,' Gael said. 'And anyway, whatever I had, my father would take. He hates Eldof and wants to depose him, although they're blood relations. It's all that matters to him – Bertil of Glevum, that's how he sees himself – and he needs Gadlyn's warriors and money to do it.'

Kerin's eyebrows rose at this unexpected information. 'You're related, then?' he said. 'You and Eldof?'

'He's a cousin to my father,' Gael said. 'My father has no brothers or sisters, though, and my mother's family were slaughtered in the Irish raids, so I've always been encouraged to look on Eldof as my uncle. And that stupid bishop too, even though my father hates the sight of them both.'

'And do you hate them?' Kerin asked.

'No,' Gael sighed. 'Eldadus is an old hypocrite, but he's never done anything to hurt me. And Eldof's kind enough, if rather dull. Glevum is far better off with him than it would be with my father, I promise you.'

Kerin looked intently at her, trying unsuccessfully to suppress the image of Gadlyn's bloated form sprawling across that slender body. 'How did you bear it?' he asked.

'I don't know,' Gael said, looking down at her hands. 'Perhaps now I should be unable to.' She glanced up, her eyes hesitant, and for the first time Kerin realised that she was probably far less composed than she looked.

'Have you thought of me a little?' he asked.

'Yes,' she said. 'And you of me?'

'I have thought of nothing else,' Kerin said. He had hardly noticed Gael move, but he could have sworn that the distance between them had diminished. 'Look,' he said, trying hard to keep his voice steady, 'you should really not come any closer, if you want me to be responsible for what I do next.'

'I don't want you to be responsible,' Gael said, her voice trembling slightly. 'I haven't waited all this time for that, have you?'

Kerin reached out and gently lifted a stray lock of hair which had fallen forward over her cheek. The pulse in his throat was beating like a hammer. 'I hope not,' he said. 'But it's for you to decide.'

Gael reached for his hands and drew him close. In the last reasoned act he was to perform for some time, Kerin loosened the laces of her bodice and eased the dress from her shoulders. She was wearing only a light shift beneath it, as frail and diaphanous as a dragonfly's wing.

'Look,' he began, in anguish, 'if –'

'Don't!' she cried, moving to silence him. Her hand never reached his lips.

8

On the evening of the fourth day, they lay together in perfect quietness, staring up at the ceiling where the flames
were weaving their ritual dance. Kerin had built a roaring
fire with logs from Morvid's abandoned wood store. The
nights were growing colder, even for two people who spent
them making love or sleeping in each other's arms. Gael
extended a lazy hand and drew a heart on Kerin's chest with
her forefinger.

'How long does it take for a strained fetlock to heal?' she
asked.

'As long as it takes me to get tired of this,' he said, taking
her hand and sliding it gently downwards.

'Mm,' she murmured, as he quickened. 'Poor horse. She'll
be lame forever.'

This time there was no attempt to delay the moment. It
was over in no time, a brief, trembling ecstasy. They rolled
apart and lay, catching their breath.

'I love it when you do that,' he said.

'Playing the lyre,' Gael gasped. 'Strengthens the fingers.'
Kerin smothered a laugh on her bare shoulder. 'It wasn't
quite a jest, though,' she said, rising on her elbow. 'How
long?'

'One more night,' he said. 'Two at the most. Any longer
and someone may come looking for me.' He got up and
pulled on his clothes. There was a little cauldron under the

table, containing the remains of the rabbit stew Gael had made the evening before. Kerin put it to heat, fetched the lyre from the corner and laid it on the bed. 'Come on, then. Play something for me.'

Gael flung on a nightdress and took the instrument in her hands. 'It was my mother's,' she said, arranging herself cross-legged. 'She used to play for me. I'm nowhere near as good as she was. She taught me songs, and she'd play while I sang them. She used to call me her singing bird.' Her face clouded. Kerin suspected that she was trying hard not to weep.

'It's me,' he said. 'Not Gadlyn. Not your father.' She smiled and allowed the tears to fall.

'I'll play,' she said. 'And then I'll tell you about her.'

The melody was beautiful and completely unfamiliar. Her mother must have had a rare talent, if she could make the lyre sing more sweetly. The musicians in Londinium were far more plangent, perhaps because they were competing with pipes and drums, or simply trying to impress some pompous patron. Gael sang a short verse in a language Kerin couldn't understand, then reverted to the melody. Kerin found himself wondering about the woman who taught her. He had told Gael all there was to tell about himself. She had sat for a while without speaking while his dread deepened. He supposed that his revelations must have been hard to take in. Usually, when a girl enquired about a man's family, she'd expect to be told that his father was a warrior, a craftsman, a labourer. She'd try to understand what her own life might be like, if her choice or her family's settled upon him. What could she possibly deduce from his tale of death, wolves and abandonment? Her small hand had closed over one of his. 'Thank God for that,' she'd said. 'No relatives for me to please or offend.' It almost made him weep, even now.

She played the final chord, set the lyre aside and smiled. He sat down beside her and kissed her brow.

'That was wonderful. The lyre and the singing. Was that your mother's tongue?'

'Yes,' Gael said. 'She learned British to please my father, of course, but she often spoke Irish to me and my brother. I was only nine years old when they died, but it's still here, in my head.'

'I thought you were younger when they passed,' Kerin said. 'Vortigern and I came across your father, in Eldof's company. I asked who he was. Vortigern told me that he'd married an Irish woman who was captured down in Dyfed. But he thought that she'd died in the plague that killed my people, you and your brother too.'

'No,' Gael said. 'Years afterwards. There wasn't much plague about at all, except in little pockets amongst the poorest people. But my loving father visited a whorehouse in Glevum and brought it home with him. I was lucky. My uncle Eldof's wife was pregnant with a fourth child, and I'd been sent over there to keep the other three from under her feet. My mother sent me off with a little basket full of fruit and sweetmeats. I never saw her again.' She tilted her head back, eyes defiantly dry. There was probably a vein of simmering anger within her still, entwined with the Irish language and the memories.

'What was her name?' Kerin asked.

'Aislinn. A beautiful Irish name. If – ' she broke off and looked away.

'If?' Kerin asked.

'If I had a daughter, I'd like to name her after my mother,' Gael said, fiddling with the lyre. Kerin took it from her and laid it aside.

'You could be with child now,' he said. 'We've hardly left this bed for days.'

She looked up. 'It's unlikely. I know my body well, Master Brightspear. Its rhythms are as regular as Father Septimus's prayers. I don't suppose you have much to do with the wise woman, do you, but we girls study these things. My servant's an expert. She's – well, let's say she doesn't live like a nun. Before I was made to marry Gadlyn, I asked her for the best way to make sure that I didn't fall with child of the old goat. My lady, my darling, she said, learn to count and with luck you'll avoid it. Even better, shove this in his drink before bed. If he doesn't pass out, he'll be as limp as a wet flannel.' She grinned. 'I've no idea what it was, but it tasted disgusting. I had to mix it up with honey. I'll be truthful, when I saw him choking to death after you speared him in the throat, the first thing I thought was, thank God I'll never have to do that again.' She laughed out loud. Kerin laughed too. The sound petered away. 'It's possible, though,' she said, lowering her eyes. 'Unlikely, but still possible.'

He took her in his arms. 'It won't matter,' he said. 'One day, I hope you'll have at least one child. That you'll be my wife and share my home, and bear our children. Can I hope for that?'

She drew back. 'With all my heart,' she said. 'But I fear for you so much. For you and for all the people we love. How would we manage, without people trying to kill each other over it? My father hates you. He hates you anyway, without even knowing about us, because you killed Brennan and Gadlyn and shamed him on his own ground, in front of Balin and the old man and the boy. He'll never forgive you. I don't care for his opinion, because he's treated me worse than his animals, but I care about what he might do. About the consequences for all of us. You think he's a cruel man, I expect, but you don't know the half of it.'

I cannot lose her because of this, Kerin thought. 'Are you

saying that it's impossible?' he asked, trying to appear calm while everything within him churned like a mill race.

'No!' she exclaimed. 'No, no, no. I couldn't bear to say that. But I can't make you a false promise, either. I must think, and try to see a way through this – ' she broke off, clasping her head in her hands. He cupped her chin gently.

'There will be a way,' he said. 'I don't know what it is yet, but I will find it. Your Father Septimus told me that we should both take time to be sure. I don't think I could be more sure, but he's probably a wiser man than I am. Do you want this back, while you think about things?' He held out the silver ring on its chain.

'No,' Gael said, closing a hand around the ring and his fingers. 'I want you to keep it.'

'A man in Londinium noticed it,' Kerin said. 'He asked if it was a token from my wife. I said yes, because I didn't know what else to say. Then I realised how much I wished it was true. There will be a way, if you wish it too. I will find it.'

Gael's eyes shone in the firelight. 'Not if we both die of starvation.' She rolled off the bed, crawled on hands and knees to the fireside and stirred the cauldron. 'Done to a turn. Come on, bring the bowls. I warn you, I may not be very big but I eat like a horse. My mother used to say it was the Irish in me. Big eaters, all of them.'

'We're big eaters in Cambria, too,' Kerin said. He fetched bowls and spoons, and settled down beside her.

'I wouldn't know,' Gael said, ladling out the stew. 'You've only been hungry for one thing so far.' She gave him a lecherous grin and tucked into her food. This is how I want my life to be, he thought. A house that feels like home, even a tiny shack like this; a good fire, good food. This woman, without whom all the rest would be meaningless. My singing bird. And perhaps one day a child called Aislinn, if it's a girl.

9

Eryr stood patiently, eyes half closed, while Kerin examined her feet. Unlike many warhorses she seemed to relish this invasion of her privacy. Gael came from the hut with a dry crust and offered it on open palm. The mare extended her elegant neck and delicately took the morsel in her teeth.

'You're honoured,' Kerin said. 'She'd kick most people into the river.'

'Do you mind it?' Gael asked. 'My father won't let me anywhere near his warhorses. He says it turns them soft if you treat them like ordinary animals.'

'No, I don't mind,' Kerin came out of the pen and they leaned together on the rail. 'She's a killer in battle, nothing's going to change that. And anyway, I'd prefer her to like you. Then I can send you out to feed her when it's pouring with rain and I'd sooner stay in bed. Ouch, Christ!' Gael had hit him over the head with a water bucket.

'You speak as if we were already betrothed,' she said.

'I hope we will be,' he said. 'I've felt more at home these past few days, in this little hut, than I've done for years. And that's thanks to you. It was just a shack before, the sort of place you'd keep your dogs or geese.'

'I expect your house is bigger,' she speculated.

'Yes, much bigger. You could fit this hut into the part where the cook and the others live.'

Gael drew back. 'The cook and the others?'

Kerin closed his eyes. I have blundered, I have blundered, he thought. At that moment he could have cut out his own tongue. 'I'm sorry. I should have told you. I would have told you. But there's been so much else –'

'Never mind so much else,' Gael said, folding her arms. 'Tell me now.'

Kerin sat down on a log beside the ashes of the cooking fire where he had ended Gadlyn's life. Gael sat beside him. 'When we moved into the praetor's house in Londinium, I went snooping around to find out how the household worked,' he said. 'I found the kitchen, and there was a cook there. A Saxon cook called Cheldric. He'd been captured down in Kent, and ended up cooking for Garagon's family. They treated him like dirt. Then the praetor bought him, and it was more of the same. We started talking. He said that his people would soon attack Britain again, trying to grab land. Thousands of them. I don't know how aware Glevum is about all this. In Cambria, people know that the Saxons have been raiding the south coast for years, but to most of them it's something that happens somewhere else. No concern of theirs. I can't agree with that. I thought that if Cheldric was right, and his people were coming back, then at least one of us should be able to speak their tongue. I bought Cheldric from the praetor, so that he could teach me. And – ' he hesitated. 'For God's sake don't repeat this to anyone else, but I was sorry for him. His own people had abandoned him and he'd had a dog's life ever since, so I was sorry for him. What's so funny about that? It'll ruin my good name with the warriors, if anyone else finds out.'

Gael composed herself and leaned into him. 'You're really not at all like the rest of them, are you,' she said.

'No,' Kerin said. 'So I'm told.' One day, he realised, he would have to tell her that the praetorian guard would probably have beaten him to death without Cheldric's intervention; but that would mean admitting what he was doing in the forbidden darkness of the slaves' quarters. He felt no guilt for his association with Faria, but it was not something he wished to explain to the woman he loved, on the spot where he had killed her husband. There would be better moments, and perhaps an amphora of wine to help things along. 'I'm in debt to Cheldric, anyway,' he said. 'One day I'll explain. He helped me out of a dangerous spot in Londinium, and his own life was at risk, so I couldn't leave him there. I took him back to Henfelin and put him in my house. It was empty, there was no reason not to.'

'And the others?' Gael enquired.

'The old man and the boy who were living in this hut,' Kerin said. 'Morvid and Marc. If I'd left them here, your father would have butchered them, so I told them to get themselves to Henfelin and move in with the cook. I haven't been back since, so I've no idea if they got there in one piece. That's all.'

Gael sat with elbows resting on her knees, chin supported by one hand. There was a very lengthy silence. 'Is he a good cook?' she asked.

'Yes,' Kerin said. 'A very good cook. And a good man. I couldn't leave any of these people behind, but if you'd sooner they lived somewhere else – '

Gael pressed her finger to his lips. 'I'm not used to good men,' she said. 'It's not what I'm used to, that's all. I'm glad you didn't leave them behind. And that you put them in your house. That's what good men do, I expect. Let's leave it there, for now.' She leaned forward and kissed him. They might have moved from the log, but behind them, Eryr gave a sudden, strident whinny. Her warning note. Kerin stood up. He recognised the rider immediately; Father Septimus, on his sleek grey mule. The monk hailed them and pushed the animal into a trot.

'Father!' Gael exclaimed as he dismounted. 'Will you take breakfast? There's gruel in the pot.'

'No,' Septimus said, 'there's no time for that. Eldof's party is approaching Corinium. They expect to make Glevum by nightfall. And if your father's ridden ahead, he could be here at any time.' He turned to Kerin. 'You should be on the road. And Gael, you need to pack up your things and get yourself back to your father's house. He wouldn't be too pleased to find you here, I'm sure.'

'I'll help you load the cart,' Kerin said.

'I'll do that,' the abbot said. 'Go on, take a few moments together and I'll harness the pony.'

Kerin took Gael's hand and they retreated inside the hut. Neither could find words for this. They simply clung together in the darkness. Outside Septimus chirruped to the pony and the cart creaked as he raised the shafts to back her in.

'I'll come back,' Kerin said. 'I promise.'

'Before you go to the North!' Gael cried, flinging her arms around his neck.

'Yes,' Kerin said. 'Before we go to war. I promise.' He grabbed his weapons and saddlebag, left her in the hut and walked out into the clear morning.

'I'll look out for her,' Septimus said. 'Her father will probably leave her alone for a bit. He's a good fighting man, if nothing else, so he'll be busy schooling his men and horses ready for the spring. I brought this.' He held out a little sack tied at the neck. 'Bread and cheese. We make our own. And a little flask of cider. We make that too. Should keep you going for a while.'

'Bless you, Father,' Kerin said. 'For this and for everything else.' He let Eryr out of the pen, flung on her tack, secured his spear and baggage to the saddle and rode away through the beech woods towards the Roman road.

10

The settlement beside the river was waking to a fine, wind-swept day when Kerin reached the head of his home valley. Men and women who had gathered at the mill to grind corn looked up and hailed the familiar rider. As he rounded the bend in the track under the ivy-clad rocks, something small and hard hit him between the shoulder-blades. Kerin spun in the saddle and saw a smooth round pebble rolling into the grass. Vortigern came down the side of the valley on a fine young liver chestnut horse. He chuckled at Kerin's bewilderment and they rode side by side down the broad track beside the river. Vortigern reached out and slapped Eryr's neck.

'Is she recovered?' he asked.

'Yes,' Kerin said, feeling miserably guilty. 'I had to wait until I was sure. I can't spare her.'

'Of course not,' Vortigern said. 'Where did you stay?'

'At a village not far from where it happened. They were hospitable and didn't ask many questions. I told them I was on my way to visit Eldof. Some horse-dealers arrived as I was leaving, and you know what they're like, full of gossip. They said he'd just reached Corinium.'

Vortigern drew rein. 'No news of Rufus?'

'No, lord. Not that I've heard.'

Vortigern shrugged. Whatever Rufus's absence meant to him, he looked transformed, like a man who had woken whole and refreshed from a night of healing sleep.

'The city doesn't agree with you, does it,' Kerin said.

'No. But the business of the world is transacted in cities, so there'll be more of it to come. No matter. We have a feast to look forward to first. The feast you told me I should have. It's in ten days' time. I'm on my way to Carneddlas, to invite them all. I could have sent a messenger, I suppose, but I thought Hefydd deserved a personal visit. He was a damned nuisance in our younger days, but he and his brother have been strong men for us this year. You can come along, if you like. They're bound to tap a cask of ale.'

'I might come later,' Kerin said. 'My clothes stink to heaven and I need to change horses.' It was neither of those things, of course, although both were true. Vortigern's ready invitation had made him feel more guilty than ever, and besides, he had a mission to accomplish before he lost his nerve.

* * *

It was less than an hour's ride from Henfelin. Circumstances rather than distance had drawn the line. Kerin reined in on the hilltop, looking northward across the valley towards the high ridge of the Cribin. On the next hilltop, clearly visible although veiled by sea mist, was the citadel; a modest chieftain's hall and perhaps twenty other smaller houses, with their outbuildings and animal pens. They were sur-rounded by a wooden stockade which looked far too high, and a ditch which was far too deep and wide, for a peaceful stretch of country where all the enemies had been driven off or slaughtered years ago. After all this time, Gwyndaf still had his guard up.

It was enough to have embittered any man, of course.

Gwyndaf of Craig Goch loved his wife and two young daughters with the sort of passionate, enduring commitment which Kerin had yet to experience; and as if losing them were not enough, he was forced to watch, bound hand and foot, while a boatload of pirates raped them and burned them to death in the house he had built for them. Vortigern, faced with an invading fleet of fifty Irish war galleys, had decided that he needed every man at his disposal to protect Henfelin, with its vulnerable valley settlement and hundreds of inhabitants. Gwyndaf pleaded for a defence force while the galleys massed out in the channel, and Vortigern refused, telling Gwyndaf that he should bring his people to Henfelin for protection, like Hefydd and many others had done. Gwyndaf was too proud and headstrong to have anything to do with that idea. In his heart he probably reasoned that the war fleet would ignore his little settlement in favour of the richer prize to the east. He reckoned without the maverick ships which followed the fleet, crewed by freebooters who spat on the Irish commanders and feasted on the spoils of their battles. The men who came ashore had been at sea for weeks, and it had made them savage. They beached their boats in a muddy creek, killed the fishermen who lived there and got drunk on their ale. By the time they sighted Gwyndaf's citadel they were crazy for blood and flesh. The distant flames were sighted from Henfelin. By that time the main battle was over, and most of the Irish galleys were burning on the beach at the valley mouth. Vortigern and Lud led a rescue party which Kerin and Rufus, youngsters at the time, were forbidden to join. They were back within hours with the few survivors. These did not include Gwyndaf, who ran howling into the hills the moment his bonds were cut.

It was fifteen years since all this happened. For much

of that time Gwyndaf had avoided Vortigern entirely, apart from a couple of frosty and ill-tempered occasions when they met by accident. The raiders never returned, and Gwyndaf recovered with time, insofar as anyone could. He rebuilt his citadel, married a girl who accepted that she could never replace his first wife, and fathered two more children. But his hatred of Vortigern manifested itself in all sorts of irritating ways, like his refusal to pay the tribute tax, or to allow Henfelin tradesmen to pass through his territory without searching their baggage. His craftsmen turned out superb swords, which he would not sell to Vortigern's warriors, and he refused to return any Henfelin cattle which strayed onto his land; although all the land in Glywysing, in the nature of things, belonged to Vortigern in any case. Vortigern never exacted the tribute or complained about the cattle. Gwyndaf, of course, took this as an admission of guilt.

As Kerin rode down from the hilltop, wondering what on earth he was going to say, a horseman appeared high up on the great buttress of sandstone rock which had given Craig Goch its name. Gwyndaf came down the hillside at a fast clip, his mare's hooves drumming on the short brown turf. Kerin raised his hands to indicate peaceful intentions. Gwyndaf was armed as if for battle with a spear, a fine double-edged sword, two knives and a sling, which he had a reputation for using with deadly accuracy. A few horse-lengths away he reined in and circled Kerin warily, a lean, rangy man with short brown hair and a heavy, drooping moustache, both flecked with grey. He could not have been more than forty years of age, but with that gaunt, lined face he looked a little older.

'Kerin Brightspear,' he said, without a flicker of a smile. 'What are you doing here? Was he afraid to come himself?'

'It was my idea to come here, Gwyndaf,' Kerin said.

'No-one else knows I'm here, and no-one sent me. I'd like to talk to you.'

Gwyndaf looked straight at him with his sharp, hard grey eyes. 'What for? Why should I talk to someone who lives in Vortigern's pocket?'

'Because I want to ask you something. Some things are more important than a feud with one man, whatever caused it.'

Gwyndaf regarded him curiously. 'I don't think you know what you're talking about. But you've got nerve, I'll give you that. Come on, we'll talk over meat. It won't be poisoned, by the way. I don't believe in killing the messenger.'

'I'm no-one's messenger,' Kerin said. 'I've already told you that.'

Gwyndaf shook his head as if he didn't believe a word of it, and turned his mare's head towards the citadel.

The house was as bare of luxuries as a hermit's cell. Gwyndaf invited Kerin to sit and brought out a platter of cooked meats; mutton, salt pork and pheasant. A thin, dark woman with shy eyes brought a pitcher of water.

'I don't drink ale at this time of day,' Gwyndaf said, without apology. 'It addles the brain.'

'I can ill afford that,' Kerin said. Gwyndaf looked up with the trace of a smile. Three young warriors, as fit and sharp as he was, peered in through the door and drifted away. Kerin knew that he had made the right decision, however uncomfortable he felt sitting here. No king, however confident, however strong, could afford to have living right under his nose an adversary as disruptive and damaging as Gwyndaf was capable of being. The woman brought bread and beakers, then vanished into an adjoining room. A child's laughter greeted her.

'I take it the news is true,' Gwyndaf said.

'The news?'

'That he's killed off that monk and made himself king. It's no more or less than I'd have expected.'

'It wasn't quite like that, but it's true that he's king now,' Kerin said. 'Almost everyone wanted it in the end, even Eldof of Glevum and some of the Romans.'

Gwyndaf laughed and looked up at the dark roof. 'There's no limit to it, is there?'

'To what?'

'To people's stupidity,' Gwyndaf said darkly. 'I suppose he's spun them some yarn about it being for their own good.'

'It is for their own good,' Kerin said. Gwyndaf snorted and tore at his meat.

'I wouldn't expect you to say anything else. He did save your skin after all, though God knows why; it was out of character, to say the least.'

Kerin knew that he was more than half right, but it was hardly the time to admit it. 'I don't want to argue with you, Gwyndaf,' he said.

'Then why did you come here? What is there to agree about?'

'Keeping your family safe, possibly?'

Gwyndaf's eyes narrowed. 'What the hell are you talking about?'

'Fighting the Picts,' Kerin said. 'We're raising an army to fight them in the spring. They've already overrun most of the North, and their galleys are threatening the merchant fleet. If we don't fight them soon, there's nothing to stop them ravaging the rest of the country. And if you don't think that's got anything to do with us, imagine what would happen if they joined up with the Irish and started attacking these coasts too.'

Gwyndaf put down his meat. His hand closed around Kerin's wrist. 'If you're lying about this to make me listen to you, I'll cut your throat,' he said.

'I'm not lying,' Kerin said. 'Why should I? Don't you think it would have been easier for me to stay at home in Henfelin and get drunk or bed a few girls?'

Gwyndaf raised his eyebrows. 'The answer must be yes, given your legendary capacity for both. So, let's suppose that you're telling the truth. What do you expect me to do about it?'

'Come with us in the spring,' Kerin said. 'They say you've got a better warband than most.'

Gwyndaf laughed out loud. 'You're actually asking me to fight for him?'

'No. Vortigern wouldn't ask that of you, and neither would I. But I thought you might want to fight for Cambria. And to keep your family safe. Someone's got to do it, Gwyndaf, and I can't believe that you'd trust any of us.'

'You're right about that,' Gwyndaf said, with the cold bitterness which always lay within him, ready to flash out at the slightest provocation. 'Come with me.' Kerin followed him, between the buildings and up a wooden stairway to the top of the stockade. It was almost like standing on the prow of a ship, high above a great blue expanse stretching from the dark headlands in the east to the wide estuary of the river which met the rising tide at Leucarum. Sea merged into sky on a distant, invisible horizon. High above, gulls wheeled in the thin cloud. On the hill's north-western flank, the ground sloped gently away towards the saltmarsh where Gwyndaf's people grazed their sheep. The three young warriors who had appeared at the door were out on the slope with some others, racing their horses back and forth, hurling spears at a sack of straw nailed to a post. Their aim and horsemanship were as good as most Kerin had seen. Gwyndaf watched them critically.

'They're good,' Kerin said. Gwyndaf nodded.

'As good as any of yours. That boy on the dun mare – Derfyn, the thin lad – he's a better swordsman than I am. And now you want me to take them off to fight for Vortigern. That is what you're asking, of course, however you put it. Anyone who rides with him must defer to him. It was ever so, and the kingship will hardly have changed things.'

'Do you think we could have chosen a better leader, then?' Kerin asked. 'Eldof of Glevum, or one of the old Romans?'

Gwyndaf spat over the wall. 'No. Eldof's a self-important oaf, not half the warrior he thinks he is. I never said that Vortigern was a bad leader, anyway. Sacrificing another man's family to save your own might make you a bastard, but it doesn't make you a bad leader.'

It was not quite like that, of course, and Kerin suspected that Gwyndaf knew it as well as anyone. 'How many fighting men do you have?' he asked.

'Thirty in all. Hardly an army, but enough for my needs. They're all between your age and mine, and they can all fight as well as you or I can. A few of them are relations, and the rest are nobodies who turned up here looking for something to do.'

'A bit like me, then,' Kerin said. 'What made you take them in?'

Gwyndaf looked round. 'They're the best of them. Blood relations – sometimes you don't know whether they're with you because they're loyal or because they feel they should be. The others are different. Nothing's forcing them to stay, but they think they owe it to me, because I've given them a chance they wouldn't have had otherwise. I'd say that they're exactly like you, in fact.'

His gaze was steady and without irony. Kerin knew that it was the closest thing to a compliment he could ever expect to get from Gwyndaf.

'We need them,' he said. 'We need them, and we need you. Vortigern will never ask, but I can. We're trying to make an army out of all sorts – Eldof, Gorlois and his Kernow boys, the Kentishmen, even any Roman military men who've come over to us. It's like trying to keep six separate wolf packs in order sometimes. If it's ever going to work, we need enough men we can trust at the heart of it, people whose loyalty we don't even have to think about.'

'And you think of me like that?' Gwyndaf said. 'I'd have knifed him after it happened if I'd had the chance.'

'I know. But who is it best to knife now, Vortigern or a Pict? I'm not asking you to change what you feel, Gwyndaf, just to see what matters most.'

Gwyndaf's face set hard with resentment. 'There's only one thing that matters to me, Kerin Brightspear, and that's to make sure that what happened to my family never happens again.' He looked out across the hillside where the sea mist was thinning under a pale sun. The young warriors were still charging back and forth and a little crowd of women and children had gathered to watch them, cheering when they hit their straw target and laughing raucously when they missed. Gwyndaf watched with unconcealed affection and pride. 'If fighting under the same flag as Vortigern is the only way to protect all this, then I'll do it. I'll hate him until the day I rot, and I'll never swear allegiance to him, but I will do it. He'll have to ask me himself, though. I've got time for you because you're a good warrior and it must have taken some guts for you to come here like this, but in the end it's not enough. He'll have to ask me himself, and he'll have to ask me here, because I'm not going to Henfelin.'

'I'll tell him that,' Kerin said. Gwyndaf looked at him curiously.

'He really didn't send you, did he.'

'No. I wouldn't have lied to you about that.'

'Alright.' Gwyndaf folded his arms. 'If he wants to see me, tell him to come here tomorrow morning at sunrise. Alone and unarmed. It's easy to be brave when you've got a warband as good as his. I'll meet him down there in the valley.'

'Alone and unarmed?' Kerin asked.

'Of course,' Gwyndaf said resentfully. 'I'm a man of honour, even if others aren't.'

'I'll tell him,' Kerin said, hoping as he spoke that Vortigern would not, for whatever reason, refuse to go along with it. He was here because he had talked himself into a corner back in Londinium, but there was far more at stake than his own reputation. He left Gwyndaf on the rampart and rode away, wondering how he himself would have felt about meeting, alone and unarmed, a man who had wished him dead for fifteen years.

11

It was not the shortest way home, but after months of roads and inland tracks, Kerin could not resist the coast. Eryr, as happy as her rider, pranced and cavorted along the low watermark like a filly. At first Kerin tried to ignore the voice which was shouting at him, but it persisted. Father Iustig came over the crest of the dunes on his shabby donkey.

'Kerin!' he bellowed. 'Kerin Brightspear! Wait!'

Kerin waited. The donkey had got up some momentum, and Iustig had to drag on her reins as he came alongside. She dug all four hooves into the sand and stopped dead, sending the abbot straight over her head. Kerin looked away, trying hard not to laugh, while the donkey trotted away towards the woods. He dismounted and helped the abbot to his feet.

'Thank you, lad,' Iustig gasped. 'That's the devil's creature.' He paused. 'I've heard. But I want to hear it from you.'

Kerin looked up at the clear sky and the circling gulls. 'Constans is dead, Vortigern is king, and we're going to war in the spring.'

'And who killed Constans?'

'A bunch of Picts who were supposed to be guarding him. Lud and the boys caught them out on the coast, and Vortigern thought they might come in useful.' Iustig gave him a look which required no interpretation. 'Father, Vortigern didn't kill Constans,' Kerin said, wishing that the abbot had been able to see things in the same light as the pragmatic Marcellus. 'Perhaps he did wish him dead. I wished him gone myself, although I'd have preferred it done without blood. But whatever happened, we're better off without him.'

'Kerin!' Iustig protested. 'There are many ways to do God's will, but murdering his servants can't possibly be one of them.'

Kerin stared out at the glistening sea. Its calmness seemed to mock his confusion. 'He wasn't God's servant, Iustig. Not any more. And there are worse things to worry about now, anyway.'

'I know,' Iustig said. Some sharpness in his tone made Kerin turn. 'Rufus is here. He came back last night, with a monk from the north country. He asked me to look out for you. I know there's a feast coming up. A celebration. He says he wants to talk to you before it happens.' Iustig paused, as if bracing himself for something. 'He told me where he's been.'

'Well, Vortigern doesn't know,' Kerin said, 'so for God's sake, keep it to yourself. Whoever this needs to come from, it's not you.'

'I'm well aware of that,' the abbot said, avoiding his eyes. Kerin took a steadying breath. He knew that this was no time for raising obscure old feuds, but it was beyond him not to feel a ripple of hostility on Vortigern's behalf.

'What do you think about it, then?' he asked. 'Rufus's little expedition?' He knew that his voice had sounded harsher than he intended. Iustig looked pained.

'I told him he should have stayed at home, for what it's worth. Vortigern's king now, for better or worse, and he can't afford a squabble with his oldest son. What's done is done, and I never want to see another war galley out in this bay. That is what we might see, I take it, if the men of power decide to fight each other, not the invaders?'

'It's more than likely,' Kerin said. 'Do you think Rufus listened to you?'

'God knows. The faith I tried to teach you is about love and redemption. Now men are making it a warriors' code, a blood-letters' excuse. Rufus was the gentlest of lads. If men like him can take up the sword and say they're doing it all for God, what hope is there for the stupid, unthinking brutes who make up most men's warbands?'

'Very little, Father,' Kerin said, realising that what was coming to him now was worse than any of the angry disputes in Londinium, and that he would have to deal with it alone. 'Send Rufus down here to me. I'm not running after him. He's the one who left.' They walked to the point where a stream curved out from the salt marsh behind the grassy dunes. Ahead, wooded cliffs rose steeply towards the hidden chapel and the monks' cold caves. 'I'll wait here,' Kerin said. He tied Eryr to a sun-bleached log and sat down on it.

'You've changed,' Iustig said. 'Or something's changed. You speak as if you had authority.'

'I do,' Kerin said. 'There were things that had to be done, and I did them. In Londinium, I'm known as the king's right arm. His words, not mine. I'd never have presumed.'

Iustig gave him a look of some misgiving. 'Please, be careful what you say to Rufus. He loves you, whatever's happened, and I know he cares for your opinion. I don't know how much faith you have these days, but please, try to remember the things you learned here as children. They haven't changed, however some men pervert them. And if the faith doesn't come before all things, it's nothing.'

'That's easy enough for you to say,' Kerin snapped. He was quite unprepared for the way the abbot flinched, as if he had torn the scar from some half-healed wound.

'No,' Iustig said. 'That's quite untrue, as it happens.' He

turned and trudged off along the bank of the stream. Kerin watched him go, as bemused as ever. Leather soles slapped on rock as the abbot toiled up the rough path through the wood. The distant sea rumbled, wind hissed in the sea grass. Kerin closed his eyes, trying to let the sounds calm him, and waited for his blood brother to come.

* * *

'Did he send you?' Rufus was standing in front of Kerin, still in his travelling clothes, looking like a wary animal.

'For God's sake, sit down,' Kerin said. When Rufus didn't respond, he stood up. They faced each other on the soft sand beside the driftwood log. It had not been Kerin's intention at all, but already, with scarcely a word spoken, this felt like a confrontation. 'No, your father didn't send me. He has no idea that you're here, and even less that you've been to Gallia.'

'I asked Iustig not to mention that,' Rufus said, with patent surprise.

'He didn't mention it,' Kerin said. Rufus's eyes narrowed.

'Who on earth told you? No-one knew.'

'I heard it in Londinium,' Kerin said. There was nothing he wished to add.

'Well,' Rufus said, 'if you know where I've been, then I'm sure you'll know why I went.'

'Yes,' Kerin said curtly. 'So, what do you want? A civil war? Because on my life, Rufus, that's what we'll have, if this carries on. Either that, or a bloody invasion. Your father's king now, whether you like it or not, and the Picts –'

'The Picts!' Rufus said scornfully. 'Will you blame them for everything? If all my father wanted to do was kill Picts, he'd have hanged those savages in Londinium.' He raised his hands defensively. 'And before you speak, I know we have to drive them back behind that wall, and yes, I'll fight them with you. But as for dragging a monk from his cell –'

'Constans wasn't dragged!' Kerin shouted, his temper fraying dangerously. 'He wanted it, Rufus. He wanted to get out of that stinking hovel and have the power and get drunk and bed boys like Lupinus. And anyway, did you have a better plan?'

'We should have sent for his brother Ambrosius,' Rufus said, white with anger. 'But you were never going to listen to me, were you? Alright then, burn in hell with my father, if you must.'

'My life belongs to him!' Kerin protested.

'Yes,' Rufus said, 'and he'll cast you off just as he did Constans, the moment he no longer needs you.'

Kerin lashed out with a howl of anger. Rufus staggered backwards and fell on his back in the sand.

'I'm sorry!' Kerin cried, seizing him by the shoulders. Rufus struggled to his feet, wiping a trickle of blood from his mouth.

'No.' He avoided Kerin's eyes. 'It's I who should be sorry.'

'Why did you say that?' Kerin blurted. Rufus's eyes brimmed with tears.

'Because my brothers will never be what you are. And my father doesn't deserve your love.'

Kerin walked across to the log and untied his horse. 'That's not for you to say. You might see things differently, if you'd been born as I was.'

'Yes,' Rufus conceded. 'I know that's true.'

'Are you coming to the feast? Everyone will be there.' Kerin paused. 'For God's sake, Rufus. You know how it'll look, if you don't come.'

'Alright,' Rufus said, without enthusiasm. 'I'll come, I

promise.' He looked out across the beach, where flocks of seabirds were gathering to feed as the tide rose. 'I should go to Carneddlas first, really, to make my peace with Branwen.'

'You'll need to make your peace with Hefydd and his boys, too,' Kerin said. 'I think they were hoping for a marriage.'

'A marriage?' Rufus looked stunned.

'Well, you courted the girl, didn't you?' Kerin asked.

'Courted her a little, yes, but that's all.'

Kerin snorted. 'You're the fool, then,' he said, mounting up. 'Now she thinks you're putting your sword in someone else's scabbard, as Mabli so delicately put it.'

'That's nonsense.' Rufus coloured violently. 'How could I possibly think about that, with things as they are? Let alone marriage, if that's what she was hoping for.'

Kerin did not respond. He was finding it difficult to think about anything else. 'Next you'll be telling me that the faith comes before the flesh,' he said.

'Well, it does,' Rufus said. 'It must.'

Kerin raised his eyebrows. 'Rather you than me, trying to explain that to Branwen.'

Rufus looked up. 'I never said I didn't want the girl. But at the moment, there are other things which have to come first. Do you think she'll understand that?'

Kerin grimaced. 'No. Perhaps a jug of wine would help. She's bound to be at the feast.'

'Look, I've already told you I'll be there,' Rufus said tetchily. 'You don't have to dangle the girl in front of me.'

'I wasn't. But if you want her, you should do something about it, before she dangles herself in front of somebody else.'

Rufus looked up at him in mild horror, as if despite everything, this possibility had not occurred to him. Perhaps it was something to do with being Vortigern's son and sure of his station in the world, Kerin thought, turning his horse towards the valley before Rufus had time to change his mind.

12

Vortigern was riding along the beach on his beautiful dappled grey stallion. No saddle or bridle, just a rope headcollar. Kerin sat on the river bank, throwing sticks into the dark water, and waited for them to arrive. Banks of heavy cloud to the south-east suggested that snow might be imminent, but the evening still seemed mild after the freezing weather in Londinium. The stallion came through the river by the stepping stones in a shower of spray. Vortigern turned him loose and threw himself down on the bank beside Kerin. He lay on his back and stared up at the sky.

'God,' he said softly, 'this is the water of life.' Kerin leaned on his elbow, picking at a tussock of grass. 'I found an old man on the beach,' Vortigern said. 'Collecting seaweed. I'd have kicked him into the tide, but he said he belonged to you.'

Kerin's hand flew to his forehead. 'Morvid!' he exclaimed. Since arriving home, he had not even had time to visit his own house, let alone given a thought to the old man and his grandson. 'He's the one who saved my leg. Is he well?'

'Well enough to give me a mouthful of abuse,' Vortigern said. Kerin groaned aloud.

'He couldn't have known who you were, lord.'

Vortigern grinned. 'No saddle and a peasant's clothes? Anyone could guess that I was King of all the Britons. What's he doing here, anyway?'

'I told him to come here with his grandson. I couldn't leave him there to get butchered by Bertil Redknife. And he might come in useful when we go off to fight.'

Vortigern shrugged. 'Very well,' he conceded. 'Let him stay.' The stallion sauntered over and nuzzled his shoulder. As a colt, he had kicked his way out of a pen and torn his neck on a splintered plank, opening a broad gash which left behind a strange, elongated scar when it healed. The stable lads, thinking it looked like a fish, started calling him the Pike; and everyone still did, even now, when the scar had become a patch of white hair, and the horse was a weapon of war. Vortigern sat up. 'Is Rufus back?'

'Yes, lord. He'll be at the feast.'

'Well,' Vortigern said, 'if he comes, it'll be for you.'

Kerin wondered whether to leave the other matter, but all in all it seemed better to get it over with. 'I saw Gwyndaf this morning,' he said. 'After we met by the river.'

'Gwyndaf? Where did you run into him?'

'I didn't run into him. I went to look for him. He said that he'll fight for us in the spring.'

Vortigern laughed out loud. 'Gwyndaf, fight for me? Don't be ridiculous. He'd fight for the Picts first.'

'No,' Kerin said. 'Not if he thinks it's the best way to protect his family.'

'What on earth did you tell him?'

'That the only way to guarantee the safety of Cambria is to make sure that the Picts never push south-west and link up with the Irish,' Kerin said. 'It might be a threat, I don't really know, but I wanted to tell Gwyndaf something he could believe. He's got a first-rate bunch of warriors over there, just the sort we need.'

'Is there something else?' Vortigern asked. 'It *cannot* be as simple as that.'

'Well,' Kerin said carefully, 'he says he won't swear allegiance, but I think that's just for appearances' sake. He wants you to ask him, though. He won't take it from me.'

'You mean he wants me to crawl to him.'

'No. But to satisfy his pride, he wants to be asked by you.'

'Well, I hope that's all he wants. I know we could do with his fighting men and I'm sorry in my heart for what happened to his family, but you must see that I can't apologise to him for something which I know was right, and which I'd do again, if need be.'

'I know that,' Kerin said, 'and I'm sure Gwyndaf knows it too. Will you go to him?'

'How can I refuse?' Vortigern's tone held a trace of irritation. 'If I do, he'll tell everyone in creation that I'm afraid to do it, won't he?'

'Yes,' Kerin said. 'I think you can count on that.'

'Then I'll go to him, since you've left me no choice.' Vortigern's eyes glittered resentfully. 'Perhaps you'd like to tell me what you have agreed on my behalf.'

'Nothing,' Kerin said. 'They're Gwyndaf's terms, not mine, and I haven't agreed to anything. But if you want to meet him, he'll be in the valley below his citadel at sunrise tomorrow. Alone and unarmed.'

'Alone and unarmed?' Vortigern said sceptically. 'Do you believe that?'

'Yes. Whatever's happened between you, I think he's honourable.'

Vortigern rose to his feet and whistled softly to the Pike. 'Honour doesn't come into it.'

'What do you mean?' Kerin asked. Vortigern caught the stallion's halter rope.

'No man can be entirely honourable when he bears that sort of grudge. One day you'll take a wife and father some children. Then you'll know what I mean.'

Kerin looked up, suddenly filled with foreboding. A host of images flooded into his mind, coming straight from Morvid's valley. 'Lord, I'd never put you at risk.'

'No, I know that. And in a way, it's for the best. It'll never work if we can't turn our backs on each other without fear.'

'I'll ride with you as far as the Cribin.' Kerin was beginning to wish that he had never been near Gwyndaf's citadel.

'No,' Vortigern said, swinging easily onto the stallion's back. 'There'd be no point. If Gwyndaf has lied to you and comes armed, how long do you think it would take him to kill me? Half a second? Even you can't move that fast.'

Kerin watched him ride away – loose rein, one with the horse – and knew that he was looking at a man in his element. Londinium and the kingship seemed very distant. He knew that there could be no turning from the path Vortigern had chosen. If they abandoned it now, everything would be lost. But at that moment he could have wished them both back where they were a year ago; lords of the West, with a border at the river and no concerns beyond the roots which bound them to this blessed earth.

13

Morvid sat cross-legged on the floor beside the fire in Kerin's house, drinking a bowl of steaming gruel which Cheldric had prepared to welcome the cold new day.

'How was I to know who he was?' he said indignantly. 'Would you expect the king to turn up wearing something the dog might have dragged in?'

'Alright,' Kerin raised his hand. 'Just watch your step in the future.'

Morvid cackled and slurped his gruel. 'I'll bet it's years since anyone called him a cheeky young bastard.' Kerin groaned and shut his eyes. Marc, who was sitting on the table whittling a chunk of wood, smothered a giggle. Cheldric ladled out a bowl of gruel for Kerin and gave the boy a baleful look.

'You know him, you don't laugh.'

Marc gave him an evil grin. 'I'll laugh at you falling over the pig, then,' he said. Cheldric emitted a threatening growl and raised the ladle. Marc dropped his wood and fled, screeching with laughter. Kerin sipped his gruel, hardly able to believe the noisy, convivial place which his house had become. Despite the bickering, it was plain that Cheldric, Morvid and the boy had struck up a friendship, if only because they were all strangers in a place where everyone else had known each other from birth. Cheldric hurled his ladle at the wall and stalked out of the door. Morvid chuckled.

'He's a good lad, but no sense of humour. I wonder if they're all the same?'

'The Saxons, you mean?'

'Yes. Never set eyes on one until now. Please God, he's the only one I'll ever see.'

There was a rap on the door, the smart crack of wood striking wood. Kerin got up, but he was too late; Caradog the archdruid had already let himself in. He hobbled over to the fire on his wooden staff and sniffed at Cheldric's cauldron.

'Help yourself,' Kerin said. 'It's only gruel, but there's plenty of it.'

'Ha!' said the druid, grabbing an abandoned bowl and filling it up. 'You've still got that cook, then. Take my advice and keep him over here where the monks can't get hold of him, or he'll have you on bread and water in no time. As if we were given all the earth's bounty, just so that we could starve ourselves.' He gave Morvid a suspicious look. 'Who are you, then? You're not one of the Christians, are you?'

'No, no,' Morvid said reassuringly. 'I'm Morvid, and I don't care much about religion. I'm more interested in pigs, really. My father worshipped the old gods, so I suppose I believe in them, if anything.'

'Good, good.' The archdruid gave an approving nod.

'Morvid's a healer,' Kerin said. 'I was wounded in a fight, and he saved my leg.'

The archdruid drained his bowl, filled it up again and gave him a quizzical look. 'Well, Kerin Brightspear, you're acquiring quite a household, aren't you? All you need now is a woman.'

Morvid chuckled. 'I know one who'd have him,' he said. Kerin turned. He knew that he lacked Vortigern's capacity for the assassin's stare, but the look he directed at Morvid had an adequate effect. The old man smiled sweetly and broke into a tuneless whistle, while Caradog went on wolfing his gruel. Kerin left them to their breakfast and went outside. The air was crisp and cold, but the sun was rising above the moors behind the citadel, and its pale light cast a surprising warmth over the sheltered spaces between the buildings. Kerin sat down on the bench outside his door and examined the little silver ring, still hanging from the chain around his neck. Mabli, perhaps sensing a change in him, had kept her distance, and he was grateful.

'Glad to be home, lad?' It was the archdruid, coming out to sit in the sun with his bowl of gruel.

'Very glad, Caradog,' Kerin said. 'You've never been to a big city, have you?'

'Never, boy.' Caradog sat down with a grunt. 'I've never seen the point, when the gods gave us trees and caves for shelter. It must have driven the Lord mad, being there for as long as he was.'

'Yes, it did. But he's king now, so there'll be more of it to put up with, I expect.'

Caradog put down his bowl and leaned closer. 'Did he kill that monk, then?'

'No,' Kerin said. 'And neither did I.'

The archdruid chuckled mischievously. 'You're both glad to see him dead, though.'

'Well, he was never going to make a leader. The country needs a strong king; someone who can pull men together, and lead an army.'

The sound of trapping hooves came up the track from the valley. Abbot Iustig rode through the open gates on his ageing donkey. Brother Padarn was close behind, on one of the grey horses Kerin had pilfered from the praetor's stables to get to Eldof's camp.

'That monk,' Caradog sighed. 'And he's brought another one. A new one.'

'Brother Padarn,' Kerin said. 'He's a good, sensible man, and he's coming to the North with us. The Picts killed his family, and it turned his head. I think he became a monk because he thought it might be a way to get over it.'

Caradog stood up as the monks dismounted and tied their animals to the hitching rail. 'What are you doing up here, then, Iustig?' he asked.

'I've every right to be here,' the abbot said, with strained patience. 'At least as much right as you, because there are as many Christians as pagans here, if not more. And anyway, I've been asked to bless a new child.'

Padarn cleared his throat awkwardly and looked at Kerin.

'Brother Padarn, this is Caradog, our archdruid,' Kerin said, ushering the old priest forward. Padarn smiled and extended a large hand.

'I'm honoured,' he said. The archdruid looked profoundly shocked.

'Honoured?' He clasped Padarn's hand in his mottled claw. 'Well, that makes a pleasant change.'

'Everyone must come to God in his own way,' Padarn said. 'Why should I damn anyone for following his father's gods? And there's good and bad in both camps, surely.'

'Oh yes,' the archdruid said, giving Iustig a sly glance. 'There are some terrible people who worship the old gods, and I suppose there must be one or two good Christians about somewhere.' He chuckled, and Iustig gave him a pained look. There were times, Kerin thought, when the abbot's undoubted goodness could have benefited from being leavened with a sense of humour.

'Have you found somewhere to live, Padarn?' he asked.

'Oh yes,' the monk said happily. 'Father Iustig's lent me

an excellent cave. It might not sound like much to you, but believe me, if you'd lived in one of those hovels in Venta Belgarum, you'd think you were in paradise.'

'Venta Belgarum?' The archdruid pricked up his ears. 'That's the place we call Caerwynt, isn't it? The place where that little weasel monk came from?'

'Caradog, we should pity poor Constans, not revile him,' Iustig sighed. The archdruid looked up at the sky.

'Well, I don't know about that. They say he lay with boys, not to mention a few juicy slave girls. Is that right, Kerin Brightspear? Did he lie with boys?'

'Yes,' Kerin said. 'One or two.'

The archdruid shook his head. 'Not much of a loss, Father. And at least now we've got a king we can support. That can't be a bad thing, can it?'

'No,' Iustig said, tight-lipped. 'Vortigern's got what he wanted, so what's a dead monk here or there? And before you open your mouth, I know he's the king we need. But don't ask me to approve what he did. Vortigern sacrificed that poor, pathetic young man on the altar of his own ambition. And yes, I'll support his kingship because no-one else can save the kingdom. But if your faith can condone something like that, then I'm sorry for you.' Scarlet-faced, he turned and stalked off between the houses.

'Short-sighted old fool,' Caradog said, watching him go.

'Why do you say that?' Kerin asked. Caradog looked up, narrowing his weak eyes against the sun.

'It'll do for him, Kerin Brightspear.'

'What?'

'The Lord,' said the druid. 'I've known him since the day he was born. Of course he wanted to be king. But you know, power's for stupid men, really. Men like the Romans, who could enjoy its fruits and still get a good night's sleep.

Vortigern always had too much going on in that head of his. He's walking into the fire with this, and he knows it.'

'But he's the best king we could have,' Kerin said. 'The only man who can possibly hold the kingdom together.'

'Oh, I know all that,' Caradog said. 'He'll lead the armies and beat those savages into the middle of next year, and everybody will say there's never been a king like him. But it'll do for him; you see if it doesn't.' He patted Kerin's shoulder, then, picking up his oak staff, he gave Padarn a sociable wave and set off towards the valley.

* * *

Vortigern came back at midday. Kerin ran out as he heard the horse come in. 'Well?' he said. Vortigern followed him into the house. Cheldric looked up from tending the fire.

'You eat, lord?'

'Yes,' Vortigern said. 'Some of that stuff you made yesterday, if there's any left.'

'Well?' Kerin was on fire with impatience.

'He'll fight for us,' Vortigern said. Kerin blew his cheeks out in relief. Vortigern took off his cloak as they sat down beside the fire. He had gone unarmed, as requested. The plain, close-cut tunic and breeches seemed chosen to make that obvious.

'Did Gwyndaf keep his side of the bargain?'

'Yes. His warriors were all sitting up on the stockade, though. They could easily have finished me off, but there was no trouble.'

There was a clang and a thud. Cheldric came marching back with a small iron pot. 'The pig,' he said, setting it on the fire. 'Is hot soon. Then you eat.' He trotted off to his store room again and returned with two bowls, spoons and a pair of tankards. Rather to Kerin's surprise, he had maintained the cleanliness inflicted upon him in Londinium. His fair hair was glinting in the firelight, his face was pink and shiny and even his apron had barely a speck of dirt on it.

'What's in it?' Vortigern asked as a steaming bowl was placed in front of him.

'Two pigs,' Cheldric said. 'Fresh pig, smoked pig. Roots I dig in the woods, herbs I have from Morvid.'

Vortigern nodded. 'It's good. And I never thought I'd say that about anything produced by a Saxon.'

Cheldric looked as wounded as he dared. 'Saxons not all bad,' he said. 'I cook, I work hard all day. And I hate Roman bastards. You too, I think, lord.'

Vortigern looked up. 'Yes. And with more reason than you'll ever have.'

Cheldric looked at him intently. He was staring, Kerin realised, at the clipeum. Vortigern took off the medallion and handed it to him. Cheldric studied it, running a stubby finger over the inscription around the rim. '*Redditor lucis aeternae*,' Vortigern said, observing his bewilderment. 'It means "restorer of the eternal light."' Kerin looked away and he grinned. 'Yes, alright, you're not the first person to see the humour in that.' Cheldric returned the medallion with a respectful bow.

'You kill Roman warrior and take it from him, lord?'

'No,' Vortigern said, spinning the clipeum on its chain. 'It was freely given.'

'Ah!' Cheldric smiled. 'Friend to friend.'

Vortigern nodded. 'Something like that.'

'Then Roman bastards too are not all bad,' Cheldric said affably. He emptied the remains of his stew into the bowls and clattered away with his pot and ladle.

14

Darkness came early, and with it the snow. Kerin put on a splendid green tunic and fastened it with a silver-buckled belt. He wrapped himself in his finest cloak, a flowing black garment trimmed with ermine, and walked across the square to the great hall of the chieftains. A servant bowed and drew aside the blanket screening the inner doorway. The vast interior was lit by torches and flickering tallow lamps. Fires crackled on the hearth at the far end. Above their vivid flames huge joints of beef and whole sheep's carcasses sizzled on spits, and enormous cauldrons bubbled vigorously. In the bays between the stout posts supporting the roof, rows of tables had been set up, laden with tankards and bowls. Each table had its own amphora and its own cask of ale. The guests were gathering. Kerin strode up the hall, feeling a sudden glow of pride in this spectacle and his place in it. The leading warriors of Henfelin were congregating, all dressed in their best and dripping with ornaments of silver, gold and bronze. Katigern and Paschent were there with Lud and his sons, talking to Hefydd's likeable brother, Hefin.

'Kerin!' Hefin exclaimed, seizing him by the arms. 'Have a cup of wine with me, lad. I've got news! Good news. Tirion's expecting. I know, after all this time and effort. Due at harvest time, she tells me. What do you think of that?'

'I think it's worth an amphora, never mind a cup,' Kerin said, laughing and slapping Hefin on the back. No child had ever been more longed for than this one. Tirion lost her first not long after the marriage, and over time, both parents had resigned themselves to dying childless. 'Fill a jar for me,' Kerin said. 'I'd better see the King of all the Britons first, while I'm still sober enough to speak.'

'He's preening himself,' Lud said, with a wink. 'Go on in; I think he's waiting for you.'

Kerin smiled and passed through the open doorway leading to the private apartments at the rear. There were guest rooms, three spacious bedchambers belonging to Rufus and his brothers, and a square room with a long polished table where Vortigern received envoys, dealt with disputes and met the men who managed his estates. Beyond all this was an inner sanctum which few people entered without express permission. It contained only three rooms. First was the library, the sanctuary where Vortigern kept his books, and went to sit when he wanted some peace. Opposite was a small, stark bath-house with a capacious wooden tub; far removed from the Roman bath, complete with steam-room, which the family was said to have maintained at its palatial townhouse in Isca. Adjoining it was the bedchamber where Vortigern slept alone.

The library was deserted except for the shaggy grey deerhound, Fanw, who was stretched out beside the fire. She opened one eye and thumped her tail lazily as Kerin looked in. Vortigern was in the bath-house, adjusting the gold shoulder-pin of a red cloak.

'Mm,' Kerin said, looking the garment up and down.

Vortigern scowled. 'Don't mock. Where is he?'

'He'll come, lord. He's given me his word.'

'Damn his soul!' Vortigern spat. 'My oldest son, and he can't be here to welcome my guests.'

'Kat and Paschent are there,' Kerin said. 'They seem to be making a good job of it.'

'It's not the same.' Vortigern paced up and down beside the bath. 'It's Rufus's place, not theirs. People are talking already.'

'He will be here,' Kerin insisted.

'Yes. Because you asked him, not because he wants to be. Are all the others here?'

'Most of them,' Kerin said. 'And Hefin's wife is with child, did you know?'

'No,' Vortigern said. His eyes were bleak. 'I'll have to try not to get him killed in the North. Fate's cruel sometimes. All these years, then she conceives before a battle.'

Kerin went to the door of the main hall and peered through. The place was full to the walls. Hefydd was arriving with his boys, shepherding a tall girl with black hair and sparkling dark eyes. Branwen! Kerin hadn't seen her since they were both children, and now the child was a woman, with a slender waist and a pair of ample white breasts which looked eager to escape from her clinging red gown. Kerin wondered if Rufus had thought much about the implications before disappointing her. Branwen was a goddess at Carneddlas, born to Hefydd and his ageing wife when the youngest of their four sons was seventeen years old. They had not expected to be blessed with a daughter, let alone one who looked like Branwen. It seemed unlikely that Hefydd, a shaky Christian at best, would have much patience with anyone who put God above her. Branwen had linked arms with Hefin's wife, Tirion, a gently-spoken woman with soft brown hair. Branwen was wearing enough jewellery for both of them, and looked none too distressed about Rufus's absence as she circulated amongst the young warriors, smiling merrily and accepting a goblet of wine here and there. The bard Cynfawr swept in behind her, resplendent in a voluminous white robe and a green cloak shot through with gold.

'They're nearly all here, lord,' Kerin said.

'Alright,' Vortigern said. 'I'm not waiting any longer.' He marched towards the doorway, then stopped. His hands travelled slowly over the red cloak. 'Does it look well?' Kerin smiled.

'Yes, lord. It looks very well.' He followed Vortigern down the passage and into the hall. Lud leapt from his seat and hammered an empty tankard on the high table.

'Silence!' he bellowed above the din. 'Silence for the Lord Vortigern, King of all the Britons!'

The gathering rose and roared. Vortigern raised his arms, smiling as he took his seat. Lud drew his sword and hacked a huge chunk of meat from the nearest leg of beef.

'The champion's portion, lord!' He presented it on the point of the sword. Vortigern seized the meat and tore at it with relish. Cheers reverberated around the hall again. Cheldric and Vortigern's cooks started carving generous slices of beef and lamb, loading them onto platters for the servants. The whole company fell to eating and drinking as if they had been starved for a month. Hefin arrived, beaming, and handed Kerin a huge tankard brimming with red wine. Katigern had taken the place at Vortigern's right hand without asking. Vortigern loved his second son, but he had little patience with slow wits and a lack of imagination, particularly after drink. Kerin noticed a flicker of irritation, but nothing was said. Katigern swallowed his fifth tankard of ale and looked around the hall with glee.

'By God, it's good to be the son of a king!'

'It's a pity your brother doesn't agree,' Vortigern said. Kerin sat down next to Katigern, watching the door, then felt his attention drawn. Hefydd's daughter was gazing at him intently. She lowered her eyes. Kerin watched. After a while she looked up, dark eyes glowing beneath long, flickering lashes, and gave him a knowing smile.

'Who's the woman you're looking at?' Vortigern asked.

'Hefydd's daughter, Branwen,' Kerin said. Lud's eyes twinkled with amusement.

'Hefydd's been hiding her for years. But she's no stranger in Henfelin these days.'

'Well, that's true,' Kat chuckled, pouring himself more ale. 'She stays in that empty cottage next to Cilydd's, where his sister lived before she married the blacksmith. Branwen's a bosom-friend of Cilydd's daughter, Mabli. But it's my older brother you should ask. He was all over her until God got in the way.'

Vortigern swallowed his wine at one gulp. Kerin ate half-heartedly. From his seat next to Katigern he watched the main entrance.

'God, Kat, where's Rufus?' he murmured. Katigern spluttered into his tankard.

'I don't think Branwen's too worried,' he said, already too drunk to care how loudly he was speaking. 'Look, she's like a bitch on heat. I'd be in there myself if I didn't think Hefydd would cut my balls off.'

Around the hall, the furious pace of eating slowed down. The diners were bubbling. Even Paschent was singing rowdily with Dull Bened. Kerin tensed as the door screen was drawn. Gwyndaf strode in, brushing snow from a bearskin cloak. He had brought a tall old man and dark-haired Derfyn, the fine swordsman. The pair found a seat amongst Hefydd's people while Gwyndaf marched up the centre of the hall to the high table.

'Welcome, Gwyndaf!' Vortigern rose and extended his hand. Gwyndaf looked long and hard at him, then shook his hand firmly. A murmur of approval rippled out. Vortigern sat and reached for a silver goblet. 'Cenydd,' he said, 'wine for the Lord Gwyndaf of Craig Goch.'

Cenydd brought another of the elegant jugs. Kerin filled the silver goblet.

'Pardon us for being late,' Gwyndaf said. 'Have you seen the snow? It'll be as deep as the Hafren before the night's out.' Kerin watched him uneasily. The lean, scarred face and fierce eyes looked altogether too sanguine for his liking. 'Lords of Cambria!' Gwyndaf said, raising his goblet. 'A health to the King of all the Britons!' He looked down with a faint smile as Vortigern acknowledged the cheers. 'And may he rule his kingdom better than he rules his sons.' A subdued muttering travelled down the hall. There was a sudden outbreak of head-shaking and mischievous, half-concealed smiles. Gwyndaf bowed with a flourish and strode off to join his companions. Vortigern watched him go, his eyes burning with the savagery of hurt pride.

'Enough!' Kerin leapt up. He had drunk enough to lose his patience, without any assistance.

'Where are you going?' Katigern chortled. 'To rip off Branwen's dress?'

Vortigern's hand gripped Kerin's arm. 'Stay!' he hissed. Kerin glared mutinously at him. 'For the love of God, stay.' Kerin sank back into his seat. Vortigern reached across to pat the bard's shoulder. 'Give us one of your poems, Cynfawr. Nothing about the kingship, that will have to wait. And for God's sake not the one about Hefydd and the cauldron.'

The bard threw his head back. 'Lord, you shall hear the story of the mighty victory on the banks of the River Hafren.'

Kerin watched, drinking steadily, as Cynfawr swept out into the centre of the hall. The old man's grey locks tossed like a wild mane as he warmed to his theme, the beating of Eldof of Glevum in a bloody skirmish at the river, long before Kerin's time. Every warrior in Henfelin knew the poem by heart, but they never tired of it.

'Have you seen Rufus?' Lud whispered.

'This morning,' Kerin said. 'He promised me he'd come.'

'The people are talking. And that's without Gwyndaf adding his pinch of salt. They're saying Rufus won't fight the Picts with us.'

'He will,' Kerin murmured. 'He's promised, whatever he believes about God and Jesus Christ.' He could hear his desperation, but the wine stopped him silencing it.

'Kerin, I've known the boy from birth,' Lud said. 'I know he's no traitor, not in the ordinary way. But there's something else. He looks mad sometimes. Possessed. Like men who've been in one too many battles, and their heads go. Iustig's to blame, and that bloodthirsty little menace Paulinus.'

Kerin reached for his wine, torn between longing for oblivion and the need for a clear head. Macsen and Hefin were having a clumsy wrestling match. Branwen had transferred her coy attentions to Derfyn, who was resisting temptation so far, despite her breasts being barely a hand-span from his nose. Hefydd and his family always referred to her as 'little Branwen', because she was a small child when her brothers were grown men; but this thought would not readily have occurred to any red-blooded male without a family connection. Hefydd, too far gone to notice, was arm-wrestling with one of his boys. Kerin did not want to contemplate what would happen if Derfyn decided to take Branwen out to the stables, setting off an argument between Gwyndaf and a bunch of drunken well-armed warriors. Out on the floor, Cynfawr was reaching the familiar climax of his poem.

'Then came Vortigern, the mighty warrior,'
he roared, eyes glistening with tears of pride.
'Then came the Parthian, prince amongst horses.
The spears flew with the speed of the falcon's flight,

The swords sang like wind in the trees of Glywysing.
Then did Eldof know fear!
Then did the blood of his strong men flow like the waters of
Hafren!
So triumphed the mighty lord, the eagle of Henfelin;
Long may he rule in our fair land, the prince of warriors.'

Through the haze of lamplight and wine Kerin looked
across at Vortigern and saw that his lips were moving in
silent unison with Cynfawr's, cynically framing every word.

* * *

It was past midnight when it ended. Some drifted away to
their homes or the houses of friends. Those who had fallen
asleep amidst the debris of the feast were heaved outside
by Cenydd and his underlings. Kerin had drunk himself
sober. He leaned against one of the uprights, watching
Macsen trying to pick himself up by the seat of his breeches.
Everyone else had gone, except for Vortigern, who sat alone
at the high table staring silently at the hall. Kerin hoisted
Macsen to his feet and bundled him outside into the bitter
night air.

'Leave it,' Vortigern said sharply, as a servant clattered
by with a pile of plates. Kerin sat down, wondering what to
do next, while flakes of snow whirled around the doorway
and the lamps burned low in their holders. No-one living
had ever seen Vortigern weep, but there was a peculiar large
brightness about his eyes that night as he sat, watching the
door and quietly fiddling with the clipeum. Something
was cutting him to the bone; whether Rufus's absence or
something older and darker, Kerin could not tell. He felt as
tense as if he were standing next to a bow-string stretched
too tight. He knew suddenly that he must break the string,

before it snapped and stung him like a whiplash. He filled a tankard and thrust it at Vortigern.

'Drink,' he said. Vortigern scowled and pushed the tankard away. There was a movement at the doorway. Rufus stepped from the pool of shadow. He was dressed as if for the feast, with an ermine-trimmed cloak and a silver-hilted sword at his belt.

'You gave me your word!' Kerin exclaimed.

'I'm sorry,' Rufus said, avoiding his eyes.

'Sorry!' Vortigern's eyes were savage. 'Have you come to mock me, now that they've gone?'

'No, father,' Rufus said. 'Not to mock.'

'Then what? Gwyndaf has already humiliated me in front of all of them. In front of my own people, for God's sake. Is that what you wanted? Is that what your God of love tells you to do?'

Rufus closed his eyes. 'Look, I came dressed for the feast. As you can see. But I've been outside freezing all night, because I knew that if I came in and drank with you, I'd tell the truth. And God knows, that would have shamed you more than my absence.'

'Damn you,' Vortigern said, 'you don't care about shame, yours or mine. You're afraid to defy me, that's all.'

'I am not!' Rufus cried angrily.

'Oh, but you are!' Vortigern drew his sword and raised the point to his son's throat. Rufus pushed the blade aside.

'I'm not afraid of you. And I'm not afraid of death, either. Hang me if you like, but don't defile me with that thing. The blood of Constans is on that sword. You might not have killed him yourself, but you knew what you were doing from the beginning. You used him, as you've used the praetor, and those Picts. As you use Kerin, and every poor, trusting bastard who comes to you.'

The weapon dropped from Vortigern's hand. 'Merciful God,' he whispered, 'if your sainted mother were here –'

'Then she'd spit on you, as I do,' Rufus bellowed. Vortigern stared at him, his lips mouthing an inaudible response. He seized the fallen sword in both hands, drove the point into the ground at Rufus's feet and ran from the hall. Rufus stared at the blade quivering in the ground beside him.

'For God's sake,' Kerin said, incredulous. 'Why did you have to say that? Of all things?'

'I shouldn't have done,' Rufus said. 'Even if it's true.'

'You can't possibly know if it's true!' Kerin said. 'You were seven years old when your mother died. You can't know how it stood between them. And you broke your word to me. After all those years.'

Rufus turned away. 'Forgive me,' he said. 'You deserved better, at least.'

Kerin stared at the silent hall. 'God, where will this end?' he murmured.

'If I believed in your powers of foresight, I'd be worried,' Rufus said. Kerin smarted at the note of mockery.

'You don't believe in all that nonsense, do you. Why not ask God for a prophecy?'

Rufus sank into the chair beside him and they sat for what seemed like eternity, gazing at the dereliction. Kerin drank the wine which he had poured for Vortigern and wondered whether it would have been better, after all, to stay well away from Craig Goch. One by one the torches burned out. The fire died to a heap of glowing embers.

'I'm leaving tomorrow if the snow's not too deep,' Rufus said. 'You have my word that I'll fight Picts with you, but I can't stay here now.'

'You gave me your word that you'd come to this feast,' Kerin said sullenly. 'Why not go tonight? I'm sure God will protect you from the weather.'

'No,' Rufus said. 'I'm going to Cilydd's cottage, to make peace or war with Branwen. She may understand, she may want to kill me, but you were right. I should at least be honest.'

Kerin said nothing, but could not help wondering whether Derfyn's resolve had held up once away from the public gaze. The last time he looked, Branwen was stroking the hand of Gwyndaf's expert swordsman and feeding him honeyed apples from a spoon. He and Rufus each took a last draught of wine then walked together down the hall, picking their way over mislaid cloaks and discarded bowls. The night outside was still and black, strung with gliding stars. Their footsteps crunched in the frozen snow as they trudged down the hillside. At the door of the cottage Rufus paused.

'May we still be friends?'

'I suppose so,' Kerin said, without conviction. 'But it's in your hands. I'm the same as I ever was.'

They embraced briefly, then Rufus frowned. The frosted silence of the night was disturbed by the muffled sound of a woman's voice. They both turned as the door-screen was drawn aside from within. Vortigern stepped from the doorway, trailing his red cloak. He laughed cruelly. Rufus's expression changed from astonishment to silent horror. He tore aside the skin and plunged into the darkness within. Vortigern caught Kerin's eye, and the laughter ended abruptly in a harsh sob of despair.

'Hurt for hurt,' he whispered, and went into the encircling darkness.

15

Winter passed quickly. It seemed only days after the feast and its bitter aftermath that the hills were alive with lambs. It was an easy winter, blessed with overflowing bins of corn from the previous summer's rich harvest; a time of recovery for men and beasts. Those who knew what might await them in the North gave thanks to whatever gods they worshipped.

The king had set up his administration at Caerwent. It was still Venta Silurum to many, merely through force of habit. There Vortigern held court throughout the winter, settling disputes and hearing complaints with a tolerance Kerin could hardly credit. People came from all over Cambria to pay tribute and pledge their allegiance. The only man of any standing who did not make an appearance was Rufus. He had found his way home at the turn of the year, and there he had stayed, grimly practising his fighting skills.

On a fine cool day in the month which the Romans called Februarius, after their festival of purification, the riders came from Kent. Kerin was standing on the town's rampart enjoying some unexpected sunshine with Publius Luca, who had come to report on his military preparations. The commander looked like a wealthy landowner in his well-made breeches and travelling cloak, although an odd gold shoulder-pin depicting a goat with a lobster's tail recalled his links with the Second Legion.

Kerin liked Caerwent. It was a friendly town, its houses set in regimented lines about a cluster of grand Roman buildings still kept in good repair by the prosperous community. There was a fine basilica where an efficient ordo met, a row of workshops occupied by skilled craftsmen, and a busy marketplace where you could buy anything from Samian pottery and amber jewellery to Italian olive oil and wine, as well as the silverware and leather goods produced within the walls. Kerin and Publius Luca were leaning on the battlement beside the eastern gatehouse, looking out across bare cornfields and meadows where well-bred cattle picked at the sparse grass. Below them, the town went about its business. Its merchants were in conclave, and the lads from the inn inside the gate were doing a brisk trade, meeting new arrivals and leading their horses away for food and stabling.

'Who is it today?' the commander asked.

'The merchants officially, but at the moment it's Gorlois and his notables,' Kerin said. 'It was good to see them; I do like Gorlois.'

'Indeed,' Publius Luca said. 'He seems like a grand leader, loved by his warriors.'

Kerin looked out across the rooftops of the modest town. Towards the centre the pale stone basilica gleamed. In the street below, a pretty girl who was not Gael had paused to greet a small child. Lud and Custennin were talking to a tall old druid in a green robe. 'Thank you for what you told me,' Kerin said. 'It's never spoken about, so I had no idea.'

'Most of Vortigern's inner circle were killed,' Publius said. 'Lud must know what went on, but he's no talker. And as for the ordinary warriors and townsfolk, I think it washed straight over them. They all thought Vortigern was immortal.' He gave a wry smile. 'Nothing's changed, has it.'

'It has,' Kerin said. 'I'm here to slay the demons.'

Publius Luca sighed and patted his shoulder. Kerin smiled uneasily. He would never have done that except to a young lad who had said something painfully naive.

'Look,' he said. 'Here comes Gorlois.'

The Kernow contingent had emerged from the basilica. Gorlois was riding down the street, his great woolly mane ruffled by the cool breeze.

'The Bear of Kernow!' Publius Luca smiled. 'Let's go to meet them.' He waved to Gorlois, who roared a greeting. As they reached the flight of steps leading down from the wall, the riders appeared, distant specks on the good road running north-east towards Glevum. Kerin narrowed his eyes against the light.

'Brennius!' he exclaimed. 'Commander, it's Brennius, Garagon's adjutant. What on earth can he be doing here?'

'The gods know. But it surely means trouble.'

They hurried down the steps. Gorlois had dismounted and was striding towards them. 'Kerin Brightspear!' he cried, flinging his great arms around Kerin in a rib-crushing embrace. 'And Publius Luca! By the gods, commander, I wasn't expecting to see you down here. Come to see if the Cambrian army's up to scratch, eh?'

Publius Luca chuckled. 'I'm sure the Cambrian army can get along quite well without my help, Lord Gorlois. It's more a case of reporting progress to the king.'

'Well,' Gorlois said, 'if your Roman boys can fight as well as Vortigern's Cambrians and my lot, we'll beat the Picts hollow. Have you seen him, by the way? Have you seen Vortigern? I never thought he had it in him. I thought he was like me, just a horse-warrior and a head-splitter, but by the gods, I was wrong.'

'Yes,' Publius Luca said courteously. 'I think many people were.'

And there the conversation ended, as the town gates swung open to admit Brennius and his three companions. The boys from the inn led away their exhausted, steaming horses. Brennius looked round, intense relief on his face as he recognised the three men beside the wall. He walked quickly across and clasped Kerin's hand, acknowledging Gorlois and Publius Luca with a brief smile. For once the shrieking laugh was silenced.

'We must talk,' he said, 'but not here in the street.'

Kerin knew the innkeeper well enough to trust his discretion. The handful of old men who were inside gave them some curious looks. How often did their drinking companions include the Lord of Kernow, a senior Roman military man, the king's confidant and four well-dressed strangers with unfamiliar accents? Kerin caught the landlord's arm.

'Get rid of those and send word to the king,' he murmured. The landlord winked and ushered his customers outside with a jug of ale. The seven men within sat down at a corner table, and everyone looked expectantly at Brennius. The landlord and his daughter brought brimming tankards. Brennius drained his at one draught and held it out for replenishment. The landlord knew better than to keep a well-armed man waiting. He placed jugs on the table and withdrew to the back room where he stored his casks. Kerin, Gorlois and Publius Luca waited. Brennius took another gulp of ale and leaned forward on his elbows.

'Saxons,' he said hoarsely. The word fell amongst them like a stone into a pool. They all sat quite still as the ripples spread, and each man's mind drew its own picture.

'Where?' Kerin asked.

'Everywhere.' Brennius looked desperate. 'Everywhere, all along our coast. They never land. They appear just off-shore in their ships – hundreds of them, armed to the teeth

– just beyond an arrow's range, but close enough for us to see the sun shining on their swords and axes.' He shivered involuntarily. 'And then they're off out to sea again, and the next thing you know, they've sprung up somewhere else. It's enough to drive a man mad.' He seized his tankard with a shaking hand and took another gulp.

'Brennius, did Garagon send you?' Publius Luca asked.

'No. He doesn't know I'm here. Garagon would never ask for help from anyone, let alone Vortigern.' He glanced up at Kerin with a nervous smile. 'He's my best friend, but that doesn't prevent me from seeing his faults. I know he can be pompous and vain, but he's not a bad man. Just a stupid one, sometimes.'

'So,' Publius Luca said. 'If you think that Kent needs defending, why not go to the military authorities in Londinium?'

'Because I need to see the king,' Brennius said. 'I mean no disrespect to you, commander, but I need to see Vortigern. He may well tell me to go and jump in the sea, but I must try.' He hesitated and took another mouthful of ale. 'Again, I mean no disrespect, but no-one knew what to do about the Picts until Vortigern turned up. Now it looks as if we're on the point of marching off to fight them; and what's more, that we might manage to do it without killing each other. I can think of no-one else who could have done that, and no-one else who'll have the first idea what to do about the Saxons. And you must know how hard it is for me to say that, about a man of the West.'

Publius Luca's face was sober but without resentment. 'You're right, of course,' he conceded. There was a commotion in the street; horses trampling the cobbles, men shouting. Vortigern came into the inn. All eyes turned to him. He looked hard at the gathering in the corner, waving aside the ale which the landlord offered.

'Alright,' he said. 'Brennius, stay where you are. Publius, please take Brennius's companions and quarter them in the barracks, with the garrison. Tell the commander to feed them, but don't let them leave or speak to anyone. Come back here when it's done. Gorlois, go back to the basilica and tell the merchants to wait for me. And if you breathe a word of whatever Brennius has said, I'll cut your tongue out and feed it to the buzzards.' Gorlois gave him a wounded look. Vortigern nodded to the landlord. 'Take everyone out by the back door, then sit outside and let no-one pass.' Kerin remained where he was. Brennius looked scared witless. Vortigern sat down opposite him. Outside, the sounds of the town continued; a dog barked, men talked as they walked by in the street. Inside the small, dark room the silence was so intense that Kerin felt he could have grabbed it and torn it, like a veil.

'Alright, Brennius,' Vortigern said. 'You've half-killed your horse, and Garagon hasn't sent you, or you'd have arrived with twenty marching musicians and an escort of dancing girls. So why are you here without his knowledge?'

Brennius closed his eyes. 'Lord, there are Saxons in Kent. Hundreds of them. They're lying offshore, just close enough to show how well-armed they are. All along the coast.'

'So soon!' Vortigern said. Brennius stared down at his tankard.

'What do you think we should do, lord?'

'Perhaps you should ask Garagon, not me,' Vortigern said. 'He usually seems to have plenty to say.'

'Garagon knows nothing about fighting!' Brennius blurted. 'We call ourselves warriors, and we ride around on our pretty horses, flashing swords that have never tasted blood. I don't know why I'm telling you this, lord, because I'm sure you must have seen it for yourself.'

'I think you have a lot to learn,' Vortigern said. 'But at least you're honest enough to admit it, and you wouldn't be here if you were a coward. Garagon, of course, has no idea that you are here.'

'Of course not,' Brennius said bitterly. 'Garagon grew up believing that civilisation ends at Glevum. He'd run on his sword before he'd ask you for help. But someone had to do it, because if those savages land we'll be mincemeat. And if Garagon's too proud or too stupid to understand that, then he needs saving from himself, never mind from the Saxons.' He broke off, staring at his empty tankard. He had said his piece, and had possibly said far more than he intended.

'So,' Vortigern said softly. 'You think that I should take my army of half-witted barbarians and tell them to die for the sake of Garagon's cornfields.'

'No, lord. I think you should probably let us burn in hell. But all my family and friends are in Kent, and I'd be less than a man if I hadn't tried. Garagon may kill me for it, all the same.'

'He may thank you, in the end,' Vortigern said. 'Go back to your friends. I'll send for you in the morning.' He went to the doorway and called the landlord. 'Take this man to Publius Luca at the barracks. And remember what I said to the Lord of Kernow.' The landlord bowed hurriedly and led Brennius away. 'Brennius!' Vortigern said. The Kentishman turned. 'You're a braver man than you know. I won't see you burn.'

Kerin leaned back on his bench and stared at the cob-webbed ceiling as the back door closed. Vortigern sat down beside him with the jug of ale which he had refused earlier.

'We can't fight Picts *and* Saxons,' Kerin said, filling two tankards.

'No,' Vortigern said. 'But if we waste our time killing

Saxons now, the Picts could be in Londinium before the summer. And if we do nothing, and there are as many Saxons as Brennius thinks, they could have the whole of the south coast in their hand by the time we're done in the North.' He took a judicious mouthful of ale and smiled. 'You had better finish this; I can't go drunk to a meeting of merchants.'

'What do they want?' Kerin asked.

'A guarantee of safe passage to Londinium for their goods, I expect. The seas are dangerous these days, and Eldof doesn't keep his roads as secure as he should. It doesn't matter. There'll be time enough to harass Eldof before long.'

'We're leaving?' Kerin asked.

'Yes. They can smell the blood now. We'll pick up Eldof's army in Glevum. Publius must go ahead to call up his infantry and cavalry.'

'And the Saxons?'

'That can't be decided now. I need to know how strong they are, what their intentions are –' Vortigern raised his eyes when Kerin failed to respond. 'Look, you know that if I had twice the army, I'd ride to Kent and send them packing. Do you think I should do that, and let the Picts burn their way across the country?'

'No, of course not. But you saw Brennius. That was no ordinary fear.'

'I know. It makes me wonder if there might be something worse waiting in Kent than anything the Picts can do. Do you think so?'

'Yes,' Kerin said. 'I can feel it from here.'

Vortigern shook his head. 'One more year. We could have dealt with the Picts, then settled things in Kent.'

'Yes,' Kerin said. 'It would have been very straightforward.'

Vortigern laughed quietly but did not reply. Kerin became aware of the silence again, clinging like cobwebs.

'I take it we're riding at dawn?'

'No. At midday, perhaps, but not at dawn.' Vortigern smiled at Kerin's visible surprise. 'Yes, I know it's unusual for the eve of a march. But tonight, perhaps for the last time, I should like to be quite simply Vortigern of Glywysing. Decisions are for kings, and God knows I shall have enough of them to make when we get to Kent.' He looked up, and for the first time ever, Kerin thought he saw a trace of apprehension where there had always been fire and blinding certainty.

'I'm glad in my heart that I don't have to make them,' he said. There was a knock at the door. Kerin opened it to Publius Luca.

'Those men are frightened to death,' the commander said. 'Did Brennius say any more?'

'Nothing worth hearing,' Vortigern said. 'Sit down and drink this. I have to keep my head clear. You only have to be sober enough to stay on your horse on the way home.'

'A burden shared?' Publius Luca asked.

'No. I wouldn't share this with an enemy. And besides, nothing can be decided yet, however much it offends your Roman sense of order and clarity. We're not even talking about one people. Everyone calls them Saxons, but there are Jutes, Frisians and Angles too. Who knows if they'd sooner fight each other than fight us? Who knows if their leaders are clever or stupid? If they're clever, they'll soon work out that I have both Picts and Irish to think about, let alone a bunch of mad Christians; and what can we do then? Fight them? Pay them? God knows. I don't.' He took a mouthful of ale, despite all he had said, and passed the tankard to Publius Luca.

'Your men sound restless,' the commander said. 'Lud and Gorlois, not to mention Hefin and his mad brother.'

'I know,' Vortigern said. 'I've already told Kerin that we're leaving tomorrow. We'll ride for Henfelin as soon as I've finished with the merchants. And after that, to Kent or Londinium; it depends what news comes to us on the march. Go back and muster your troops, and I'll send word. I expect to be in the east within fifteen days. I'd say less, but I have to allow for getting Eldof out of bed.'

Publius Luca gave a guarded smile. 'Don't disparage him. I know you're old rivals, but he's a good fighter, and so are most of his warriors. A little rough around the edges, but none the worse for it.'

'Rough around the edges?' Vortigern laughed.

'Alright,' Publius said. 'Eldof's warriors look like the Valeria Victrix, compared to some of yours. But yours have something that Eldof's warriors will never have, don't they.'

Vortigern looked straight back at him. 'Yes,' he said. 'And the rest of you had all better pray that it works.'

16

Kerin awoke on the floor of Cilydd's workshop. Some muffled grunts were coming from the lean-to where the apprentice usually slept. Kerin could not remember how he got there, although a vision of Macsen falling headfirst into the river surfaced as he drifted back to sleep. When he awoke for the second time, Mabli was standing over him, and Elir was trying to sneak out without being noticed.

'Come on, get up,' she said, hauling him to his feet. He sat down on Cilydd's bench. Mabli came back with two beakers of some hot brew her mother had made. She sat down and leaned into him. Kerin played idly with a lock of her dark hair, thinking about Gael, far away in her father's citadel.

'Must you leave today?' Mabli sighed.

'You know we must,' Kerin said. 'And you know why.'

'Yes,' Mabli said, her voice flat and lifeless. Kerin rubbed his eyes.

'Did I dream it, or did Macsen fall in the river?'

'Oh yes,' Mabli giggled. 'Cheldric and Marc fished him out and threw him in the stable. I expect he's still there, unless Eleri came looking for him.' Kerin grinned. He wouldn't have liked to be in Macsen's boots, although Eleri was barely half his size. 'We've made a banner,' Mabli said, in one of her usual grasshopper leaps.

'A banner?'

'Yes. A huge one. It was Mora's idea. We've all been stitching for weeks. We thought the Lord should have a new banner, now that he's king and going off to war.'

Kerin reached for her hand. 'It's a fine idea, Mabli. What sort of a banner is it?'

Mabli pursed her lips. 'Well –' she said cautiously.

'Come on. It must be good, if you've all spent so long on it.'

'Oh, it's very good,' Mabli said hastily. 'But – well, it's a dragon, that's all. Do you think the Lord will mind? We did wonder, because the Romans used them. But Mora said that when she was a little girl, she used to see the patrols riding out, and they always had their *draca – dracon –*'

'*Draco*,' Kerin said. 'I'm not old enough to remember them, but I know what you mean. It looked like a great hollow dragon's head on a pole.'

'Yes, yes!' Mabli exclaimed, all excitement. 'And a long tube of material to fly behind it, and something in the dragon's mouth to make him scream when the horseman gallops! Oh Kerin, they used to frighten the daylights out of everyone, so why not the Picts?'

Kerin laughed and hugged her. 'Why not? If Vortigern won't have the dragon, I will.' He got up, stretched and went to the door. It was a beautiful day, which made things worse. The sky was blue and clear, laced with high, windspun clouds which thinned and vanished as they crossed the sun. Up by the citadel the stable lads were preparing the warhorses, looking for undetected injuries, checking every last stitch of saddle and bridle. Just along the well-worn path from Cilydd's house, in the open space enclosed by the big, lazy bend in the river, ox-carts and baggage animals had been mustered ready for loading. The air reeked with smoked meat and tallow and dung.

'Midday,' a hard voice said damningly. 'What's wrong with him? We should have been gone at dawn.'

Gwyndaf had approached as silently as a hunting cat. His thin young protégé, Derfyn, was standing behind him holding the horses; big, powerful brown mares, fast-looking, almost identical.

'Sisters?' Kerin asked, ignoring the remark.

'Mother and daughter,' Gwyndaf said tersely, not quite managing to disguise his irritation at Kerin's refusal to rise to his bait.

'It'll make no difference.' Kerin gave a sociable smile. 'I'll eat my riding boots if Eldof's ready to leave when we get to Glevum.'

Gwyndaf snorted. 'You're right about that. At least Vortigern doesn't take all his worldly goods with him. Eldof's like an old woman fussing around with her bits and pieces. A fighting man shouldn't need anything more than he can carry on his horse.'

'I agree with you,' Kerin said. 'But I've had good training.'

Gwyndaf's lip curled. 'Alright,' he said grudgingly. 'I won't argue with that.'

Derfyn tied the horses to a hazel bush and came over to join them. He was a handsome lad with curly dark hair and smiling brown eyes which suggested considerable wickedness. 'Ready to go?' he asked.

'Yes,' Kerin said, 'More ready than I look, I suspect.'

Derfyn chuckled. Mabli peered round the door-post of her father's workshop and inspected him with interest. Kerin laughed out loud. It was minutes since Elir had left her bed, but all the same she couldn't resist the sound of a promising male laugh. Derfyn looked at him enquiringly.

'This is Mabli,' Kerin said, 'Cilydd the silversmith's daughter. We've been friends since we were children.'

It was true, of course, and he had no intention of saying anything which might make things awkward for Mabli, given the way she and Derfyn were looking each other up and down. Mabli pulled her long, dark curls back from her face, fluttered her eyelashes and smiled. 'Would you like some wine?' she asked cheerfully.

'No, you saucy bitch,' Gwyndaf said, with a threatening scowl. 'Or at least, I wouldn't, and if Derfyn would, he can forget it. There'll be no drinking between here and Glevum, and precious little afterwards.'

'We'll have some when we come back,' Derfyn said encouragingly. Mabli pouted.

'Next winter,' she said. 'And that's if the Picts don't kill you first.' She flounced back into the workshop. Derfyn's eyes followed her.

'Come on,' Gwyndaf said sourly. 'You haven't got time for that.'

He loosed the horses, tossed Derfyn his reins and vaulted into the saddle. Derfyn looked back and winked at Kerin as they rode away up the hillside to join the swelling band outside the citadel. Further up the valley, rooks flew squawking from the treetops as Hefydd and his boys came pounding down the track beside the river, cloaks streaming. It's time, Kerin thought. It's almost time. He walked briskly away from Cilydd's house. There were the cooks' carts, packed with pots and utensils and provisions, but outnumbered ten to one by the big, heavy wagons which carried the artefacts of war; the spare horse tack, the spears and shields, the swords and daggers and whetstones and quivers full of arrows, and all the craftsmen's tools which would be needed to hold everything together on the long road north. Cenydd finished tying off a waxed sheet and came to meet Kerin, smiling and slightly breathless.

'Where's Cheldric?' Kerin asked. The two men had grown so close that, where one appeared, the other was likely to be close behind.

'Gone up to your house to get his knives.' Cenydd mopped his brow. 'Did you see the abbot?'

'No,' Kerin said. 'Was he looking for me?'

'Yes. He had another monk with him. A big chap with rough hands and a scar on his head. I've seen him about the citadel.'

'Padarn!' Kerin smiled. 'I didn't think he'd be far away. Where did they go?'

'Down by the stepping stones, last time I saw them. Father Iustig was arguing with the druids.'

'I'll leave them to it, then,' Kerin said. It was not what he needed to take with him as a reminder of home.

* * *

On the stroke of midday, with the sun at its zenith and the wind gusting off the sea, Vortigern came down from the citadel. He was riding the Pike, saving the black mare for what lay ahead. Lud rode out to meet him. A crackling urgency ran through the gathering beside the river. The great jostling column snaked around the perimeter of the open ground, enclosing the strings of spare horses, baggage trains and wagons which would follow it out of the valley. Rufus and his brothers were in the first rank, accompanied by Macsen; just behind them were Custennin, Hefin, Gwyndaf and Derfyn. They were followed by the remainder of Vortigern's own warband, Hefydd and his boys, Gwyndaf's warriors on their smart brown horses and every other able-bodied man of the southern coast who was strong enough to lift a sword and endure a punishing journey on horseback. Kerin glimpsed Idris amongst them with a bunch of unfamiliar young men. For the time being, he supposed, he should be glad that they were there and ready to fight.

'Lord Kerin!' a voice hailed him. It was one of the youngsters he had brought in for training. Kerin was fiercely proud of the way these boys stood out, with their alertness and proud bearing. He and Lud had worked tirelessly to pass on their skills with the spear. Macsen and Custennin had fought the green lads up and down the training ground until some of them sank down exhausted and slept where they lay. Only in the North would Kerin learn if it had been worth it. In the rear were all the other bands of warriors who had turned up; a mad, fulminating mass of flashing blades and competing banners. There would be time enough to weed out the hopeless and knock the others into shape on the long trek to the Wall.

All the talk sank to a murmur as Vortigern raised his hand for silence. He rode slowly along the column, observing everything it had to offer, and reined in on a low hillock. The assembled company had swelled and spread until it occupied the whole of the land enclosed by the river bend. The murmur dissipated and was replaced by an expectant silence. Vortigern drew himself up to speak, then stopped short. Something was going on amongst the baggage animals. The crowd grumbled and parted. Iustig and Padarn elbowed their way through and arrived at the foot of the hillock.

'Well!' Vortigern said, all attention. 'The men of God. You've left this rather late, Iustig. It would have been pleasant if you had seen fit to visit the king even once during his brief time at home.'

Iustig looked up at him without a blink. 'It would have been pleasant if the king had seen fit to visit the House of God,' he said. Vortigern raised his eyebrows.

'I only visit the house where I am welcome.'

The abbot's eyes narrowed. 'Everyone is welcome in God's house, as you well know,' he said. Vortigern chuckled.

'I wouldn't be too sure about that, Iustig. God has cursed me, according to your brother Paulinus.'

Iustig tutted impatiently. 'I can't speak for Paulinus. But on this occasion, I think I might presume to speak for God. *All* men are welcome in his house, no matter what they may have done.'

'Ah,' Vortigern said. 'I thought we'd come to that.'

Iustig raised his hands. 'I haven't come to argue.'

'Then why? To pray for good Christians like my son?'

'To ask for God's blessing on the king and his warriors.' Iustig folded his arms.

'Do it, then,' Vortigern said. 'The rest of them deserve it.'

Iustig gave him a pained look, then closed his eyes and folded his hands. Most of the warriors, even those to whom the monks were an inexplicable curiosity, followed suit.

'God our Father,' Iustig said, 'have mercy on the souls of these your servants. Shield them in battle, give them the victory and bring them safely home.' He looked up at Vortigern, who was watching him with interest. 'And grant wisdom and courage to the king, for he will surely need both in the days to come.'

Vortigern gave the abbot a withering smile and turned to his companion. 'What about you, Brother Padarn? Have you come to pray for the damned as well?'

'No more than usual, lord,' Padarn said stoically. 'I'd like to go with you, though, if you'll have me. Some of your warriors might like to have a priest along, and it's the least I can do if you're marching against the bastards who slaughtered my family.'

Vortigern nodded. 'Alright, Padarn. At least we speak the same language.'

Iustig reached up and caught Vortigern's sleeve. 'I shall pray for you, whatever you think,' he said. Vortigern shook off his hand with a bitter laugh.

'You'd pray for a dog, Iustig,' he said, turning his horse away. Iustig stared up at him reproachfully and retreated. Padarn shrugged, gave Kerin an amiable wink and made for the wagons.

'Come on,' Vortigern said, wheeling his horse. 'It's time. For God's sake, let's leave.'

'Lord!' Lud called him. The women were coming from the village in a tight, muttering bunch. They were carrying something rolled up in a blanket. There were about twenty of them, led by Mabli and stout, waddling Mora. Just behind them, holding one end of whatever it was, were Macsen's girl Eleri and a chastened Branwen. They went up to the foot of Vortigern's hillock and stopped dead. There was a huddled consultation. Mora and Eleri seized Mabli by the shoulders and propelled her forward. She stood in front of Vortigern's horse and looked up at him with a nervous smile.

'Well?' he enquired.

'We've made you a banner, lord,' Mabli mouthed, so quietly that Kerin only understood her because he knew what she was saying.

'What?' Vortigern said curiously.

'We've made you a banner, lord,' Mabli whispered, only slightly more loudly.

Vortigern frowned. 'I can't hear you, child. Speak up, for the love of God.'

'Lord, we've made you a dragon!' Mabli blurted, loud enough for the monks to have heard her in their caves. Her hand flew to her mouth.

'A dragon?' Vortigern said.

'Yes, lord. A banner. A *draco – dracon - draconunculus*.

We hope you won't be offended, lord, because we know the Romans used them, but we wanted to make something to bring you good luck in battle, and to remind you all of Henfelin, and –' the torrent of words dried up, and Mabli lowered her eyes. 'He's a very fine dragon, lord,' she said wistfully.

'Then you had better show him to me, Mabli,' Vortigern said gravely. Mabli dug Mora in the ribs. The blanket was unrolled. Mora held up the head of the draco on its tall, stout pole while Eleri and Branwen unfurled the long, snaking banner. Kerin stared at it in awe. The dragon's head gleamed in copper-gold, exquisitely moulded, from its scaly neck and flared nostrils to the gaping jaws and savage teeth. The banner itself, of a deep and vivid green, had been embroidered along its whole length with a swirling tapestry of images; fish with lashing tails, boughs in leaf, fierce-eyed hawks and prancing horses, painstakingly worked in bright red thread. Red streamers hung from its tail, and from a point below the dragon's head, binding it to the pole. Vortigern ran his hand over the fearsome head. He picked up the trailing banner and passed it through his hands.

'Your fingers must have bled making this,' he said. Mora stiffened.

'They did, lord. We have been stitching every day, and far into the night, until our lamps burned out. Thank God the thread was red, or you would have seen the blood of Henfelin on your banner already.'

'My father Cilydd made the head,' Mabli said, with a shy smile. 'He's wonderfully good with bronze, even though he usually works in silver. Cenydd cut the pole from the woods, and Cynfawr has set flutes below the dragon's head, so that he can sing in the wind when you ride. And Gwynfi wove the cloth; red for the blood of your enemies, and green for the hills of Cambria.'

Vortigern shook his head silently. For once, he seemed lost for words.

'Will you take the dragon, lord?' Mabli asked anxiously. Vortigern leaned down from the saddle, took her hand and pressed it to his lips.

'Yes, Mabli, I will take the dragon.' The women laughed and cheered and wept and hugged each other. Vortigern seized the draco. 'And now,' he said, circling his horse, 'I need a standard-bearer.' The warriors surged forward, roaring their competing claims. Kerin checked his horse, knowing that this honour was not for him. His skill with the spear was unmatched in their company. His only purpose could ever be to use that skill to its most lethal effect, and to protect Vortigern. Lud moved up alongside him.

'Who would you pick, then, lad?' he asked.

'Some mad bastard who can fight one-handed. And he'll need more nerve and stronger arms than most men have got.'

Vortigern sat quite still as the warriors milled around him. His eyes moved over the brawling mass, found Gwyndaf and rested. Gwyndaf stared straight back at him with his unforgiving eyes. Lud gave a low whistle. The other warriors fell back. The silence rippled out again.

'Gwyndaf,' Vortigern said. 'Will you ride with me at the head of this army, and carry the dragon against our enemies?'

Gwyndaf said nothing. Kerin knew, as Lud knew, as Gwyndaf and every man watching must know, what Vortigern was asking. To bear the draco was more than an honour. It was a fearful responsibility. The king's standard could turn battles. It could never be entrusted to any man whose courage and loyalty were not beyond question. Gwyndaf had chosen to humiliate Vortigern in his own hall, in front of many of the men who watched and waited now.

It was within his power to do it again, here, before this raw and disparate army. Should he refuse, it would damn the whole enterprise before a single man set foot outside the valley. Kerin watched silently, his heart hammering, for in a few words Vortigern had placed his own authority and everything they had done in the hands of a man who had hated him for almost half his life. Lud closed his eyes and shook his head silently. Kerin looked at Gwyndaf, and saw to his great surprise that his eyes were full of tears.

'Gwyndaf?' Vortigern said. Gwyndaf threw back his head and squared his shoulders.

'Yes. I will carry the dragon.'

The warriors cheered and shrieked and waved their swords in the air. The pale sunlight caught the blades, flashing out like a shower of sparks. Vortigern wound the banner around the pole, secured the bindings and offered the draco to Gwyndaf. He seized it in both hands and raised it high above his head.

'Gods,' Lud murmured, 'I thought we were done for there.'

Kerin caught Vortigern's eye across the pandemonium of horses and warriors and brandished swords. Vortigern acknowledged him with a nod and the trace of a smile. It was a look of triumph, and of fervent relief. Someday, Kerin thought, you will do it once too often.

The women and children had gathered on the grassy banks, singing and laughing bravely, fighting tears. Gwyndaf's quiet, dark-haired wife was amongst them, with her two little daughters. The druids had come from the woods and the monks from their caves, arguments silenced for once. Behind them the old men, who had seen it all before, stood back with sombre eyes. The sun came out from the thin cloud, flooding the valley with light and illuminating every rock and twig with cruel clarity, as if to engrave them forever upon the souls of the men who were leaving. Vortigern drove his stallion up to the head of the column.

'It is time,' he breathed, and turned to face his army. 'It is time! Men of Cambria, blood of my blood, may we burn with the dragon's fire!'

A roar went up from the banks. Biting his lip, Gwyndaf raised the draco, loosed its bindings and flung the banner to the wind. With the horses whinnying and fretting at their bits and the wild breeze shrieking in the dragon's head, the banner flew out with a crack, and Vortigern's army rode from Henfelin.

17

'We shouldn't have come,' Morvid said. He perched on the seat of Cheldric's wagon, head twisting from side to side like a nervous bird's. 'If Bertil finds out, he'll have all our hides.'

'Be quiet, you old fool.' Kerin smiled as his horse ambled alongside. 'Bertil's not coming anywhere near you.'

Beside them, the gentle waters of the Hafren winked in the late afternoon sun as their company moved slowly over the pleasant green plain towards Glevum. A warm breeze shook the hazel catkins and primroses covered the grassy banks below. Morvid shivered, despite the sunshine.

'It'll be freezing in the North. Did you hear what those lads said yesterday? The ones we met by the Roman bridge? No wonder their ponies had coats like bears, if it's snowing like they said it was.'

'The Britons are babies,' Cheldric said. 'You have been on a boat when there is ice in the sea? When the snow is in your eyes and in your mouth?'

'No,' Morvid said. 'I'd sooner live on your horrible gruel than do that.'

Kerin drew his sword and slapped Morvid's back with the flat of the blade. 'Prophet of misery,' he said. 'Watch your grandson.' Marc was riding beside the track on the fine grey colt which Kerin had bought for him.

'He rides like a warrior already,' Morvid said, overcome

with pride. For Kerin, delight was suffused with guilt. He would never pitch a youngster into battle, and there would be plenty for the boy to do in the North, helping out in sick-tents or with the animals; but no-one could foretell where danger might strike. Encampments could be attacked, marching warbands ambushed; there was no certainty that Marc and his grandfather could be protected. Just ahead Vortigern had reined in to watch the passage of his army. Kerin rode up onto the bank to join him.

'Tonight we shall dine with Eldof,' Vortigern said. 'For us, he will kill his best cattle. An army like this never came out of Cambria.' He ran his eyes over the jogging horse-men, proud smile fading as his gaze fell on the head of the procession, where his sons were riding. Scarcely a word had passed between Rufus and his father since the night of the feast, although they had maintained a brittle screen of civil-ity. Mabli, ever the source of inside information, had made a point of reassuring Rufus that Branwen had not been taken by force. Kerin had no idea if that made things better or worse for him.

'They should stop squabbling,' he said, as one of Gwyndaf's youngsters picked an unnecessary argument with Hefydd's boys.

'They will,' Vortigern said, 'as soon as we reach Glevum. Nothing compares with a common enemy. These may dislike each other, but not nearly as much as they dislike Eldof's people. By tonight this army will be a devoted Cambrian brotherhood, committed to hating the men of Glevum. And when we arrive in Kent, both parties will discover that all men of the West hate the Kentishmen far more than they hate each other. Then all we shall have to do is find a few Saxons, to remind them that there's something they can all agree about. In that way we shall get them to the Wall, I hope.' He looked round with an optimistic grin. *I hope.*

Kerin looked straight back at him. 'Gwyndaf could have refused, you know,' he said. Vortigern stared up at the cloudless sky.

'I know,' he said. Ahead of them, the argument resolved itself and everyone fell back into line. Gwyndaf rode past and acknowledged them with an unsmiling nod. The draco was slung from his saddle, wrapped in a horse blanket. He slept with it lashed to his arm.

'It was mad,' Kerin said. 'Everything could have gone.' He would have liked to say that in twenty years of blood and risk it was the most courageous thing he had ever seen Vortigern do, but he remembered the grey afternoon in Marcellus's garden, and the cautionary words of the haruspex.

'You are becoming increasingly free with your opinions.' Vortigern had spoken without hostility, but there was a warning there.

'I'm sorry, lord,' Kerin said, 'but I can't lie to you. And I wasn't thinking of myself.'

'I know,' Vortigern said. And then, with a sudden sharpness, 'perhaps you should. You're not my keeper, Kerin.'

An image glowed in Kerin's mind; a scrubbed table in a bare, stone-flagged room, a faded fresco. The faint smell of melissa sweetened with honey. 'Why not, lord? You've been mine for long enough.'

Vortigern turned, rather too quickly. 'That's gone. Don't you understand? Yes, I know I could have left you where I found you. I chose not to, but it doesn't make me a saint. You make too much of it.'

Kerin was nonplussed. The outburst seemed to have come from nowhere, but that was impossible. 'You saved my life, lord,' he said. 'It's hard to make too much of that, don't you think?'

Vortigern shook his head. The look held more sadness than reproach, and that confused matters further. 'You make too much of it,' he said, turning his horse towards the track. Kerin made to follow him, then changed his mind and let him go.

'Everything alright?' Brother Padarn was approaching on a fat brown mule.

'Yes,' Kerin said. He was growing to like Padarn, but none of this needed to be the monk's concern. Padarn watched Vortigern ride away.

'What's between him and the abbot, then?'

'What do you mean?' Kerin asked. 'Did Iustig say anything to you?'

'About the Lord Vortigern? Not much. But before we marched, he seemed to think he should give me some advice. Little things, like not mentioning Gwyndaf's family. Now, I'd have thought it was quite important for a man like me to avoid upsetting the Lord, because he doesn't have too much respect for the cloth, you must admit. So I asked the abbot how to stay on the right side of him, and he just gave me a funny look, as if I'd made a bad joke. I was wondering if you might know why.'

'No,' Kerin said. 'But for as long as I can remember, it's been as it is.'

'Nothing to do with Brother Constans, then.'

'No, not at all. Possibly Vortigern upset Iustig years ago.'

Padarn's brows rose. 'I'm not a gambling man, but if I were, I'd lay you any odds that it's the other way round.' He circled his mule, perhaps judging from Kerin's expression that he had said something shocking.

'What do you mean?'

'I don't know,' Padarn said. 'But it'll come out one day. I've spent years hanging around with armies. Everything comes out in the end.' He reached over and patted Kerin's arm in a friendly way, then turned back towards the wagons and laden donkeys.

* * *

It was a while since Kerin had been in Glevum, and so much had happened in the meantime that he had almost forgotten how beautiful the city was, rising warm and golden beside the river. The fine Roman houses and administrative quarter were still there, and to give Eldof credit he had maintained them without stinting. Kerin could quite see why he was anxious to protect the place, even – or perhaps especially – from Vortigern. The army passed well-tended meadows and a cluster of small, solid houses set out squarely, in the Roman style; a community of retired legionary soldiers, someone said. Eldof sent out an advance party to greet his guests, immaculate red-caped guardsmen on matched grey horses. It was quite different from their last visit, when Vortigern was just another mad chieftain coming out of Cambria. Kerin recognised their leader from Londinium, a fresh-faced blonde lad wearing fancy gold armlets which must have cost his family a few denarii. He bowed to the king, introduced himself as Tullius, the youngest of Eldof's sons, and invited the notables to enter the city whilst everyone else set up camp below the walls. As the studded gates swung wide, Vortigern waited for Kerin to catch up with him.

'There will be no trouble tonight,' he said.

'Lord?' Kerin queried.

'I mean there will be no private war with Bertil Redknife.' Kerin's face fell. 'But, lord,' he protested, 'I –'

'No more. You know we need Eldof, and I won't have you butchering his minions under my nose.'

Kerin sighed. 'Very well,' he said reluctantly. Vortigern nodded and rode on.

'What was that about?' Morvid arrived on his little brown pony.

'Bertil. Vortigern wants me to keep the peace with him.'

'Well, of course,' the old man said. 'I'd love to see you cut Bertil up and feed the bits to the buzzards, but what would happen then? Eldof would find out, his men would have to fight your men –'

Kerin stared at the procession jogging along into the city. One of Hefydd's sons, a dark-haired scarecrow known as Mad Mabon, was baiting one of Eldof's guardsmen. Vortigern banged their heads together and the argument subsided. 'You're right, Morvid,' Kerin admitted. There was no point in making things more complicated than they already were. The sun had dipped below the low hills to the west. Darkness would fall soon. 'I know one thing, though. I will see Bertil's daughter.'

Morvid spread his hands. 'How?'

'Bertil will be at the feast with his warriors. If I go to his citadel –'

'And if he takes his daughter to the feast with him?'

'Lord!' Marc piped up. Kerin had not noticed him, listening in and sitting his handsome colt like an old hand. 'I know this country. If I go to the citadel, I could find Lady Gael.'

'No!' Kerin exclaimed. 'Do you think I've wasted my time teaching you to ride and fight so that Bertil can roast you on a spit?'

Marc smiled impishly. 'Lord, if you've taught me properly, Bertil won't catch me.'

Kerin clenched his fists. His affection for the boy cried out against unnecessary risk, but the knowledge that Gael was almost within reach did not encourage selflessness and restraint.

'It's your choice,' Morvid said. 'If you hadn't come along, we'd be dead already.'

'Lord, please!' Marc begged.

'Alright.' Kerin unfastened his crucifix, slipped the ring from the chain and pressed it into Marc's hand. 'Give this to Gael. Tell her that if she wants, I'll come to her tonight when her father's at the feast. The ring is hers, so she'll know you're telling the truth. I'll wait for you at the city gate when it gets dark.'

'Done!' Marc said eagerly. He slipped the ring onto his little finger and drove his colt down the bank into the river. The grey head of the swimming horse moved slowly out across the gliding mass of water.

'God forgive me!' Kerin murmured, as horse and rider plunged through the mud on the far bank and vanished into the belt of trees.

18

Eldof of Glevum lived in a house which, whilst about half the size of the praetor's residence in Londinium, shared many of the same comforts; spacious rooms with mosaic floors, a courtyard with a statue of some Roman god or other and a bath-house with a steaming pool, heated by the furnaces which provided the under-floor heating. There were stables with tiled roofs, and chambers with tapestry hangings imported from the eastern fringe of the Empire by the high-ranking official who once lived within the walls of honey-coloured stone. The house stood alongside the basilica where the city's ordo met, and not far from the residence of Eldof's brother, the bishop, reputed to be almost as grand.

'It's pleasant, for a house of this sort,' Vortigern said, as he and Kerin dismounted in the courtyard. 'I can see why Eldof gets nervous whenever I come anywhere near it.'

The Lord of Glevum was approaching, accompanied by a pair of servants in formal white tunics. 'Vortigern!' he said warmly, and extended his large freckled hand. Vortigern raised expectant eyebrows. Eldof sighed. 'Do I really have to call you "Lord King"?'

'No,' Vortigern said. 'We've known each other too long for that. But I hope your warriors are ready to march.'

'As ready as can be,' Eldof said. 'They're good, keen fighting men, as you know. But it can be hard convincing men to go and fight in some godforsaken place they've never set eyes on. If the Picts were about to burn Glevum, it would be different. As things stand, they're just as interested in fighting your warriors, unfortunately.'

'Then it's up to you to remind them of what might happen if they're stupid enough to do it,' Vortigern said. 'My men have had the warning already. I won't hesitate to hang anyone who causes trouble, whether he's yours or mine.'

'Well, that sounds fair enough,' Eldof said. He looked around as the other leading warriors rode in. 'I have chambers prepared for you and your sons. I take it that the ordinary warriors will camp alongside the wall, but I have beds enough here for a few more of your notables; Lud and his sons, perhaps? And of course there's room at my brother's house for anyone who can't find himself a warm bed elsewhere.' He winked, as if sure that no man of experience could fail to understand what he meant by that. Vortigern smiled and looked about him.

'May God strike me dead if the only warm bed I can find belongs to a bishop,' he said airily. Eldof snorted.

'Warm beds have always come looking for you, as I recall,' he said sourly. 'The men who say you live a monk's life must be blind and deaf.'

Vortigern chuckled. 'Not at all, Eldof. I'm the King of all the Ascetics these days, unless you count the odd drop of ale or wine. But first things first. I've left Lud in charge of the warriors' camp. You can give his bed to this man.'

Eldof looked Kerin up and down with unspoken disgust. *To a robber's bastard?* he might have liked to say, Kerin suspected; but in fairness, he seemed to be making every effort to maintain a degree of cordiality.

'Very well,' he said grudgingly, and nodded to his servants. 'Show the Lord King and the Lord Kerin Brightspear to their chambers, and see that they have everything they need.'

It would have been much easier to be quartered with the men outside the walls, Kerin thought, as he was shown into a large, cold room with a large, cold bed. He would need a credible excuse for not attending Eldof's feast, and the excuse must be conveyed to Vortigern; but this would not be easy to manage from a bedchamber under the noses of Eldof's household. He sat down on the bed and pulled off his riding boots. Almost immediately, there was a tap at the door. Kerin padded over in his bare feet and drew the bolt. Flora was standing outside, with a tray which held a jug of wine, a goblet and a bowl of dried fruit. She was dressed in a simple, formal style, like the male servants; a white sleeveless tunic belted at the waist, sandals, hair twisted into a coil at the neck. She smiled a greeting as Kerin opened the door.

'I was told that this was your room, Lord Kerin,' she said, offering the tray. 'We are to serve all the members of your company. Just some light refreshment after your journey.'

'Come in,' Kerin said, opening the door wider. 'Come on, put the tray down over there. Do you still serve Lord Eldof's wife?'

'I do. And I suppose I should be grateful. They do at least feed and clothe us. Many girls would kill for this work, I'm sure.'

'You look better than you did in Londinium,' Kerin said. 'Not quite so thin.' He paused, unsure how to continue. For her own sake, he hoped that her obsession with Vortigern had passed; although it was partially responsible for all that followed. Who knew if Vortigern would have been wearing the crown now, if her attempt to help Constans escape had not misfired as it did? 'I'm sorry about what happened to

Constans. My intention was to keep him safe. That's why I took him back to the city. If I'd known what was going to happen, I might even have let him get away on the ship. Because that was your plan, wasn't it. To get Constans out of the way, so that Vortigern could take the crown. I'm sure you meant him no harm.'

'Of course I didn't,' Flora said. 'I was sorry for him. All he really wanted was to go to some quiet place with Lupinus. And I thought I was acting for the best, but I didn't see how things would turn out. That it might end in blood. We have you to thank that it didn't. I'm in your debt, lord.' She poured Kerin a goblet of wine and held out the bowl of fruit.

'There's no debt, Flora,' he said. 'But for all our sakes, don't do anything mad like that again. I suppose your grandfather and your young men are getting ready to join our army. Please, whatever happens, don't try to follow them. Stay here, or with your family.'

Flora put the bowl down rather hard. 'Why not? You have a huge army, everyone says so. There'll be work enough preparing food, and caring for the wounded.'

'There will,' Kerin said, 'but the king has very strict rules about what happens in a marching army. No strong drink and no female servants. Eldof may have different ideas, but Eldof's not in command.'

Flora turned away. For a moment she was silent. 'Edryd has courted me,' she said. 'The smith from Calleva, who helped us in Londinium. I know he speaks out of turn sometimes, but he's a good man. Brave and kind and honest. My family wants me to accept him.'

'Perhaps you should,' Kerin said. Flora turned and came closer to him.

'I let Edryd take me to his bed. More than once. And if a woman can't give her body to the man she loves, perhaps it makes no difference who she does give it to, or why. I'm not with child of it, thank God, and it was pleasant enough. You're a warrior. All the warriors lie with women they don't care for, and no-one thinks anything of it. When a woman does it, she's a slut and a whore. Perhaps I should redeem myself, and marry Edryd. Would you marry a woman you didn't love?'

'No,' Kerin said. 'But I hope I wouldn't waste my life pining after a woman who didn't love me.'

Flora's eyes met his, hurt and angry. 'You speak as if it were a choice.'

'It is a choice. Not who we love, but what we do about it.' He took her hands lightly. 'I love a woman, Flora. I believe that she loves me back. And if she does, one day, I'll make her my wife. But if I found out that I was deceiving myself – that she was simply being kind, or grateful for something – then I hope I'd wish her well, and let her go with a good grace.'

Flora withdrew her hands. 'You'd simply forget about her.'

'No. That would be impossible. But I wouldn't follow her around like a dog, hoping that she might spare me a smile or a word. The king did you a kindness – something most people wouldn't give him credit for, believe me, but he did it, and now it's done. Let it be. I can't tell you if you should marry Edryd. He's a good man, as you say. Perhaps he sees how it is with you, and doesn't care. I've no idea. But I do know that you should stop dreaming about the king.'

Flora glared mutinously at him. Kerin didn't want her at all, but she had moved a little too close for comfort. His head was full of Gael and hope and desire, and the last thing he needed was to find himself next to an empty bed with a woman who didn't care what she did with her body. There was a loud hammering at the door.

141

'I don't know who that is, but you must go,' he said. Flora stepped back, her eyes defiant.

'I know you mean well,' she said. 'But I have only one flame, and I will keep it.'

Kerin opened the door. Outside was Gwyndaf, looking uncharacteristically agitated. Kerin ushered Flora out. Gwyndaf followed him inside.

'Do you know this bastard city?'

'Not very well,' Kerin said. 'Why do you ask?'

'Because Derfyn and some of my other boys have gone missing. Not one of them has ever been anywhere bigger than Leucarum, and their eyes nearly fell out when we were riding in. There'll be hell to pay if they're not back for the feast.'

'I'll help you look,' Kerin said, pulling on his boots and uttering a silent thanksgiving. A credible reason for leaving Eldof's house, and a companion who would back him up.

'Thank you,' Gwyndaf said. 'I'd sooner not trouble a man I hardly know, but I thought there was a fighting chance that you'd know where the alehouses and the whorehouses are.'

Kerin had absolutely no idea where the alehouses and the whorehouses were, but it was not the moment to say so. They went out through Eldof's gates, acknowledging the guards, and into a crowded street where torches were being lit as darkness gathered. 'It's this way,' Kerin said confidently, for no better reason than a general movement of people along the street. To his relief a large amount of noise greeted them, growing louder as they walked; the particular mingled shouting, laughter and singing which usually signified a busy alehouse where the night's trade was well underway. 'This is the biggest one,' Kerin said as the building came into view; and it was probably true, because he had never seen a larger alehouse anywhere. It had two storeys, both full to the rafters. On the ground floor men were hanging out of the open windows with their tankards, while others spilled out into the street to sit on the cobblestones. As Kerin and Gwyndaf approached, one of the drinkers ducked into an alley with a furtive glance over his shoulder and disappeared through a low doorway. 'The whorehouse is down there,' Kerin said, making an educated guess. 'I'll wait for you here, if you like.' A pair of hands grabbed him by the collar and he hit the wall of the alehouse with a force which winded him. Gwyndaf's eyes blazed into his as he gulped for breath.

'I have never, ever been unfaithful to my wife,' Gwyndaf growled.

'I'm sorry,' Kerin gasped. 'It was a jest, nothing more. You know what it's like amongst warriors. Most men laugh at that sort of thing.'

'Alright,' Gwyndaf said grudgingly and released him. 'I'll let it pass this time. You're right, most men do laugh at things like that. And you're just a young lad who's never had any grief in his life. Forget about it, and I will, too.'

Kerin took a deep breath and straightened his tunic. 'I won't forget about it. And I won't make the same mistake again.'

They fought their way into the alehouse. Derfyn was in the far corner with three companions. Pottery tankards brimming with ale were on the table. Some girls had found them, and it looked as if thoughts of Eldof's feast were far from their heads.

'Young rams,' Gwyndaf said under his breath.

'Do you want any help?' Kerin asked.

'No,' Gwyndaf said. Almost before Kerin could see what he was doing, he had taken out his sling, fitted a stone to it and let fly. The tankard Derfyn was holding exploded in pieces, drenching him and a few others with ale. The drinkers on the adjoining tables cheered and bellowed. Derfyn looked up, open-mouthed. Gwyndaf gave him a frozen stare and beckoned grimly. 'You can leave them to me now,' he said. Kerin elbowed his way out, stifling laughter. Outside, the sky was black and the moon was up. He found a street leading to the city gate, and went in search of Marc and an excuse.

19

The night was utterly still. Not a breath of wind disturbed the hazel copse on the north side of the settlement. Kerin and Marc tethered their horses and crept forward through the undergrowth. A dry twig snapped, splitting the silence. Marc stopped and pressed his finger to his lips. Ahead of them, where the trees thinned out, Bertil Redknife's citadel was clearly visible in the bright moonlight. It stood on a slight rise, the inner circle of notables' houses protected by a ditch and a wooden palisade.

'Two men on the gate,' Marc whispered, 'but all the others are at the feast. I climbed the wall before, and no-one saw me.'

They edged forward to the fringe of the copse. The guards were leaning on their spears in the gateway, exchanging the odd lethargic word as their long night wore on. A tawny owl hooted mournfully in a solitary elm. Kerin felt about for a pebble and sent it spinning into a tussock of dead grass. The guards turned, fumbling with their spears. Kerin and Marc bolted across the open ground and away round the base of the stockade.

'I'll lift you,' Kerin whispered as they reached the shelter of the south wall. He raised the boy until his eyes were level with the top of the palisade.

'Clear,' Marc hissed. Kerin tossed him up onto the top of the barrier and scrambled after him. They dropped lightly on the other side and ran for the shadow of the nearest house. The muffled sound of women's voices filtered through the walls. Everyone was indoors except for the guards, pacing uneasily up and down at the edge of the copse and prodding the bushes with their spears.

'Keep watch,' Kerin said softly. 'Can you signal if they come back?'

'Yes, lord. I can hoot just like the brown owl.'

Kerin closed his eyes. 'How will I know that it isn't the brown owl?'

'Lord, I'll hoot three times. One short, one long, one short. The brown owl doesn't do it quite like that.'

Kerin slipped from the shadows and scuttled up to Bertil Redknife's hall. A strip of yellow light leaked around the door-flap. A sudden wave of panic swept over him. What if she had had second thoughts? If she had summoned him, simply to explain that she could not love him? It would be typical of her, to want to tell him to his face. Kerin breathed deeply and told himself that he had not risked Marc's life and his own so that he could spend the night dithering on the woman's doorstep. He seized the door-flap in both hands and pulled it aside.

She was standing facing the doorway, dressed in an exquisite sea-green gown embroidered with gold thread and pearls, and fastened at the shoulder by a jewelled brooch resembling a slender leaf. She would have graced anyone's feast. The ring which Kerin had carried for so long was on her finger, clearly visible as she faced him with her hands clasped just below her breasts. She was smiling, and looked far less frightened than he felt.

'Should you be in Glevum?' he asked.

'Yes,' Gael said. 'I told my father I was sick. In fact I made sure that I was sick, and sent my woman to show it to him.'

'That was resourceful,' Kerin said, with a nervous smile. The sword which she had worn at her belt in Morvid's valley was lying on a side table. 'What's that for?'

'For anyone else who might have come,' Gael said. 'I thought the boy was telling the truth, but you can't be sure, in these times.' She turned, beckoning, and he followed. They passed through a chamber lit by a flickering fire. There was a couch strewn with sheepskins and tapestries.

'Take off your cloak,' Gael said. 'My father's safe where he is, and you'll be cold when you leave.'

Kerin slipped off his light woollen cape and unbuckled his sword-belt. Gael took them from him and laid them on the couch. Her hands travelled fleetingly over the cape as she put it down.

'You shouldn't have come,' she said. 'Have you any idea what my father would do if he found out?'

'I have a fair idea. But how could I come so close, without seeing you?' Her face was illuminated by the warm, shifting light of the flames. Kerin thought how beautiful she looked, and how vulnerable. He tried vainly to keep his body in check as he stood next to the couch, so different from the bed where he had first made love to her. 'Have you thought of what we talked about, the last time we were together? Of what I asked you to think about?'

'Of course I have,' she said. 'Come, please. Come with me.' He followed her out of the room and down a dim passage. She opened the door at the end. They were in a small room lit by a single tallow lamp. There was a wide bed, with a vivid blue and green coverlet which she had already drawn back. 'Of course I have,' she repeated, bolting the door. 'I will love you for as long as I have breath. I will be your wife, if that's still what you want. I will share your house with the cook and the others, and bear your children, and care for you, and yes, yes, that's how the brooch unfastens, the dress slips off like so, yes. Love me. Love me.'

In the end, she slept. Kerin, who needed all his willpower not to do the same, lay with her head resting on his chest, listening for a signal from Marc or any other sound which might mean danger. He could hear only the faint crackling of the hearth fire in the other chamber, the occasional snort from horses in the pens. Gael was breathing steadily, her face peaceful and bearing, even in sleep, the trace of a smile. There was a low table in the corner, barely visible in the darkness. A wine jug and two goblets were standing on it, alongside Gael's lyre. She must have hoped that they could share the wine, that she could play for him again. Kerin closed his eyes and folded her in his arms. If only there were time for such things. Before long the feast would be over, and someone would start looking for him. It would have been futile to expect his absence to pass unnoticed, so he had despatched Morvid to explain that he had taken to bed with a grievous stomach cramp, for which the old man had administered one of his remedies. Gael stirred and snuggled closer.

'What's the matter?' she asked drowsily.

'Nothing. I'm the happiest man on earth. But I'd be happier still if I had more time. And if I knew exactly where your father was.'

'Drunk by now, probably,' Gael said. 'He might not expect you to be at the feast. If he were king, he'd only have the high-born there. But I don't know how he sees it. Your position with Vortigern, how much status you have. He doesn't speak of it, and I couldn't possibly ask him.' Kerin kissed her, rolled out of bed and pulled on his clothes. She sighed and reached for his hand. 'Do you have to go? So soon?'

'I wish I didn't,' he said. 'But we're marching at first light. We have a battle to fight.' Gael's eyes met his. He saw the shadow of apprehension and sat down beside her. 'Don't worry. No, that's a stupid thing to say. What I mean is that I have a better chance than most. That's not bragging. I'm as good with the spear as they say, and decent with the sword. I've got the best weapons and the best horse I could have. The best warriors beside me. And more reason than any other man to live, and come home.'

Gael drew back and sat with arms clasped around her knees. 'I have been thinking,' she said. 'Ever since you asked me. About how we would manage this. If I go with you, and my father finds out, he'll come after us. There'd be bloodshed. People we care for could be killed. How could we live with that?'

'I don't know,' Kerin said. 'And I don't know how to manage it either. Not yet. All I know is that I love you, and want you with me for the rest of my life. That's a promise. A pledge. Whatever you like.'

'I know,' Gael said, clasping his hands. 'And I know you're a man who would never break a pledge. I couldn't wish it otherwise. But it's our curse, too. You were pledged to Vortigern, long before you even knew that I existed. From the moment he saved your life in that freezing wood. I can see it in you, I can hear it whenever you speak of him. And you wouldn't break your pledge to him, any more than to me. So what if he forbids this?'

'I don't know,' Kerin said. She had found words for all he had dared not say, for fear of losing her, and he was still no closer to an answer. 'Of course I'm loyal to him. How could I not be? You'd think less of me if I were not. And I know that doesn't help us. But I will find a way. Please God, Vortigern will accept this if he knows that I won't give you up. And I won't. If we had a priest here, I'd marry you now, this moment. I'd – ' he stumbled to a halt, blushing to the roots of his hair. 'I'm sorry. I've said too much now.'

'No, no, you have not,' Gael cried, pulling him close, smiling and weeping all at once. 'But unfortunately I don't have Father Septimus hiding in the cupboard. Bless his soul, I know he'd do it, even though he's risked so much for me already.' She drew back and grabbed Kerin's hands. 'Let's make vows. To each other, here, now, just ourselves. A promise before God. A betrothal. We don't need a priest for that.'

'We could swear on this,' Kerin said. He took off his crucifix and laid it on the bed.

'We could,' Gael said, her eyes shining with tears. He laid the crucifix on her palm, and closed his hand over it. 'You first,' Gael whispered. 'That's the way the priests do it.' Kerin stared at their joined hands, struck dumb. The only marriage he had ever witnessed was Hefin's, and that was ten years ago when he was a gawky sixteen-year-old, blind drunk on some disgusting liquor that Macsen had pilfered from his mother's larder. Gael looked up. 'Just say whatever you want. Whatever you feel.'

'I love you, that's all,' Kerin stammered. 'I will love you always, whatever it costs. And when the battle's over, if I'm spared, I swear that I will come back and find you, and I will love you and protect you for the rest of our lives.'

Gael bent her head to kiss their joined hands. He could feel her tears falling on his fingers. 'Those were beautiful words,' she said. 'I can do no better. I'll love you always, whatever it costs. I'll wait until you come back from the battle. I'll wait and I'll wait and I'll wait, and I'll pray and pray, because God knows I'll never want another man for as long as I live. And that's a promise.'

The pledge made, they held each other quietly in the warm darkness. It was impossible to say more, or to ask more of God's mercy, when the road ahead was so perilous and so cold.

* * *

The lamps were burning low in Eldof's hall. The banquet over, drink and merriment were still flowing. A guard at the door politely requested Kerin's sword, assuring him that everyone else had complied, and that the weapon would be returned. Kerin slipped in unobtrusively and found an empty seat between Rufus and some elderly dignitary. The hall was a monstrous room, like the praetor's.

'How was it?' he asked.

'The usual thing,' Rufus said. 'Too much to eat and some arguments. But Eldof and my father are still speaking, so I suppose we'll march together.'

Vortigern was engaged in a spiritless conversation with Eldof. Bertil Redknife was sitting near the entrance, observing the proceedings in silence. Kerin seized a stray chunk of meat and devoured it.

'You've been missed,' Rufus murmured. A hand landed on Kerin's shoulder. Vortigern dismissed Rufus and took his seat.

'Where have you been?'

'Didn't anyone tell you, lord?' Kerin looked plausibly surprised. Vortigern removed his hand.

'Well, I've been told the pack of lies you intended for me.'

Kerin smiled half-heartedly. 'You told me to keep away from Bertil, so I did.'

'You lying toad,' Vortigern said. 'There's a woman. It isn't so many hundred years since I was your age.'

Kerin stared up at the wall on the far side of the hall. A goddess carrying a scythe and a bundle of corn stared unhelpfully back at him from a peeling fresco. It was sure to be Ceres. Probably they were destined never to be any good to each other.

'Did she please you?' Vortigern enquired. Kerin's temper snapped.

'Yes,' he spat. 'More than Hefydd's daughter pleased you, probably.'

Vortigern blenched. 'That wasn't for lust.'

'No,' Kerin said, tight-lipped. 'I know what it was for.' He waited for the reprisal, but none came. An uneasy silence settled. Rufus leaned across and tapped his arm. Bertil Redknife was approaching. He marched straight up to the table and stopped short. The muscles in his neck were taut and his hands were shaking, as if it were all he could do not to seize Kerin by the throat. Vortigern leaned back in his seat and waited. Bertil swallowed hard and planted his hands on the table.

'I see your servant has arrived at last, Lord King,' he said. Vortigern's eyes darkened. His hands closed around Bertil's wrists.

'This is not my servant,' he said, his grip tightening viciously. 'This is Kerin Brightspear, a warrior of Cambria. He is my right arm, and worth ten of you and your makeweights.'

Bertil's face twisted in pain. He wrenched his hands free and opened his mouth, but a frigid glance from Eldof silenced him.

'Enough,' said the Lord of Glevum 'We have enough problems to solve without this. Get out, and see to your men.' Bertil gave him a venomous look, swallowed his rage and stalked out of the hall. Eldof grunted and got up, shaking his head. 'Sleep and cool your tempers. It's a long way to the Wall.'

Vortigern waited for him to go. 'Why are you staring at me like that?'

'No reason, lord.' Kerin lowered his eyes. The king's right arm? He had associated that with Londinium, with the clash of orators in the curia and the rituals of a dark chapel. He had not expected the writ to run here, in the rough and ready company of fighting men. Vortigern got up and stretched, and looked out over the bleak hall. They were alone in it now, except for a brown-skinned slave clearing the wreckage of the feast. The boy had let the lamps burn down, and soon they would all go out. Vortigern turned, a dark figure against the fading light.

'It was true, you know,' he said. 'What I told Bertil. It was nothing but the truth.'

There was something else, Kerin knew, and for a moment he felt as if he had only to find the right response to release it. But then he remembered what had been said on the road to Glevum, and the moment passed.

'Thank you, lord,' he said, with a grave, affectionate smile. 'This time, I shall try not to make too much of it.'

20

'They're waiting at the crossroads,' said Hefin, who had ridden ahead to assess the lie of the land. 'That old goat who was roaring outside the curia in Londinium, and a few hundred men ready to kill someone. Some on foot, some on rough ponies. Wagons full of tools. Not much shape and not many weapons, but by God, I don't think I'd want to cross them.'

'You'd better go and tell the king, then,' Kerin said, with a wink. 'He told them he wanted able-bodied men and craftsmen who can forge weapons.' And I, for my sins, told them that we'd train them in battlecraft and turn them into warriors, he thought as Hefin rode off, chuckling. It might have been a rash promise, but Kerin could not regret it. He had fired these people, he had brought them to the right place at the right moment; but it was their voice which had silenced the orators, their force which had given Vortigern the crown.

A horseman was approaching, riding alone down the middle of the Roman road. Kerin recognised the brawny, curly-headed figure from a distance. Edryd the smith, still on the praetor's horse, and looking more secure in the saddle than he had been on the day they crowned the king.

'Lord Kerin!' Edryd saluted. 'They're waiting down the road, I expect your man told you. But I wanted to speak to you alone. It's old Malan. He thinks we can't manage without him, and he does have a point, the lads do listen to him. He's an old man, though. It's a long way to the North, and the weather will freeze his old bones. But the king told him he could come, didn't he – "I'll look no further than you, Malan", we've heard nothing else since the day it was said.'

They turned their horses to the roadside, letting the other warriors pass by. 'Well, we can't leave him,' Kerin said. 'Not after all he's done. What about that black mule of his? The last time I saw it I thought it was going to lie down and die in the road.'

'Oh, the mule is fine.' Edryd gave a wry smile. 'He's been feeding it up for the journey. It's been stuffed with food even if the rest of us have had to go without. Strong enough to pull a cart, without a doubt.'

'I'll think of something.' Kerin paused. 'I saw Flora in Glevum a few days ago. She said you'd courted her a little. Will anything come of it?'

Edryd looked away down the road. 'No, lord. I made my feelings plain, but I've got too much pride to marry a woman who loves another man. There wouldn't be much point, would there?'

'None at all,' Kerin said. 'Perhaps she'll wake up one day.'

'Well, I'm not counting the moments.' Edryd shrugged. 'She's got nothing in her head except the king. It's mad, isn't it, even if he did do her a kindness. The high-born go for the high-born, if they bother at all. And everyone knows that the king's heart broke when his wife died all those years ago.'

Kerin had been about to ride away. He reined back sharply. In his head, he said, are you sure about that? He had been raised on something quite different. 'Is that what people believe?' Edryd looked surprised that the question had even been asked.

'Of course, lord. You know what it's like. People love talking about the high-born, don't they? They gossip about them when they're sitting around the fire. Everyone knows that the Lord Vortigern had run-ins with the Roman soldiers when he was a lad. They say the powers-that-be offered him old Emperor Magnus Maximus's daughter just to keep him in line, as if anything ever would. But he must have loved the woman, surely. Most men take another wife after a while, however much they cared for the first one.'

'Yes,' Kerin said. 'I suppose they do.' And yet Vortigern had not. This man who could have had any woman in the kingdom, according to Mabli; a man whose dim-witted, affectionate son had said that, if his father ever married again, he would eat his horse's saddle. 'Take my advice, Edryd,' Kerin said, pushing the question aside. 'Concentrate on the weapons, and keeping the wagons going. There'll be time enough to think about women when we come back.' The smith grinned, perhaps recognising a fellow-sufferer, and rode off to rejoin his people.

Vortigern and Lud were riding abreast at the head of the army. Kerin moved alongside, careful to keep his distance. He was riding his warhorse-in-training, Blaidd, and the Pike wasn't too keen on the upstart youngster.

'Hefin tells me we have company,' Vortigern said.

'We do,' Kerin said, trying to dismiss an image of his childhood; of firelight dancing along rows of books and manuscripts, while two small boys shared a sweet apple and a young man laughed as he flung an arm around the shoulders of a smiling, dark-haired woman. Vortigern gave him a curious look. 'Edryd the smith came to me,' Kerin said. 'You must remember him. He's a good, solid man, and he's concerned about Malan. The old one is determined to come with us, but Edryd's afraid that the journey might kill him.'

'It might,' Lud said. 'Before we even get to Hadrian's Wall, if the old wreck is looking as rough as before.'

'We'll all die sometime,' Vortigern said. 'And Malan would sooner die in a freezing ditch than get left behind. I told him that he could come, anyway. We owe all these people who rose up after Constans was killed. They'll still be on our side after we've dealt with the Picts. So go and find Malan, Kerin, and bring him here. Speaking of old wrecks, I might make him my chief warrior. This one next to me is well past it.'

An outraged roar burst from the man beside him. Kerin rode away, loving the sounds of raucous mirth and warriors' banter coming from behind him. Please God, let it last, he thought.

Malan was wearing his best clothes; a brown tunic and breeches, neatly patched but clean, and a grey woollen cloak secured at the shoulder by a Roman fibula brooch. 'Lord King,' he said, with a reverence.

'Malan,' Vortigern acknowledged him. 'Ready for the journey?'

'Yes, lord. We both are.' Malan patted the mule's neck.

'Does he have a name?'

'Yes, Lord King. He's called Virtus. Latin for manly courage, I'm told.'

'That'll do,' Vortigern said. A cooks' wagon was passing by, laden with sacks of cornmeal. 'Is he strong enough to pull a cart like that one?'

'Ha,' Malan said. 'He'd pull two of those, Lord King.'

'Then I have work for you both,' Vortigern said. 'Another cart will arrive soon. Our priest, Brother Padarn, is the escort. This cart contains my personal possessions, and a chest full of gold and denarii for purchasing necessities. I'm putting you in charge of this cart, and all it contains. I'm sure you understand the weight of this responsibility.'

'I'll kill anyone who touches the stuff, Lord King,' Malan said, showing his teeth.

'I don't doubt it. But remember that if anything goes missing, I'll be doing the killing. You can drive the cart. Tie Virtus Apertus to the back for now, he can take it in turns with the draught horse. Now, I have matters to attend to.' He smiled cheerily. 'Lord Kerin can stay and explain all this to Brother Padarn, and the man who's driving the cart.'

'Lord!' Kerin protested, but Vortigern had gone, chuckling as he cantered away.

'Don't waste your breath,' Lud said.

* * *

Kerin's horse told him that something was afoot as they passed Corinium, skirting the city walls where townspeople had gathered to wave and shout their good wishes. Vortigern and Lud stopped to size up the horsemen and foot soldiers pouring out of the gates to join them. Looking away southwards, Kerin's keen eyes picked out a rider approaching along the good old track running east of the Roman road, down towards the fine city of Aquae Sulis and deep into Gorlois's country. For a moment, Kerin thought that it was Gorlois himself. The same build, the same mass of woolly hair, a big, raw-boned horse with feathers on the fetlocks, like most of the Kernow men rode. Then he saw that this man was younger, brown-haired, carrying less weight. A relation, surely. He raised a hand and smiled.

'A lord of Kernow!'

'Not much of a lord.' The other man laughed as he reined

in. 'I'm Gorlois's brother, Gerdan. The youngest of the brood, and the youngest always get the crumbs. But I've come to fight, for sure. And you're Kerin Brightspear, the king's right arm. Saw you at the curia in Londinium. You wouldn't have noticed me, I can't get a word in when my brother's around.' He chuckled and slapped his horse's sweaty neck, not a bad talker himself, by the sound of it.

'Is Gorlois far behind you?'

'No distance. He's leading the horse warriors, and the foot are half a day behind. Good, hard boys. They'll be worth their weight in the North.' He paused, as if there were some other piece of news coming.

'Is something wrong?' Kerin asked.

'I don't know. A messenger came in the other day. We didn't know quite what to think, so Gorlois sent me to tell the king.'

'There's no point in saying it twice,' Kerin said. 'Come on. We'll go together.'

Vortigern had decreed a halt while Lud, Macsen and Hefin marshalled the new recruits, scrutinising men and weapons. Elir was assessing their horses and mules, assisted by Gwyndaf, who had taken to Lud's unassuming youngest son. The Sword of God had gathered out on the fringe, talking amongst themselves. Katigern was sitting under a tree, drinking something he probably shouldn't have had with him. Vortigern put aside the manuscript he was reading.

'Lord King!' Gerdan bowed from the waist. Vortigern grinned.

'A kinsmen of Gorlois, if ever I saw one.'

'Indeed, Lord King. The youngest brother, so I get sent on all the errands. Gorlois and the horse warriors are no distance away, they'll be with us within the hour the way they ride, and the foot soldiers and wagons less than half a day, and as for – '

'Enough!' Vortigern exclaimed. 'The words pour out of your family like shit out of a sick man's arse. Now shut up, and tell me why you are here and your brother is not.'

Gerdan cleared his throat. 'A message, Lord King. From one of my brother's lookouts. Attached to our household for years, but he's a fisherman's son by birth, from a village on the south coast. A few days ago, he rode down to visit his family. But there was no-one there, Lord King. Not a soul. No destruction. No burning. But no people either. Not even a dog or a donkey. And no grain in the corn bins, which there always is, even if most of it has been used up over winter. So Margon – that's the man's name – rode east along the coast until he came across two lads in a boat. They'd been fishing, and they'd put into a village where they go to trade. The people there make beautiful woven goods, they're famous for it. But that village was the same. Completely deserted. No corn, no beasts or chickens, nothing. And even if it was the plague, which you might think – well, there'd be animals, wouldn't there? And bodies. There'd be a few bodies. And there was nothing.' Gerdan shrugged and waited for someone to speak, but no-one did. 'We didn't know what to make of it, and the soothsayers weren't any help, so Gorlois said, "we'd better tell the king." And here I am.'

Kerin sat quite still, sifting the possibilities. Whatever the threat or temptation, he could not imagine any circumstances which would have driven him to abandon Henfelin without a fight, especially given enough time to gather livestock and load material possessions onto a wagon. Such time could have been used to organise some resistance and raise defences, even in a poorly protected coastal village. Vortigern too was silent. Perhaps his mind was making the same calculations.

'Lord King?' Gerdan said, with a flicker of anxiety.

'Go back to your brother,' Vortigern said. 'Thank him for his message, and tell him to make his usual good time. We'll speak of this tonight.' Gerdan bowed, retrieved his horse and cantered away towards the south-west. 'What do you make of that?'

'I don't know,' Kerin said. 'I can't imagine abandoning my home for any reason. But then, I'm a warrior. Those people are not.'

Vortigern looked round as Gwyndaf and Elir passed by, their inspection of the animals complete. 'Gwyndaf. A word.' The standard-bearer strolled over, in no hurry at all. 'Suppose you came across a fishing village. Completely deserted. No people, no livestock, no food, nothing. And then you rode a little further along the coast and found another village, exactly the same. No slaughter or burning, just completely abandoned. What would you think?'

Gwyndaf's face darkened. 'Why the hell are you asking me this?'

'Because I think your opinion might be worth hearing. What would you think?'

Gwyndaf's jaw clamped. 'I would think that whoever ran that village was so frightened that he decided to get his people out. I would think that those people were lucky, for having a wise headman and the time to do what he told them. So, are you going to stand there and wait for me to say that another man had the sense to do what I did not? That he made a choice which saved his people, when I did not?' He broke off, breathing hard.

'No,' Vortigern said. 'I want to know what you'd do next, if you found a village like that. Because the Kernow lookouts have found two of them east of their territory, and when Gorlois gets here, that's the first question he's going to ask me.'

Gwyndaf steadied himself, perhaps disconcerted that his opinion had been sought. 'I'd keep on riding along the coast until I found a village with some people in it. I'd ask them if they knew what had happened. If they didn't, I'd tell them to run. And then I'd keep riding until I found the answer. A burned village and a lot of bodies, unless I'm much mistaken. And if that's happened here, you'll have to deal with it, whatever's going on in the North. And if you don't deal with it, I will deal with it myself, however many I have to take with me.' Gwyndaf nodded, an acknowledgment quite devoid of respect, and marched off towards the horse lines.

* * *

Seven men sat around the fire. Beyond them, in the darkness, the encampment murmured and hummed. Nothing it might have thrown up, short of pitched battle, could have torn the web of concentration enveloping these seven. Gorlois of Kernow and his youngest brother. Chief warrior Lud. Gwyndaf the standard-bearer. Cheldric the cook. The king and his right arm.

'We couldn't make sense of it,' Gorlois said, short of words for once. 'Gwyndaf here may well be right. Perhaps the poor devils were running from something. But if they were, what? And why haven't they come back?'

No-one spoke. Kerin, who had little to draw on in his own limited experience of life, turned to the one thing which was sounding a slow, persistent alarm note in the back of his mind. 'I've only once seen the sort of fear which might make people abandon their homes. And that was last month, in Caerwent, when Garagon's friend came from Kent to tell us that Saxons were threatening their coast.'

'Saxons!' Gorlois's tone was dismissive, but his eyes were not.

'This far west?' Gerdan said. 'They've never been this far west. I know the Romans built that enormous fort to protect their fleet, but that's over by Vectis. And it was for ordinary pirates as much as Saxons, wasn't it?'

'It was for any possible threat,' Vortigern said. 'Most of the Saxon incursions were further east, but the Romans left nothing to chance. What do you think, Cheldric?'

'I think that if I am Saxon leader, I go anywhere my ship can go,' the cook said. 'Everyone talks about the man who comes from Kent. This man is warrior. This man is frightened enough to die. I have seen this thing. The ships come. The ships go. The people on land say, we will run, run before they come back. They never go back to their place by the sea. They go where the ships cannot go. Their fathers and their mothers have told them about warriors from the sea who will cut off heads and hands and hang them on their ships for the birds to eat.'

'Alright,' Vortigern said. 'Gorlois, pick ten good men, including your brother, and send them east by the coast road. Gwyndaf, you have leave to go with them. Take a few of your own boys. Send word if you have trouble or find anything. When we reach Calleva, I'll decide whether to make for Londinium or bear south-east for Kent. There are two places we could muster; there, or the Campus Martius. If I choose the Campus, I'll send a messenger and you can ride back with Garagon's forces.'

'I'll do it,' Gwyndaf said. 'But what about the draco? I can't take it on a scouting expedition.'

'What do you want to do with it?' Vortigern asked.

Gwyndaf grimaced and nodded to Kerin. 'I'll leave it with him. He's as good as any of you, and better than most. Don't worry, Kerin Brightspear, I don't expect you to carry it. Haven't got the arms for the long haul, have you? Just don't let anyone interfere with it until I come back. Understood?'

'Understood,' Kerin said. 'And it's an honour. No-one will touch it.'

Cheldric remained as the others dispersed. 'Lord, this is Saxon work, I swear. Please do not show me to them, if they come.'

'I won't,' Kerin said. If he had had men to spare, he would have sent them to search inland, but there were no spare men and no easy answers. 'Go back to your wagon,' he said. 'You're safe here. And make room for the dragon. Gwyndaf's right, I haven't got the arms for the long haul.'

21

'He's insane.' Custennin flung the saddle onto his mare's back. 'The Picts are swarming over the North like flies over a corpse, and he brings us here to frighten Saxons. And where are the Saxons?' He spat on the ground and jerked his saddle-girth tight. The mare winced and squealed. Custennin thumped her on the muzzle with his clenched fist. Kerin stood back and kept quiet. There would have been no point in admitting that Kent was his doing. Three days back at Calleva, Vortigern had halted at the crossroads.

'Londinium or Kent? It's your call.'

'Kent,' Kerin said, without a moment's hesitation. 'Something's going to happen.' And so here they were, the huge, diverse mounted army of the Britons, camped on the outskirts of Garagon's flashy capital, waiting for the storm to break. 'Where are you going?' Kerin asked.

'Into the town to get drunk,' Custennin said, mounting up. 'What else is there to do in this hell hole?'

Lud seized the rein. 'If you cause one moment's trouble with Garagon –'

'Garagon's out hunting with Brennius and his cousins,' Custennin scoffed. 'They're never back until sunset. By then I'll be eating meat with you and my brothers.'

Lud scowled and released the rein. Kerin watched as Custennin clattered off along the Roman road. He couldn't understand men who mistreated their warhorses. A mile distant, the white citadel of Durovernum gleamed under the early sun. Around here, its Roman name had clung. Back in the West most people called it Caer Ceint, if anything; it was merely a shadow in their imagination, vague and insubstantial like Londinium and all the other places they would never see. Kerin sat down, leaning against the grey, gnarled trunk of the oak where they had gathered. Lud squatted beside him on a fallen branch, sharpening his dagger.

'Do you want me to follow him?' Kerin asked.

'No.'

'But if there's trouble –'

'There will be trouble. It's not just Custennin. Half of them are spoiling for a fight.'

Around them the pleasant green meadows of Kent smiled in the late morning sunlight, but the tranquillity was brittle. Close by, the Cambrian animals grazed beside the makeshift village housing their owners. There were tents, sparse timber shelters and nothing at all for men like Hefydd and his boys, who said that luxury was for girls, and slept under the stars. To the right lay the grander accommodation belonging to Eldof of Glevum and his entourage. There were hitching rails and carriages, and any number of large tents containing comfortable beds; the sort of thing Vortigern wouldn't tolerate in his own following because he said it turned fighting men soft. Any stranger might have gone to the wrong encampment to look for the king. Vortigern's only concession was a large, sparsely furnished tent known as the praetorium; the name the Romans used for the general's tent in their military camps, the older men said. It was one of two things which distinguished the headquarters of the Cambrian army from the domain of Gorlois and his men. The other was the smell of ale occasionally drifting from the Kernow area, when someone slipped up and forgot that the king was particular about abstention in a fighting force. Kerin ran his eye over it all, filled with admiration, whatever private fears he might have entertained. He doubted whether Publius Luca would have much criticism to offer when he arrived to inspect the troops.

'It's quite an army, you know,' he said. Lud gave a grim smile.

'I know. That's the trouble. It's a fine, big army with nothing to do, and that always means grief. If we don't go and kill someone before those boys start killing each other, we won't have an army. When's Publius Luca coming from Londinium?'

'This afternoon. We'll be on the march before you know it.'

'Not a moment too soon.' Lud slid his dagger into its leather sheath. Gwyndaf came up from the meadow. He and the Kernow men had found no bodies or burned villages. Kerin couldn't decide whether the standard-bearer was glad or a little disappointed about that.

'Trouble?' Gwyndaf asked, sensing the tension.

'No,' Kerin said. He still didn't trust Gwyndaf not to exploit an advantage if it arose.

'But there will be,' Lud said, to his chagrin. Gwyndaf smiled faintly.

'That's interesting. Where's Vortigern?'

Lud nodded towards the praetorium. 'In there, talking to some priests.'

Gwyndaf winked. 'Good for the soul, I'm sure,' he said, and strode off, chuckling.

'What's it about, anyway?' Kerin asked.

'I've no idea. One of them's Giraldus, that old crow from the chapel of St Alban. Brother Padarn brought them, so you could try asking him.'

* * *

After the priests had gone, Kerin went to the praetorium and drew the door-flap aside. Vortigern, looking tired and drawn for the time of day, was sitting at the long table.

'Don't ask,' he said. 'We'll talk about it tonight, after meat. Is everything quiet out there?' Kerin sat down and helped himself from a pitcher of cool water. 'On the face of things. But I wouldn't turn my back. You've done well to get them this far without trouble.'

'It's not done yet,' Vortigern said. 'The slightest thing could set them off. Most of Eldof's men at least have a gloss of civility. But the Kentishmen put our warriors on the level of the beasts. It would only take one piece of stupidity to start a bloodbath.'

'You haven't slept,' Kerin said.

'No. Would you?'

'Perhaps not. I've never borne a weight like this, so I can't tell. But I do know that it's a long way to the Wall. Sleep now, while you can. I'll watch things.'

'Alright.' Vortigern went out, patting Kerin's shoulder, and disappeared into the small tent alongside the praetorium where he usually spent the night. Quietly satisfied with the responsibility entrusted to him, Kerin set off to survey the encampment. Most men greeted him with respect. His stock had risen steadily during the long ride from Glevum. Everyone seemed to have heard what was said after Eldof's feast, and Vortigern was not known for scattering compliments like rose petals, even when deserved. The robber's bastard had gone up a notch in most men's estimation. His inspection complete, Kerin went in search of Padarn. He found the monk sitting on the bank of a stream, feet dangling in the clear water.

'What was that meeting about?' he asked.

'Bishop Germanus and his war against the Pelagian heretics, unfortunately.' Padarn gave him a look of utter weariness. 'I'd have spared Vortigern the grief, because I know he's got no patience with it. But there's talk of armies being raised. If I'd said nothing, that wouldn't be right either.'

'Who was with Giraldus?'

'Two young friends of his who've just landed from Gallia. Very clever lads, very sharp. Giraldus sent them to study with a good teacher he knew when he was a young man. They bumped into Paulinus at a prayer meeting. He must have gone out there after Constans was killed. You don't need too much of a brain to work out why, do you?'

'Unfortunately not,' Kerin said. 'Why was Giraldus keen to tell Vortigern, though?'

'I couldn't quite put my finger on that,' Padarn said. 'In a funny sort of way, it sounded as if he felt he had to look out for him.'

Kerin had no time to speculate. At that moment a band of riders appeared, coming from the thinly-wooded country north of the city; five noblemen and a few servants leading pack-horses laden with fresh deer carcasses. Lud came running.

'Garagon, home early!' he shouted. Kerin sprang to his feet. 'Bened!' Lud bellowed. 'Get my horse!'

Kerin looked around for Marc and found him loitering outside the praetorium. Putting two fingers to his lips, he let out a piercing whistle. The boy sped off to catch the horses. Lud ran for his saddlery and weapons. Gwyndaf, who had not gone far enough to miss anything, came sauntering back.

'Custennin,' Kerin said. 'He's gone into the town to get drunk, and his father thinks he may stir up trouble. We have to find him, in case he picks a fight and it gets out of hand.'

'I'll come if you want me to,' Gwyndaf said.

'Yes,' Kerin said. 'Bring Derfyn too.' Another sword-arm might not go amiss; there was no point in expecting Lud to keep a level head where his son was concerned. Marc brought up the horses, eyes bright with excitement. It was all another adventure to him, so far.

It was market day in Durovernum, and the narrow streets leading to the main square were choked with people and baggage animals. The four warriors dismounted, left their horses with a disgruntled Marc and fought their way through flocks of sheep, strings of bleating goats and crowds of jovial revellers. The square was crammed with stalls full of pottery, clothing, jewellery and sweetmeats. Garagon's jaunty musicians were playing somewhere, and on a tall, bare plinth a half-naked old man was leaning on a rough wooden cross, roaring about the wages of sin.

'Who's that madman?' Kerin asked one of the goat-herds.

'God knows,' the herdsman said. 'It's that plinth. It draws them. Garagon sent all the way to Italy for a statue, but some idiot knocked it off a wagon in Londinium.'

'Ale and food!' a voice bellowed above the din. 'Ale and food, best in the city!' In the corner of the square was a cart loaded with barrels. A very big, bearded man was taking the money and three well-blessed girls were handing out tankards. A tipsy, good-natured crowd had gathered; stall-holders, craftsmen in working clothes and four smart middle-aged men with a military air. Gwyndaf nodded towards the wagon.

'Go on,' he said to Kerin. 'You're better at this sort of thing than the rest of us.'

Unsure whether that was a compliment or a veiled insult, Kerin wandered casually over to the wagon and paid the bearded man for ale. The three girls fell over each other to serve him. They grabbed for the tankards and screamed and spat and pulled each other's hair.

'Here you are,' gasped the victor, a big, dark-haired girl who looked rather as Branwen might have done after a year's rough living. Kerin took the tankard and thanked the girl. The beer was warm and disgusting.

'Cambrian, aren't you?' the bearded man asked, happily fleecing the next customer. 'One of the king's lot?'

'That's right.'

'Not before time.' The bearded man mopped his forehead. 'I'm Nanus. I keep the alehouse by the gate, but I do this on market days. Venison stew at the alehouse later, I'm famous for it.'

'Nanus,' said Kerin. 'That's a Latin name, isn't it? You don't look Roman, if you don't mind my saying so.'

'Take after my mother. My father was in the Victrix. He didn't marry her, of course, just had his way and went marching off, but it didn't stop her giving me a Roman name.' He guffawed. 'She must have had a sense of humour. Nanus means "little dwarf".'

Kerin laughed too, then had to remind himself why he had come. 'What did you mean, not before time?'

'Well, it's a shambles round here, isn't it.' Nanus waved his hand about. 'It was alright when the old man was alive; he had his airs and graces, but he did keep things in order. Now nobody knows who's in charge, and all Garagon can do is ride around on that racehorse. They can't even fix the buildings or fill up the potholes in the streets. And now we might have those bastard Saxons about to land on us.' He shook his head and sat down on the tailboard, probably a lot more frightened than he wanted to admit.

'Has Garagon done anything about defences?' Kerin asked. Nanus snorted.

'There are the defences.' He nodded towards the military men, probably on their fourth or fifth tankard. 'Decent enough, but no commander, no pay – well, what would you do? So *that's* what I meant by not before time. And to be honest, we've never been too keen on men of the West.'

'A bit wild and uncivilised?' Kerin enquired. Nanus chuckled.

'Your words, lad. But I could see straight away that the king was going to knock a few heads together.' He took two tankards from the back of the wagon and filled them from a small cask hidden under the seat. 'Here, give me back that piss and try this.'

Kerin sipped the powerful ale cautiously. 'Have you seen many of our warriors in the city?'

'Not many,' said Nanus. 'You're supposed to keep off the ale really, aren't you? There's one lad I've seen a few times. Taller than you, thin face, red hair. A bit wild-looking, I suppose. Bloody good drinker, though, I'll give him that.'

'Oh?' Kerin said nonchalantly, sweat prickling on the back of his neck. 'Have you seen him today?'

'Yes, yes,' Nanus said, 'not long ago. Didn't stop long. Just downed a few jars, gave me a bit of a wink and rode off towards the rich men's quarter. He's found himself some tasty little morsel, I expect. The city's full of bored wives and reluctant virgins.'

Kerin leaned towards Nanus. 'I could do with some of that myself,' he murmured. 'It's like being a monk in the king's army.'

Nanus grinned, making an obvious gesture with his fore-arm. 'Over that way, down the potters' street and past the basilica. Garagon's got any amount of pretty cousins. Keep your hands off his sister, she's promised to some Roman toff, but there's a warm welcome from the cousins when their men are off doing what men do. Or if you fancy, there's the world's best whorehouse behind the barracks. Smile nicely, and you can have it any way you like.'

Kerin put down the tankard. Whatever was coming, it was likely to require a clear head.

'Thank you, Nanus,' he said, patting the big man's shoulder. 'I'll see you later for the venison stew.'

'Well?' Lud said as they cleared the square and arrived in the potters' street.

'Custennin's here somewhere' Kerin said. 'He's been drinking, but now he's probably looking for a woman. The landlord said that Garagon has a house full of female relations. Either that, or the whorehouse behind the barracks.'

'Well that's it, then,' Gwyndaf said. 'No disrespect, Lud, but I'm sure your son's just like my young idiots. Put them in a city and they're like bulls in a field full of cows on heat.'

Lud's face coloured with embarrassment. 'They're young men! What do you expect?'

'Leave it!' Kerin exclaimed. 'Come on, for the gods' sake, let's find Garagon's house.'

They found it soon enough. Following Nanus's directions, Kerin realised that everyone they encountered was heading the same way, and that everyone was running. The sweaty, panting crowd of which they were now a part ended up at the open gates of a packed courtyard. One look confirmed that everyone in there was out for blood. Under the portico of the grand house, Kerin glimpsed the horses he had seen returning from the hunt. Fired up and terrified by the commotion, they were plunging about as a trio of servants tried vainly to calm them. Of Garagon and his companions, there was no sign.

'Oh gods, what's passed?' Lud elbowed his way forward. Kerin caught his arm.

'Lud, something's happened here. I hope Custennin is nothing to do with it, but if he is, for God's sake, keep a cool head.'

'A cool head?' Lud shouted, jerking free. 'He's my son!'

The crowd surged forward with a savage roar and they struggled to see above the bobbing heads. Something was happening under the portico. Kerin launched himself forward, hurling aside a big man with a wooden stave, and fought his way to the foot of the steps. Four men were holding Custennin in front of the pillars. He was struggling manically, and it took all their strength to restrain him. The main door behind them was open, and a sound like the howling of caged beasts was coming from deep within the belly of the house. Someone had split Custennin's lip. A thin stream of blood was trickling down his neck. Garagon came flying out of the house, raging and weeping. There was blood on his pale grey tunic. It appeared not to be his own. Kerin knew that, however many deer he had dropped out in the woods, Garagon would not have stooped to slit their throats himself. He glanced around. Gwyndaf was not far away, with Derfyn at his shoulder, but there was no sign of another Cambrian or even a Kernow man in the whole wild, baying mob.

'Right!' Garagon whipped out his sword. 'Now you'll answer for it.'

'No!' Lud bellowed, stumbling up the steps. 'Let my son go!'

'Your son's an animal, Lud,' Garagon panted. Kerin saw Lud go for his sword but could not reach him. Something hissed in the air. Lud dropped as the stone hit. Gwyndaf and Derfyn hoisted him up as he fell and hauled him away through the crowd. Garagon turned as Kerin mounted the steps. Whatever had happened to stir his fury and grief, he had mastered himself now.

'Stay where you are,' he said, raising his sword. 'I don't want to use this, but I will if you try to protect him.'

'What's happened here?' Kerin asked. Custennin stared sullenly at the ground. The question triggered something in Garagon.

'Tell him!' he howled. The sword flashed out and nicked Custennin's forehead. Kerin found Brennius beside him, ashen-faced, as he was in Caerwent.

'This is the end of everything,' he stammered.

'Stop!' a voice roared. Vortigern was at the gates, with Eldof and a troop of mounted warriors. Marc was with them. Kerin thanked the gods that he had brought him along. The crowd parted. Vortigern rode up to the foot of the steps and dismounted. Garagon's sword-arm sank back to his side. Vortigern came up the steps with Eldof following.

'Alright.' He looked from Garagon to Custennin. 'What's going on here?'

Garagon flung down his sword. 'This savage of yours ravished my sister!'

'It's a lie,' Custennin spat. 'The bitch was a ready partner.'

Garagon dived for his sword. Vortigern caught him long before he reached it and held him, encircled by one arm, in a grip he was powerless to break. Garagon struggled impotently, weeping with rage. Kerin sprang up the steps and grabbed the sword.

'Bring the woman,' Vortigern said.

'No!' Garagon exclaimed. 'Hasn't she suffered enough?'

Vortigern released him. 'Bring her. One of them's lying. If it's your sister, I'll hang you both.'

Garagon closed his eyes. 'Alright. Brennius, bring Livia.'

Brennius's footsteps thudded away down an unseen corridor. He was soon back, with Edlym. Between them, arms linked through theirs, was a slender girl, the hood of her cloak drawn tightly around her face. As they reached the top of the steps she twisted free and spat in Custennin's face. Vortigern took her by the shoulders and turned her round. She flinched and cowered at his touch. He let his hands fall. The girl stood silently in front of him. Vortigern reached forward and drew back her hood. Garagon's breath escaped in a hiss of rage. Her face – and Kerin could see from the unblemished side how beautiful it had been – was swollen and disfigured by an ugly red weal which extended from her right eyebrow to her chin. Vortigern's face hardened.

'Did he do this?' The girl stared vacantly at him. Her long dark hair fell about her face in a tangled mess.

'Yes, Lord King.' Her voice was expressionless, but the blood throbbed in her face, making the bruise look even angrier. 'I'd sooner hang than come before you like this, but better to die of shame, than for him to go free and do this to another poor girl.'

Vortigern gently lifted the tangle of hair and examined the bruise. 'Is this all he did?'

'No!' the girl shrieked. Seizing the edges of her cloak, she flung it open. Her white silk dress was torn from shoulder to hem. Her exposed breasts were blackened with bruises, her thighs smeared with drying blood. Kerin stared at her in horror, and in that awful moment of blinding truth he knew that he had seen this before, and where.

'Faria,' he whispered hoarsely. Vortigern turned, frowning. 'Faria!' Kerin howled, and lunged forward. Vortigern seized him round the neck. As he did it, Kerin felt two other pairs of hands grab him from behind. Gwyndaf and Derfyn had come from the crowd.

'Leave it, boy, leave it,' Gwyndaf hissed in his ear.

'I can't leave it,' Kerin choked, struggling against their grip. Gwyndaf's fingers dug into his arm.

'Leave it,' he said calmly. 'You can't settle this.'

Kerin closed his eyes, but that only wakened a vision of Faria lying broken on her narrow bed in the slaves' quarters. By the time he opened them again, Vortigern had Custennin by the throat.

'Did you do this?' He gritted his teeth as Custennin thrashed in the crook of his arm. Custennin screwed up his face, clenched his jaw and said nothing. 'Did you do it?' Vortigern bellowed. Custennin's eyes bulged and he clawed helplessly at Vortigern's arm.

'She was as hot as a rutting doe,' he bawled. 'She drove me mad for it, then spat in my face.'

Vortigern's eyes moved to Garagon's sister, standing trembling and defiant beside her brother. His eyes questioned her. If they had held a shred of contempt or brutality, pride might have sustained her, but there was neither, and her composure disintegrated.

'It's a lie,' she sobbed, clinging to Garagon. 'I'm betrothed to a good man, and I love him dearly. How could I betray him with this – this thing?'

She flung her cloak about her and stumbled, weeping, into the house. Vortigern hurled Custennin against the wall with a force which sent him sprawling on the ground, retching and gulping for breath; then he dragged him to his feet by the collar of his tunic and pinned him against one of the pillars of the portico.

'Now,' he breathed, twisting the collar tight. 'The slave girl.'

Kerin lunged forward, but found himself restrained as if by iron bands. Gwyndaf was stronger than he had ever imagined, and now Derfyn had been joined by Eldof to ensure that he remained where he was, struggling impotently at the top of the steps.

'Slave girl?' Custennin faltered. Kerin had always supposed that nothing much frightened him, but now he was plainly terrified. Vortigern leaned closer to him.

'Oh yes,' he said softly. 'The Phoenician girl. Faria. The girl who drank poison because some savage raped her twice.'

Custennin giggled hysterically. 'You can't rape a slave,' he yelped, in a strangled voice which became a shriek of pain as Vortigern cracked his head against the pillar and let him drop.

'Well?' Garagon demanded.

'He did it,' Vortigern said.

Garagon's eyes glowed. 'God's blood, if he doesn't die for this, I swear on my father's grave that we'll slaughter every last one of your barbarians before tonight.'

He had spoken quietly, but the crowd in the courtyard caught the inference if not the words. They screamed and stamped and yelled for blood; those who had weapons drew them, and those who had only their fists pumped them above their heads as they poured towards the steps in a lethal, brawling mass. Garagon raised his hands and begged for restraint. Kerin found himself penned up under the portico with Eldof and Gwyndaf. They had released him now that his temper was cool enough to control.

'Mother of God,' Eldof said, 'they'll butcher the lot of us if they don't get their way.'

Garagon circled Custennin, who had hauled himself to his feet and was clinging to one of the columns. Distraught or not, the young lord of Kent was revelling in his moment of power. 'You're going to die here,' he said earnestly. Custennin clutched Vortigern's sleeve.

'Lord, save me!' he whispered. Vortigern shook off his hand. He turned and spoke quietly to Garagon, who looked around and pointed towards the crowd. Kerin picked out a bunch of four young warriors; big, strong fellows who looked as if their brains were not quite a match for their muscles. Vortigern beckoned them and bent his head to speak to them. The young men looked taken aback, as if even their outraged sense of justice did not quite allow for what he was saying. But then they weighed the alternatives, exchanged furtive smiles and changed their collective mind. When Vortigern gave them the nod, there was no hesitation. They grabbed Custennin, stripped off his breeches and undergarments and spread-eagled him face down on the steps. Vortigern drew his sword. Custennin fought and screamed for mercy. The crowd roared like a river in flood. Garagon smiled nervously, his face white as marble.

'What's the matter?' Vortigern asked. 'Do you want him left in a fit state to do it again?' Eldof touched Vortigern's arm.

'You could just kill him, you know,' he said uneasily. 'He'd be better off dead than gelded like a packhorse.'

'Too good for the bastard,' Vortigern said. The sword swung back and fell. Custennin howled in agony and rolled senseless down the steps. Vortigern turned to Garagon, slamming his sword into its scabbard. 'That's that, then,' he said crisply. 'No more talk of bloodbaths, please.' Garagon stared silently at him with something between admiration and terror. Behind them, Gwyndaf and Derfyn were dragging Custennin up the steps. 'Send for your physicians. He should survive if they can stop him bleeding like a stuck pig.'

Garagon swallowed hard. 'Eldof was right. He'd be better off dead, don't you think?'

'Not to me,' Vortigern said. 'Now, go and comfort the

girl. Her beloved will wash his hands of her, if he's like most men I know.'

He turned and strode back down the steps. The crowd parted before him, muttering and exchanging cowed glances. Kerin felt a hand on his arm. It was Nanus the landlord.

'Well,' the big man said shakily, 'that'll give them something to talk about over the venison stew.'

22

The news had reached the encampment, conveyed by a hysterically excited Marc. The men took it with a pinch of salt. Only when Gwyndaf the standard bearer came back and told them exactly the same tale did they understand that it was the truth. He had related the events calmly and with a relish which probably had its roots in the fate of his first wife.

Kerin rode back to the camp with Derfyn and turned his horse loose in the meadow. Hefydd and his boys had lit a small fire on the bank of the stream, and a cauldron was steaming over the flames. Kerin felt bitter and deflated. Faria had been avenged, no doubt, but he had been denied the satisfaction of inflicting his own justice. Now Vortigern had done something which would live in the mind far longer than any execution. Warriors saw death almost every day, they became inured to it, but Custennin's punishment would make them all wince every time they thought about it. And it had been done, not only for the women who had suffered, but to stop the king's army descending into a bloodbath which would wreck it even before it left Kent. For Faria and for Garagon's sister, but not wholly so. It had been done out of necessity, and Kerin had had no part in it. He felt cheated. There was no redemption.

'My God, boy,' said Hefydd, and handed Kerin a mug of brew. They all sat and drank in silence, because it was hard to know what more to say.

'Where's Macsen?' Kerin asked.

'With Elir,' said Mad Mabon. 'They've gone to look for their father.'

Another silence followed.

'I don't know,' Hefin said. 'All of us and Custennin, we've fought together for years, and saved each other's lives, and all the rest. But an animal wouldn't do that, would it? Suppose he'd done it to little Branwen, or Mabli? And we all know what the Kent boys would have done if the bastard had been left to get away with it. But by God, I don't think I could have done what the Lord did.'

There was little to add to that. Hefin had spoken for every man around the fire, so in the end they simply sat and drank Hefydd's brew until the cauldron was empty.

* * *

Late in the afternoon, a cloud of dust loomed on the Roman road. Marc spotted it first and wakened Kerin, who had fallen into a fitful sleep.

'Riders, lord,' the boy said. 'Three of them.'

Kerin got up, rubbing his eyes, and went to investigate. It was Publius Luca, accompanied by two soldiers of the city garrison. Gwyndaf, Varro and Gorlois were already greeting them. All in all, Kerin was happy for someone else to relate what had happened at Garagon's house.

'Aren't you going to meet them, lord?' Marc asked.

'Yes,' Kerin said, 'but Gorlois can go first. At least he's never short of something to say.'

Marc gave him an uneasy look. 'Do you think it was a cruel thing to do?'

'No more cruel than what Custennin did,' Kerin said. 'If you ever hurt a girl like that, I'd cut you up with Cheldric's meat cleaver and feed you to the dogs.'

Marc lowered his eyes. 'I saw my grandfather chop a pig's balls off once. But at least he knocked him out with a sledgehammer first.'

The sound of voices drifted on the light wind. Publius Luca came out of Eldof's tent and marched towards the praetorium.

'Can I go riding with Derfyn?' Marc asked. 'He said he'd show me a few sword tricks.'

'Yes, of course. Be back before dark.'

Kerin went down to the stream and ducked his head in the water. The kitchen lads were there busily cleaning mackerel, but he had no appetite for the bread and salt pork they offered. As he left them, Publius Luca emerged from the praetorium.

'I came ahead of the others,' Publius said. 'I wanted to make my own assessment without Severus Maximus and that half-wit Alberius looking over my shoulder. They'll be military experts when they arrive here tomorrow.'

'What do you make of it all?' Kerin asked.

'Better than I could have hoped for. Knowing Vortigern as I do, I'm not surprised. But that said, too much optimism seemed unfair. The gods know how he managed it.'

'He'll tell you that he hasn't managed it,' Kerin said. 'I suppose he'll have managed it when we beat the Picts. Do you know where he is?'

'In the praetorium, playing backgammon with Eldof of Glevum. More than I could do, under the circumstances, but your standard-bearer was well impressed.'

'Gwyndaf has good reason,' Kerin said. 'And if nothing had been done, you wouldn't have found an army here. You'd have found a slaughterhouse.'

'I know,' Publius Luca said. 'All I'm saying is that I'd probably have hanged the boy. Not that it would have frightened people in the same way, however dead he was. I'm thankful that nothing quite like this ever happened to me in the Second Augusta.'

* * *

Towards evening, when the men were gathering for food, Kerin sat on his blanket in the tent he shared with Macsen, mending a broken bridle. As he worked, more for distraction than from necessity, the tent flap was drawn and Vortigern came in.

'Ride with me, for God's sake,' he said.

The horses moved slowly along the bank of the tide-channel, side by side. Their hooves made a soft, sucking sound as they trod the grey mud. A strong sea breeze lifted their manes and swelled their riders' cloaks. The sky was leaden. Vortigern stared at the colourless flats rolling towards the sea. 'This is a horrible place,' he said. 'Even the birds don't stay here long.' He drew rein and glanced down at the winding channels, their sluggish water eerily reflecting the glow of sunset. 'Streams of blood,' he said under his breath. Kerin slowed his horse.

'Pictish blood? Saxon blood? Custennin's blood?'

Vortigern shrugged. 'Custennin got what he asked for. I'd have thought that you, of all people, would agree with that.'

'I do. I'd have killed him myself, with my bare hands. But wouldn't killing him have been better? I know you had to keep the peace, but how can Lud live with that?'

'Lud's got two more sons to bear his name, and his daughters have already given him more grandchildren than he wants,' Vortigern said. 'And anyway, you'd be surprised what Lud can live with.' They rode on as the wind freshened, bringing a scattering of rain. 'What did Publius Luca say to you?'

'That he admired what you'd done,' Kerin said. 'That he couldn't have done it himself. And that things were a bit different in the Second.'

'You mean he thinks I'm a bloodletting savage.'

'No, lord,' Kerin sighed. 'He said that he'd have hanged Custennin, that's all.'

Vortigern turned. 'Look, as you pointed out, this isn't the Second Augusta. There are no laws, no rules. Half of these men are brutes, with a brute's sensibilities. And so I gave them a brute's solution. Let it rest.'

'I'm sorry,' Kerin avoided his eyes. 'For what it's worth, I haven't found one man who thinks it was undeserved. All they're saying is that they couldn't have done it them-selves. And for most of them that means admiration, not disapproval.'

'As I told you,' Vortigern said harshly. 'They're brutes.'

They rode on in silence. The land grew bleaker as they neared the sea. Kerin thought that if he had been a Saxon, he would have thought twice about risking death to get his hands on it.

'That girl you went to in Glevum,' Vortigern said. 'The one whose ring you wear around your neck.' Kerin started, wondering what association of ideas had brought him to this point. His hand moved to the silver chain, and Vortigern laughed. 'Idiot. We both know you've been wearing it for months.'

Kerin smiled half-heartedly. He had supposed that there was no worse subject to talk about than Custennin's castration, but here it was. Vortigern circled until they were face to face.

'Well? Do you love her?'

'Yes, lord, I do.' Kerin felt a wave of hot colour rise to his face.

'And is she beautiful?'

'Oh yes,' Kerin said, unable to prevent a smile. 'Her hair's red and gold, like the colour of autumn leaves. And her eyes are as blue as – well, as blue as hare-bells.'

Vortigern chuckled. 'And who is this paragon?'

Kerin stared down at the filthy, clinging mud. He had hoped for better circumstances, but they might never arise. Sooner or later the truth would surface, like some gruesome creature rearing its head from a murky pool. He knew that it was better to haul it out himself than let it slither out on its own. 'Bertil Redknife's daughter,' he said quickly, and waited for the storm to break. Vortigern's face darkened.

'Bertil Redknife's daughter? I've forbidden you to feud with him, and now you've bedded his daughter under my nose?'

'Lord, I love the woman,' Kerin said. 'For God's sake, you must see that I'd prefer it any other way. But I love her. More than my life, and that's the end of it. I lied about my horse going lame on the way home. Don't blame Elir, I put him up to it. I spent that time with Gael. And I went to her again on the night of Eldof's feast, as you know. You can say what you like. We've exchanged vows, and I'm going to marry her one day, with or without your blessing.'

Vortigern's face drained of colour. For a moment he sat quite still, as if incapable of movement or speech. Kerin was appalled. Until that moment, he had had no idea what sort of weapon he was wielding.

'Better with than without, lord,' he said hastily. Vortigern shook his head and recovered himself.

'With my blessing? You'll never have my blessing, and if

you lay another hand on that bitch without it, you won't live long enough to marry her.'

More would have followed, probably, but in the same instant they both heard the galloping horse. A rider was coming in from the east, where mud and sand spits ran into the sea.

'Marc!' Kerin said. The boy was riding flat to his colt's neck.

'Lord!' he yelled. 'Lord!' Kerin grabbed the colt's rein as he skidded to a halt, showering mud. Marc's eyes were wide with alarm. 'Lord, you'd better go down to the beach,' he stammered. 'They're down there, three great ships, and – '

'Quiet!' Vortigern snapped. He seized the boy by the shoulder. 'Start again.'

'Lord King, warriors, down there on the beach beyond the shingle bank,' Marc said, struggling to compose himself. 'And boats, big boats. I didn't wait to count the men, I just took off.'

Vortigern released him. 'Alright. Ride back to the camp and find Lud or Gwyndaf, tell them what's happening and tell them to come to the beach with two hundred men.' He wheeled his mare and set off towards the sea. Kerin followed, racked with dread. A mile on, a shingle bank ran between the salt-marsh and the beach. They dismounted, scrambled up the bank and peered cautiously over the top. Three galleys were riding on the calm water beyond the waves, sales reefed. Another vessel, broader in the beam, was lashed to one of them; a cargo boat, its deck crammed with crates and barrels. Men were moving about on board the galleys, quick and sure-footed, black figures against the darkening sea.

'Saxons!' Vortigern murmured. A man leapt from the prow of the leading galley and waded ashore through the surf. A shout went up as a hundred warriors sprang to their oars and drove the vessels up onto the beach. Their leader strode up across the shingle and paused, hands planted on hips. His shoulders were broad, and his bare, muscular arms were scarred from the wrists to the point where they disappeared beneath the short sleeves of his brown tunic. His long hair and thick beard, which must once have been the colour of ripe corn, were heavily streaked with grey. Probably he was around Vortigern's age. He bawled an order to his men, and they set about hauling galleys and cargo boat up the beach towards the high water mark. They were dressed like their leader, in rough tunics and cross-gartered breeches tucked into light, supple boots which looked well-suited for moving about on a slippery deck. Their studded belts bristled with daggers and short-bladed swords.

The faint rumble of hoofbeats echoed across the flats. The Saxon leader tensed and drew his sword. To Kerin's horror, Vortigern rose up and stood, arms folded, on the summit of the shingle bank. The Saxon warriors roared forward, but their leader raised a hand and stopped them. Vortigern strode down the bank. Kerin leapt up and hurried after him. Vortigern and the Saxon looked each other up and down.

'I am Vortigern, Lord of the West, King of all the Britons,' Vortigern said. 'If you can understand me, you should tell me who you are. No-one lands a hundred armed men here without my leave.'

The Saxon did not flinch. His pale blue eyes peered keenly from beneath heavy fair brows. 'I am Hengist, a prince of the Jutes,' he said, speaking in the British tongue. His speech was heavily accented but clear. He nodded towards a tall, loose-limbed man who had emerged from the band of seafarers. 'My brother, Horsa.'

'You speak our language,' Vortigern said. 'And you speak it well. Where did you learn?'

'From a young man of my following,' Hengist said. 'My brother also. The young man was shipwrecked. He was a prisoner. He spent many seasons here. When he came home, he could speak of nothing but Britain. Her forests, her rich cornfields. I thought, "One day, Hengist will go and see for himself." And so I asked him to teach us your tongue.'

Kerin caught his eye, uneasy despite the Saxon's lack of hostility. Hengist's eyes flicked upwards as hooves crunched on shingle and Lud appeared with a bunch of warriors, ranged along the top of the bank.

'Are you thinking of fighting us?' Vortigern asked.

'No, of course not, Lord King,' Hengist said. 'We have not come here to fight. We come as brothers, to offer ourselves in your service.'

'Indeed,' Vortigern said. 'And what's wrong with the country of the Jutes? My warriors wouldn't go sailing off to fight for someone else.'

Hengist spread his hands and sighed. 'Our young men are lusty, lord. Our young women are fruitful. Sometimes the increase of children is too much for our poor land. The country of the Jutes is not a rich and beautiful land like Britain, of course.' He smiled appealingly. 'I cannot let my people starve. That cannot be Odin's will. All we ask is a little land, just enough to grow corn for our needs, and perhaps to keep a cow or two, for milk. For this, we will serve you as true men.'

Vortigern folded his arms. 'And what about the men who grow our corn now? How pleased do you think they will be, if I give their land to you?'

'Lord, we seek no other man's land.' Hengist looked mildly indignant, as if the suggestion had offended his warrior's sense of fair play. 'Give us only the poor land, where nothing will grow. We are used to poor land. You will soon see corn growing where there are now only rocks and miserable weeds.'

Vortigern raised his eyebrows. 'You're a good talker, Hengist.'

'Then will you accept us?' Hengist asked. His face radiated hope. Vortigern snorted.

'Britain's full of good talkers. I saw through it at my mother's breast. What do you really want?'

'I want what is best for my people, Lord King,' Hengist said. 'The same as you want for yours, I expect. They need food and shelter. I want a place where I can give them these things. We have no gold. But we have our swords and spears and axes. We are strong. Good warriors. We know you make a great army, to fight the men who try to take your kingdom. Give us just a little land and enough food to live on, and we will fight for you. You have seen Saxons fight?'

'Yes,' Vortigern said. 'I killed a few near here, around ten years ago. They'd caused trouble, and they shouldn't have been here, so they deserved it. Good fighters, though. Quick and brave. I'll grant you that.'

'You will let us stay, then?' Hengist asked. Vortigern raised a finger.

'Take your time. Your people may decide things on a wet beach, but here we do things differently. I shall consider, and speak with the lords of the Britons and my chief warriors.'

Hengist inclined his head politely. 'Then we stay here with our boats, and we wait. If you tell us to go, we go. We are only a few, and I am not stupid enough to think that we could win a fight with the King of all the Britons.'

'Good,' Vortigern said. 'If we fight, it'll be your choice. But if it is your choice, remember that quite a few men have picked fights with me over the years, and that they're all in the graveyard.'

Hengist made a respectful bow. Vortigern nodded and strode back up the beach. Kerin caught the Saxon's eye. An unspoken animosity crackled in the air between them, the more ominous because there was no reason for it.

'Who are you?' the Saxon asked.

'Kerin Brightspear,' Kerin said. 'The king's chief warrior.' He felt disinclined to play down his importance. Hengist turned and spoke to his brother. Horsa chuckled but did not reply. He had a ready smile and wide-set blue eyes which gave his face an air of genial openness. This did not prevent Kerin from noticing the length of his arms, which would give him a formidable reach when he was swinging a sword. Hengist had said, "If this is the chief warrior, we should have brought the boys, not the men." Kerin was galled, but kept his counsel. It would have been self-defeating, to let them know that they had been understood. Instead he laughed along with them and raised a cheery hand before trudging back up the beach to join the others. Marc was holding the horses. Beside them Lud sat his raw-boned roan, watching the proceedings. His face looked hard and grey, like a statue's. Kerin swung unto his mare's back and gave him an uneasy nod. They sat quite still, moving only to pull their cloaks tight as the cutting wind brought a wall of fine rain.

'I've told Gwyndaf and his boys to stay here and keep an eye on these,' Lud said stiffly.

'Good,' Kerin said. 'Hengist sounds friendly enough, but I don't trust him at all.'

Lud turned. 'Kerin, I could die of shame for what Custennin did. If you ever have a son, I hope he serves you better than that.'

Kerin raised his eyebrows. 'I hope so, too,' he said. Lud stared out at the sea.

'I wish to the gods he'd killed him,' he said, blinking

away tears. Down on the beach, against all odds, the Saxons had managed to kindle a fire. Hengist was standing braced against the wind, giving unobtrusive orders. His warriors split into two groups, one foraging along the tidemark for fuel whilst the other dealt with the boats. They moved methodically, never making a false move or getting in each others' way. Kerin wondered if they fought with the same detachment. He thought for a moment of Hefydd's boys and the Kernow men, tipsy and carrying King Constans on their shoulders after his coronation, and the thought filled him with dread.

'What do you think?' Lud asked.

'That I'd rather fight the Picts any day,' Kerin said. Lud's eyebrows rose.

'Those savages?'

'Yes. Any day.'

Lud watched as the Saxons stowed the oars and drove stakes deep into the shingle, securing their vessels with stout ropes in case of a high tide. 'The Romans hired barbarians all the time. There was a troop of them in Isca when we were lads. Batavians, or something. Horrible bastards. They sent them up to the Wall, thank the gods. We had enough trouble without them.'

'Yes,' Kerin said. 'Publius Luca told me a few things.'

Lud looked round. 'You should respect that man.'

'I do. Why do you say it?'

Lud stared out at the rain-swept sea. 'The last time they locked Vortigern up,' he said. 'The time they almost killed him. If Publius Luca hadn't stepped in, he wouldn't be here now. And if Vortigern had died in Isca, you'd have been a wolf's breakfast, so you owe Publius a debt. Don't forget it.'

'I won't,' Kerin said, realising that there were still many things he did not know. He fastened his cloak against the rain, which had grown suddenly colder. The Saxons had unloaded a big basket of fresh herrings. Two of them set about gutting the slippery, gleaming fish whilst another constructed a makeshift spit from two pieces of driftwood and a grappling hook. Hengist turned and looked up at the two horsemen on the shingle bank. He smiled and raised his hand in a friendly salute. The chill rain flattened his wild hair, dripped off his beard and ran down his sinewy arms, troubling him not at all. Lud grinned.

'Mad bastard,' he said, raising his hand in response. But Kerin could not respond. He simply turned his mare and rode away across the grey, desolate flats.

23

Rush lights flickered in the praetorium. The servants, sent by Garagon as a gesture of goodwill, had set up tables and benches. The king had made it clear that no-one should feel crowded or disadvantaged. He explained this to the servants in a calm, undramatic fashion, ending with a disarming smile which seemed to have no place on the lips of a man who had castrated his chief warrior's son the day before.

The names of the delegates were announced by a stout, businesslike man called Cenydd, who ticked them off on his fingers as he spoke. Men who had never been more than a rumour in Kent, but would soon become flesh. Eldof of Glevum, with his brother Bishop Eldadus and chief warrior, Varro; Gorlois and Gerdan of Kernow; Publius Luca and Lucius Arrius, luminaries of the legionary army; the re-nowned merchant Gallus, Master of the War Fleet; Severus Maximus, praetor of Londinium, with his one-armed aco-lyte Alberius; and Flavius of Eburacum, a city so far north that the servants thought it lay under a permanent mantle of snow. The familiar figures followed. Lord Garagon with his affable companion, Brennius; the king's chief warrior, Lud; his fierce standard-bearer, Gwyndaf; his holier-than-thou son, the Lord Vortimer, and that odd young man Kerin Brightspear, who had the king's ear despite being a by-blow from some plague-ridden hole in the West.

The robber's bastard was the first to arrive. He winked

at the servants, gave them a few denarii for ale and sent them packing. The tent-flap was drawn aside and Eldof of Glevum appeared, brushing droplets of fine rain from his cloak. His gaunt grey-haired brother came behind him, sporting a bejewelled crucifix. Varro followed, acknowledging Kerin with a courteous smile.

'You may have been expecting Bertil Redknife,' Eldof said. 'I don't know what's made the bad blood between you, but I don't want it spilling over here. I've warned him to keep away. I hope this thing won't make trouble amongst the warriors.'

'If it does, I won't be the one to start it,' Kerin said. Eldof's expression held no resentment. Perhaps that was because he loathed Bertil, but Kerin was prepared to give him credit for a degree of fairness and good sense.

'This meeting had better pass peacefully,' Eldof said. 'There are enough ingredients here to light a bonfire without including the Saxons.'

His brother pulled a disapproving face. 'Heathen savages,' he said tartly. 'Aren't there enough heathen savages around as it is?'

'More than enough,' Eldof said, 'but these Saxons are a minor irritation. You should worry about the ones who'll be coming down the north road, if we don't get moving soon.'

Kerin kept his concerns to himself. Riders and chariots were arriving. The fading light flared with torches. Rufus was outside, greeting Severus Maximus, Alberius and Flavius of Eburacum. Kerin was astonished. For months Rufus had done anything he could to dissociate himself from Vortigern's activities, and now here he was, smiling and wringing the praetor's limp hand as if they were long-lost friends. Kerin gave Severus a courteous greeting as he approached the tent, but found it impossible to appear more enthusiastic than he felt. The quiet air held a premonition of disaster, and he could not ignore it, although it was in fact rather pleasant to see the silly, ineffectual man again.

'Kerin Brightspear!' A thin voice in the darkness. Kerin looked up.

'Marcellus!' he exclaimed, with delight. He flung open his arms and the old man came shuffling into them. Kerin ushered him into the tent and sat him down at the table. 'What brings you here?' he asked.

'Severus Maximus,' Marcellus murmured behind his hand. 'He would have had me disembowelling every unfortunate creature we passed on the way here. Let's talk before all this gets out of hand.'

'Come on,' Kerin said, taking his arm. They left the tent and walked as quickly as Marcellus's aged legs would allow, to the spreading oak where Kerin and Lud had watched Custennin riding away; something he wouldn't repeat for a while. Kerin sat down on the fallen branch. Marcellus lowered himself gingerly, settling beside him with a grunt of discomfort.

'Even I do not have a potion for old age,' he sighed. They sat in silence, watching the swimming lights of the torches. Beyond them horses moved invisibly in the darkness. 'The Saxons have come, then.'

'Yes,' Kerin said. 'We could fight them and delay marching north, but I can see why most men think it's the least of our worries. We have to decide something quickly. I wish I had a good feeling about this meeting, but I don't.'

'And the king?' Marcellus asked. 'What does he want?'
Kerin shrugged. 'Who knows?'
Marcellus leaned forward intently. 'What has happened?'
Kerin frowned. 'I don't know what you mean.'
Marcellus looked up at him with a grave, knowing smile.

'My young friend, you have every right to keep your counsel, but please do not lie to me. There was never a time when you did not have at least some idea of what Vortigern thought or felt.'

Kerin raised his hands. 'Alright. We fell out over something. No, it wasn't even that. There's something I haven't told you about, or someone, rather. A girl in Glevum. We're betrothed, she's everything I could want, but she's Bertil Redknife's daughter, and we've got enough trouble with him already. Something happened, and I had to tell Vortigern.'

'Ah,' Marcellus said. 'The Lord Vortigern thought it unwise for you to court the daughter of a blood-enemy, I imagine.'

'To say the least,' Kerin said. 'But I love the girl, and it changes things, doesn't it. In a way you could never have imagined. He forbade me to see her, and I had to tell him that I meant to have her, whether he liked it or not. He was furious, of course, but it was worse than that. Far worse. He looked at me as if I'd pulled my dagger out and knifed him.' Marcellus rested his sharp chin on one bony hand. 'Well?' Kerin said, apprehensive at his silence. 'Do you think I did the wrong thing?'

'If you love the girl, then you probably did the only thing you could have done,' Marcellus said. 'But then again, there are ways of saying and doing things; if I were removing the bad flesh from a wound, for example, then I should do my best to use the surgeon's scalpel, not the butcher's axe.'

Kerin winced. 'You have a way with words, Marcellus.'

'It comes with age, like blindness and aching bones.' Marcellus flexed his stiff limbs. 'Please the gods, it may come to you before the other two. And preferably before the king does something regrettable because he believes that you are about to put lust before obligation.'

'I'm not about to do anything of the sort,' Kerin protested. 'It isn't just lust, anyway. I told you, I love the girl. And nothing can ever change my obligation to Vortigern. I don't see why I shouldn't be his warrior *and* take a wife, that's all.'

'Well, of course not,' Marcellus said. 'And I'm sure that the Lord Vortigern would be the last man to say otherwise. But you know as well as I do that he cannot be told. Do you not think that it might have been, shall we say, more judicious to have asked?'

Kerin snorted. 'What should I have said, then? Lord, please give me permission to marry Bertil Redknife's daughter? Despite the fact that Bertil will want to rip my heart out and feed it to his dogs, and you will then have to make war on his cousin Eldof?'

'No, you young idiot,' Marcellus said tartly, 'that isn't what I think you should have said. And whatever you mean to do, it will surely have to keep until the Picts have been dealt with. If you love this woman, you will wait for her, and you will want to be able to take her home to Cambria, to live amongst the people who have loved and cared for you from your childhood. You will not achieve that by breaking with Vortigern, and if you think you can be happy without the benefit of his approval, you're more of a fool than I take you for.' He stopped with an emphatic nod, his sharp little eyes gleaming like jet. Kerin stared up at the sky.

'Alright,' he said. 'You're right. I know you're right. But what now?'

'If I knew that, I should not need the entrails,' Marcellus said. 'But you will never find out if you don't go to him, and you should do it now, before the meeting. Perhaps you could do worse than ask for his help. He may spit on you, but don't be put off. Most men like to be asked, whatever they would have you think.'

Kerin felt relieved, although the idea of confronting Vortigern filled him with dread. 'Thank you, Marcellus *magister*,' he said, clasping the haruspex's bony hands. 'Publius Luca said that you were a good judge of men's hearts.'

'Well,' Marcellus said, 'I don't pretend to understand what's in Vortigern's heart, but I think I have a good idea of what might be in yours. Believe me, you will feel better for trying, whatever happens.' He paused, as if weighing something, then drew a small pouch of soft lambskin from within his robe. 'I have something for you. I have wondered about it ever since it was entrusted to me, but thanks to our conversation, I do now have an idea what this may be. It was given to me by an old friend, a physician named Gratius. We were boys together in Ravenna, we studied medicine together and came to Londinium together. Some years ago, Gratius was offered employment by Eldof of Glevum, and has been with his household ever since; but he does come back to Londinium from time to time, to obtain remedies, and we always meet to exchange ideas and talk about old times. This time Gratius was troubled, however. He dropped this little item into my hand as if it were a hot coal, and asked if I could make sure that it reached a young lord of the king's following, named Kerin Brightspear.' He held out the little lambskin pouch. Rather hesitantly, Kerin took it. 'I don't expect you to open it in front of me, or to tell me what it contains. But bear in mind, if you will, that Gratius took a risk of some sort in bringing it to me. Now go, quickly; most of them are here already. All my instincts tell me that you should speak to Vortigern before this meeting, and the consequences which you think it may bring.'

Kerin walked away from the tents to a deserted spot on the perimeter of the camp, lit by a lantern on a pole. He sat on the ground in the pool of yellow light and undid the draw-strings of the lambskin pouch. His fingers felt as clumsy as dogs' paws. Very carefully, he felt inside the pouch; there was something in there wrapped in soft fabric, which he drew out onto the ground between his knees. He knew at once. He had only ever seen that particular shade of luminous sea green once in his life. Gently unfolding it, he found within a lock of red-gold hair, a sprig of rosemary and the same delicate jewelled brooch which had fastened this fabric, this dress, at her shoulder; on that night in her bedchamber, deep within her father's hall. He sat quite still for a moment, staring at the three objects; then he wrapped them up again, slipped them back into the pouch and pressed it to his lips. The thought of parting with it pierced him through, but a man could not go into battle carrying something so fragile and so precious. He would return it to Marcellus for safe-keeping. And if I should fall, he thought, Marcellus must find her and give it back; and then she will know beyond doubt that I have gone, for she must surely know that I would never part with it while I can still draw breath.

Macsen was on guard outside the king's tent. 'Have you come for him?' he asked. 'They're waiting, you know. Everyone's here except Gallus, and they're getting impatient.'

'They can wait,' Kerin said. He drew aside the flap. The interior of the tent was dim, after the blazing brightness of the praetorium. Vortigern was sitting at the bare table, reading a book by the light of a single lamp. The chest containing his writing materials was on the floor beside him. Kerin had not seen it for a while. He wondered how much of the past few days' events would be preserved for posterity.

'Lord,' he said. Vortigern looked up and acknowledged him, but did not reply. Kerin sat down at the end of the table. As his eyes became accustomed to the light he was able to pick out the detail of the manuscript, with its indecipherable inscriptions.

'What's that, lord?' he asked.

'The letters of Marcus Tullius Cicero to his friend Atticus,' Vortigern said, without taking his eyes from the page. 'If you'd paid attention when Iustig was trying to teach you Latin, you wouldn't have to ask me questions like that. And you wouldn't have to waste your money paying the praetor's scribe.'

'I know,' Kerin said guiltily. 'I never imagined that it would be of any use to me.'

Vortigern put the book down. 'Your foresight is not infallible, then.'

'No, lord. If it had been, I'd have kept my mouth shut.'

'You weren't lying, though. You do love Bertil Redknife's daughter.'

'Yes. I wish I didn't.'

'This began months ago,' Vortigern said. 'When Bertil wounded you, and that old buffoon saved your leg.'

'Yes. Bertil had his daughter with him. The old man I killed was her husband.'

Vortigern looked at him in sour disbelief. 'You killed the girl's husband? How much worse does this get?'

'They're all blood-relations,' Kerin said. 'I thought Bertil was just an ally of Eldof's. But they're cousins. Gael regards Eldof and the bishop as her uncles.'

Vortigern stared up at the roof of the tent. 'Kerin, why are you telling me this now, when I'm about to preside over a meeting which may determine the fate of the kingdom?'

'Because I don't want to go into the meeting with this hanging between us,' Kerin said. 'I don't want to do anything without your blessing, whatever I said. But I do love

Bertil's daughter, and nothing can alter that. I can't give her up. I was hoping that you might know what to do about it.'

Vortigern leaned towards him. 'Kerin, you know what to do about it. If you take the woman against her father's will, he'll come after you with every man he can raise, and I'll have to fight him. I'll have to fight Eldof, too, because he's bound by blood to support Bertil, however much he hates him. Then Gorlois will side with us, probably, and Garagon will side with Eldof, and we'll end up with two thousand dead and the rest at the mercy of the Picts. Is that what you want?'

'No,' Kerin said, closing his eyes, as if that could keep out the black tide of despair.

'For the love of God,' Vortigern said softly, 'Cambria's full of women.' Kerin's silence must have signalled the futility of that argument. Vortigern stood up and reached for his sword belt. 'You'll marry her even if I forbid it, won't you.'

Kerin looked up. 'Lord, that's the last thing I want.'

'I'm sure it is. But you'll do it if you have to. You'd be less of a man if it were not so. But please, not until we have dealt with the Picts. And not if it might cause some catastrophe that splits the kingdom in half. Everything I have done could come to nothing because of this. I thought that you and I had passed beyond the point where I had to ask for a pledge of good faith. But no. I want your word on it.'

'You have it,' Kerin said. Mortified though he was to be asked, loyalty and practicality both dictated that there could be no other answer.

'Good. And don't bring this to me again until we're done in the North. I have to lead these men and give them a victory, for God's sake. I have no room for it. No room.'

And none for me, after this, Kerin thought. 'I won't be the one to raise it, lord.'

'Don't be,' Vortigern said. 'Now let's settle this before they all kill each other at the table.'

Gallus's chariot passed them as they left the tent, the fine white horses prancing and spitting foam. The merchant hailed them; smiling, animated, self-possessed. At the entrance to the praetorium, Vortigern paused.

'Do you think I should let Hengist stay?'

'No, lord,' Kerin said. 'Not if it can be avoided.'

'Is there any good reason for this?'

'Nothing I can explain,' Kerin said. 'Not even to you. It's no more than a feeling in my gut. And you can't lay that on the table in front of the others, can you?'

'No. And having spent a year persuading them to fight Picts, I can't hold them back, now that they're straining at the leash.'

'Lord!' Lud hissed from inside. 'They're beginning to argue.'

Vortigern plunged into the brightness within. It took only seconds for the meeting to come to order. Vortigern took his seat, Lud hammered the table with the hilt of his sword and the conversation ceased as suddenly as if someone had driven a stopper into a bottle. Silence followed, broken only by the guttering of the lamps, and all eyes rested on Vortigern.

'Lords and warriors,' he said, 'you know why we are here. Our armies are ready to march. But something has happened which demands a decision. Hengist and Horsa, princes of the Jutes, have come ashore with three galleys full of warriors. We could easily ride down there and kill them; but as we know, the men of Kent better than anyone, there are many more where they came from. Hengist has offered his warriors to my service in return for enough land to support him and his company. He claims that he will be satisfied with the poorest land we can give him.' He paused and looked slowly along the two rows of pale, intent faces which lined the walls of the tent. For once, it seemed, no-one was prepared to make the first move. 'Garagon, Lord of Kent,' Vortigern said, 'you should speak first, since it's your land we are discussing.'

Garagon rose to his feet. He looked tense, even frightened, but his flashing dark eyes had not lost their insolent pride.

'Lord King, it's my birthright we are discussing,' he said. 'The land my father fought and bled for, willed to me and my sister on his deathbed. I am sure that the rest of you would not be looking so calm, if these savages had landed on your doorstep instead of ours.'

Eldof coughed and drew back his shoulders. 'That's probably true, Garagon. But by the will of God or sheer bad luck, it's your doorstep they're sitting on, so we must decide what to do.'

'Lord King, what precisely are these men asking for?' Severus Maximus asked.

'For enough land to live on, in the first instance,' Vortigern said.

'In the first instance?' Garagon spluttered. 'In the first instance? What are they going to ask for in the second instance? Would you like to give them Durovernum while you're about it?'

'Garagon, cool your temper,' Vortigern said. 'I've seen the land Hengist wants, between the Roman road and the sea. It's a bog. There's nothing living on it except the marsh birds and a few toothless sheep.'

'And the second instance? You haven't said anything about the second instance.'

Vortigern leaned forward on the table. 'What I am saying

is that it would be unrealistic – indeed, unfair – to expect men to fight for us without reward.' He looked around at the silent delegates. 'If we let the Saxons stay and fight on our behalf, then we are going to have to pay them.' He turned to Publius Luca. 'Such arrangements are not unprecedented.'

'No, sir,' the commander said, 'they were commonplace throughout the Empire. As new lands were conquered, it was normal to recruit auxiliary troops from amongst the inhabitants.'

'Ah, the *foederati!*' Severus Maximus said wistfully.

'The *foederati!*' Alberius exclaimed. 'A bit before my time, of course, but when my uncle was in the Twentieth he campaigned alongside a barbarian unit, and by Jupiter, they fought like wildcats. Tooth and claw, lords, tooth and claw, not to mention knives and axes and anything else –' he broke off as Vortigern gave him a look.

'The old man should have cut off the tongue,' someone murmured.

'Thank you, Alberius,' said Severus. 'I think most of us have heard of the *foederati*. The arrangement worked well for the Empire, and I can see no reason why it should not work for us.'

Vortigern nodded. 'The alternative, of course, is to fight the Saxons. We have raised this army to beat the Picts. Should we deal with the Saxons before we march?'

'Lord, we cannot!' Varro's voice rasped. The gathering came to attention. Everyone knew that speech was a struggle for Varro since his neck wound, and that he would only speak if unable to keep silent. 'I am not a statesman, Lord King. I am a warrior. I speak for the ordinary fighting men under my command, because I know their hearts. I expect that I speak for all such men, because in the end I think that warriors are much the same, wherever they come from.'

He paused and swallowed hard. 'You summoned us all to Londinium to choose a king. Most of us were expecting a man of politics, and we all know what these men are like. They argue and line their pockets while the ordinary man starves in the cold. But you spoke with a warrior's voice. You told us that we must defeat the Picts or perish. We believed you, and we have carried that flame in our hearts to this day. You cannot ask us to extinguish it now.' He bowed his head. Vortigern gave him a look of the utmost respect.

'So, you don't want to fight the Saxons?'

'I do!' Varro growled. 'But if we fight them now, we'll have thousands of them on that beach in weeks. We may well have to fight them one day, but the Picts must come first.'

'And what about my land?' Garagon yelped.

'Use your head, man.' Varro gave a hoarse chuckle. 'If we don't see the Picts off, you might lose the best of your land, never mind that old bog.' He gave a determined nod and planted his elbows firmly on the table.

'Alright,' Garagon conceded. 'You're probably right about the land. But there must be safeguards.' He lowered his eyes. Brennius, for once the more assured of the two, gave his shoulder a brotherly pat. Vortigern looked about him.

'Does anyone else wish to speak?' His eyes rested on Severus Maximus, Alberius and Flavius. 'The men of politics, perhaps?' he enquired.

'There's nothing to add,' Severus said, with wounded dignity. 'I can hardly disapprove of a practice which generations of Roman emperors found acceptable.'

A rumble of approval travelled around the table. Vortigern looked steadily from man to man. 'Alright. Everyone agrees that we must deal with the Picts first. Are we also agreed that, with Garagon's consent, we should grant Hengist the land he has asked for?'

'Give it to them!' Gallus brought his fist down on the table. 'The Saxons are seafarers. It's in them from the womb. If nothing else, engage them to fight the Picts by sea. My fleet can keep the Picts out of Londinium, but no more. And it doesn't take a military genius to know that if the enemy can move by sea, he can land a force to the rear of a marching army, and attack it from both sides.'

'I agree with Gallus, lords,' Gorlois said. 'But can we trust these men?'

'We're not talking about trusting them,' Vortigern said. 'We're talking about engaging them as mercenaries, and we're talking about paying them. Either in gold or as payments in kind; corn or cattle, or whatever. The Romans called it *annona*. I'll be calling it taxes when I come to get it.'

Severus raised his hand. 'Lord King, I'm sure that we all understand the principle.'

'Good,' Vortigern said, 'because I want no quibbling after the event. You've all had to pay the fleet tax; with a miserable bad grace in some instances. Please understand now that if we employ the Saxons, we will have to pay them, and *all* of you will contribute, if I have to hang you by the balls until you pay up. Is this understood?' There was a silence, and a few weak smiles. 'Good,' Vortigern said. 'So, is there anyone here who thinks that we should not employ the Saxons?'

'Yes!' a voice rang out, sharp and clear, and so wholly un-expected that it made Kerin start in his seat. Rufus was on his feet, burning with a righteous ferocity which Kerin had last seen in the eyes of Abbot Paulinus. Vortigern appeared nonplussed.

'Why?' he asked blankly.

'Why?' Rufus shouted. 'Because they're heathen savages. How can you possibly consider giving them a piece of this country? They're pagans. Devil-worshippers. We should fight them now, and have done with it.'

'Lord Vortimer, the Picts are heathen savages too!' Flavius exclaimed in horror.

'So, you want to deal with one bloodthirsty bunch of pagans by making friends with another?' Rufus said. 'No. It's all wrong. If they want to take our land and fight alongside us, they should embrace our faith.'

'Whose faith, though?' Publius Luca protested. 'With respect, Lord Vortimer, most of my infantrymen have some Roman blood, and many of them worship the gods of their fathers. So should the Saxons worship Jesus Christ or Mithras? Or the gods of the druids, perhaps?'

'There is only one true God,' Rufus retorted. Publius Luca raised his hands in resignation. Vortigern, who had seemed paralysed by disbelief, came violently to life. He lunged past Kerin, seized Rufus by the collar of his tunic and pulled him back down into his seat.

'Are you saying that you won't fight the Picts if the Saxons join us?'

'I'll fight anyone who does what the Picts have done.' Rufus straightened his tunic with a look of disgust.

'Yes,' Vortigern said. 'And you were quite prepared to fight them alongside Publius Luca's infantry. Half those men are pagans. Publius Luca's a pagan. For the love of God, *I'm* a pagan on a bad day. Why should a pagan mercenary be any worse?'

'Because at least all those men have a Briton's loyalties,' Rufus said. 'If you engage the Saxons, it'll end in disaster; and if you don't believe me, ask him.'

Kerin felt his courage shrivel as Rufus's eyes burned into him with a fanatic's fury. He clutched vainly at the sweet memories of their childhood, and realised that Vortigern was waiting.

'Well?' Vortigern said. He was taut with apprehension.

You know the truth, Kerin thought. You have known it since that night in Londinium, when we talked about Cheldric and Garagon's statue, and got drunk on the praetor's wine. But it was not the truth Vortigern wanted. He wanted to be told that the reasonable, eminently practical course he had suggested was correct, and he wanted to be told here, in front of the men whose approval he needed. Those men were all sitting quite still, looking expectantly at Kerin.

'Lord, we have spoken of this,' he said, looking straight at Vortigern. 'I have told you what I think.'

'Then tell everyone else,' Vortigern said. You are asking me to lie for you, Kerin thought. He remembered that bleak moment on the marsh; understanding, for the first time and in an eye's blink, the damage he could do. For conscience and love, and for the sake of every man who had pledged himself to the campaign in the North, he could not do it again. All those thousands of lives, and the fate of the kingdom itself, rested on the shoulders of one man. He remembered a dining hall in Glevum, a quiet green garden full of sociable doves, and the sweet, lingering scent of melissa laced with honey.

'Lord, I can give you no sensible reason for not engaging the Saxons as mercenaries,' he said. As the words came out, Rufus gave a mad animal howl. In his entire life, Kerin had not heard him make a sound remotely like it.

'You've really sold your soul to him, haven't you.' Rufus turned from Kerin to Eldadus. 'What about you, Bishop? You call yourself a man of God. Have you nothing to say?'

Eldadus recoiled. 'We can only fight one set of heathens at a time,' he quavered. Rufus gritted his teeth, hurled his chair aside and stalked out into the darkness. Lud jumped up.

'No,' Vortigern said, watching the gaping doorway. Everyone waited for him to speak. He seemed to have lost the will.

'We must come to a decision, sir,' Publius Luca said. Vortigern stood up.

'Does everyone else think that we should employ the Saxons?' There was no reply, but a collective muttering and nodding indicated acceptance. 'It's not enough. If you think we should engage the Saxons as mercenaries, raise your hands.' Every man at the table complied, except for Kerin, who did nothing at all until he noticed Publius Luca looking at him, and reluctantly followed suit. 'Alright,' Vortigern said. It sounded like relief rather than pleasure. 'Garagon, you and I will meet the leaders tomorrow to set the boundaries of their land. Publius Luca, you have dealt with mercenaries before, so I shall leave the negotiation of the *annona* to you.'

'Lord King,' Severus Maximus ventured, 'are we to meet the Saxon leaders?'

'Yes. They should swear an oath of loyalty here, in front of us all. Lud, ride down to the shore and tell Hengist that his presence is expected. He can bring Horsa, but no more.'

Lud bowed his head and went out. Kerin sat silently at the table and listened to the horse galloping away. He wondered exactly what he had done, and how far it went towards repairing what had fractured out on the cold marsh. Men started to mill around talking, or slipped outside to get some fresh air and relieve themselves. The cooks stoked their fires and the pleasing aroma of Cheldric's pork stew drifted into the praetorium. The entrance flap was drawn aside and the praetor came back in, making his way towards the high table with courteous gestures in all directions.

'Thank you,' Vortigern said, in the last few seconds available. 'I knew what I was asking of you.'

'Yes,' Kerin said. 'And I knew what I was doing. So whatever comes of this, it's on both our heads.'

Vortigern's eyes held an uneasy acquiescence. 'Go and look for him. I don't expect you to bring him back, just find out where he's gone.'

Kerin went out into the darkness. There was no sign of Rufus, but he soon found Katigern, sitting on a grain cask outside the cooks' tent clutching a flask of wine. Kerin fetched another cask and sat down beside him.

'Hello, Kat. What's worrying you?'

Katigern turned, his usually cloudless eyes dark with dread. 'Do you really think we'll burn in hell if we let the Saxons stay?'

'No,' Kerin said. Katigern swallowed some wine and passed Kerin the flask.

'Rufus says we'll burn in hell. He wanted me to go to Caerwynt with him.'

'Is that where he's gone?'

'Yes. He said he'd catch up with us on the road. Him and his – well, the Sword of God, or whatever they are.'

'Why didn't you go?' Kerin asked. Katigern grimaced.

'If Vortigern was your father, would you cross him?'

'No, probably not,' Kerin said. 'And certainly not over this. I don't like Hengist at all, but I can see that we need his fighting men. Will Rufus come back, do you think?'

'Oh yes. He's mad keen to fight the Picts. But he said he had to see Father Paulinus first. Can I have the wine back if you're not going to drink it? I don't want to burn in hell, Kerin. I love my father, but I don't want that.'

Kerin walked back towards the praetorium. Marcellus's carriage was standing nearby. The blinds, drawn down for privacy, glowed with a warm orange light. As Kerin approached it, a hand gripped his arm.

'I saw that in there,' Gwyndaf said. 'Rufus put you on the spot. And so did Vortigern, in a different way. Don't worry.

I'll stand with you on this, because I know we need the warriors. But I also know that you don't trust those Jutes, and neither do I. I'd have searched their cargo boat if there'd been a chance. I'd love to know what they had in all those casks.'

'So would I,' Kerin said. 'Perhaps a chance will come. And thank you for telling me. But it should stay between us.'

'It's not going anywhere,' Gwyndaf said, and slipped off into the darkness. Kerin tapped the door of the carriage. It opened a crack and Marcellus peered out.

'What happened?' he asked. 'I saw Rufus leave. He took horse and galloped away like a madman.'

'He fell out with his father over the Saxons,' Kerin said. 'And with me,' he added reluctantly. Marcellus raised thin eyebrows. 'There was no way out of it. Everyone else was in favour of engaging the Saxons as mercenaries. Rufus put me in a position where I had to side with him or with Vortigern, in front of everyone. I'd have done anything to avoid it. Except, of course, what he asked me to do.'

They looked round, hearing the sound of voices. Lud was riding back into the encampment with Hengist and Horsa trotting alongside. The two brothers had combed out their long, pale hair and flung on fine black tunics over their cross-gartered breeches and seafarers' boots. Horsa wore a heavy wine-red cape with a silver clasp. He was smiling broadly, not only with his lips, but with his large, friendly eyes. Hengist was wearing a cloak of bright leaf green, fastened at the shoulder with a gold pin depicting a leaping salmon. He too was smiling, albeit less broadly than his brother, and his eyes were everywhere.

'They've come to swear the loyal oath,' Kerin said. 'I must go in. Will you come with me?'

'Is it my place?' Marcellus asked.

'Yes. I hope I've got that much credit left. Please. I've only got a handful of true friends here. I want everyone to know exactly what's said, so there can be no going back on it later.'

Marcellus reached out to clasp his hand. 'Thank you for including me in that company, my young friend.' The tent flap was drawn aside and Vortigern appeared at the entrance to the praetorium. 'He is waiting for you,' Marcellus said. 'Go to him now. There are things I need to bring along. I will be sitting with the praetor's people, should you need me.'

Kerin made his way to the high table. There was no doubt that the vacant chair at Vortigern's right hand had been reserved for him. All the other seats were full, and all the men who mattered were occupying them. Kerin sat down. That wretched old wild man who laid a newborn child out to die on a freezing rock had surely not expected him to land on the same table as the most powerful men in the kingdom, any more than the child would have expected it himself, until very recently.

Lud brought the two Saxons to the open floor. There they stood, like two prize beasts set out for inspection in a market pen, while the lords, warriors, priests and politicians looked them up and down and exchanged comments. Hengist was looking remarkably confident, under the circumstances. He stood with legs braced and arms folded, watching all that went on and making an inspection of his own. Horsa, perhaps a little less at ease, returned smiles when they were offered and made gestures of greeting with one of his large hands.

'Lords and warriors,' Vortigern said, rising to his feet, 'I present to you Hengist and Horsa, princes of the Jutes. They have offered to serve me in good faith, and to fight beside us in the battles to come. You have all agreed to accept this offer. Please make them welcome.'

The gathering murmured its approval. Hengist bowed his head.

'Lord, we are your true servants.'

'I trust you will remain so,' Vortigern said. 'And that both of you are now ready to swear an oath of loyalty, to me and to the cause of the Britons, in the sight of every man here.'

'We are ready, lord,' Hengist said solemnly.

'We are ready,' Horsa agreed. Marcellus had taken his place amongst Severus Maximus's retainers. He was writing rapidly on a large tablet.

'The terms of your service have been agreed,' Vortigern said. 'The land which you requested will be granted. And you will be paid for your service in corn and coinage, the amounts to be agreed with my commander of infantry, Publius Luca. Do you have anything to say?'

'Only that we are truly grateful for such generosity, Lord King,' Hengist said gravely. Vortigern looked at the rows of intent faces.

'Good. And now, lords of the Britons. You have already agreed how Hengist and his warriors should be rewarded. To ensure that there are no misunderstandings, I should like you all to confirm now, in front of them, that you agree with the gift of the land, and will contribute your share of the *annona* when it is due.' There was a palpable silence. 'Raise your hands and swear,' Vortigern said, in a voice which could have frightened a marching army. Hands were raised. Everyone swore. Marcellus went on writing. Vortigern drew his sword and placed it on the table in front of the Jutes. 'Hengist, kiss this sword and swear by your own gods that you will serve me and the cause of the Britons until death, or until I release you from this oath.'

Hengist knelt. 'I swear on Odin's head, and on the blood of my fathers and their spirits departed,' he said, and pressed his lips to the cold blade. He stood up. Horsa knelt and swore. Marcellus stood and displayed his writing tablet for all to see, the script bold and clear enough to be read by anyone with the facility. Both Jutes shook hands with Vortigern and, at his signal, moved along the high table, clasping the proffered hands of all the men who sat there. In front of Kerin, Hengist paused.

'I thought you lied to me when you said you were the chief warrior,' he said. 'Now I see that you did not. You sit with the men of power. In my hall, amongst our young men, only my sons would have this honour. You must give more than a warrior's service to the king, for it to be so.'

Kerin looked straight back at him. 'Yes, I do,' he said. 'I tell him the truth.'

Hengist stepped back from the table. His pale eyes were as cold as the sea which had brought him to the coast of Kent. They narrowed slightly, and he gave a little nod which signified that he knew what he had been told. Lud and Macsen had come to see the brothers back to their ships. The Jutes bowed courteously to the king and then they were gone, exchanging jovial banter with their escorts. Kerin watched them leave. There had been no handshake.

Around the tent conversations were resumed as pitchers of water were brought in; there would be no strong drink, on the eve of a dawn march. Extra tables were set up and some of the lesser warriors were invited to share the food. It was the last formal meal that any of the men-at-arms would eat for weeks to come. For some there would never be another. Vortigern moved amongst the men; a patrician for the well-born, a bluff comrade for the warriors, a reassuring old hand for the nervous youngsters facing their first campaign. Soon, on some pitiless frozen wasteland, all the guises would be ripped away, revealing the battle commander's face in all its savage fury. Tomorrow the army would muster, and they would be on the road to the North. Now, more than ever, Kerin wished for it all to begin.

24

The day they reached Hadrian's Wall would remain burned into Kerin's memory forever, but not for any of the reasons he might have expected. Even he had not foreseen it. Afterwards, he blamed himself; but it had been easy to dismiss a feeling of vague dread when the most terrifying battle of his life was days away.

It began when he came upon Brother Padarn, sitting on his mule and staring soulfully at some indeterminate point amongst the bald, treeless hills to the east of the encampment. Lud had chosen the site well. It was on a level plateau, elevated enough to give good views of the surrounding countryside and of the Wall itself, gleaming like a ribbon under the cold sun. Below and to the south was a tangled wood which might hold game, and to the north a clear, swift-flowing river teeming with fish. Up here there was still frost every night, and sharp white pockets clung all day in the hollows where the sun did not reach. Beyond the wood was a partially ruined village which, miraculously, had a working alehouse with two large rooms. The tough, grizzled landlord swore that he would find ale for the king's warriors, if they could rid the place of the savages who had killed his sons. Up on the windy plateau the army came to rest, hoping for a few days' respite in which men could sleep, tend horses and make repairs to wagons and harness. There was not much else to be done until Publius Luca's spies came back, and the Saxon foot-soldiers marched from the coast.

Padarn looked distraught. Kerin was saddened; on the long trek north the monk had been the life and soul of the army, chivvying men along when they got down-hearted, comforting the homesick and praying with them when asked.

'Tie your mule up and come with me,' he said. 'Hefydd's boys have got a brew going, and it's just the thing on a cold day.'

Padarn shrugged and went to tether the mule. Kerin took a deep breath of the clear, cold air. Nothing he had heard about or imagined had prepared him for the sheer awful desolation of these bleak hills. Most of the people had fled, if they had not been butchered, and only the blackened ruins of their houses remained, along with the empty pig-pens, ravaged crops and bleached bones. Kerin had seen burned villages when Vortigern fought the Irish, but at least the Irish had buried the dead and left the churches alone. Here the churches were razed, and the corpses had been left for the carrion birds and the wolves, whose chilling chorus could be heard echoing through deserted valleys as night fell.

Hefydd's boys had lit a fire, and their brew was steaming away in a small iron cauldron. Hefin invited Kerin and Padarn to sit on his horse blanket. 'Are you going to have some, Brother?' he asked. 'I couldn't help noticing that you enjoy a jar. I've got nothing at all against holy men, but most of them seem to think we should spend our lives being miserable. What's the point of that?'

'There's no point,' Padarn said, picking up one of the mugs. 'Life's hard enough as it is, without refusing God's bounty. Fill it up, man.'

Hefin chuckled and filled two mugs. Mad Mabon and a few of the boys were having a disorganised wrestling match. At least it made Padarn smile. 'My village was over there,' he said. 'The other side of that ridge. Just a handful of houses in the bottom of a valley, with a stream and a patch of ground where we grew stuff for the pot.'

'Did you see much of the Romans?' Kerin asked.

'All the time. There was a villa next door, where they sent their wounded soldiers. Some of us lads used to go up and work in their gardens, and they'd give us plants and cuttings to take home. My mother had a herb garden, and a little tree with white blossom in spring and lovely sweet fruits in the autumn. I can taste those fruits now. When I was older, I worked on the Romans' farm. Tilling the ground, sowing corn. It was hard work, but I was happy. I had my own pony and cart, and a girl I was planning to marry. We built a house next to my father's workshop. Of course, once the Picts started raiding again, the Romans moved their men away. They'd stopped defending the Wall, and they couldn't leave a bunch of invalids to fend for themselves. One day the place was full of wagons and the next everyone had gone. Only one man stayed on, a centurion called Gaius who'd married a girl from my village. He'd lost part of his right arm, so he couldn't fight. Nice enough, but one of those dyed-in-the-wool soldiers. The last I saw of him, he was loading his family onto an ox-cart.'

'How long ago was that?' Kerin asked. Padarn shrugged.

'Ten years, I suppose. It was the day before the Picts slaughtered my family. I only escaped because I'd gone with a couple of the lads to find out where Gaius and his wife were heading. We never found them, but a bunch of Picts found us, alright.' He tapped the scar on his head. 'They must have thought they'd killed me, because when I woke up they'd taken our ponies, and the other two lads were dead. I started walking home. I smelt the burning a mile away, but I didn't expect what I found.' He took a deep draught of Hefin's brew and rubbed his eyes. 'I couldn't bury the whole village, so I just dug graves for my parents and my brother and my girl. My hands were bleeding by then. The other bodies I just piled in a heap and set fire to them. I still feel badly about it, but it seemed better than leaving them for the birds and the wolves.'

Kerin wondered how any man could possibly have borne all that. 'What did you do?'

'Walked until I came across some soldiers. They'd had a pounding up at the Wall, and their commander had been killed. They took me as far as Eburacum. I spent a while getting drunk, then I met up with a horse-dealer. He asked me to go south with him, and I thought, why not? On the way we met a monk, a kind old man from Kent. He rode on my wagon and we did nothing but talk. It got me thinking. I'd always been a God-fearing man, and there wasn't anyone else left to care about. I started praying with the old monk and ended up with Abbot Paulinus. Now and again I look around and wish I had a home and a family, but there's more to this life than meets the eye. I think I made the right choice.'

'I'm glad of it, anyway,' Kerin said, looking out over the camp. Vortigern and Publius Luca were inspecting the lines of horses, wagons and tents. The two men had been constant companions on the march. There was an easy familiarity between them which Vortigern rarely shared with anyone. Kerin was envious. Vortigern had had little to say to him since the night of the meeting in Kent. If battle had not been imminent, if Rufus had been more loyal and Kat more solid, if his own fighting skills had not made him invaluable, he wondered whether he would even have been here. A horseman came out of the wood below the plateau. Rufus dismounted outside Eldof's tent and went inside. Kerin watched, wondering what he was doing there.

'I probably shouldn't ask,' Padarn said, 'but you could help me. I have to look at my village. Would you and a few of the other lads come along?'

'Of course,' Kerin said, realising that he had not even measured the risk. 'You know this country, Padarn. How dangerous is it? An honest answer. I don't want to get killed before the first battle.'

'Well, I expect most of the Picts are up in the hills sharpening their swords. But you might get a few marauders. I'll understand if you'd rather not come.'

'You'll go anyway, though,' Kerin said.

'Yes. I owe my family that much.'

'Alright,' Kerin said, getting up. 'When's the safest time to go?'

'Nightfall. If it stays this cold, the Picts will be snoring in their beds, like any sane men.' Padarn paused. 'Will you tell Vortigern?'

'Yes. I can't lie to him. And it would be stupid, anyway, because if we get into trouble we'll need help. If he stops me, I'll have to respect it.'

'I can't ask more than that,' Padarn said. Kerin hoisted him to his feet.

'Go and get ready, then. I'll find you a sword and a horse. Meet me by the cooks' tent at sunset.' Hefydd's brawling boys were far too preoccupied to notice, so he picked up the iron cauldron and a pair of cups, and strode off to complete his side of the arrangements.

Kerin had hoped to find Vortigern alone, but Garagon was there, and Brennius, and a handful of their young warriors.

Garagon was standing, arms folded, in the middle of the king's tent. It made Eldof's tent look like a palace. Any warrior would have had what was in it; a blanket or two beside the small fire, a lamp hung from the main pole, a saddle which served as a pillow. Vortigern was sitting on the ground beside the fire, leaning on his elbow.

'What's all this about?' Kerin asked. Garagon turned.

'What's it about? I didn't march my picked warriors all the way to this godforsaken hole so that we could form a reserve. A reserve! You put your has-beens and cowards in a reserve.'

'Garagon, I'm sure no insult was intended.' Brennius glanced at Kerin. 'Publius Luca has asked us to form a reserve. To support the main force if they need to fall back. He says we don't have enough battle experience to fight in the front line.'

'It's common sense,' Kerin said.

'It's an insult.' Garagon was tight-lipped. 'How can I tell my picked men they have to hide behind a bunch of louts from the West? I'd sooner –'

Kerin saw Vortigern move, although Garagon did not. It looked no more than a lazy flick of the hand, but the knife had sliced the shoulder of Garagon's tunic and pinned him to the tent pole before anyone found out what he would sooner do. Garagon gulped, and the picked men took a hasty step backwards as Vortigern leapt from the fireside, seized the corner of Garagon's cloak and whipped it round his neck and the pole.

'What would you sooner do?' He jerked the cloak tight. 'Lead the charge with me, so that you can take the first spear? Have your throat ripped out or your legs cut off because you didn't see the sword coming? Who'll save you then, Garagon, the louts from the West?'

'I won't be humiliated!' Garagon's face turned purple and beads of sweat ran down his forehead as the cloak throttled him. Vortigern snorted with disgust and let him go. There was a rending sound as Garagon sank to his knees, sobbing for breath. A fragment of his tunic remained behind, impaled on the pole. Vortigern dropped to the ground beside him.

'Now, hear me. When this army rides, every man's life is in my hands. I wouldn't risk the worst of them to save your pride.'

Garagon's shoulders shook. 'I don't want to risk any man's life.'

'Then go back to Publius Luca and do what he tells you.' Vortigern hoisted Garagon to his feet by the scruff of the neck. The warriors recoiled. Vortigern gave a grim smile. 'God help you all if this frightens you.'

The Lord of Kent withdrew, straightening his damaged tunic. 'We'll prove you wrong, you know,' he blurted, shooing his men outside.

'I'm depending on that,' Vortigern said, as the disgruntled band marched off. Kerin dumped Hefydd's little cauldron on the fire and sat down. Vortigern jerked his knife from the pole. The sliver of Garagon's tunic fluttered to the ground. The cauldron began to hiss.

'What the hell's that?' Vortigern asked.

'A brew of some sort,' Kerin said. 'Hefydd and his boys make it, so it must be something that grows near Carneddlas.'

'Heat it up, then,' Vortigern sighed. He sat down beside the fire. After a while, Kerin picked up the cauldron with the aid of a blanket and tipped out two cups of steaming liquid. Vortigern closed his eyes and sipped. 'This is a pestilent place. God knows why anyone wants it.'

'Lord, there's something I want to do,' Kerin said. Vortigern looked up.

'What can you possibly want to do on the eve of a battle, except sleep and prepare yourself?'

'It's Brother Padarn, lord. You know the Picts slaughtered his family. His village is just over there. He wants to go back. Just to see the place.'

Vortigern stared up at the roof of the tent. 'And you, of course, have volunteered to act as his bodyguard. Have you any idea how dangerous this country is?'

'Yes, I have. That's why I thought he shouldn't go alone.'

Vortigern refilled his cup. 'You'll go whatever I say.' It was not a question. Kerin felt the chill wind of the Kentish saltmarsh.

'No,' he said. 'Not without your permission.'

'Alright. But take two or three others with you. You're here because I can't spare you.'

'We'll go at dusk,' Kerin said. 'The sky's clear. We should be back by midnight.'

'And if you're not, I shall have to risk yet more men finding out why. What's Padarn to you, anyway?'

'He's a good man,' Kerin said. 'And an asset to the army.'

'You're right about that,' Vortigern conceded. Kerin wondered what was happening in Eldof's tent. Only a fool would pick a quarrel now, but the Lord of Glevum was powerful enough to be a threat later, if he survived the battle. Kerin sipped Hefydd's brew, trying not to contemplate the consequences of a war against Gael's father and family.

'What are you thinking about?' Vortigern asked.

'Padarn's village,' Kerin said. He couldn't tell that particular truth. Vortigern examined the contents of his cup.

'There's something in this,' he said, reaching for the cauldron.

'I know,' Kerin said. 'Hefydd's boys swear that it makes them the warriors they are.'

Vortigern's hand stopped short. They both grinned and drained their cups. For a brief moment the shadow had lifted, and the small, dark tent had become a corner of Henfelin.

* * *

The voices were coming from the woodland fringe, just below the rim of the plateau. There was something odd about the sound; it didn't have the cadences of normal conversation. Kerin was on his way to spy on Eldof's tent, but the sound distracted him. He followed it, treading silently in his smooth-soled riding boots. The ground fell away sharply towards the wood. He stood quite still. Below him a group of warriors had gathered. They were kneeling in a circle; Rufus, Idris and some other men, around twenty in all. Their heads were bowed but Kerin recognised a few by sight. Two of Eldof's youngsters; a Kentishman; a lad from Caerwent. Rufus was reciting, from memory, something which sounded like a Latin prayer. Every so often his companions chimed in with a response. On and on it droned. *In nomine Patris, Filii et Spiritus Sancti.* Even Kerin, in his ignorance, recognised an ending. Amen, murmured the young warriors. Everyone crossed himself and started to get up. Kerin tiptoed away and trotted back towards the encampment. He knew that he had every right to be where he was, watching the proceedings, but simple common sense told him to keep it to himself. An argument would be lunacy. For now, all that really mattered was that Rufus and his band of zealots were well-armed and raring to fight.

There was something going on inside Eldof's tent. The sound of voices drifted out; muted by distance but earnest, not gossiping about women or the price of cattle. Kerin crept up to the back wall, put down the saddlery he was carrying and stood still.

'There's nothing to be done until the Picts have been crushed.' Eldof's sonorous voice was unmistakable. 'You're fools if you think anything else.'

'And if we lose?' a sceptical voice enquired; Balin's, Kerin thought.

'If we lose, we're all ravens' meat,' Eldof said. 'But suppose we beat them? Beat them once and for all? Vortigern believes it with a passion, and love him or hate him, he's usually right about that sort of thing. If we win – ' he was interrupted by a loud bang, followed by a grating exclamation which could only have come from Varro. Kerin couldn't hear what followed, only that it sounded angry and aggrieved.

'Cool your head,' Eldof said sharply. 'You're my chief warrior, not my conscience.' There was a crash, and something hit the wall of the tent. Varro burst from the entrance and stalked away towards the wood. There were mutterings within, and a rather hollow laugh.

'Let him go,' Bertil Redknife sneered. 'Decency was always his weakness.'

'Never yours, though,' Eldof said. 'Go to your beds. And tread carefully around that young idiot and his brothers in Christ. They don't need any encouragement from us.'

Kerin crouched in the shadows as the tent emptied, consumed with indignation. Inside, Eldof yawned and dimmed the lamps. The moon was rising above the woods. Kerin walked across to the grazing horses and saddled one of Macsen's spare animals for Padarn. He had not asked, but it didn't matter. At least with Macsen, he knew exactly where he stood.

25

Padarn had borrowed a tunic, brown breeches and a woollen cap. 'Don't worry,' he said. 'I haven't renounced the faith. But if I have to fight, I'll be better off like this.' He drew the sword and made a few experimental thrusts. It was immediately obvious that he knew what he was doing. 'Are these two coming with us, then?' He looked over Kerin's shoulder at the two young warriors on their wiry ponies.

'Yes,' Kerin said. 'Leil and Cadfan. They belong to Gwyndaf, the standard-bearer.'

Padarn grunted as he scrambled aboard Macsen's horse. 'It'll be safe enough if we keep our eyes open.' Kerin hoped that he was right, but he had chosen his companions with care, just in case. They could scarcely have looked more different. Cadfan stocky and muscular, with wispy dark hair and a wrestler's shoulders; Leil lithe and fair-haired, with the long, lean legs of a swift runner. But both could sit a horse, use a sword and land a spear. Like all Gwyndaf's boys, they were confident but respectful of the leading warriors.

They rode down off the plateau then eastward along a shallow ravine. The moon illuminated their path, gleaming on the frozen waterfalls which hung in sheets of ice from the rock walls. Kerin's eyes searched every crevice. He found it hard to share Padarn's confidence. After a mile or two they emerged on a bleak hilltop, bright as daylight under the moon.

'It's over there.' Padarn pointed. 'Over that ridge, then down along the edge of the birch woods.'

'At least you can see for miles up here,' Cadfan said, flinging his arms about to keep warm. An owl floated above them, white as a ghost, and glided away across the bare hillside. An unearthly shriek rang out and hung in the frozen air.

'God, what was that?' Leil whispered.

'Picts!' Padarn hissed, and kicked his horse. A spear trimmed with eagles' feathers skimmed past Kerin's ear and thudded into the ground ahead of them. They took off across the hill at a headlong gallop, flattened over their horses' necks. Glancing behind, Kerin glimpsed six Picts pounding after them. Another spear flashed past, grazing the shoulder of Leil's pony. By the time the ground started to rise beneath them, the Picts were far away, tiny figures in the middle of the moonlit moor.

'This way!' Padarn shouted as they gained the crest of the ridge. A steep, rocky path plunged through scrub and brambles into the heart of the birch woods. Kerin dropped the reins and let his mare find her own way down. At the bottom, a scream and a crash came from behind. Cadfan's pony rolled down the bank and landed beside them, foaming and thrashing. Cadfan was sitting on a rock halfway down the slope, nursing his arm. Kerin dismounted. Leil dropped to the ground, gently stroking the pony's neck.

'Broken leg,' he said matter-of-factly. He drew his dagger and calmly slit the animal's throat. The pony died noisily but fast. Cadfan picked his way down.

'Don't do that to me,' he said, wincing. 'My arm's gone, for sure.'

Kerin cursed their luck. 'I thought the Picts didn't come out at night.'

'I'm sorry,' Padarn groaned.

'Never mind,' Kerin said, 'we're here now. Leil, stay with Cadfan. I'll come for you on the way back.'

'Alright,' Leil said. He was normally steady as a rock, but there was no disguising his fear at being left alone in the dark wood with his injured companion.

'You go with them if you like,' Cadfan said manfully.

Leil grinned. 'And leave you here on your own? Not likely.' He winked at Kerin. 'We'll survive. Gwyndaf taught us.'

It was midnight when they reached the village, judging by the moon. The thriving little cluster of houses was long gone. Its boundary was only a matter of paces from the stone outbuildings of the Roman farm. To the east lay a thin wood of rowan and stunted birches.

'That was my parents' house.' Padarn pointed. 'Look, the fruit trees are still there. And that was the house I built for myself.' Kerin looked. There was nothing to see, apart from a few charred stumps. It was hard to imagine that this had once been a house, where Padarn had eaten and worked and lit fires and made love to his girl. They rode into the village and splashed through the stream. Something caught Kerin's eye.

'Someone's been here,' he murmured. 'They've lit a fire by the stream. It's quite fresh. And look, the pointed stick. Someone's speared a fish and cooked it there.' He looked carefully around. There was no prospect of tracks in the iron-hard ground, but a pile of firewood lay against one of the Roman walls. 'There's someone living here,' Kerin said quietly. 'Get off your horse, get your sword out and follow me.'

They trod warily amongst the ruins. Kerin led, reins looped over his arm, spear in hand.

'That wasn't here before!' Padarn was looking at a hut, a large, rickety affair propped up by timbers driven at an angle into the ground. The thatched roof was half gone. Slivers of wan yellow light filtered out through the wattle walls and around the ill-fitting door. Kerin pressed his finger to his lips, passed his reins to Padarn and crept forward. The door was barred from within, the cross-piece visible through the gap at the side. He drew back, then kicked it with all his force. The door flew in with a crash and a woman shrieked. Kerin stood in the doorway, blinking in the dim yellow lamplight. Padarn pushed in behind him. A woman was standing in the middle of the room with two small children clinging to her knees. Her lank hair was drawn tightly back from a thin white face. An older child, a girl, was sitting at the rough table with a grey-faced old man, who was clutching a filthy bowl of gruel in his gnarled hands. The place reeked, and the floor was thick with cow dung. Kerin could hear the animal chewing quietly in the adjoining room.

'Henwyn's son!' the woman whispered, staring at Padarn. 'You're Padarn, Henwyn's son!'

'Edra!' Padarn exclaimed. He pushed past Kerin and flung his arms around the woman. She clung to him, weeping softly. 'Gaius's wife,' he said, across the top of her greying head. 'These must be her children and their grandfather. Is that right, Edra?'

'Yes,' the woman said, bending to pick up the smallest child. Padarn looked at the squalor around him and shook his head. 'Gaius is dead,' she said sharply, as if that excused it all. 'Not the Picts. A dog bit him, and the wound turned poisonous and killed him. A big strong man like that, it's mad, isn't it.' She looked down at the floor self-consciously. 'We've got to keep the cow in; she's all we've got left, and she'd be taken if we left her outside. Wolves or Picts, what difference does it make?'

'Not much,' Padarn said, stroking her hair, 'but don't worry. We won't leave you here like this.' Kerin caught the monk's eye and shook his head. We can't go back to a battle-ready army with a woman, three children and a half-dead old man. Padarn ignored him. 'Get your things together. Have you got a pony or anything?'

'I told you,' Edra said expressionlessly. 'Just the cow.'

'I'll think of something,' Padarn looked imploringly at Kerin. 'I'm going to look at the graves. I've got to do it on my own. Can you stay here for a moment?'

'Yes,' Kerin said, 'but for the love of God, don't be long. It's way past midnight. They're probably looking for us by now.' Edra moved away from him as Padarn went out. 'It's alright,' Kerin said, leaning his spear against the wall. 'I won't hurt you.'

She looked up at him with her defeated eyes. 'Just keep away from the children and their grandfather, alright?'

'I've told you,' Kerin said. 'I won't hurt any of you.'

'Who are you, anyway?' the old man asked. It was almost shocking to discover that the wasted body had a voice.

'Just a warrior,' Kerin said. 'We've brought an army to fight the Picts.'

The old man cackled and drained his gruel. 'An army?' he said. 'I doubt it.'

Kerin felt the woman's hand on his arm. 'Please forgive Gaius's father,' she murmured. 'I swear he thinks he's still in the legion.' The old man eyed her balefully. Kerin smiled.

'Don't worry. We've suffered worse insults than that.' He heard his mare whinny and looked out through the door. There was no sign of movement, but the mare's head was up, testing the air.

'What is it?' Edra asked.

'I don't know.' Kerin reached for his spear. 'Picts? Or it might be someone coming to look for us.'

Edra put down her toddler and shooed him back inside. 'I know you can't take us with you.'

Kerin shook his head. 'I'd like to, but I can't.' The mare whinnied again, but without hostility. Riders were coming down the valley; Vortigern and Publius Luca, followed by Gwyndaf and a warband of twenty men. Kerin chuckled with relief. 'Don't worry,' he said. 'They're friends.'

Edra looked at him as if she doubted the existence of such things. The warband had fanned out, searching the woods. Vortigern and Publius Luca were dismounting in the square outside the hut.

'In here,' Kerin called. 'It's alright. There's no danger.'

The two men came in, Vortigern leading. The yellow lamplight illuminated their faces.

'It's alright,' Kerin said. 'Padarn's safe too. He's gone –' he got no further. The old man was staring at Vortigern and Publius Luca as if transfixed. Vortigern froze.

'Quintus Parvo!' he whispered. The old man flung his bowl away and hurled himself against the wall, scrabbling frantically at the wattle. Afterwards Kerin remembered the woman's screams and the frightened whimpering of the children clinging to her skirts, but at that moment only two things existed for him within that black, rancid room; the old man cowering in abject terror, and Vortigern, staring silently at him with a look which held all the unadmitted horrors of Isca. Publius Luca's hand came down on Vortigern's arm.

'Leave it, sir,' he said steadily. 'He's an old man. It would serve no purpose.'

'How in God's name can I leave it?' Vortigern said hoarsely. The spear cut the foul air like a hot knife slicing lard. It pierced Quintus Parvo's heart and skewered him to the wall behind. The old man's life expired in a horrible, rasping gurgle and he slumped forward, his blood running out onto the dirt floor. Vortigern turned, slowly, as if he already knew where the spear had come from. Kerin walked across the room, trying to ignore the howls of the woman and her children, which were now quite apparent to him as they fled past him and out through the doorway. He seized the shaft of his spear and wrenched it free, stepping aside to escape the fountain of blood. Quintus Parvo's body sprawled face down in the cow dung. Kerin stared down at him. He couldn't feel sorry.

'Go on,' Publius Luca said gruffly. 'I'll see to this.'

Kerin looked up and found that they were alone in the room. 'I don't usually kill defenceless old men,' he said shakily.

'I know that,' Publius Luca said. 'I don't blame you for it. He was my commanding officer, so I can't leave him to rot, but I don't blame you for it.' He nodded towards the doorway. 'Go on. You'd better look for him.'

Kerin went out into the clearing. Gwyndaf and Padarn were trying to calm the woman, who was shrieking hysterically. She flung out her hand and pointed at Kerin as he came out of the hut, the bloodstained spear still in his hand. Padarn stared. There was no way he could have understood, of course; and perhaps he never would. Kerin found Vortigern at the edge of the village. He was leaning against the crumbling wall of an old Roman building, a grain store, judging by the ragged remnants of sacking which still littered the ground inside.

'Are you alright, lord?' Kerin asked doubtfully. Vortigern stared up at the starlit sky.

'How did you know?'

'Publius Luca told me. In Londinium, the day Paulinus turned up. Not everything, but it was enough.'

Vortigern looked round. 'You know as much as you want to know, believe me,' he said.

'Yes,' Kerin said. 'You're probably right.' Gwyndaf was coming out of the village, leading the horses. Kerin took the animals' reins with a shake of the head. There was nothing to be said for the time being. 'You can go back without us,' he said. 'There'll be no more trouble here.' He walked back to the grain store.

'Where's Publius Luca?' Vortigern asked.

'Burying the body,' Kerin said.

'Get him. I want to finish this here.'

Kerin found the commander at the fringe of the wood. Beyond lay the graveyard which Padarn had come to see, a series of frosted mounds from which the crosses had been ripped. Four of the men were struggling to hack a grave from the frozen ground with some broken spades and pickaxes which they must have found in one of the buildings. Kerin delivered his message, then he and Publius trudged back to the village. Vortigern was waiting for them, sitting his horse in front of the ruined grain store. Publius Luca gave him his usual respectful nod.

'I trust you won't hold anything against him for killing your former commander,' Vortigern said.

'No, sir. I've already told Kerin that I don't blame him for what he did.'

'Good. It would be a pity for us to fall out at this stage of the proceedings.'

'We won't do that, sir,' Publius Luca said. 'Quintus Parvo got what was coming to him, as far as I'm concerned.'

Vortigern gave a brittle laugh. 'That's a little disloyal for a legionary veteran, don't you think?' he said flippantly. Publius Luca squared his shoulders, his eyes meeting Vortigern's directly.

'Not really, sir,' he said stiffly. 'I'd have put a stop to it there and then if it had been in a centurion's power, and I think you know that quite well.'

Vortigern looked away. 'Yes. Forgive me, commander. I know it's the truth.'

'Well, I don't think any forgiveness is called for,' Publius Luca said, 'except perhaps from yourself. Now then. I am taking the men back to the camp, and I think you should return as well, sir, if you can.'

'I've given you an army, commander,' Vortigern said. 'What more do you want?'

'You are the army, sir,' Publius Luca said equably. 'It would fall to pieces without you.'

Vortigern gave a wry smile. 'It'll fall to pieces anyway, once we've beaten the Picts,' he said. Kerin looked up. He had not realised that Vortigern, too, saw it with such brutal clarity.

'I wouldn't be too sure of that, sir,' Publius said. 'I don't think there's a man in it who doesn't respect what you've done.'

'Possibly not,' Vortigern said, 'but respect isn't enough on its own. For some of them, it might even make it worse. You must see that, surely.'

'I'll see it one day if I have to, sir,' Publius Luca said. 'But not tonight.'

The warriors came tramping back from the wood. They had given up trying to dig and had covered the body with a cairn of stones. Padarn was with them. Probably he had blessed the grave and prayed for the soul of Quintus Parvo. He untied Macsen's horse and beckoned to Edra and her children.

'What are you doing?' Vortigern said sharply.

'Taking them with me,' Padarn said. 'I don't know why Edra's father-in-law had to die like that, but I'm not leaving a woman and three children here to starve or get butchered.'

Vortigern rode over to the hut. 'Padarn, get on the horse.'

'No, lord,' Padarn said calmly. 'They can ride. I don't mind walking.'

Vortigern looked down at him, shaking with cold and temper. 'Padarn, get on the horse. And if you think I care a jot about adding one more monk's life to the tally of my sins, then think again.'

'I'm not leaving without them, lord,' Padarn said obdurately. 'You can kill me if you like, I really don't mind, but I'm not leaving them here.'

'Stay here and die, then,' Vortigern spat. Edra screamed and shrank as he leaned down from the saddle and snatched the reins of Macsen's horse. The warband was already moving away up the valley. Vortigern tossed the reins to Kerin and rode headlong after them. Publius Luca watched him go and shook his head.

'I'll take the horse for Cadfan,' he said. 'Leil told us what happened. You'd better make your peace with the monk, if you want a good night's sleep.'

Kerin handed over the reins and walked slowly back to the hut.

'Why?' Padarn said bitterly. 'He was a sick old man. What harm could he possibly have done?'

'That was done years ago,' Kerin said. 'One day I'll explain if you want, but not now.'

Padarn sighed. 'Leave it, then. I'm sorry if all this has made trouble for you. I'll come back as soon as I can, but I can't leave now. I've known Edra's family all my life, and they were good people. She doesn't deserve this, whatever Quintus Parvo had done.'

'No, I know.' Kerin broke off, caught by the woman's accusing eyes.

'Go on,' Padarn said. 'Go with the others. I'll pray for you all, if you want.'

'Although I just killed her father-in-law?' Kerin asked. Padarn raised his hands in resignation.

'Old men, monks, what difference does it make? God loves us all. Go on, get out before I change my mind.'

Gwyndaf was waiting for Kerin at the head of the valley. He had let the rest of the warband ride ahead and was sitting on his big brown mare, sharpening his dagger.

'What on earth was that about?' he asked. 'If I'd been asked to name someone who'd kill a starving old man in cold blood, you're the last I'd have thought of.'

Kerin had no wish to talk, but lying to Gwyndaf would only have made things worse. 'It happened years ago,' he said. 'Long before my time, when Vortigern was a lad. Publius Luca told me. The old man commanded the Roman garrison in Isca. Vortigern made their life hell, and they used to lock him up whenever they could catch him. Things happened.'

'Ah,' Gwyndaf said speculatively. 'I thought he had more than a normal dislike of them.' He shrugged. 'Well, that's it, then. I'd have done the same myself, without a doubt.'

Kerin gave him a sceptical look. 'For Vortigern?'

Gwyndaf chuckled. 'Oh no,' he said. 'You don't catch me that way.'

26

It did not seem like an auspicious beginning. Kerin stood at the door of the king's tent and watched the first pale streaks of dawn licking up across the leaden sky to the east. Rooks fluttered and cackled in the skeletal black trees behind the camp. Inside the gloom was thick enough to touch. Vortigern, who had not slept, was sitting beside the dying fire staring silently at the heatless flames. He had about him the dull, blank look of a man who had not fully recovered from being knocked unconscious. Kerin brought a jug of Marcellus's soothing tisane. Vortigern rejected it, with a smile which seemed to hold both gratitude and reproach.

'There is no cure for this,' he said. 'God knows, I've been long enough looking for one.'

But there was a cure, albeit temporary. It arrived in the shape of Macsen, who came blundering into the tent with a chalk-white face and blood on his hands.

'Lord, the spies!' he exclaimed. Vortigern looked up.

'They're back?'

'One of them, lord. Well, both, in a way.'

Vortigern looked at Macsen as if his sanity might be in doubt. They followed him out into the half-light. A knot of agitated spectators had formed in the open square amongst the tents. The first thing Kerin saw was the grey pony, drenched in blood. It belonged to the man she had brought home strapped to her saddle. They had cut him down and laid him out on the frozen ground, a middle-aged man, true Roman. His throat had been slit, and around his neck was the object which had led to Macsen's confusion; a grisly necklace consisting of a leather thong on which were threaded two pairs of mutilated hands. Vortigern shook himself into life like some creature casting off its carapace. Lud arrived, running. His lip curled with disgust.

'Get the commander,' Vortigern said. 'And send a man to meet Hengist. Tell him to make as much speed as possible. Then saddle the Pike and find Gwyndaf for me.'

'Lord, you can't go out there,' Kerin said as Lud ran off across the camp. 'And why Gwyndaf?'

'Because he's the best tracker we've got,' Vortigern said. 'And we're not crossing the Wall. We're going to find those Picts who attacked you last night, then we're going to do whatever we have to do to make them show us where their people are gathering.'

'I'll get ready,' Kerin said.

'No,' Vortigern said bluntly.

'Lord!' Kerin protested.

'No!' Vortigern seized him by the shoulders. 'If we both die, this whole thing dies. I can't spare you.'

'And what am I supposed to do?' Kerin said mutinously. 'Sit here and pick my teeth?'

'Lead the Cambrian spearhead if I don't come back,' Vortigern said. 'Who else could do it? How could I possibly ask Rufus? For the love of God, use your brain, if you have one.' He turned as Publius Luca came running across the square, breathless and dishevelled.

'You see?' Macsen choked, beside himself with rage. 'Brutes! Bloody savages!'

Publius Luca stared down at the corpse. 'I have known this man since he was born. He has a wife and four daughters waiting for him in Londinium.'

Vortigern nodded to Macsen. 'Bury everything in the same grave and mark it. We don't have a priest to bless it, so do it yourself.'

Macsen and Derfyn went to round up a burial party. Publius Luca still stared, silent and distraught. Vortigern moved to his side.

'My nephew,' Publius said. 'My sister's son.' He knelt and removed a gold ring from one of the crushed fingers. 'His wife's marriage gift,' he said, straightening up. 'She'll want that much of him back, I expect.' His fists clenched. 'Oh gods, I'm not a butcher, but by Mithras I'll kill ten men for every finger on those hands!'

Vortigern fetched a blanket from his tent and threw it over the bloody remains. Lud came with the grey stallion.

'Gwyndaf's ready, lord. I told him to pick a warband. And I've sent messengers to meet Hengist. Is there anything else?'

'Yes,' Vortigern said, swinging onto the stallion's back. 'Find a man who speaks Pictish. That landlord is bound to know someone. And then dig a pit. About as wide as Eldof's tent, and the same depth.' Publius Luca looked up with a grim smile, which Vortigern did not return. 'I'm sure you know what that's for, commander,' he said, and turned his horse towards the grey dawn.

* * *

Kerin could think of nothing useful to do whilst he waited. His swords and spears were as sharp as they could be, and no-one would benefit from battle-training so close to the event. Still trying to absorb the enormity of what Vortigern had told him, he trudged despondently over to the shelter which Morvid and Marc had made by stretching skins and worn blankets on a lattice of branches between their own wagon and Cheldric's. The cook was perched up on his casks of flour, grinding something with a pestle and mortar. Morvid was sitting on the ground stirring an aromatic dark green paste in an earthenware bowl.

'Can't have too much of it, can you?' he said. 'I started drying these herbs at the end of last summer.' Kerin sat down beside him and noticed the rows of jars stowed under his wagon. 'Where've they gone, then?'

'Looking for Picts,' Kerin said. 'If Vortigern can catch a few, they might lead us to their army.'

'And pigs might fly,' Morvid said. 'They're tough as ox-hide if they can stay alive in this horrible country. Why aren't you with him, then?'

'Because he told me to stay here,' Kerin said, picking up a stone and hurling it at Cheldric's cauldron. It rebounded with a clang and rolled along the iron-hard ground.

'I treated that lad Cadfan,' Morvid said. 'He thought his arm was broken, but he'd just had a bad knock.' He squinted up at Kerin. 'He said you killed an old man. Worse still, that the old man was just eating his supper and minding his own business.'

'It is true,' Kerin said. 'And I hope you know that I wouldn't have done it without a very good reason.'

Morvid put his bowl down. 'You saved our skins, boy. Cold-blooded murderers don't do that.' There was a moment's hesitation, until curiosity won. 'Who was he, then?'

'A Roman,' Kerin said, standing up. 'An old garrison commander. That's all I want to say.'

Morvid raised his hand. 'Sit down, boy. I'm sorry, I know it's not my business. Sit down and tell me what's happened to that stupid monk. Cadfan told me he'd stayed behind.'

'Yes. There were some people he felt he had to look after.'

'Christians,' Morvid sighed. 'They can't see a suffering creature anywhere without martyring themselves to help it along.'

'Keep it down,' Kerin said. 'Here comes one of them now.'

Rufus was approaching. Morvid grinned. 'Good day, Lord Vortimer. You're not looking too happy, if I may say so.'

Rufus gave him a damning look. 'How should I look, when we're about to march off and slaughter a few thousand?'

Morvid chuckled. 'Overjoyed, I should think, as they're a bunch of heathens,' he said. Rufus ignored him. It was Kerin he had come to see, although they had hardly spoken on the march.

'What's that pit for?' he asked.

'I've no idea,' Kerin said.

'Perhaps you could put the Saxons in it,' Morvid suggested. Rufus grimaced and walked briskly off towards Eldof's encampment.

'Rufus!' Kerin said sharply. Rufus looked over his shoulder but did not stop walking. Kerin trotted after him.

'I don't think we've got much to say to each other,' Rufus said.

'You put me in an impossible position,' Kerin protested.

'No. There are no impossible positions. I put you in a position where you had to make a choice, and you made it.'

'So what's going on in Eldof's tent?' Kerin asked.

'Nothing's going on,' Rufus said resentfully. 'Can't I speak to a man who's fighting on the same side?'

'Yes,' Kerin said. 'But I hope you know whose side that is.' He turned at the sound of running footsteps.

'They're back!' Lud bellowed. 'All safe, and they've got two of the bastards!'

Eldof came out, flinging a fur-lined cloak around his shoulders. He nodded to Rufus, as if he had been expecting him. The warband was coming up out of the valley. Gwyndaf and Leil were leading two Picts, bound by the hands. Both were cut and bruised and had dead leaves and bracken stalks tangled in their hair, as if they had been dragged straight through or over anything that was in the way.

'Success!' Lud smiled broadly. Vortigern dropped to the ground.

'Did you find someone who can talk to them?'

'I did. A shepherd. It cost me a full purse, but he speaks it like a Pict. I gave him half the money, and told him he'd get the rest when he'd done the work.'

'Good,' Vortigern said. 'Get him. There's no time to waste.'

The two captives were standing beside the horses, gasping for breath. Their hairy arms bore the colourful tattoos Kerin had first seen on the limbs of Constans's bodyguard. Both had thick dark hair and heavy brows; relations, probably, although one was short and thin and the other as large as Lud.

'Was it much trouble?' Kerin asked.

'No,' Vortigern said, 'but only because we outnumbered them four to one. Anyone who thinks it'll be easy to beat them had better go home now.' Lud came back with the shepherd, a squat man with thinning grey hair. 'You speak their language?' Vortigern asked.

'Yes, Lord King,' the shepherd said, in a voice as heavily accented as Padarn's. 'Things haven't always been like this. I used to trade with them – wool for fish, mostly – but these past few years it's been nothing but trouble. All my sons have been killed. They steal my sheep, they burn my house down – five houses in the past two years, if you don't mind – and last summer they took my wife and daughter. God knows what they've done with them, but if I ever –'

'Alright,' Vortigern raised his hand. 'We'll start with these ones. Tell them I'll give them a bag of gold each if they lead us to their army.'

The shepherd raised his grey brows. 'I'll tell them, Lord King, but I doubt if it'll do any good.' A brief exchange followed. The skinny little Pict spat on the ground. The shepherd shrugged. 'They're not interested in gold, Lord King.'

'Do they have a price?'

The shepherd asked the Pict. He clenched his fists, let out a roaring bellow and spat in the shepherd's face. Gwyndaf jerked the end of the rope and sent him sprawling on his back.

'He says they can't be bought, Lord King.' The shepherd wiped his face calmly.

'Well, it's up to them,' Vortigern said.

'Lord?' Lud said expectantly.

'First find a carcass. This man's bound to know for a dead sheep. The fresher the better. Build a scaffold over the pit. Around twice your own height. Put a wagon beside it, and then light a fire in the pit. An arm's length below the top.' He smiled at the Picts. 'And take them with you. They can watch what you're doing.'

'Come on then, you savages!' Lud roared, whipping out his sword. The bigger of the two Picts moved protectively in front of his companion.

'Your first mistake,' Vortigern said, as the prisoners were led away.

27

It was almost impossible to get near the pit. The sun was going down by the time Lud's preparations were complete. Every man in the army had found out what was happening; or at least that something was about to happen. No-one but Vortigern knew precisely what that was, except perhaps Publius Luca, and he had preserved a tight-lipped silence. Kerin could see him standing, arms folded, beside the pit. Lucius Arrius was there too. He had the tense, wide-eyed look of a man who, however brave and resourceful, had not experienced much unpleasantness at first hand. The scaffold reared above them, stark and black against the red dusk.

'That'll do,' Vortigern said, as Lud came to meet him. 'Now get yourself some ropes; good strong ones, the sort you'd use to tie a mad bullock. And a sword, as sharp as you can find. Tie it to a spear shaft.'

The fire was burning fiercely. Even from where he was, Kerin could feel it scorching his skin. The heat had melted the frozen ground, turning it to running mud. The shepherd gave a bloodthirsty grin, looking forward to some wholehearted enjoyment of whatever was about to happen. Lud came back with Macsen, Gwyndaf and the prisoners. Kerin noticed that, whereas Lud and Macsen simply had the no-nonsense look of warriors performing a necessary task, Gwyndaf's eyes were glowing with an eager, predatory light. He seemed to take a peculiar pleasure in exacting payment for the blood of the shepherd's sons and Padarn's family, perhaps because he had never had a chance to punish the pirates who slaughtered his wife and daughters. Not as sweet as a more personal vengeance, but perhaps it would do, much as Custennin's punishment had had to do for Kerin.

'Alright,' Vortigern said. 'Lud, bring the carcass.'

'One of mine, Lord King,' the shepherd piped up. 'Died lambing this morning, poor girl.' Macsen and Derfyn shouldered their way through the crowd, dragging the body of a black-faced ewe.

'Hang her over the fire,' Vortigern said. They tossed the carcass up onto the wagon. Gwyndaf roped the back legs, then he and Lud hoisted the ewe aloft while Derfyn seized the end of the rope, shinned up the scaffold and lashed it to the crosspiece. He leapt back down onto the wagon and the carcass swung out over the pit, barely a man's height from the fire beneath. A flame licked upwards and took hold. The fleece began to smoulder as the oil in it caught and crackled. 'Cut the rope,' Vortigern said. Lud seized the sword on its long shaft and swung. The blade whistled through the air, the rope severed and the carcass dropped. The onlookers retched and choked as the stench of burning flesh and bone rose from beneath in a pillar of stifling black smoke. The captive Picts stared in terror.

'That'll do,' Vortigern said. 'They've seen how it works. Take the small one, we'll never do anything with him. Hang him by the feet.'

Lud and Macsen seized the Pict and heaved him up to Gwyndaf and Derfyn on the wagon. He struggled, clawed and bit like a trapped cat as the four men went to work. The warriors roared and waved their swords. The Pict swung out over the pit, arms flailing. He grabbed for his long hair, desperately trying to lift it clear of the flames. Vortigern watched impassively. The shepherd looked up.

'Ask him if he wants to change his mind.' Vortigern said. The shepherd edged towards the pit and shouted through the flames. The Pict stared back at him, dangling helplessly. The skin on his face blistered and cracked. Choking in the smoke, he gasped out a response. The shepherd shook his head.

'It won't work, Lord King. He says he'll die before betraying his king.'

'Ask the other one, then,' Vortigern said. The shepherd leaned forward and put the question. 'Well?' Vortigern said. The shepherd sighed.

'An honourable fool. He's asking to die instead of his brother.'

'Tell him it'll be his turn soon enough.'

Brennius and Malan arrived beside Kerin.

'My God,' Brennius gasped, 'I thought I'd seen it all in Kent.'

'You haven't seen the half of it, young whippersnapper,' Malan cackled, jigging from foot to foot with excitement. A raucous laugh went up. One of the Pict's sleeves had caught fire, and he was frantically trying to beat out the flames with his other hand. The shepherd bellowed up into the smoke. A hoarse scream answered him.

'He won't do it, Lord King,' the shepherd said calmly. 'You may as well throw them both in the fire and have done with it.'

Vortigern looked at the remaining Pict, who was weeping silently. 'Ask him if he wants to save his brother.' The shepherd gripped the man's arm. The Pict held out, shaking his head and mumbling desperately.

'Lord King, he says that his brother has a wife and six children who will perish without him. He begs you to spare his brother, but he says that they're both loyal men, and can't betray their king.'

'They can't? Alright, then. Are you ready, Lud?'

'Yes, lord,' Lud shouted from up on the wagon. 'Shall I cut the rope?'

'No,' Vortigern said. 'Set fire to it.'

Gwyndaf leaned down into the pit, grabbed a burning brand and handed it to Lud, who held it to the rope. The flame caught and smouldered dully. Vortigern beckoned to the shepherd.

'Now,' he said, 'it takes a while for a rope like that to burn through, so explain to this fool that if he takes us to the Pictish army, he and his brother can both go free. If he refuses, his brother can fry up there until the rope breaks. Then I'll do the same to him, and there'll be two sets of widows and orphans. Tell him all that.'

The shepherd chuckled grimly and grabbed the big Pict by the hair. Above them, the first strand of the rope burned through and snapped. The warriors roared. The big Pict pleaded and wept. The man above the pit thrashed and jerked as his tunic began to smoulder. The strain came on the rope and another strand snapped, the frayed ends igniting in a burst of yellow flame. The big Pict threw himself down in the mud at Vortigern's feet, howling and beating the ground.

'Well?' Vortigern said. The shepherd nodded.

'You've won, Lord King. Spare his brother, and he'll show you where their army's hiding.'

'Good.' Vortigern raised his hand to Lud. 'Cut him down.' He took the shepherd's arm. 'Now, tell this one that we're marching at dawn. If he does as he's told, they can both go free. But his brother will be held here at the camp, and if he lies to us or tries to trick us, I'll send my warriors straight back here to throw him in the pit.'

The shepherd smiled gleefully and rubbed his hands together. 'Can I have the rest of the money now, Lord King?'

'If you like,' Vortigern said, 'but you won't be spending it for a while. You're coming with us, to tell that savage what to do. And if you're planning to double your reward by betraying us, don't do it. It's a large pit. Do you understand me?'

The shepherd smiled weakly. 'Perfectly, Lord King.'

Kerin watched as Lud marched him away alongside the big Pict. Macsen and Gwyndaf were dragging the man they had cut down from the scaffold. The warriors drifted off as they realised that the night's entertainment was over. Soon only a handful of men remained; on one side of the pit Vortigern and Kerin, on the other Publius Luca, Varro and a grey-faced Lucius.

'Kerin, send your old man to treat that Pict,' Vortigern said, shivering violently despite the heat of the fire. 'He won't be much good to us if he dies of his burns.' He pulled his cloak tight, his eyes distant, as if he were slipping back into lethargy now that the drama was over. Publius Luca trudged across, his feet squelching in the mud. Varro placed a fatherly arm around the shoulders of Lucius and shepherded him away towards the tents. Publius Luca glanced at the pit, still seething with flame and filthy smoke.

'It worked, then,' he said, without enthusiasm. Vortigern turned on him.

'*Tortoribus tormenta*,' he spat. 'How about it, commander? There's plenty of room left in the pit.'

Publius Luca looked at him with a wounded smile. 'I am not the enemy, sir,' he said gravely.

28

Hengist and his warriors arrived at midnight. Kerin heard them long before they came into sight, and as they drew nearer, the sound resolved itself into a marching song with a stirring rhythm and a bloodthirsty refrain.

'*We'll slit the bastards open like we slit the silver herring,*

And hang them from the mast for the birds to pick them clean', it went, roughly speaking. The thought that there might be danger in the darkness seemed not to have occurred to them. They sang at the tops of their voices. They carried torches. They had polished their fine bronze shields until they glowed, and the torchlight danced on them. Kerin joined the warriors who had gathered at the edge of the plateau, watching the line of yellow lights bobbing up from the ravine. There were far more men than three ships could possibly have contained. At first Kerin was alarmed, but then he supposed that, at least for the moment, he should be pleased. First to come bursting out of the darkness was Horsa.

'Kerin Brightspear!' he shouted, flinging his long arms around Kerin and hoisting him clear of the ground with disturbing ease. 'Tomorrow we'll do some killing together, my friend!'

The Saxons came pouring up onto the plateau with their torches, into the brighter light of the rush lamps about the tents. There were four hundred of them at least, lean, sharp and fit. They were carrying an enormous banner of deep luminous green, across whose rippling field a monstrous white dragon was unwinding its coils, its yawning mouth spewing flames. They were the most fearsome-looking bunch of foot-soldiers Kerin had ever seen. He knew that he had never seen the Roman army in its glory; but Publius Luca's infantrymen, brave, eager and disciplined though they appeared, lacked the blood-hunger that burned in these men. Hengist came out of their midst to meet Vortigern. His smile seemed to hold a genuine goodwill. The two men clasped hands, and all their warriors cheered and crowded in to share the warmth of their reunion. Hengist raised his hand for silence.

'We have gifts for you!' he cried, waving a group of his men forward. They came with heavy grain sacks, tied at the neck with whipcord. The ties were loosed, the sacks were upended and an avalanche of fine bone-handled daggers spilled out. Hengist seized one and sliced a lock of fair hair from one of the youngsters who had carried the sacks. The lad yelped in surprise, then burst out laughing. 'As sharp as you'll find, lord,' Hengist said, presenting the dagger to Vortigern with a ceremonial bow. 'My Jute craftsmen will sing to Odin when I tell them that they helped us to victory.'

'One for you, Kerin Brightspear!' shouted Horsa, who never said anything quietly.

'Thank you, Hengist,' Vortigern said, 'we are honoured. Lud, take them to the cooks and see that they're well fed.' He turned and laid a hand on Hengist's arm. 'Now, I don't know much about Jute ships, Hengist, but even a halfwit could work out that all these men wouldn't fit on the three ships you brought to Kent.'

Hengist gave a contrite smile. 'Lord, I have brought more warriors. I thought it would be prudent. I have brought –'

'Five hundred,' Vortigern said. 'I can count warriors like shepherds can count sheep.'

'You are correct, lord,' Hengist said. 'If a messenger could have reached you in time, I would have asked. That was not possible, so I brought them anyway. The Picts are a strong enemy. I thought more warriors would be better. After we fight, then of course I will send them home; indeed, I will send them home now, if you wish.'

Vortigern ran his eye over the warriors. 'No. Let them stay. They'll be paid for their service, like the rest of you. But understand that once the fighting is over, they must leave. You can't all live on that strip of land in Kent. Now go to your men, and tell them that we hang anyone who drinks on the eve of a battle. Then come to my tent with your brother and whoever else matters to you. You may eat there, with me and my commanders.'

Hengist bowed and withdrew. His warriors marched off towards the cooks' tents, still singing their bloodcurdling song. Vortigern watched them go.

'We are playing with fire here, Kerin,' he said softly.

* * *

Hengist brought only two men apart from his brother. There was little room to spare in the modest tent. From Cambria, Lud, Macsen and Gwyndaf, Kerin and Katigern; then two representatives from each of the remaining factions. Eldof and Varro from Glevum, Garagon and Brennius from Kent, and finally the Kernow men, Gorlois and his brother Gerdan. Publius Luca was there, as commander of infantry, and Lucius as head of cavalry. Into the midst of this well-acquainted gathering came Hengist, his familiar brother, and two younger men about whom no-one knew anything. One

252

was the fair-haired youngster who had lost a lock of his hair to Hengist's dagger. The other, probably nearer Gwyndaf's age, was tall and rangy like Horsa. He had pale, supercilious eyes, a trim beard and long sandy hair, pulled back from his high forehead and secured with a leather thong. They joined the rest of the gathering sitting cross-legged on the floor. The servants brought bowls of broth and haunches of mutton. Hardly a word was exchanged whilst the food was consumed. Every man in the tent knew that this would be his last meal before battle, and might be his last ever. When the bowls and platters had been cleared, Hengist stood.

'Lords of the Britons,' he said, 'allow me to introduce my kinsmen. My brother Horsa you know, and this is his wife's young brother, Aelle.' He turned to the older warrior. 'And here is my cousin's son, Oswi. I have spoken of a young man who was captured in this country. Oswi was that young man. When he was freed, he lodged with a family who had fine horses, and in time he mastered them all. Amongst us Jutes, he is called Oswi the Horseman. Of course, I do not expect him to deserve this name amongst the Britons, who have been horsemen from their cradles.' He smiled down at Oswi, who wrinkled his nose, as if his own expectations might be entirely different. Vortigern noticed but did not comment.

'Publius Luca,' he said, 'you know this country and this enemy better than any of us. Tell these men what is expected of them tomorrow.'

Hengist sat. Publius Luca rose. 'The king is right. As a young soldier, I served here on the Wall when needed. Most of the time just east of here, at a place called Brocolita. Lord Hengist, you must have passed it on your way from the sea.'

'We saw no soldiers,' Horsa said, leaning forward. 'But on Odin's head, we saw buildings of stone so large that they must have been raised by giants. Did you fight those giants, when you were a young man?'

'Oh yes,' Publius said. 'We slaughtered them every one.'

Horsa's eyes gleamed. 'Then truly the Roman soldiers were sons of Odin,' he said, with a reverence. Publius Luca bowed, avoiding the eyes of the men on his side of the tent.

'I would sooner fight those giants than fight the Picts,' he said. 'Hear me now, all of you. In Londinium, men call the Picts animals, without sense or reason. These men are ignorant fools. The Picts are a proud people, with their own gods and their own ways. They won't yield because we have better weapons, or armour, or horses. They will fight to the death. And you will need every scrap of your strength and courage to defeat them.' He turned to his commander of cavalry. 'The map, please, Lucius.' A scroll was produced, which Publius Luca unrolled, passing one end back to Lucius. 'This belonged to my commander at Brocolita. Look, this line here marks the Wall. Here is the sea, Lord Hengist; this is the river you must have sailed up, and this is the valley which brought you to our camp. We shall cross the Wall here, at the milecastle. When the sun rises, if you look to the north-west, you will see it clearly; a small fort, with gates to north and south. Beyond the Wall, here, is moorland. There are bogs, but also good tracks. If we bear westwards, we shall soon strike one of the old military roads. That will lead us to Liburnia, an outpost fort of Hadrian's day. From there, it's less than half a day's march to the foothills, across open moorland with patches of low scrub. Somewhere in those hills, the Picts are gathering their forces.'

Eldof frowned. 'We're going into the hills after them?'

'Lord, we might as well sign our own death warrants,' Varro croaked. 'Those men know the hills like they know their own villages. They'd have a spearman or a bowman behind every rock, waiting to pick us off.'

'You're right, Varro,' Publius Luca said. 'We must make them come to us.'

'How?' Gorlois asked. 'No disrespect, commander, but if I was a Pict I'd sit up in the hills and wait for us to lose patience, wouldn't you?'

'I might. But we're not Picts, Gorlois. I've fought these people before. They're savage fighters, as courageous as any I've met, but military planning is foreign to them. They fight with the instincts of a hunting wolf. And if you show the hungry wolf a hare, he'll chase it, won't he.'

'A hare?' Garagon sounded alarmed. 'What do you mean by that, commander?'

Publius Luca cleared his throat. 'Firstly, a warband will ride ahead with the Pict who has agreed to lead us to his king's encampment. Once they have established where the Picts are lying, they'll return to meet the army at Liburnia. The second step will follow.' He paused, rolled up the map and handed it back to Lucius. 'And in this, whilst I commend the principle, I am concerned about the detail.' His eyes met Vortigern's across the heads of the seated warriors.

'Shall I continue, commander?' Vortigern asked.

'Yes, sir,' Publius Luca said. 'It'll sound mad, coming from me.'

Vortigern stood up. 'It's simple enough. Once we know where the Pictish army is, I shall lead a band of forty mounted warriors against them. We shall attack them in daylight, from the front. They'll come out after us, naturally.'

Hengist's eyes narrowed. 'That's madness, lord.'

'No. It'll work, I promise you. Some of us will die, probably, but that's to be expected. When they come after us, we'll turn and run. They'll follow us out of the hills, onto the moors and into the arms of your Saxon warriors, Hengist, because you and Publius Luca's infantry will be lying flat on your bellies in the scrub waiting for them. They'll try to escape you, but by then Eldof's horsemen and my Cambrians will have cut off their path back to the hills. Lucius's cavalry and the men of Kernow will take them from right and left, and if any of them turn south, Garagon's Kentishmen will hold them at the Wall. Do you still think it's madness?'

Hengist considered. 'No, Lord King. I think it could succeed. But may Odin's mercy fall upon the hares.'

Vortigern smiled and looked about him. Barely a sound disturbed the silence except for the crackle of twigs on the fire, and the occasional shuffle and quiet cough as men glanced at each other, every one imagining his own part in what was to come. Eldof was the first to speak.

'Who are the lucky hares, then?'

'The forty warriors of the Cambrian spearhead,' Vortigern said. 'Please understand that I mean no disrespect to you, Eldof, or to you, Gorlois, or to any man here. But these are the men I know and trust with my life. You would surely do the same.'

'Yes,' Eldof said. 'We would all do the same. But ours is the easier part.'

'There will be no easy parts tomorrow,' Vortigern said. He looked about him, at the men who held the future of the kingdom in their hands. 'Go to your warriors now. We ride at first light. Whichever gods you pray to, may they guard your souls.'

Kerin waited until the others had gone. 'The usual bunch?' he asked.

'Everyone you would expect. Lud, Macsen and Elir, Rufus and Kat, Gwyndaf and his band. Hefin, Bened, Hefydd and the best of his boys.' He smiled wryly. 'There won't be much hope for Cambria if this fails.'

'It won't fail,' Kerin said. He felt sure of that much.

'Unless they find a way to cut us off before we get clear of the hills,' Vortigern said. He picked up a piece of brushwood and stirred the fire, sending a shower of sparks up into the darkness. 'If they do that, we're dead men.' He shrugged and tossed the wood into the fire. The sound of a Cambrian song hung lightly in the frozen air as the warriors settled down to sleep.

'You're taking Rufus, then.'

Vortigern looked up. 'Yes, of course I am. He's my son, and a fine warrior, whatever's happened.'

Kerin raised his hands. 'You're right. I don't know why I said it.'

Vortigern shook his head and let it pass. 'It doesn't matter. Go to your bed.'

Kerin looked up with the trace of a smile. 'Even gods and devils need sleep, then.'

'Not necessarily,' Vortigern said. 'But you do, if you're going to protect my back tomorrow.'

Kerin felt his throat tighten. It was as if that bleak episode on the mud-flats in Kent had never happened. 'No-one will pass me, lord.'

'Believe me, I know it,' Vortigern said. 'Whatever's happened, if I had to choose only one man to take into those hills, it would surely be you. So if this is the last thing you do for me, do it well. With heart and soul. The kingdom depends on it, and so do I.'

Kerin was aghast. 'The last thing I do for you? How could it possibly be?'

'Very easily, if you do as you intend,' Vortigern said, drawing the tent flap for him. By this time tomorrow, we could both be dead, Kerin thought.

'You were wrong on the road to Glevum,' he said. 'Telling me not to make too much of things.'

Vortigern stood, looking out over the camp. Only the watchmen's lights were burning now. 'Perhaps I was. We shall speak of it again. But not tonight.'

'But, lord!' Kerin protested.

'Don't,' Vortigern said sharply. He turned, the firelight catching him.

'I'm sorry,' Kerin whispered, and went out into the darkness. He walked away from the tent as quickly as he could without running, which would have drawn someone's attention. He thought with bitter regret about what he had told Publius Luca on the rampart at Venta; a young fool's claim, as naive as it was presumptuous. He couldn't even slay his own demons, let alone the ones which had crawled all this way from the foul, remote darkness of Isca. He went on walking until the edge of the plateau stopped him. An arresting whinny made him turn. The racehorse Ghazal was watching him from a high-sided pen behind Garagon's tent. Well, Kerin thought, the rest of us may die tomorrow, but you surely won't. Glancing around to make sure that no-one was looking, he slipped into the pen, slackened the buckle on the headcollar and eased it over the stallion's ears. Ghazal shook his head vigorously and blew through his nostrils. Kerin pressed his finger to his lips and opened the gate wide. The stallion looked at him curiously and stood still.

'Go on,' Kerin murmured. 'Get out of here.' The stallion whickered and nuzzled his sleeve. 'Go on, you stupid beast!' Kerin hissed, jerking his arm away. Ghazal snorted and trotted out of the pen. 'Go!' Kerin pleaded, waving his arms. Someone was awake inside the tent. Kerin heard a drowsy voice; Brennius's, he thought. Ghazal watched him, motionless as a carving. In desperation Kerin clenched his fist and brought it down on the stallion's soft, velvet nose. Ghazal gave a screech of pain and took off like a bolt from a crossbow. Stones rattled over rocks as he hurtled over the edge of the plateau and down into the valley below. Brennius poked his head out of the tent, rubbing sleep from his eyes.

'What the hell was that?'

'One of Hefydd's boys riding around in the dark,' Kerin said, trying to look nonchalant. 'You know how mad they all are.' Brennius grunted and crawled back inside. Kerin walked to the edge of the plateau and looked out towards the east. He thought he glimpsed Ghazal, a fast-moving dark speck on the moonlit moor.

'What are you doing out here?'

It was Rufus.

'I let Garagon's horse go,' Kerin said. 'It's a racehorse. It would have been killed in the first charge, so I thought I'd give it a chance. Garagon should thank me, anyway. He'd be better off riding some fat old plodder from the cook's carts.'

Rufus began to laugh and stifled the sound with his arm. They looked at each other silently. Neither had words for what he wished to say. A year ago they would not have had to say anything, on the eve of a battle which might kill them both.

'Whatever's happened,' Kerin began.

'I know,' Rufus said. 'I wish you nothing but good fortune tomorrow.'

'You'd better pray for me, then. If God's going to listen to anyone, it's probably you.'

'I pray for you every day of my life,' Rufus said. Kerin heard the catch in his voice. He seized him by the shoulders and they embraced.

'My dearest friend,' Rufus whispered; then he tore himself free and trudged away across the silent camp.

29

The scouting party set out first, as the eastern sky turned from black to luminous blue. Vortigern had picked Derfyn to lead it. He seemed to have taken to the young warrior, and indeed, Kerin thought, there was plenty to like about Derfyn. His nerve and fighting skills were balanced by a rogue's good humour, and appearances meant nothing to him. Having ridden all the way from Cambria on one of his smart brown mares, he turned up outside the king's tent on the most moth-eaten grey horse Kerin had ever seen. Vortigern grinned.

'What's that? Your mother's donkey?'

'That's what everyone calls him, lord,' Derfyn said. 'Asyn. And he may not look much, but if three men attack me, he'll kill one of them before I get my sword out.' He looked calm and assured at the head of his band, a mixed bunch of Cambrians and Kernow men surrounding the shepherd and the captive Pict. Gwyndaf had come to see them off. He gave Derfyn a long, unblinking look before they got moving. Afterwards, he turned to Kerin in near despair.

'He's the son I never had,' he said. 'I must have been mad to listen to you.'

They were at Liburnia within hours, and then there was little to do but wait for Derfyn to come back. The fort was well-sited on a rocky promontory rising from the gently undulating moors like an island in a pale brown sea. The solid stone walls had survived a hundred years of neglect, although the wooden gates had rotted or been hacked down for fuel. To one side were the walls and columns of a temple to Mithras, its roof destroyed long ago by wind and rain. This did not deter the god's many devotees amongst the infantry, who gathered silently about the ruins to ask for his blessing. The Saxons formed a tight circle at a safe distance, glancing towards the fort, as if they feared that the giant builders might be watching them. Padarn, who had caught up with the army on the road, parked his wagon close to the old gatehouse. A rough cross was planted in the ground alongside to reassure any Christians in the company that they could go there for prayer and comfort.

Vortigern was sitting on one of the outlying walls, looking out towards the north-west. Kerin turned his mare loose and sat down. The blue line of the foothills looked disturbingly close. For more than a year it had existed in the landscape of his imagination, but now it was here, and it was real, and within the day he and almost everyone he loved would be there, riding like madmen against an enemy thousands strong. Vortigern took off his Roman medallion and let it spin on its chain.

'What are you thinking about?' he asked.

'About what's waiting for us over there. And about something Gwyndaf said. I hope Derfyn comes back in one piece.'

'Yes,' Vortigern said. 'Probably Gwyndaf thinks I should have sent one of my sons instead of offering up another sacrifice at his expense. But I can't trust Rufus with a prisoner. God might tell him to let the bastard go.'

Kerin found himself smiling, in spite of everything.

The army lay spread out before him on the breezy moor, an edgy, bickering mass of men and horseflesh. Fluttering banners, a forest of spears. Sunlight winking on the shields and breastplates of the infantry. No such luxury for the men of the spearhead; they would ride as they had always done, unprotected save for triple-layered leather jerkins and gauntlets. Nothing to add weight. Nothing to slow speed, or hamper lightning movement. The sky above Liburnia was blue and cloudless. A few ravens circled over the fort, calling raucously, as if they bitterly resented this unexpected invasion of their lonely home.

'Did you know someone had stolen Garagon's horse?' Vortigern asked.

'No, did they?' Kerin was unable to restrain a smile.

'Last night. He was raging about it this morning. I told him he should be grateful. A mule would be more good to him in battle.'

'Perhaps the horse escaped, lord,' Kerin suggested.

'Hardly. You must have seen the pen, and the way they'd tied it up.'

'Well, perhaps someone felt sorry for it and let it go, then,' Kerin said. Vortigern stared up at the sky.

'Who'd do that? You might as well throw a bag of gold in a river, and –' he broke off. The clipeum hung motionless on its chain. Kerin got up, chuckling to himself, and walked off across the springy grass.

* * *

By midday the high sun was warm enough to melt the frost. The warriors waited, some sprawled on their backs, some sitting around playing knucklebones, others simply dozing or watching the country to the north-west. Edryd had joined them, despite being told that his blacksmith's skills entitled him to remain behind. He was chatting with Hefin, examining a dagger and pointing out some small imperfection in its construction. Someone had hog-tied Malan to stop him coming too. The horses munched, switching clouds of tiny flies which the warmth had drawn from the nearby marsh. Just when it seemed that the whole business might be postponed, a shout came from high up on the fort. Marc came stumbling down over the lichen-covered stones and landed in a heap on the grass below.

'They're coming, Lord King!' he gasped. Vortigern hauled him to his feet.

'All there?'

'Yes, Lord King.'

'Go and tell Gwyndaf.'

Kerin joined Vortigern as the riders approached. Gwyndaf arrived, running.

'Good,' Vortigern said. 'Not a mark on any of them.'

'You're lucky,' Gwyndaf said tartly. 'If there had been, I'd have cut your throat.'

The council of war was held within the walls of the fort. It included all the men who had met in the king's tent the night before, except for Hengist and his companions.

'We're almost on top of them!' Derfyn said, eyes feverish with excitement. 'Those hills are closer than they look, and once you get over the first ridge, by God, there they are, thousands of them, and –'

'Calm down, boy,' Gwyndaf said curtly.

'Did anyone see you?' Kerin asked. Derfyn steadied himself.

'No chance. There's a hillside above the valley where they're lying, covered with trees and undergrowth. The Pict took us up through the wood. Higher up there are rocks with brambles and stuff growing over them. You can hide there and see what's going on down below.'

'Alright,' Vortigern said. 'How many of them? More than us? Less?'

'I'd say a few hundred more. But Drust – the Pict – he said that reinforcements are arriving every day.'

'The approach to the camp. Could you see what it was like?'

'Not very well. But it's narrow, alright. Drust said you couldn't get a wagon through it.'

'Suppose Drust's lying to you?' Gwyndaf said.

'No,' Derfyn said. 'He worships his brother. He wouldn't do anything that might get him killed.'

'And you can find the entrance to the valley from this side?' Vortigern asked.

'Yes. Drust showed it to me on the way back. The sides are steep, covered in scrub. If they were expecting an attack, they could sit up there and pick us off, but I don't think so. They think we've just come to defend the Wall. That's what the Romans did, and they're expecting us to do the same.'

'Good,' Vortigern said, getting up. 'Pick someone you trust, and take that Pict back to the camp. Tell the guards to chain him up with his brother, and tell Cheldric to feed them. Nobody beats them, nobody kills them. Then get yourself back here, as quick as that donkey can go.' Everyone else looked up expectantly. 'It's time,' Vortigern said.

* * *

The hills did not live up to anyone's preconceptions. There were far higher hills in Cambria, but none of them concealed the latent menace of these ordinary-looking ridges. The forty hares reined in and waited.

'That's it.' Derfyn pointed. 'That gap in the hills, just there.'

They looked at the unprepossessing valley, the sort of place where they might normally have gone for a pleasant ride, and where they might all shortly be slaughtered, like rats in a drain. Kerin looked back at the army massing behind them. For a brief moment, the sight of what they had worked made him catch his breath. Everything seemed to be in swirling motion, row on row of shields, helmeted heads, bristling spears, Saxon pikes and axes; and beyond that a thousand horses of every kind and colour, jostling and plunging, some barely controlled. A sea of standards streamed above them, Hefydd's red stag leaping, the sky-blue banner of Kernow with the black bear rearing, the hideous coiling dragon of the Jutes, the white bull of Glevum snorting on a field of gold. The breath and sweat of men and beasts rose and hung over them like a cloud of foul-smelling steam.

Publius Luca rode the front line, acknowledging his commanders. Drawing Eldof, Gorlois and Lucius to him, he addressed them briefly and sent them to their men; then he reined in beside Vortigern and saluted.

'Good luck, sir. When you come out of those hills, we'll be ready for them.'

Vortigern rode up to the head of his picked band and turned to face them. The men sat motionless, as if frozen in that moment of fierce resolve; and beneath them, snorting and stamping, the warhorses; the dreaded death-bringers of the Cambrian spearhead, all gentleness snuffed out as the hour of blood drew near. No exhortation from Vortigern this time; only a smile and a clenched fist. No more was needed for this chosen few. He turned his mare's head towards the hills and held her still. Gwyndaf shouldered the draco and moved to his right hand. Lud brought up his battle-scarred roan on the left. Kerin pulled Eryr in behind them, with Rufus and Macsen to either side. Vortigern sat quite still. He closed his eyes tightly and kissed the clipeum. Gwyndaf pressed his forehead to the pole of the draco. Lud clenched a fist on his breast. Kerin clasped his crucifix and Gael's tiny ring. They moved off at a steady trot. The hills rose above them. They entered the narrow defile. Kerin's eyes scoured banks, bushes, high ridges. The horses trotted on. The sides of the defile grew higher and steeper. Pale outcrops of rock thrust out far above, god-given platforms for archers or spearmen. Did the Picts have crossbows, like the Romans used? Did they have horses now?

'In the name of the Father, the Son and the Holy Ghost,' Rufus whispered, as the horses jogged on. 'In the name of the Father, the Son and the Holy Ghost.' The ground rose ahead, the track grew wider. 'In the name of the Father, the Son –' And then Kerin smelt the wood smoke; sharp, acrid, cooking-fires. Vortigern stopped dead and raised his hand. He edged his mare forward. His hand turned palm-downward and patted the air. Absolute silence. He beckoned Kerin. The great bowl of the valley spread before them. Every Pict north of the Wall might have been swept up and funnelled into this one place. No houses, no wagons or orderly horse lines; simply a boiling mass, lethal as the fire in the pit. Campfires sent lazy plumes of smoke into the still, cold air. Around them warriors swarmed, sweeping forward and receding in great multicoloured waves, swords and spearheads glinting. A man came out of a large tent, tall, hair like a flame. The sun winked on a bronze breastplate and gold armlets. He was swept up shoulder-high, and a roar reverberated through the quiet hills. Kerin felt sweat forming on his brow, although the grass was still white with frost. A small herd of shaggy ponies was grazing on the gentle slope between the edge of the encampment and the watching horsemen. Short in the leg, but sturdy enough to carry a man. Bridles hung on a railing hastily constructed from rough branches. A well-trodden track led upwards through scrub, looking as if it might emerge high above the narrow defile. Even a moderately skilled spearman would have trouble missing his target from up there. Vortigern nodded to Kerin, Lud and Gwyndaf, drawing the three men close.

'Lud, take Macsen and Hefin and stampede the ponies. Straight ahead, if you can. The rest of us will attack the camp. Kerin, you must try to kill the leader. The rest of us will protect you.' He turned to the other warriors, crowding in behind. 'When I give the word, turn and run. Every man for himself. Don't wait for anyone.'

Lud drew Macsen and Hefin aside. Gwyndaf loosed the draco's bindings and let the banner fall. The brazen head glowed above them. Vortigern raised his hand. The warhorses, recognising the moment, shivered and snorted. Vortigern's hand fell. The horses leapt forward and hurtled down the slope, wind shrieking in the dragon's head. Lud was amongst the ponies, roaring, thwacking with the flat of his sword. Macsen and Hefin came in from the sides, sending the panicking animals straight towards the encampment. Kerin raised his spear to shoulder height. Blinded by terror the ponies poured over everything in their path; tents, fires, men who were too slow or shocked to escape. A spear flashed by, skimming the neck of Gwyndaf's mare. Kerin could see the leader's tent. He could see the big man with the flame-red hair. A shower of blood drenched Eryr's neck, and a spear clattered beneath her hooves. The leader had a sword. He was wearing a shining breastplate looted from

some Roman officer. A little band of warriors came screaming past the ponies. Gwyndaf swung down from the saddle
and sliced off the top of the first man's head. Kerin was
dimly aware of blades chopping flesh, but he saw his mark,
rose in the saddle and launched his spear. It flew straight
as a line across the tangle of limbs, swords and squealing
ponies and buried itself in the leader's throat, just above the
line of the bronze breastplate.

'Turn!' Vortigern bellowed.

Kerin spun his mare, flinging himself flat over her neck.
He glimpsed Rufus fighting off three men who were hacking
frantically at him with long-bladed knives. Katigern sent
two of them sprawling. Gwyndaf was galloping alongside,
the draco slung low. His tunic was ripped from neck to waist.
Kerin glanced behind and saw Vortigern following, blood
streaming from a head-wound. The first of the Cambrian
warriors were in the defile. Some Picts caught their frightened ponies, seized weapons and set off in pursuit. More
followed on foot, howling manically. Kerin dropped Eryr's
reins and let her run. Ahead of him were Derfyn, Lud and
Rufus, behind only Gwyndaf and Vortigern. High up on the
right, something moved.

'Derfyn, right!' Kerin yelled. Derfyn flung himself flat in
time to avoid the spear. The man who had thrown it leapt
suicidally from the outcrop where he had been standing.
Derfyn swung his sword and caught him in mid-air, slicing
head from shoulders with a surgeon's precision. The Pictish
horsemen filled the defile. The leader flung his spear. It
furrowed across the quarters of Vortigern's mare, opening
a bloody gash. Gwyndaf turned in the saddle, whirled his
sling and let fly. Knocked senseless, the Pict fell backwards
into the path of the riders behind him. Kerin spun his mare,
swung his sword and slashed the pony's jugular. It fell,

gurgling and gushing blood. The animals behind stumbled over the dying pony, throwing their riders as they went down. Flocks of jackdaws went squalling up from the woods as Vortigern's men galloped out onto open ground. Before them the moorland stretched, vast and empty. Kerin glanced behind. He could see only Picts, horsemen galloping out of the defile, waves of foot-warriors pouring down the slopes, their naked, tattooed legs devouring the ground. Ahead was nothing. Brown turf, gorse, burr reeds.

'Gods, where are they?' Lud gasped. As if in reply, the moorland came alive. Hengist sprang from a ditch just ahead of them.

'Odin!' he bellowed, raising both hands above his head, knife in one, battle-axe in the other. Warriors leapt from every gorse bush and clump of reeds; Saxons and legionaries, brandishing swords, spears and axes. Horsemen swept in from the flanks, Gorlois leading on the left, Lucius on the right, as Publius Luca marshalled the foot-soldiers. Far behind, beyond the sea of Pictish spears, Kerin glimpsed Eldof and Varro leading the men of Glevum in a flat-out chase for the gap in the hills. It's working, he thought, swinging down to grab a fallen spear. If Eldof got there with even half his warriors the Picts would be cut off here, on this merciless moor, with no cover, no escape, nothing but the ravens and the eagles, already circling high above in the cloudless sky. The armies met with a howl and a clash. Vortigern appeared at Kerin's side. He had hacked a broad strip of green cloth from the trailing banner of the draco and tied it round his head, to stop the blood pouring into his eyes. Gwyndaf was beside him. All three galloped back towards the battle, the dragon's head screaming in the air above them.

'Kerin Brightspear!' It was Oswi the Horseman. He had

grabbed a loose pony and was on the charge, whirling his axe. As the pony reached the solid, brawling mass Oswi kicked it in the flanks and drove it forward. Men howled and threw themselves sideways as it landed amongst them, lashing out in panic. The last Kerin saw of Oswi, he was standing on the pony's back with a Pict's head impaled on his axe-blade. Lud was thundering round the fringes, cutting down fugitives. Hefydd roared across the open ground, whirling something which might have been a length of someone's gut. Kerin wrenched a spear from a dead man's back and tore after Vortigern. Between them a brawling mass of Picts, one with sword swung back, about to slash the black mare's hamstrings. Kerin loosed the spear. The man choked and pitched forward, pierced through the back of the neck. His fellows turned, ten men, spears useless at this range. The long-bladed knives were coming out. Kerin dropped Eryr's reins. *'Kill, kill!'* The mare reared up with the awful throaty roar of the fighting horse. The first two didn't see much; just a flash of razor hooves in the split second before they smashed through cheekbones and eye sockets and sent them to their gods. Kerin's assailants turned to flee; straight down the throats of a wall of infantry. The last time Kerin had seen those men, they were stomping up and down the courtyard of the castra. 'We've got 'em, sir!' one bellowed. Another held up a short-handled spear. Kerin grabbed it and rode on, leaving them fighting hand to hand. There was deadlier work for a horse-warrior to do.

All sense of time and place vanished. A white horse came galloping out of the blood welter. Blue bridle trim. A rangy gelding, a Kernow horse. A Pict on a Kernow man's horse, sword whirling. Kerin steadied Eryr, kept her running. A heel in the flank, a slap on the neck. At the last second, the mare veered right. Kerin swung his legs back as her shoulder dropped, striking the rider on the knee, knocking the horse off balance. They went down in a tangle of hooves, the rider howling and clutching his shattered leg. A sword spun through the air. Kerin caught it and cut the sound short. Derfyn on the ground, his little grey warhorse spread-eagled over a boulder, front legs broken. Kerin dragged on the reins, rode a circle. Even in the chaos of battle, a man needed to kill his own horse. Derfyn crawled towards him, drenched in horse blood. Kerin leaned down, dragged him aboard. A red mare came careering past, fancy bridle, Glevum horse. 'Here!' Kerin gasped, grabbing the rein and hauling her in. Derfyn leapt astride her, shaking and weeping. 'Kill one for Asyn!' Kerin panted, tossing him the Pict's sword. Ahead was a solid line of armoured bodies, Publius Luca's infantry, grinding down a Pictish wall. The commander, sword slashing like a young man's, guarding their backs. The draco. Gwyndaf, dagger in his teeth. Vortigern, sword in each hand, shreds of fabric dangling from the mare's jaws.

'This way!' Vortigern gasped as Kerin rode alongside. 'They're falling back. But it's not the end of this.'

He threw one sword to Kerin and made some signal which the standard-bearer understood. Gwyndaf found a space big enough for a horse to stand in. The draco rose up. All flocked to it. Vortigern and Publius Luca drew them out into an inward-curving line; the dragon at the centre and to each side the crack warriors on their brave, bleeding horses. Behind them everyone else who could still ride or stand, the massed spears and bloodied axes, every man straining to go, and then Vortigern raised his hand high and bellowed, 'Wait!'

The Picts had surged back towards the hills. They were milling in a formless mass around the mouth of the defile which led to their hidden valley, the weakening sun flashing on metal; milling, turning. Turning.

'Wait!' Vortigern bawled, his raised arm shaking, as if it bore the whole effort of holding back what lay behind him. Kerin caught a movement below. Two lads had moved to his horse's shoulder, each with spare spears for him. 'It's your call,' Vortigern said. 'Raise the spear as soon as they're within range.' A smile flashed. 'Our range, not yours.'

And as Kerin looked from right to left, at the long, in-curving arc of men and horses, he thought suddenly of the bay; their bay, at the mouth of their valley, with its girdle of cliff and shingle. The way the water moved when the high tide was turning; sucked back by some unseen force, rising as a towering wave, holding, falling, crashing in foam on rock and stones. And so he stood his ground under the dragon as the howling blue and red tide rushed to meet them with its flotsam of spearheads and ragged banners. Swords, knives, bared teeth. I could drop that man now. And Macsen could drop him *now*. Kerin swung the spear up to his shoulder. Vortigern's hand fell. The spear flew to its mark, a hundred showering after it. The horses leapt forward, trampling bodies, the foot-soldiers forging behind. And the line of men and beasts held, as the rocks did; and the unseen power sucked the wave back, as the sea did, for it to rise again; rearing, holding and breaking, rising and breaking, rising and falling, faltering at last. Then the ends of the great arc swept outwards, enclosing the spent tide in a deadly embrace; leaving only the blood mist and the broken, the moan of life expiring, the chortling rasp of the carrion birds and the creeping stench of death.

Kerin rode alone across grass slippery with blood. Private battles were still going on around him. A few small groups hacking at each other; a Pict and a Kernow man, so exhausted that they were fighting on their knees. Kerin struck the Pict on the head with the butt of his spear shaft as he rode by, leaving the Kernow man to claim the glory. He had no idea how many he had killed. He could barely lift his right arm. The old thigh wound was throbbing and someone had opened a jagged gash below his left shoulder-blade. It was impossible to count the corpses. He was astounded to realise how far south they had come during the battle. Liburnia was far behind, and ahead in the distance he could see the undulating line of the Wall.

He was about to turn back when he saw the dead horse. It was lying in a bog, barely visible above the shivering brown burr reeds; an iron-grey with a Roman saddle. Kerin dismounted and crept forward. It would have been laughable to get killed by a trap at this stage. The horse had been speared through the neck. Lucius was lying on his back beside it. His helmet lay nearby, half submerged in a pool. An ugly wound in his calf was seeping blood. Kerin dropped down and found with relief that the pulse in his neck was beating strongly. He tore a strip from his tunic and bound the leg-wound tightly. Lucius's eyelids flickered.

'Kerin!' he whispered. 'Oh God, poor Dominus. He was such a brave horse.' He sat up and looked around him. 'Is it over?'

'The worst's over. A slaughter. But we can't stay here. Come on; we can ride double.'

'My sword,' Lucius said, struggling to his knees. 'I think it landed in the pool.'

Kerin squatted down and grasped the hilt. The prospect of imminent danger didn't occur to him until a spear hissed past his right ear, nicking him below the hairline. He spun round, fell on his knees in the mud, and found two Picts almost on top of him. The one on the pony must have thrown the spear, because the other man still had his, and was coming straight for him. Kerin swung Lucius's sword, catching the pony across its forelegs. Its rider slammed headfirst into the ground, knocking himself senseless. His companion fled away into the bog. Lucius picked himself up, trying not to stand on his wounded leg.

'I thought we were done for there,' he gasped. Kerin barely heard him. He was looking out across the moor towards Liburnia. Lucius followed his eyes. 'Jesus Christ,' he stammered. Vortigern and his warhorse were bearing down on them like an apparition from hell. Man and horse were head to foot in blood. Kerin and Lucius stumbled over through the sucking mud.

'Get your horse and ride for the Wall,' Vortigern panted. 'There are three hundred more coming behind me with Lud and Gorlois on their tails.'

Kerin hauled himself onto Eryr's back, hoisted Lucius up behind him and rode off after Vortigern. The milecastle was clearly visible, stark against a sky washed with gold as the sun sloped westwards. It was a long, cruel pull up the last hill and Eryr slowed as the ground rose. Kerin slackened the reins, pulled her ears, slapped her neck and sang to her. Vortigern had reined in further up the hill.

'Look. There they are.' In the distance, just short of Liburnia, Kerin saw a dark, moving mass. Now and again the sun caught a shield or spearhead, throwing up a brilliant flash of light. 'I was riding to warn Garagon. I left Eldof and his boys rounding up the remnants. They can't be far behind Lud and the Kernow men.'

'Some escaped towards the hills, lord,' Lucius said. 'We were after them when my horse got speared. The lads should have caught them by now.'

'You've done well,' Vortigern said.

A flush of pride coloured Lucius's drained face. He looked at Vortigern's shredded clothes, and the blood dripping steadily from the sodden fragment of the draco banner. 'Not as well as you, though, lord.'

Vortigern shrugged and smiled. 'You were quicker at getting out of the way, that's all,' he said. 'It's an attribute of youth.'

Garagon and Brennius rode down from the milecastle as they approached. Brennius merely looked nervous, but Garagon's face was ashen.

'It's alright,' Kerin said. 'They're on the run. But there are three hundred coming this way, running from our men, and you'll have to hold them here or they'll be all over our camp and the villages on the other side.'

'Of course we can hold them here,' Garagon snapped, but he looked less than confident.

'It shouldn't be difficult, but don't underestimate them,' Vortigern said. 'That was the hardest battle I've ever fought.' He glanced at Lucius, bleeding profusely from the wound in his calf. 'Take him back to the camp, Kerin. I'll follow when we've finished this.'

'I am not going without you,' Kerin said. 'Garagon, send one of your men with Lucius Arrius.'

Garagon had not heard. He was staring down towards the moors. That dark wave, the remnant of the Pictish army, had reached the bottom of the hill. They were close enough now for details to be visible; flying hair, bloodstained limbs, glinting spears. Kerin dismounted, helped Lucius down and heaved him up behind one of the Kentish warriors, a terrified-looking youngster who was not going to be much help in defending the Wall.

'Back to the camp with you,' he said, slapping the horse's rump. The Kentish horses were prancing and whinnying. It would be the first time they had participated in anything more than a local argument.

'Garagon, don't wait for them to come to you!' Vortigern exclaimed. 'Take your men and ride down that hill as fast as you can. You'll knock half of them over, and the rest might even run. Go on, for Jesus Christ's sake!' Garagon hesitated, eyes wild and staring.

'Follow me, lads!' Brennius roared. He drew his sword and launched his horse down the hill. The Kentishmen poured after him, carrying Garagon with them. Vortigern leaned across and caught Eryr's rein.

'Not unless it's necessary,' he said.

They watched from the sanctuary of the milecastle. Lud and his companions had caught up with the Picts' tail-end. Brennius and his warriors met them head-on halfway down to the moor. Trapped on the bare hillside, the Picts turned and fought. A horseman burst from the jostling mob and came galloping back. Garagon was riding blind, sword and spear gone. He rode straight through the milecastle and down into the *vallum* beyond the Wall. Out on the hillside, Lud and Eldof had been joined by a swarm of mounted warriors, Gorlois and Publius Luca amongst them. The howls and screams and clash of swords were soon replaced by an eerie silence.

'Well,' Vortigern said, 'that really is the end of it.' A light wind blew up from the moors, carrying the foul reek of blood. He slipped from his mare's back. Kerin followed and they embraced, drunk with exhaustion and relief. A party of Kentishmen was coming back.

'Where in hell is Garagon?' Edlym burst out. To his credit, he looked as if he had been in a fight. 'Brennius is dead. He didn't deserve it. He fought like a hero.'

Two Kentish warriors were trudging back up the hill, carrying Brennius's body between them. A sword stroke had sliced away one side of his head. The cuts on his forearms showed that he had died fighting. Vortigern patted Edlym's shoulder. 'Go on; take him back to the camp. We'll bury him with honour.' He looked up as Lud approached. His horse was gashed about the neck and looked ready to drop. Lud hesitated. 'What?' Vortigern asked, tensing.

'Lord, Publius Luca's taken a spear,' Lud said. 'He's asking to see you.'

Vortigern closed his eyes. 'Oh, merciful God,' he murmured. Kerin followed him down the hill. They had laid Publius out on the ground and covered as much of him as they could with someone's torn cloak. The head of the spear, a splintered fragment of shaft still attached, was protruding from a point just below his ribcage.

'I can see you've been in a fight, sir,' he whispered, as Vortigern dropped down beside him. Vortigern laughed quietly.

'Nothing's changed, commander. I'll always be a thorn in someone's side.'

Publius Luca smiled faintly. With the last of his strength, he raised his left arm. He was wearing the ring he had taken from his scout's hand, next to a simple gold wedding band of his own. 'Can you take these rings and give them to my wife? I don't trust anyone else to do it.'

'I'll keep them for you,' Vortigern said, easing the rings from his fingers. 'But you can give them to her yourself when we get back to Londinium.'

Publius coughed slightly. 'I do hope so, sir. I've been putting money aside to build myself a villa for years, and I'd hate anyone else to have it after all this.'

Vortigern looked despairingly at the wound. A froth of

blood and air was bubbling around the point of the spear. 'Kerin, get Marcellus,' he said sharply. 'Get Morvid.'

'Macsen's already gone to warn them, lord,' Lud said. 'And Derfyn's gone for a wagon.'

Publius Luca attempted to sit up. 'Listen to me,' he gasped, gritting his teeth against the pain. 'Don't let any of them take this victory from you. They will if they can, you know.'

'Yes,' Vortigern said. 'I know they will.' He gave a sudden grin. 'You'd better live and build your villa, commander. I'll need to hide in the hypocaust when they come to chop my head off.'

The wagon creaked to a halt beside them. The blankets in the back were already stained with other men's blood. Lud and Hefin brought a litter. As they prepared to lift him onto it, Publius reached for Vortigern's hand. 'Can I take it that you don't blame me personally for what happened all those years ago?'

'I don't,' Vortigern said. 'I never did, least of all now.'

They watched as the wagon moved off. Hengist and Horsa came panting up the hill with their warriors, some carrying their dead and injured. Horsa's right eye was closed and swollen. Hengist was cut about the arms, but given the fearless abandonment he had shown in battle, he had come off lightly. He smiled and slapped Vortigern on the back. 'What a victory! Odin's blood, the Picts are brave, brave warriors. The best I've fought. Do you think my men did well, lord?'

'You fought like dragons, Hengist,' Vortigern said. 'You'll be well rewarded, I promise you.'

Horsa gave him a curious look. 'We've won, lord!' he exclaimed, shaking Vortigern's shoulder. 'It's time to rejoice!'

'I know,' Vortigern said, 'but my friend Publius Luca is badly wounded, and may not live.'

'The old Roman,' Hengist said. 'A wise man and a valiant warrior. May Odin be merciful to him.' He turned to roar encouragement to his warriors and led them away through the milecastle.

'What are you thinking about now?' Vortigern asked. Kerin wondered what trick of the features always betrayed him.

'Publius Luca would have liked to hear you say that,' he said. 'Perhaps you should say it to his face, while you can.'

They turned away from the battlefield where some of the warriors were still collecting their wounded, catching up stray horses and looting the bodies. The rest were drifting away south-eastwards, leaving the remains to the wind and the carrion birds. Kerin and Vortigern rode through the milecastle, down into the trough of the *vallum* and towards the camp. Above them the military road was packed solid with horsemen and foot-soldiers; Cambrians and Kernow men, Saxons and Romans, men of Kent and Glevum, singing raucously, all devoted friends for once.

'Listen!' Kerin raised his hand. A light wind disturbed the scrubby hawthorns, making them hiss and creak. The two horsemen rode cautiously forward. Garagon of Kent was sitting with his back against a boulder, weeping into his hands. His horse was grazing nearby. It hadn't even broken sweat. A twig cracked under Eryr's hooves. Garagon stared up in an agony of shame and fear.

'I'm sorry,' he choked, scrambling to his feet and backing away.

'You gutless little bastard,' Vortigern said. 'How could you leave your warriors to fight and die?'

Garagon shook his head impotently. Kerin could find nothing to say to him. They turned their horses back towards the track. Vortigern looked over his shoulder.

'Brennius is dead,' he said casually. Behind them a howl of dismay was followed by rattling hooves.

'Someone should go after him,' Kerin said. 'Someone should drag him back and make him look at Brennius.'

'Do you want to do it?' Vortigern asked. Kerin sighed.

'No. I haven't got the strength.'

'No. And neither have I. But don't worry. There are some things you can't outrun, even on a fast horse.'

The drum of hooves faded, and was soon overlaid by another sound; the ring and thud of spades on rock and compacted earth. Ahead of them, at the fringe of the encampment, the grave-diggers were starting to bury the dead.

30

The camp was in chaos. The seriously wounded were waiting in line for attention from Marcellus or Morvid, or their assistants. The less seriously wounded, almost everyone else, were washing themselves in the stream and patching up each other's cuts and bruises. Horses wandered everywhere, all exhausted, some terribly injured, while the stable lads did their best to calm them and deal with the damage. The dead had been laid out at the edge of the wood, awaiting burial or cremation, according to their creed. Kerin went into the tent where Morvid was working, assisted by Marc, Cenydd and Cheldric. Even Malan had found his way in, and was binding wounds. Four men were lying on tables inside; two had lost arms, one had had an eye gouged out and the other was cut open across the midriff. Kerin's offer of help was brushed aside. 'Warriors aren't much help in a sickroom,' Morvid said. Kerin went out into the cooling air. There were still a few hours of daylight left, but he did not know what to do with them. He felt bereft of purpose, and the camp was full of others just like him; exhausted men who were too tired and too overstrung to sleep. A few paces away was a large tent, its entrance guarded by two slender young men in short-sleeved tunics. Inside, under the oil lamps which threw unnerving shadows on the white walls, Marcellus was attempting to save the life of Publius Luca.

Kerin walked round the camp for the fourth time,

trying to find those he most cared for. Eldof was directing the burial of the dead Christians. Lud was overseeing the cremation of the dead pagans. Brother Padarn was blessing everyone regardless, and he had earned so much respect that even the druids' men were grateful. Elir and the stable lads were treating the wounded horses. Gwyndaf and Cadfan were killing the ones that could not be saved. Derfyn was sitting under a tree, weeping for Asyn.

Kerin went back to Vortigern's tent and lit the lamps with a brand from the fire. The wound in his head was beginning to throb. He felt almost ashamed for noticing it, in the face of so much suffering. As the enormity of what they had done began to take hold, he sank down beside the fire and shook. Never had he imagined what a few thousand corpses would look like. The grotesque jumble of headless torsos, mutilated hands and unidentifiable chunks of flesh and bone, chopped up like meat in a slaughterhouse; the blood pooling in the marsh, the slimy welter of guts and shit and mud. Kerin stared down at his silver crucifix and Gael's tiny ring, both smeared with blood. His own? Another man's? Horse blood? He took the precious ring and pressed it to his lips, blood and all. One way or another I will find my way back, he thought. Hefydd's little cauldron was still there. Kerin stirred up the flames and pushed it into them. As a thin line of steam begin to rise, a shadow fell across the entrance of the tent and Marcellus came in. He lowered himself onto the blanket beside Kerin and closed his eyes.

'Publius is alive,' he said. 'The gods know, that was the hardest thing I've ever done. But the spearhead is out, and I have repaired as much damage as I could. He's as weak as a kitten, of course; if the wound festers, it could still kill him. But if he survives the next few days, I think he may yet build his villa and see his grandchildren grow up.'

Kerin smiled; then he laughed and hugged Marcellus around the shoulders, something the haruspex was not much used to, judging by his astonished expression. Kerin offered him a beaker of Hefydd's brew.

'Drink it yourself, my young friend. Your work is done, but I have to keep my hand steady.' He explored the spear wound above Kerin's ear. 'This is painful, to be sure.'

'A little,' Kerin admitted, 'but it hardly seems fair to mention it.'

'Stay where you are, and I'll come back with some soothing ointment for it. It'll be in the nature of light relief for me. The items you entrusted to me are safe, but will keep.'

Kerin topped up the beaker, sipped and closed his eyes. When he opened them again, Vortigern was standing in front of him. 'That thing in your head's still bleeding, lord,' he said. 'You should get it seen to.'

'How could I?' Vortigern said accusingly. 'The camp's full of men with one leg, and half a head, and –'

'I know,' Kerin said, raising his hand. Then he smiled. 'Publius Luca's alive, though. Marcellus thinks he'll recover.'

Vortigern leaned on the tent-pole and laughed, exhausted but elated. Marcellus came in with the ointment for Kerin's wound. He looked and blinked.

'What's the matter, you old fool?' Vortigern said irritably. Marcellus smiled politely.

'I've seen less blood on a sacrificial beast, lord,' he said. 'If even a quarter of it is yours, I think you should let me deal with it. Publius will live, though, please the gods. He'll never lift a sword in anger again, but I'm sure that's the least of your concerns.' He handed the little pot of ointment to Kerin and folded his arms. 'Now then, lord, I really think that you should come back to my tent and let me investigate. You may be King of all the Britons, but as far as I'm aware, that distinction has never prevented anyone from bleeding to death. Your people can't spare you, and you are not immortal, whatever you or they may think.' He looked up expectantly. To Kerin's surprise, Vortigern had nothing to say. Too weakened or too taken aback to argue, possibly both, he gave a non-committal shrug and followed Marcellus out of the tent.

31

Dusk was gathering and a bright half moon hung above the bare wood when Lud came from the village to announce that the landlord of the alehouse had been good to his word. Somehow in that ravaged countryside he had managed to find ale, and it was set out under the trees so that the men could help themselves for as long as it lasted. What could be more inviting? Kerin flung on a cloak and joined the general drift towards the village. The landlord had brought a wagon full of drinking vessels; tankards, cups, bowls, drinking horns, anything which might feasibly hold liquid. He was busily handing them out and the warriors were filling them up from a row of huge casks set up on trestles.

'We've emptied every town in the North for this,' he said proudly, passing Kerin a tankard. 'I've been hiding it in the barn. God knows what I'd have done with it if you'd lost. Everyone was happy to give it; by God, we'd give you anything.'

His gratitude seemed to be shared by the local girls, who were flocking around the trestles helping the warriors fill their drinking vessels. Vortigern was in the middle of the crowd, talking to his sons. They seemed completely good-humoured and happy with each other. Kerin turned, sensing a presence, and found himself next to Hengist. It was beyond him to be unfriendly under such circumstances.

'Come on,' he said, smiling. 'Let's get some ale.' He

grabbed another tankard and they elbowed their way towards the casks. Vortigern had left his sons with the girls. Marcellus had bound both his arms with heavy bandages and patched up the gash above his brow. Hengist watched him moving amongst the warriors.

'When I first landed in your country, men told me that he had no equal on the field of battle,' he said. 'I thought they were saying that to make me fear him. Now I know that they spoke the truth.'

Kerin looked up from filling the tankards. 'You should be glad that we're fighting on the same side, then.'

'I am,' Hengist said. 'And I pray that it will ever be so. Not because I fear to fight you, but because there would be no point. We should be friends, your people and mine. I know I came here for gain, but when men fight together as we have today, the victory is the payment. We've all seen enough blood. We'd be fools to shed each other's.' Kerin could not disagree with anything Hengist had said, but he was unable to manage anything more than a polite smile of acquiescence. Hengist looked piqued. 'You don't like me, Kerin Brightspear, do you.'

'I didn't say so,' Kerin said, handing him the ale.

'No, but a man does not always have to speak to say what he means. Is it fair? Did we not fight well today?'

'Yes,' Kerin said. 'Like demons, and that's more than I can say for some of ours. But I'm wary of any man who fights for money. I've only ever fought for one reason. Gain has nothing to do with it.'

'It is different for you, though,' Hengist said. 'You have grown up at the king's side, in a country with rich corn lands and fine fat cattle. I have had to fight all my life, just to keep my people fed. You say I fight for money, but I do not. I fight for my family, and my warriors, and their families; for all the people who depend on me. You would do the same, if you are half the man I think you are.'

'I would,' Kerin conceded. Hengist nodded.

'Come then. We will never be friends, you and I, but to-night we should drink together as brothers. To refuse would be an insult to the men who have died.'

'I agree,' Kerin said, and shook the Saxon's proffered hand. However deep his mistrust, whatever the future might hold, he knew that in this much Hengist was right. Brave men had given their lives this day, and it mattered not a jot if they were Britons, Romans or Saxons, or which god they had called on when they saw the axe coming down. Tonight they were all owed the same debt of gratitude, and Kerin would not be the man to dishonour it. 'Come on,' he said, 'let's go inside and join the others.'

There was hardly any room left inside the alehouse. Vortigern had commandeered the largest table, joined by Lud, Gorlois, Kat, Paschent and Eldof. Two tables ran at right-angles to it, with Gwyndaf, Horsa, Varro and Oswi the Horseman amongst their occupants. Vortigern waved, slapped the table and made everyone move up. Kerin and Hengist squeezed in on the bench beside him. Kerin drained his tankard, drowning in a flood of joy and relief. Vortigern chuckled and cuffed him across the head. It looked as if he had decided to allow himself a little enjoyment of his victory after all. The place reeked of stale sweat and horse dung, but no-one gave a damn.

'Ale for the Lord of Glevum!' Kat bawled. 'Let's see if he can drink as well as he talks!'

Eldof slapped him on the back as jugs of ale arrived, and they broke into a rowdy battle song. Most of the men joined in, bellowing at the tops of their voices. Kerin pounded his tankard in time and prayed that Vortigern would get drunk before he noticed that Rufus was missing. Hengist clambered over the table to join his brother and Oswi. They started throwing their arms about, boasting about the number of men they had slaughtered.

'This thing between you and Hengist,' Vortigern said. Kerin turned.

'Lord?'

'The thing you mentioned in Kent. I've seen it working now. You and Hengist can't stand the sight of each other.'

Kerin sipped his ale. 'As I told you. I don't trust Hengist at all. One way or another, I think he's deceiving you. Or will deceive you, in some way I can't fathom yet. And Hengist doesn't like me because I know it, and might put a stop to it.'

'There's no deception,' Vortigern said impatiently. 'I'm only doing what the Romans did. Would they have built their empire without the barbarians they paid to fight for them? No. And would we have beaten the Picts as soundly as we did without the Saxons? We would not. You *know* we would not. Even Eldof agrees, and he'd hang me from the nearest tree if he could. So are we both wrong? Were the Romans wrong?'

'No,' Kerin said. 'Everything you've said is right. We'd probably have had the victory anyway, but it wouldn't have been the slaughter that it was. We might have had to come back and do it again next year. And tonight's not the time to argue about it, anyway. The Saxons gave everything, as much as any of us did. It would be a disgrace not to honour them for it.'

'Yes,' Vortigern said. 'A shame and a disgrace. So unless Hengist proves you right, keep quiet about this for now.' He looked around the crowded alehouse and the tankard halted halfway to his lips. 'Where's Rufus?' Kerin said nothing. Vortigern seized Katigern's arm. 'Where's your brother?'

'My brother?' Kat said evasively. 'Which one?'

'Your older brother, you simpleton. The other one's sitting next to you. Where is he? Why isn't he here, drinking to our victory?'

'He's outside with the warriors.' Kat looked as if he'd sooner have been anywhere else.

'*Why?* I left Macsen and Hefin with our men. Does Rufus think they need his help?'

Kat's eyes dropped. 'Father, he says he won't drink with the pagans.'

Vortigern stared up at the cobwebbed roof. 'He won't drink with the pagans. Did you hear that, Lud? My son won't drink with the pagans. Go and find him. Find him, and bring him to me. I don't care how you do it.' Lud grimaced and went out. Kerin rose to follow him but Vortigern had anticipated the movement. 'Oh no. Not you.'

Kerin sank back into his seat. As they waited, Hengist moved across and occupied Lud's place. Oswi passed him a pitcher of something which looked like *falernum*. If Kerin was right about the wine, it was hard to imagine how anyone could have got hold of it in the bleak desert of the North, unless they had brought it with them.

'A gift for the victor,' Hengist said jovially, filling Vortigern's tankard. The gesture made, he began laughing and jesting with Katigern. After a while Kerin noticed that Hengist had stopped drinking. His tankard stood on the table in front of him, still almost full. He's keeping his head clear for a reason, Kerin thought. After a while, Hengist leaned forward on his elbows. 'Lord, may I speak?'

Vortigern was watching the doorway. 'Not now,' he said.

'I fear for the safety of my people, lord. Many of your warriors hate us, although we fought well today. Would it, perhaps, be possible to grant us another poor piece of land like the one in Kent? Just large enough to build a few houses and a stockade, and to tie up two or three ships? Then we could defend ourselves, and you would always be able to call on us. If the Picts troubled your seaways again, for instance. Or if some of these lords were not as loyal as they should be.'

'Lord, think,' Kerin said quietly. Hengist glared venomously at him.

'Will you grant me that, lord? Tomorrow we shall return to our ships, to sail back to Kent. If you could give me an answer before we leave –'

There was a movement at the door. Rufus appeared, flanked by Lud and Hefin. There was an ugly red bruise below his right eye. From the stiffness of his bearing, Kerin guessed that the point of Lud's dagger was at his back.

'Lord?' Hengist persisted.

'Go,' Vortigern said, his eyes not leaving Rufus's. 'This can wait.' As Hengist withdrew, he gave Kerin a knowing little smile. Lud propelled Rufus towards Vortigern's table. The men shifted uneasily in their seats. Vortigern leaned forward. 'Your brother tells me that you won't drink with these men.'

'That's right,' Rufus said. Vortigern leapt to his feet.

'Why? It's an insult to them, and to their dead. Look how many they've lost. You've spent all day slaughtering Picts with them, so why can't you drink with them, for God's sake?'

Rufus folded his arms. 'I won't do it.' Vortigern shoved his tankard forward. Rufus stared back. Britons and Saxons muttered amongst themselves.

'Drink!' Vortigern bellowed, forcing the tankard against Rufus's lips. Rufus turned aside. The wine spilled down his tunic and soaked into the earth floor. Vortigern hurled the tankard against the wall. 'I could kill you for this,' he breathed.

'Do it, then,' Rufus said. 'If it's death or drinking with Hengist, you'll have to kill me, because I swear on the cross of Jesus Christ that I won't do it.'

Vortigern's fist pounded the table. 'Fight me man to man, then, if that's what you want.'

'It's not what I want,' Rufus shouted. 'But better that than drink with these godless bastards. I'll meet you in the clearing next to the river. It may as well be a fight to the death.' He turned and stalked out of the alehouse.

* * *

The river was shallow there, babbling noisily over a bed of shingle and scattered rocks. The warriors had lit fires in the thickets on the north side and they sparked and crackled in the darkness, sending columns of blue smoke into the still air. The moon was up and cast a ghostly white light over the clearing.

'Rufus, you can't do this,' Kerin panted, half running to keep up with his blood brother as he marched towards the river.

'Why not? What else can I do?' Rufus stopped as they reached the edge of the clearing. 'What else can I do, Kerin? Tell me, if you can.'

Kerin threw his hands up in despair. 'You could have drunk, for God's sake. You shamed him in front of all of them. These men have bled and died for us, and you've spat on them. He *has* to fight you now, or lose his honour.'

'Honour?' Rufus said. 'What do you think I'd have lost, if I'd obeyed him?'

'Rufus, he's your father. Not only that, he's lost enough blood to drop an ox. He's drunk and his sword-arm's cut to pieces.'

'Well, that should make us just about equal, then.' Rufus gave a bitter smile. 'I've never had a hope with the sword, according to my father.'

'Look, you know that's nonsense,' Kerin protested. 'Men say these things, especially in battle training. But you take it with a pinch of salt, don't you?'

'No,' Rufus said. 'Not in my case. So let's find out who's right. He'll kill me anyway unless I drink with Hengist. Better this way than hanged like a common thief.'

Kerin turned and walked to the river's edge, where Vortigern was sitting on his grey stallion. Gorlois of Kernow, barely able to believe what was happening, shook his head as Kerin passed him. Vortigern dismounted.

'Well? Does he really want to do this?'

'Yes, lord.' Kerin's voice was dull with defeat. Rufus's blood brother, the king's right arm – at least for a while – and yet it was beyond his power to stop these men from trying to kill each other.

'So be it, then,' Vortigern said. Across the clearing Rufus had been joined by Katigern, who looked terrified.

'Lord, you can't fight Rufus.'

'Why not? Because I might actually kill him?'

'Because you're not fit to fight anyone,' Kerin said brutally. 'You're dog-tired, you're drunk and your sword-arm's in a bandage. One slip and you're a dead man, because he'll do it this time, I promise you.'

'Let him,' Vortigern said, and walked out into the middle of the clearing. 'Rufus! Have you made your peace with God?'

Rufus came from the darkness and stood facing him. 'I did that long ago.'

The British warriors had gathered at the fringe of the wood. To their left, slightly apart, a crowd of Hengist's

Saxons. To the right, a tight little knot of Rufus's supporters, wild-eyed Idris to the fore. There wasn't a man there without a battle-wound. Everyone's clothes were blood-stained. Everyone was exhausted and wound up like a spring and slightly drunk. Everyone was armed. There was no way of knowing how this would end, whichever way the fight went. Dull Bened gave a great rumbling growl and began banging the end of his spear-shaft on the hard ground. Others joined in. Vortigern laughed hoarsely and whipped out his sword. Slowly, Rufus drew his.

'May the gods favour the righteous!' Hengist roared above the rising din. The two men circled each other warily. The warriors surged together, forming an unbroken ring around the clearing. Vortigern lunged forward. His sword-blade glinted in the moonlight. Rufus side-stepped neatly and the blade sliced the air. They circled each other again. Rufus's sword flashed out with the speed of a striking viper. The blade bit deep into Vortigern's right forearm. He recoiled with a howl of pain and astonishment. Blood spurted from the wound. He lunged forward and they closed, fighting hand to hand. The warriors roared them on. Rufus was wounded; just a shallow cut across the forehead, but enough to send blood trickling into his eyes. He brushed it aside and slashed the shoulder of his father's tunic. Blood was still streaming from Vortigern's arm as they battled towards the river bank. Eldof and his men backed away. Lud stared blankly, his lips framing an inaudible prayer. Kerin had never seen Rufus fight with such fury. Loose pebbles clattered down the bank as Vortigern was driven back towards the water.

'Rufus! Fight, man! You've got him now!'

The bellow had come from Katigern. Vortigern's arm froze in mid-stroke. He stared at his second son. Rufus sent the weapon spinning from his hand. The sword crashed amongst the rocks and the spell broke. Vortigern hurled himself sideways as Rufus's blade came down. Without even thinking, Kerin drew his own sword and tossed it to him. Vortigern turned on his son, hacked him back across the clearing and swung the sword with all his remaining strength. Rufus's weapon broke clean in half just above the handle. Helpless, he stumbled over a tree-root and fell sprawling on his back. Vortigern stood staring down at him, sobbing for breath, the point of his sword resting on Rufus's throat. Britons and Saxons swarmed around them, yelling and brandishing their weapons.

'Kill!' Oswi shouted. 'Kill the traitor!'

Rufus looked up. 'Go on,' he panted. 'It's what you want.'

Gritting his teeth, Vortigern gripped the sword with both hands and drove the point into the earth. 'Get up,' he gasped. Rufus staggered to his feet, wiping blood from his face. 'Now go. Get out of my sight. And if you ever set foot in Henfelin again, I'll burn you alive.'

'You won't have to, father,' Rufus said, staring at the blood-soaked ground. 'I won't come back while Hengist sits at your table.'

Vortigern turned away. 'Don't call me father. You're no son to me after this.'

'So be it,' Rufus said. 'I've made my choice.' He picked up his broken blade and trudged off towards the edge of the wood. The Sword of God hurried after him. However convinced they were of God's protection, no-one wanted to test its efficacy against the Cambrian army. Vortigern glanced wildly about.

'Well? Does anyone else want to fight me? What about you, Kat?'

Katigern stared at his father, tears streaming. He ran after

Rufus, crashing away through the underbrush. The rest of the warriors dispersed, some with uneasy backward glances. The Saxons marched off singing heartily. Vortigern stood in the centre of the moonlit clearing, alone but for Kerin.

'Well,' he said gruffly, 'this time he has really gone.'

'Yes, lord. God's won, I'm afraid.'

Vortigern stared at his arm, gashed almost to the bone. 'You know, I never thought he'd do it,' he said, with grudging admiration.

'He's your son.' Kerin said.

Vortigern gave him a bitter look. 'I have no sons. Rufus has gone for good now, and soon Kat will go too.' He raised his hand. 'Yes, don't deny it. You saw him. He'll go soon, if not tonight, because Rufus has frightened him to death. And Paschent – well, Paschent will do what Paschent wants, as usual.' He bent to retrieve his sword and sank on one knee, suddenly dizzy with loss of blood. Kerin hurried over and helped him to his feet. Vortigern brushed him away impatiently. 'Well? What about you?'

'What about me, lord?'

'He's your friend.' Vortigern avoided his eyes. 'Your blood-brother. You could take his side – Eldof's side. They'd give you Bertil's daughter on a platter as a gift of thanks. Will you go to him? To them? To her?'

Kerin bent to pick up the sword and handed it back. After a day of such terror and slaughter, he barely felt capable of moving, let alone answering a question like that. 'Go to Marcellus or Morvid,' he said. 'If you don't let one of them look at that, you deserve to bleed to death.' He walked slowly back across the clearing and jerked his own sword from the ground.

'Kerin!' Vortigern called after him. Kerin turned. 'Do what no other man will do. Speak the truth to my face. Should I give Hengist what he wants?'

'No lord, you should not,' Kerin said. But you will, he thought, as he trudged away through the woods. You will make this one small, irreproachable concession, so time-honoured, so well deserved; and it will open the hair-line crack. The tiny, barely perceptible fracture which one day will split and gape until the bone breaks and the abyss opens beneath us.

By the time Kerin returned to the camp, the cold, grey light of the new day was seeping upwards from the east. He stood quite still at the edge of the woodland, beside a wind-bent ash, and looked down over the dark, quivering mass of men and animals; the endless rows of tents and the huge circle of wagons. The warriors were sleeping, poleaxed by exhaustion and drink; dumb brutes, most of them, who would rise to any man's call, if he could find the right levers to crank them into motion.

Only two lights were burning in the encampment, apart from the watchmen's lanterns around the perimeter; one in Marcellus's sanatorium, the other in the large, pretentious tent belonging to Eldof of Glevum. Black shadows lay along its walls, men seated around a table, heads bent forward in a conspirators' huddle. Kerin leaned against the trunk of the stunted ash, struggling to see the gentle, open-hearted lad of his golden childhood in the man Rufus had become. He wondered if that man understood what was stirring in the frozen darkness now, or exactly what he had killed in the clearing beside the river. Had he seen the murderous, crooked road open ahead of them, or was he so dazzled by the blinding light of the one true god that he had seen only a vision of beauty and eternal love?

A spear's throw from the physicians' tent, the Saxons were stretched out under the open sky; most of them sleeping, a few still chatting softly as they watched the dawn come up over the moors. Not far away, a curl of foul smoke was still rising from the pit, where the stable lads had been burning the dead horses. Above the muted crackle of the doused fire, Kerin could have sworn that he heard Hengist laughing.

32

The messenger bowed from the waist.

'The Lord Kerin Brightspear?' he enquired politely.

'Yes,' Kerin said. His mount, the well-drilled bay saddle horse of a dead cavalryman, pricked its ears and stood to attention. His dress marked him out as a man of rank, he supposed; the finely-stitched grey tunic and breeches, the black travelling cloak, discreetly lined with fox fur; a wealthy landowner's travelling clothes, bought for a song in the market at Eburacum. A year ago he would have bridled at the honorific, but not any more. Two men excepted, he no longer deferred to anyone. The messenger opened his saddlebag and drew out something slim and flat – a writing tablet, probably. It was wrapped in sacking and secured with black cords, the knot sealed with a blob of cream-coloured wax.

'For you, lord.' He held out the package. Kerin took it. The messenger wasn't much more than a boy, thin, with olive skin and tousled black hair; Roman or Hispanic blood, possibly. His escort was a fat thug with scarred hands and a boozer's nose. The horses were caked in dust and sweat and looked as if they'd come a fair distance.

'Who's it from?' Kerin asked, keeping his eyes from the package.

'I don't know, lord. They don't tell us stuff like that. One of the other lads handed it over at Durobrivae. I'm to say that there's no need of a reply.'

Kerin turned, sensing a presence. Gwyndaf had come to see what was happening. He must have decided, from some distance, that the two new arrivals were nothing to worry about. If Gwyndaf had discerned any form of threat, at least one of them would have been lying dead in the road by now.

'What's this about?' he asked.

'I don't know yet.' Kerin held up the sealed package. 'Take these two to Cheldric and tell him to feed them. Whatever's in this, it's nothing to do with them.'

'Thank you, lord!' and 'God bless you, sir!' exclaimed the two horsemen, almost weeping with gratitude and astonishment. Not many people bothered to feed the messengers, by the look of things. Gwyndaf chuckled, shaking his head at this pathetic display of generosity, and led them away. They would pass several hundred mounted warriors, many displaying gruesome battle wounds; strings of injured horses; thousands of tramping foot soldiers, cheery enough despite an array of bruises and bloody bandages; the closed carriages of the exhausted physicians; a throng of swaying baggage mules and beyond them a rumbling procession of horse-drawn wagons and ox carts carrying tents, weapons, battle-loot and all the men who were too badly injured to ride or march. By the time the messengers reached the cooks' carts, they would have seen enough grotesque leg stumps, gouged eyes, slashed-off ears and handless arms to remind them that a mouthful of dust and a few saddle sores were a fair price for staying out of a war.

Kerin looked down at the sealed message, lying inertly in his hands like a phial of poison waiting to be tipped down his throat. Someone else would have to read it for him. But Kerin did not need his powers of foresight to know that it would be bad news. In the whole of his acquaintance, only a handful of people could read and write well enough to frame a letter, and almost all of them were here, riding south with the army. Of the absentees, most were eliminated by one criterion or another. Severus Maximus would write directly to Vortigern; indeed, the praetor had already written, his messengers unmistakable in their smart red livery. Titus Luca would write to his father. Iustig would never do it. Dimos had no reason. And Gael – who knew if Gael could read, let alone put stylus to tablet? It was not the first thing a man thought to ask a girl, when his main concern was to bed her before someone came to batter the door down. It could be Abbot Giraldus, he supposed; but as his mind toyed with the idea, the unwelcome truth elbowed its way forward and stared him in the face with its sullen logic. The letter would be from Rufus, and it would tell him something he did not wish to know.

'Well?' Gwyndaf said. Kerin prickled with annoyance and embarrassment.

'I can't read the bastard, can I,' he snapped.

Gwyndaf threw his head back and laughed. 'I'd taken it for granted that you could, after growing up under Vortigern's roof. Did he save it for the sons, then?'

'Not at all. I was packed off to Father Iustig with them, but I usually managed to sneak away and spend all day swimming in the river. Someone should have kicked my arse. I can understand some Latin because Vortigern speaks it like a Roman, but as for this –'

'Take it to the monk,' Gwyndaf said. 'Padarn, the one they're calling the warriors' priest. He's bound to be able to read, after being shut up in a monastery for years. I know he was raging when you killed the old man, but I think you'll find he's got over that.'

'Why should he? He'd known that woman for years. I killed her father-in-law, in front of her and her children.'

'Her father-in-law deserved what he got,' Gwyndaf said. 'In fact, he deserved a much dirtier death than you gave him. Someone had to tell the monk why, so I did.' He nodded. 'Go on. I'll lead until you come back.'

Padarn was driving a heavy wagon drawn by a pair of white oxen. Horatius, Marcellus's assistant, was perched alongside him, keeping an eye on the six invalids riding in the back. They had a vacant look about them, probably induced by battle-shock and a dose of whatever Marcellus used to pole-axe Vortigern's warhorse before stitching up the gash in her hindquarters. One man had had a leg amputated above the knee. Another had lost an arm, and probably an eye as well, judging by the bloody head-bandage. Kerin raised his hand and Padarn reined in the oxen. The other wagons flowed on past with their cargo of pain and misery.

'Can you ride?' Kerin asked Horatius.

'Er – yes, lord, not expertly but I can stay on,' said the young man, looking rather nervous.

'Alright, then. I need to talk to Brother Padarn, so jump on this horse and leave us

Horatius got down and Kerin legged him up onto the gelding's back. The animal was wearing its own traditional Roman saddle, high at the front and back, so there was plenty to reassure an uncertain rider. Kerin climbed aboard, took the reins and dropped the package into Padarn's lap.

'I hope you can read,' he said, as the oxen moved off again.

'I'm not the world's best. Came to it too late, I suppose. But yes, I can read and write, as long as it's not too compli-cated.' He paused. 'I don't like to open another man's letter.'

'I'm asking you to,' Kerin said. 'I can't read it myself, so I'm asking you. As a favour, and because I trust you.'

Padarn drew on one end of the fine black cord. The

301

bindings loosened and the pellet of wax fell, down between the planks of the seat onto the rutted track below. Kerin stared at the gently rolling rumps of the oxen, trying not to watch as Padarn's finger moved laboriously along the lines of characters. He waited for what seemed an eternity, racked by impatience and blind dread, and thought of the way Vortigern read, his eyes skimming vast sheets of script like a dragonfly over water. The monk glanced up.

'Well, it's from your friend, the Lord Vortimer.' He seemed reluctant to proceed.

'Yes, I'd guessed that much. What does he have to say?'

'Well, he says –'

'No,' Kerin said. 'Just read it out, word for word. Exactly as it's written.'

Padarn cleared his throat. '*To Kerin Brightspear, from the Lord Vortimer,*' he began.

'He calls himself that? To me?'

'Yes. You told me to read out exactly what's here, I thought –'

'Yes,' Kerin said, as the reins slid through his sweaty fingers. 'I'm sorry. Go on.'

The monk began again. '*To Kerin Brightspear from the Lord Vortimer, greetings. We did not part as friends, but it is not too late. The light of God has shown me the path I must take. Others have joined me, and more will come. I pray that you will be amongst them. My father does not own your soul. Meet me at the church of Saint Amphibalus in Sarum, on Saint Alban's day. If you do not come, I will know that you have made your choice.*'

Padarn looked up. 'That's it, then. That's all he says.'

'That's all!' Kerin said softly. He took the tablet from the monk, who retrieved the reins and chirruped to the oxen. He knew that he was looking at a declaration of war. 'It doesn't look like enough words to say all that.'

Padarn shrugged. 'That's Latin for you. It's more – what's the word? Concise.'

'Yes.' Kerin looked up. 'Do you understand what this means?'

'It means he's going to fight his father, if he can raise enough men to do it.'

'Yes,' Kerin said. 'He's not stupid. He won't do it unless he thinks he can win. But in the end, if he's strong enough, he will do it. There will be war.' He looked around at the wagons full of horribly damaged men. 'Again.'

Padarn stopped the cart. 'The night you killed Quintus Parvo. I don't hold anything against you for it. I had no idea what the man had done until Gwyndaf put me wise. It goes against everything I believe to kill a defenceless old bugger like that, but it shouldn't make things difficult between us. You helped me when I needed it, when no-one else would have done. I'd still do the same for you.'

'Look,' Kerin said. 'Please, can I ask you – '

'I won't breathe a word about this,' Padarn said, handing the letter back. 'And if you want to know when the feast of St Alban is, it's on the twenty-second day of the month the Romans call Junius. About ten weeks from now, if I haven't completely lost count. You might want to check with some-one like Publius Luca, who keeps a journal.'

Vortigern was riding with Gorlois. It was the first truly warm day of spring, and both men had shed their cloaks and heavy winter over-tunics. Whether its therapeutic effects were real or imagined, the sunlight seemed to benefit healing battle-wounds and overstretched muscles. There was a lively conversation going on, punctuated by laughter and the usual expansive gestures from Gorlois. Even the horses looked happy, enjoying the ambling pace of the oxen instead of their usual raking forced-march trot. The Roman road was in good repair, and the wagons bowled along easily across a level plain whose scattering of silver birches sparkled in the sun, their slender white trunks rising from a sea of bluebells.

'Aha!' Gorlois boomed as Kerin rode alongside. 'Come to crack the whip on the old men, then?'

Kerin grinned. If he had any whip-cracking to do, it would hardly be on these two.

'You couldn't crack your own knuckles riding that thing,' Vortigern said. 'What's the cripple's saddle for? To stop you falling off?'

'It's a good saddle.' Kerin said amiably. 'Well padded. Just the thing for a sore arse that's been stuck with a Pictish spear. I'm going – ' *to ride all the way to Londinium on it,* he was about to say; but the cheery statement ended in a yelp of surprise as the placid cavalry horse screeched and leapt forward, throwing him against the high pommel of the Roman saddle. The Bear of Kernow roared. Vortigern had leaned over and yanked the gelding's tail. Kerin righted himself, laughing and gasping for breath. Gorlois reached out and cuffed him over the head.

'I'm off to see my lads,' he said. 'One of you mad bastards is enough for me.'

Vortigern watched him go, still chuckling to himself. He had been in good spirits over the past weeks. Perhaps it was hard not to be when every town and village along the road, alerted by delirious warriors galloping south, had come out in force to cheer the victors. In a small, impoverished settlement, someone who must have seen the army pass by on its way north had fashioned his own triumphal banner; a worn bed sheet strung between two thatched houses, the rough-edged image of a dragon's head daubed across it in red ochre. Perhaps any man would have been a little drunk on all that glory. But Vortigern had read something in Kerin's face.

'What?' he asked.

'This,' Kerin said, and drew the tablet from his saddlebag. Vortigern gestured to him and they pulled their horses aside into the fringe of trees. It was a place of ethereal, unseemly beauty; the pale young birch leaves fluttering in the light wind; the tiny twittering birds hunting insects over the bluebells. Vortigern took the tablet. He read it, absorbed its contents and calculated their implications in the time it had taken Padarn to loose the bindings. It was impossible to judge whether he had been expecting this or not.

'What will you do?' he asked.

'What do you mean, what will I do?' Kerin had not meant to sound affronted, but the question was not the one he had expected. 'You can't think I'll join him.'

'No. But will you go to Sarum? Send someone else? Send a reply?'

'No,' Kerin said. 'The messenger had been told to say that no reply was required.' I could send a few trained killers instead, he thought; but he was not convinced that that was something Vortigern would wish to hear, even now. 'Anyway, Rufus is right. If I don't go, he'll know what it means. Not that he didn't know it already. He'd have killed you without a second thought if I hadn't thrown you my sword.'

'Yes,' Vortigern said. 'I know.'

He was more shaken than he looked, probably. Kerin would have given anything not to continue with what he had to say; but he remembered how he had felt when Publius Luca told him about Quintus Parvo and Isca. Whatever the consequences, he knew that they were his to deal with.

'There are two things I haven't told you. The first won't be a surprise. Eldof and his people have already been plotting against you. I overheard them talking in the tent. Just before the battle, so there was no point in saying anything then. All the Glevum men were there. Varro threw a table or something and stormed out. Rufus wasn't involved, but he was back and fore to that tent all the time, so Eldof must have told him. I've no idea how far it's gone.' Vortigern snapped the tablet in half and handed it back. Kerin slipped the two halves into his saddlebag. He would burn them later. There was no way to deaden the blow, so he chose to be direct. 'Rufus has been to Gallia. Do you remember that time in Londinium, when we couldn't find out where he was? It must have been then. I've no idea what happened, or who else was with him, but I do know that they were there to raise arms against you. Perhaps to meet others who have the same intention.'

Vortigern had turned white. The scar above his brow stood out, an ugly purple. 'Why in God's name didn't you tell me this before?'

'Because I couldn't see what good it would do,' Kerin said. 'I was told the morning after Constans was killed. It was in confidence, so I can't say who told me. But a man of honour and integrity, completely on our side. He told me because he couldn't face telling you. And neither could I, if the truth be told. You'd just become king. You had enough to contend with. And anyway, what could you have done? Broken with Rufus? Split your alliance in half? I decided that there'd be time enough to tell you, if something happened to make it unavoidable. And now it has.'

Vortigern rode his horse round in a circle; out to the edge of the birch wood and back again. Kerin waited for him. In the branches above his head, little warblers sang; *chiff chaff, chiff chaff.* For evermore, that sweet, blameless song would remind him of this horrible moment. Vortigern reined in beside him. The Pike didn't like the cavalry horse, and started blowing and baring his teeth. Vortigern spoke sharply to him, impatient with the animal for once.

'Who read the letter for you?' he asked.

'Brother Padarn. I could have brought it straight to you, I suppose, but I wanted to know what was in it first. You needn't worry about Padarn; he'll keep his mouth shut. But even he could see where this is leading.' Vortigern said nothing; watching, as Kerin had, the slow procession of damaged men and animals. He flexed his sword arm, still bound with the heavy bandage which Morvid had applied after Rufus cut it to the bone. 'I can't believe he called himself the Lord Vortimer!' Kerin exclaimed. He took a deep breath, knowing that it was up to him to hold things steady 'We do have a little time. Padarn says it's around ten weeks until the feast of St Alban. I don't think Rufus will do much unless something forces his hand. He's not stupid enough to confront you until he has the numbers. And most of the decent fighting men are here with us.'

'Yes,' Vortigern said. 'But who knows if we can keep them? They think they're invincible at the moment. It's no-one's fault. It's the way men are. It happens every time.'

'Will you tell Publius Luca?' Kerin asked. Vortigern did not reply. 'Lord?' Kerin said.

'Tell him for me,' Vortigern said, and rode away towards the moving mass of men and animals without another word.

33

Gwyndaf the standard-bearer examined the dagger he had drawn, spat on the blade and ran his finger gently along the cutting edge.

'I can go down there and kill him for you if you like,' he said.

'No,' Kerin said, slipping the letter back into his saddlebag.

'Because you still see him as a friend?' Gwyndaf said, with unveiled disgust.

'No. Because if we killed him now, the priests would have a martyr. And Vortigern's enemies would have an excuse.'

Gwyndaf replaced the dagger at his belt, alongside the sling and the bone-handled filleting knife. 'You're still not indifferent, though.'

'I can't be,' Kerin said. 'I've loved him like a brother for my whole life. And that didn't change, through all the arguments and falling out. Nothing changed until that fight. And then he changed it himself.'

Gwyndaf chirruped to his mare and they moved off. 'I watched that. You probably didn't see me.'

'No. I thought you'd stayed at the camp.'

'I kept out of the way. Over in that thicket, where the horses were tied. I watched the whole thing. Rufus was lucky. He's a fine swordsman. But it would have been a different fight if Vortigern had been sober, and if he hadn't taken all those battle wounds.'

'I know,' Kerin said. 'I'm as good as Rufus, probably, but Vortigern has something else. It's not just skill or speed.'

'Anticipation,' Gwyndaf said. 'He knows what the other man's going to do, even a split second before the man knows it himself. You can't teach that. Derfyn's got it, up to a point. I've never had it. I'm stronger, I'm more of a dog, but I don't have that. And of course, Vortigern doesn't have the smallest shadow of a doubt that he's better than anyone else who walks the earth. It's a hard call, to beat a man like that. Rufus was never going to kill him, though.'

Kerin reined back, letting the ranks of jogging horsemen stream past. 'Of course he was. Vortigern was defenceless when Rufus knocked the sword out of his hand.'

'That's not what I mean,' Gwyndaf said. 'You threw Vortigern your sword. If he hadn't caught it, would you have stood there and let Rufus butcher him?'

'No. I wouldn't.'

'No,' Gwyndaf said. 'You'd have grabbed anything that came to hand and killed your best friend stone dead. In fact, Rufus should thank almighty God that his father did catch the sword. I don't think you'd have let him off the hook so easily. And neither would I. I was standing in that thicket with a stone in my sling, ready to go. It would have ended there, and we'd have had another body to bury.'

* * *

Vortigern had sequestrated the elegant carriage in Eburacum. Drawn by two horses, it had a covered back and windows with blinds which could be rolled down and secured in bad weather. The seats had been stripped out and replaced with a bed, a bench and a chest for medicines and personal necessities. The second of the men to whom Kerin still deferred was sitting propped up against a pile of cushions; Publius Luca, hailed Imperator by his victorious soldiers even as he lay fighting for his life in Marcellus's tent. Lucius was driving, whistling tunelessly as they travelled southwards, through countryside which grew gentler and greener by the mile. Kerin sat on the bench, poring over a book, while Publius ate the food Cheldric had prepared for him.

'What's this about?' he asked.

'Julius Caesar's conquest of Britain,' Publius Luca said. 'You gave him a hard time of it over here.'

Kerin took the empty bowl which Publius handed to him. Vortigern had returned the rings, he noticed. 'I've engaged a man to teach me to read. One of the praetor's scribes. I hope he's waiting in Londinium with some manuscripts and a bottomless bucket of patience.'

'Well done,' Publius said. 'It's never too late to learn, although that's easily said by a man with time to kill. Marcellus tells me that I have spent my last day in uniform.'

Kerin put the book down. 'I'm sure that'll please your family.'

'You'd be even more sure if you knew my wife,' Publius said. 'She's much fiercer than I am.'

Kerin held out the two halves of his letter. 'You'd better read this, commander.' Publius Luca fitted the broken tablet together and studied the script. A deep-throated growl broke from him. He slammed the tablet to the floor and turned to reach for a little stoppered bottle, gasping as the movement pulled on his wound.

'No, please, I've got to do these things for myself,' he said, as Kerin went to assist him. 'And Marcellus will have me on his altar with the goats if I don't drink this. Has Vortigern seen that thing?'

'Yes, I had to show it to him. Brother Padarn read it for

me, and I've told Gwyndaf. No one else knows, or should know. Vortigern asked me to tell you. I don't think he wanted to discuss it himself. I've no idea what he'll do. Nothing, probably. He could have killed Rufus after the battle if he'd wanted him dead. What would you do?'

'To that faithless little bastard?' Publius glared at the broken tablet.

'No. To Titus, if he'd just done his best to kill you.'

Publius looked up. There was a silence, broken by the creaking of the carriage and Lucius's tone-deaf whistling. 'I don't know. I can't even conceive of it.' He reached under the bed and drew out a writing tablet of his own. 'I've had a letter too, from Severus Maximus. It seems we've been granted a triumph. Do you know what that is?'

'Some sort of a procession?' Kerin asked.

'Yes,' Publius Luca sighed. 'A victory parade, if you like, complete with chariots, marching armies, musicians, captives in chains, wild beasts, acrobats - ' he raised his hands in resignation. 'I was planning to go quietly home to my wife, but I think it was too much for Severus and his friends to resist.'

The sound of hoofbeats interrupted him. Lud's nephew, Bened, rode up alongside, flung his reins to Lucius and climbed in. 'Sorry, commander. This can't wait.' Kerin and Publius Luca exchanged an uneasy glance. Most things washed straight over Dull Bened. 'One of the scouts just came back. Hefydd's boy, Mabon. There's a bunch of Saxons waiting by the road for us. About an hour away. Hengist and a few others. They're riding.' He guffawed and shook his woolly head. 'Saxons, riding! Nothing much, mind. Scruffy old ponies.'

Kerin gave Publius a wry smile. The quality of the horse-flesh was not the issue, whatever Bened thought. 'Does Vortigern know?' he asked.

'Yes, yes,' Bened said. 'I told him first. He's up at the front, with Gwyndaf and my uncle. Get Kerin, he said. Not another word. I saw your horse tied to the back of this contraption, so here I am.'

'Alright,' Kerin said. 'Go and find my lad Marc and tell him to bring me my warhorse. The mare, Eryr.'

Bened's bushy eyebrows shot up. 'We're not going to fight them, are we?'

'No, of course not. But I don't want to meet Hengist riding a Roman cavalry horse. It doesn't matter why. Please, Bened, just do as I've asked, or they'll be here before I'm ready.'

Bened raised his hands, gave Publius Luca a little half-bow and jumped out, bawling obscenities at Lucius as he rode away.

'What do you make of it?' the commander asked.

'Hengist wants more land,' Kerin said. 'He brought it up after the battle. He was very persuasive. He knows that our alliances aren't as sound as they look. He was trying to put himself forward as the honest soldier, the man we could depend on. Vortigern couldn't be bothered with it at the time. He told Hengist to come back in the morning. But then the fight happened. I haven't seen Hengist since; I thought they'd all gone back to Kent. But perhaps he was just biding his time, giving Vortigern time to think about what Rufus had done. What all the others might do.'

'That man's too clever by half,' Publius Luca said. 'I prefer my barbarian captains to be halfwits. Have you heard of Alaric the Visigoth?'

'No. If it's important, you'd better tell me.'

'Alaric was a barbarian leader. An ally of ours. Quite like Hengist, really – brave, resourceful, a brilliant battle-leader. Around twenty years ago, his people were living as settlers within the Empire. It was going well, but Alaric knew that he was strong enough to cause trouble, so he gave Rome a price for leaving the city alone. It was quite modest, really – no more than a single rich senator might accumulate in one year. But the rich men wouldn't pay up, so Alaric did exactly as he'd promised. He sacked Rome and left with everything he could grab, including the emperor's sister.'

Kerin gathered up the remains of his letter. 'Are you telling me that we should give Hengist more land, then?'

Publius Luca leaned back against the cushions and breathed deeply. It was probably true, as Marcellus said, that the spear had inflicted damage to his lungs which might never fully heal. 'Hear him out,' he said. 'We know the Saxons were once capable of raising an invasion force – that's why the Shore Forts were built. Anything could happen if we make enemies of them instead of allies. And don't misunderstand Vortigern's position. He doesn't trust Hengist, any more than you do.'

Kerin put the letter in his saddlebag and banged on the wall of the carriage, signalling Lucius to stop. 'I've no idea how much Vortigern has told you,' he said. 'About – well, the way I see things. The superstitious ones think I have dreams. I don't. When I was a child, Lud told me that Vortigern only tolerated me because they all thought I was a prophet. I didn't want to get thrown out, so I trained myself. To study people and work out why they did or didn't do things, and what the results might be. Quite often, I'm right. Hengist will betray us one day, in some way I can't fathom yet. But now, of course, it seems irrelevant. A distraction. He's going to come riding up this road, smiling like a bosom friend and offering us a big bunch of well-armed men. What the hell can I say to Vortigern? How can I possibly tell him to get rid of Hengist, when his own son might start a war against him?'

Publius looked up. 'You can't. And I will tell you something else. You might end up in command of this army, what's left of it, because if it lines up against Rufus, someone will have to tell it to fight. And it may not be Rufus's father.'

34

The sunlight was bright and brittle, the high moor alive with larks. Eryr had recovered enough to arch her neck and throw out her feet as Kerin rode towards the head of the marching army. He was not alone. He had Eldof of Glevum and his formidable chief warrior, Varro. He had Edlym of Kent and Andrius, a cousin to brave, fallen Brennius. He had Gorlois of Kernow and his jaunty brother, Gerdan; Hefydd, Hefin and Derfyn of the Cambrian spearhead, and Lucius Arrius, commander of cavalry, who had had to grit his teeth and ignore his leg wound. He even had Brother Padarn, back in his brown clerical robe and sporting a modest crucifix. It would do Hengist no harm to feel the heat of the monk's steadfast faith. Any man who could believe that Roman fortresses were built by giants might be susceptible to a spiritual shock. Padarn excepted, each man had been told to bring the companion he would have chosen to watch his back in a hopeless, outnumbered fight. They were a formidable-looking crew.

Vortigern heard the approaching horsemen and turned in the saddle. His eyes narrowed.

'I sent for you,' he said. 'Not this mothers' meeting.'

'It's necessary,' Kerin said. 'Hengist needs to think that we're as united as we should be, not as divided as we are. And anyway, whatever he's coming to ask for, if you decide to give it to him, they need to agree.'

Vortigern's eyes returned to the road. 'You're right, of course.' Gwyndaf checked his horse. Ahead, the Roman road bisected a track which rose towards a distant villa to the right, and dipped left into a shallow valley. Beyond it the sea gleamed. A group of riders was waiting at the crossroads. Kerin shaded his eyes from the high sun.

'Hengist. I haven't seen the other three before.'

The Pike's head went up. He snorted and flattened his ears, and made a low, rumbling noise like his mother did when she was about to send someone to the afterlife.

'What's that for?' Kerin asked.

'Saxons,' Vortigern said, stroking the horse's neck. 'He can't stand the sight of them. God knows why. The mare doesn't like anyone, but Pike's usually civil, away from the battlefield.'

'Well, don't let him kill them here,' Kerin said. Vortigern looked round.

'He'll have his day soon enough.' The eyes which met Kerin's held a bitter, weary acknowledgement. Publius Luca was right. There was probably no feasible consequence of this tainted alliance which Vortigern had not explored in the sleepless nights since the battle.

The Saxons were talking amongst themselves. Hengist raised one hand in a perfunctory greeting. Kerin grinned as the hand moved swiftly back to grasp the pony's spiky mane. It wasn't far to fall, but the ground was littered with sharp-edged stones which could damage anyone hitting them face first. Kerin was glad that he had taken the trouble to assemble his reception party. Riding south he had thought, more than once, about an incident at the height of the battle. Twenty or more Picts, blood to the armpits, swords and axes swinging, spearmen following. Kerin and Vortigern raised swords and dropped reins. The black mare leapt from the spot, bringing five men down as she landed. Eryr went in with hooves and teeth. A shriek of agony as her head jerked up, teeth clamped on a man's jawbone. And there was Hengist, staring. For the briefest of moments, there was a look in the Saxon's eyes Kerin had never expected to see. Today he wanted Hengist to relive that moment. This was why he had chosen to ride Eryr, and not the sweet dumb cavalry horse. He wanted Hengist to witness once again the awesome meshed power of warrior and fighting horse, and to remember what that power could do to a man on foot, however strong his arm and sharp his blade.

Hengist was accompanied by three smart young warriors. None of them had made an appearance in the North. Kerin wondered where he had got them, not to mention the well-made cloak and tunic which had replaced his battle gear.

'Greetings, Lord King!' Hengist cried, keeping a precautionary hand knotted in his pony's mane. Vortigern grinned.

'What's this? I thought you Saxons were foot-soldiers, apart from that madman Oswi.'

'So we are, lord,' Hengist said, 'but today we come as friends, not as warriors. And if we are to spend time amongst the Britons – well, perhaps we should try to do as the Britons do. Don't you think so, Kerin Brightspear?'

Kerin ignored the question. 'What are you doing here, Hengist?' he asked, trying to keep his tone civil. 'I thought you were on your way to Kent.'

'Well, so we are, Kerin Brightspear,' Hengist said, with a humourless smile. 'But on our way we came across two Pictish boats, and we simply had to sink them. We landed to make repairs, and Odin be praised, we found something rather interesting.' His eyes had moved to Vortigern's. They held an unspoken question.

'Well?' Vortigern asked. He wanted this settled quickly. A simple yea or nay; no nit-picking arguments.

'My request, lord. If you are minded to grant it, perhaps you would like to look at the place we have found over here.' He nodded towards the valley. 'It is, I promise you, a very small piece of land.'

Vortigern grimaced. 'Alright, I'll look, but I'm making no promises.' He waved an arm to Kerin's entourage. 'You're here, so you may as well come too.'

The seaward rim of the valley overlooked a sheltered bay, and the land which Hengist hoped to claim. Kerin would not have wanted it, but its value to a man with a boat was clear. A low spit of land lay off the valley mouth. The presence of thick grass carpeted with sea-pinks suggested that it was rarely covered by the sea. It was linked to the mainland by a muddy causeway just wide enough for a large wagon, probably submerged at high tide. The sides of the valley fell away steeply. There were no trees, apart from a scatter of stunted hawthorns which had survived the salt-laden gales. A shallow river met the sea alongside the causeway. The land on its north bank was broad and flat, probably large enough to grow a little corn and graze enough cattle for the needs of a modest village. North of the causeway lay a calm lagoon with a shingle beach, sheltered from wind and tide. Two galleys were drawn up on the beach. The lagoon could have accommodated another ten with ease.

'Well?' Hengist said. Vortigern gave him a curious glance. The valley didn't look like much compensation for all the blood spilt north of the Wall. Kerin himself would have lived in a cave, rather than on that bare land spit exposed to every extremity of the weather.

'Is that what you want?' Vortigern asked. Hengist spread his hands.

'It may not look like much to you, lord, but remember

that the Jutes are a poor people, not accustomed to rich land. The most important thing for us is a safe harbour. We could build a few small houses on the island, and grow enough corn for our needs. And of course, we could guard the seaways for you, in case the Picts cause trouble again.' He looked from Eldof and Varro to Edlym and Gorlois, to Lucius and Padarn and the Cambrians and back again. Kerin noted, with satisfaction, the way his gaze lingered over the monk. Padarn cast his eyes skywards then fixed the Saxon with an unblinking stare, crossed himself and folded his arms. Hengist acknowledged him with a nod and gave the others a questioning smile.

'For the love of God, give it to him!' Eldof exclaimed. 'It's useless to us, and he does have a point about the seaways.' Edlym murmured something which made him chuckle. Kerin was too far away to hear, but from the movement of Edlym's lips, it could well have been *And it's a long way from Kent.*'

'Well, I agree with Eldof, for once,' Gorlois said. 'The land's no good to us, is it, and by the gods, these men did their share against the Picts.'

'Alright,' Vortigern said. 'Hengist, you can have the land. The spit and the valley, no more. And you are to bring over no more men and ships than you can easily accommodate here. In return, you'll stop any Pictish raiders putting to sea. Is all that agreed?'

Hengist bowed his head. 'Lord, I am your true servant.'

'See that you remain so. The *annona* will be distributed after our return to Londinium, and until then I don't want to see your people anywhere other than here and your land in Kent. Is that understood?'

Hengist looked up with that deathless, polite smile of his. 'I am sure we understand each other, Lord King,' he said. Kerin checked Eryr as the others turned their horses away. He and Hengist remained, facing each other alone on the rim of the valley. 'What's the matter, Kerin Brightspear?' Hengist enquired. 'It's not much to ask, surely.'

Kerin leaned down and caught the collar of his fine tunic. 'Betray his trust, and one day I'll kill you,' he said. Hengist freed himself and reined his pony back out of harm's way.

'What trust?' he asked. 'He trusts no-one, Kerin Brightspear. Not even you.'

Kerin blinked. He knew that his face must have betrayed something – how could anyone have guarded against anything so unexpected? Hengist smiled again, as if satisfied that he had created enough havoc for one day, and rode gingerly away down the steep track into his new domain.

35

Moonrise found them well south of the high moors, in a shallow valley where a sprawling town had grown up alongside the Roman road. Eldof and Edlym fell behind with their leading men, making for the villa visible from the crossroads. It looked big enough to be the centre of an extensive estate, so there was sure to be food and drink to pilfer, and low-born girls who would share their beds with the victorious warriors, whether they wanted to or not.

The remainder of the army set up camp at the edge of the town, beside a river fringed with trees. The cooks lit fires and set to work and the horses were turned loose to rest and drink from the river. Some of the men set off for the town to look for ale and women, with a troop of disgruntled guards forbidden to indulge in either. The night was clear and still. Kerin wandered aimlessly along the riverbank then made his way back to the camp. Vortigern was sitting alone beside one of the fires, watching everything that went on. One of the physicians had put a fresh bandage on his right arm. Kerin noticed the way his fists clenched and unclenched, like a hawk's clawed feet. And that's what you look like, he thought; a grounded hawk, damaged and dangerous.

A short distance away Publius Luca was snoring in the back of his carriage. Morvid and Marcellus were sitting on the ground, leaning against one of the large wheels. Some initial frostiness had mellowed into tolerance and a mutual interest in each other's arts. Kerin sat down beside the fire, picked up a chunk of wood and hurled it at the flames. Vortigern looked round.

'I take it you disapprove, then,' he said. Kerin shrugged.

'About Hengist's land? Yes, I suppose I do. And before you say anything, I don't have a better solution. At least all the others agreed with you. But I don't trust Hengist at all.' He picked up a second piece of wood, and sent it the way of the first.

'Do you suppose that I do?' Vortigern asked.

'I don't know,' Kerin said curtly. 'According to Hengist you don't trust anyone.'

Vortigern chuckled. 'Is that what all this is about?' he asked. 'For the love of God, Kerin, you spend half your time telling me the man's a liar. As it happens, there are three people I trust to a greater or lesser degree.'

'And am I one of them?' Kerin asked stiffly. Vortigern's eyes narrowed.

'How can you possibly ask me that?'

'Why shouldn't I ask you, lord?' Kerin said. 'I don't know where I stand since that thing out on the marsh. I didn't expect to be asked for a pledge of good faith, whatever I said about Bertil's daughter. Everyone else calls me your prophet, but you don't listen to a word I say.' Vortigern grinned and lay down on his horse blanket. Kerin drove his fingers into his hair, mad with frustration. 'Lord, this isn't a jest,' he said.

'Everything's a jest,' Vortigern said. 'How poor a jest, I hope you never find out.'

Kerin picked up a stick and stirred the fire. There were times when he felt as if he were walking through a fog. 'What's going to happen when we get to Londinium?' he asked.

Vortigern turned onto his back and looked up at the

stars. 'It's simple,' he said. 'Utterly, completely simple. We should garrison the coastal defences, to keep out people like Hengist's pirates. I only need Hengist because it's impossible to depend on most of the others. And we should maintain a small standing army, to keep vigilance on the Wall and deal with trouble at home. It wouldn't cost much, as things go; perhaps one week's income every year from every villa-owner and merchant. They won't pay, of course; and do you know what the next problem's going to be? Hengist's *annona*. They won't even want to pay that, and it'll be difficult for us to make them, whatever I said in Kent. They're too stupid to see what the consequences might be, naturally.'

'You mean that Hengist will try to take what he's owed if we don't give it to him?'

'Of course he will. I'd do the same myself, wouldn't you?'

'Yes,' Kerin said. 'Especially if I had families to feed. Can we force our people to pay?'

'Only up to a point. It would be simple enough to ride down to Kent and requisition fifty wagons full of corn, but we'd need a mounted army to wring money out of landowners all over the country. And of course, those landowners are the ones who'd have to pay for the mounted army.' He rose gingerly to his feet, wincing as one or other of his battle-wounds caught him out. The sounds of singing and raucous laughter were drifting from the town.

'Where are you going, lord?' Kerin asked.

'To sleep, if I can,' Vortigern said. 'You should do the same. I can promise you that there are no answers where the men are looking.'

Kerin walked away towards the trees. Cheldric was sitting on the ground, sharpening a kitchen knife.

'The Lord gives Hengist some land,' he said, without looking up.

'Yes,' Kerin said. 'What do you think?'

Cheldric put down his knife and whetstone. 'I am Saxon. Hengist is Jute. But I understand his people. We talk almost the same. I keep away, pretend I am Briton, but sometimes I hear things. They like this country.'

'Do you trust them?' Kerin asked.

'I trust you and the Lord,' Cheldric said. 'Cenydd and Morvid.'

'And the Jutes? Can they be trusted?'

Cheldric grimaced. 'Horsa, yes. Oswi the Horseman, maybe. But Hengist is *wyrmcynn*. You use long stick. I hear more, I tell you.'

* * *

Kerin woke from a fractured dream. A hand was clutching his arm. A pair of eyes gleamed in the light of the dying fire. A substantial black lump was squatting beside him. Nerves screaming, Kerin grabbed for his dagger.

'No!' a voice yelped.

'Padarn,' Kerin sighed. He shoved the dagger away and sat up. 'For God's sake, don't do that to a man who's just fought a battle.'

'Sorry,' the monk whispered. 'But no-one else needs to hear this. Get up, please, and come with me.'

Kerin struggled to his feet, catching his breath as the movement pulled on the wound in his back. He followed Padarn through the litter of snoring bodies, saddlery and dead fires towards the river bank, where hungry mules and horses had stripped the underbrush to bare twigs. The kitchen carts were drawn up in a circle, the oxen which hauled them penned safely within. The sides of the carts were draped with worn blankets, offering a little shelter and privacy to the cooks and servants sleeping beneath. Padarn tapped lightly on the side of the nearest cart.

'Come out,' he hissed. 'He's here.'

The blanket moved and Marc crawled out, followed by a girl and a small white dog. Padarn fished around in the back of the cart, found a torch and lit it with a spark from his flint. Marc looked pale and large-eyed, but he had looked like that most of the time since his stint in the physicians' tent. The girl was younger, probably; twelve or thirteen years old, at most. She was thin and sallow-skinned with dark hair chopped off at chin length; no-one's idea of a beauty, poor child, even if someone had scraped off the layers of grime. There were white trails in the grime, but she had finished weeping now, and simply looked terrified.

'I won't hurt you,' Kerin said.

'He won't,' Marc said. 'I told you. He's one of the good ones.'

The girl looked unconvinced. Padarn took her arm and led them all down to the water's edge, where a little tributary stream had carved a channel in the hard earth. A slew of pebbles lay where the stream met the river and some rotting logs had washed up on it. They sat down in a circle on the logs; Kerin and the monk, the children and the dog.

'Come on.' Padarn gave Marc a prod. 'Tell him what happened. She won't talk until she's calmed down a bit.'

'I found her up on the moor,' Marc said. 'Running around in the dark like a rabbit.'

'Up on the moor in the dark? What the hell were you doing up there?'

'I went for a ride. I can't sleep sometimes. I get nightmares. Ever since the battle. All those men with their heads chopped open and their insides hanging out. Does it go away, after a bit?'

'It gets better,' Kerin said. 'But it doesn't entirely go away. I won't lie to you about it; there'd be no point. It's part of being a warrior.' He looked at the girl. She had stopped shaking and was watching him attentively.

'She started to run from me, too,' Marc said. 'She thought I was one of them. You know, Eldof and all the high-ups who went off to that villa. That's where she's from. They went in there and told the owner that he'd better give them all food and drink, or else.'

'Why did she run away?' Kerin asked. 'She's a servant, surely. Didn't they need her in the kitchen?'

Marc gave him a world-weary look which Kerin would have preferred not to see on the face of a fifteen-year-old. 'Go on, Catula, tell him before I do.'

The girl picked up the little dog and sat it on her lap. 'I was with my friend,' she said, to the dog. 'Her hair's fair, almost white, so her mother called her Alba. She'd come from another place. Her old owner was a cruel bastard, he whipped and starved her all the time, so she got frightened when she saw all those high-born riding in. Please, come and hide in the stables with me, she said. There was a big pile of fodder there, so we hid behind it. A man came in; a warrior. A big man, leading a grey horse. I think he was just looking for somewhere to tie the horse, in the first place. But then the dust from the fodder got in Alba's nose and she sneezed. He saw us straight away. Alba and me, we're the same age I think, but she's a big, tall girl and prettier than me. He started laughing and dragged her out by the foot. She's a wild girl, she screeched like a cat and bit his hand. That was the end of the laughing. He tore her shift off and stuffed it in her mouth and threw her down on the floor. I knew I'd be next, even though I'm little and ugly, so I ran.' She kissed the dog on the nose, tears coursing down her cheeks and dripping onto its muzzle. 'She's my friend. I should have helped her, but I ran.' The dog licked its chops, enjoying the salty liquid, and gave her an uncritical kiss. 'Thank you, Hadrian,' she whispered, and kissed it back.

'You couldn't have helped her,' Marc said. 'Sometimes you can't help. All you can do is run, and wait to grow up.' He looked at Kerin, the torchlight hollowing his cheeks. It was hard to recognise the child who had rammed his grandfather's spear into Bertil Redknife's back. 'It was Balin. Bertil's chief warrior.'

'Balin!' Kerin exclaimed. 'How do you know that?'

'I went to find out,' Marc said. Kerin blinked.

'You went to the villa?'

'Yes. I wanted to know who did it. I'm not afraid of those bastards any more. And anyway, I couldn't leave Catula out on the moor on her own, and she wouldn't go without her dog. So we went to get him from the slaves' quarters, and Alba was there crying her eyes out. They'd put a big table in the courtyard, and Eldof and the others were all sitting there getting drunk. The girls pointed out Balin. So that's how I know. He was laughing and bragging about it. When he'd finished with Alba he knocked her front teeth out for biting his hand. They all had a good laugh about that.' He clamped his jaw, quivering with anger. Kerin looked at the enraged boy and the distraught girl, unable to suppress a feeling that, revolting though it was, there was some other unwelcome piece of intelligence waiting to be revealed. 'What?' he asked. 'What else?'

Marc looked uneasily at Padarn. 'Can you take her somewhere for a bit, Brother? This isn't her business, really.'

'Nor mine, lad,' Padarn said, gathering girl and dog up in his arms. 'Come on now, child. You and that mutt are both thin as sticks, and there's bound to be some food in one of these carts somewhere.' He melted into the darkness, the girl sobbing quietly into his shoulder.

'The owner of the villa was sitting at the table with them,' Marc said. 'Brianus. Catula says he's a good, kind man, doesn't beat his slaves or anything. The men started talking about the North. About the battle. About who'd killed the most Picts, and all that. All except chief warrior Varro. He looked like it was the last place he wanted to be. I was watching Balin, wondering how easy it would be to get a knife and stick it in him, but then Brianus got up. He held up his jar and asked them to drink to the king, and the way he'd led the armies and saved us all. But no-one got up to drink. No-one except chief warrior Varro. Everyone else just sat where they were, Eldof and Bertil and all their men, and all the Kentishmen. And then they started to laugh. Poor Brianus, I was sorry for him, they'd made him look a right fool. Chief warrior Varro, he looked angry fit to burst, but he kept it all in. He just put down his jar, said sorry to Brianus and that he didn't mean to insult him, and walked out of the courtyard. He walked right past where I was hiding in the bushes. There was tears coming all down his face. He went and grabbed his horse and rode off as fast as he could go. Then Eldof got Brianus by the collar and sat him back down, and told him to shut up about the king because there might be a new one before long. And that he hoped Brianus was a good Christian, because once the new king and the priests were in charge, they'd be calling on him for warriors and horses. And that was it, really. Brianus went inside and left them to it. And I sneaked away and stuck Catula and the dog on my horse, and here we are.'

And here you are, Kerin thought, and here am I, trying to suppress this wave of nausea which is driving the food in my stomach towards my throat. He breathed deeply and steadily, trying to master himself. It would have done no good to vomit two bowls of mutton broth into Marc's lap; no good to his warrior's credibility, or to the boy's peace of mind. It was the brazenness which had caught him out. The bare-faced openness, the detail which spoke of prior discussions. The twilight mutterings in a soldier's tent had become a resolution, a plan with form and substance. And a new king? A new king, hand in glove with priests? Where the hell had that come from? How could they possibly have had more than one man in mind, and how could they have made common cause with that man, if he was hundreds of miles away in Venta Belgarum? Did he know? Had he always known, or were they saving him up like the last, elusive piece of a puzzle, to be slotted handily into place once their design was complete?

'Lord?' Marc said anxiously. Kerin took the boy by the shoulders.

'Marc, what you did was stupid,' he said. 'Stupid and reckless. Any of them could have caught you, and believe me, I'd never have found out what happened. They'd just have killed you and thrown you in a hole up on the moor.' He paused, letting his hands fall. 'It was also very brave, and I hope I'd have done the same thing myself. Now. The things you heard Eldof say to Brianus. Did anyone else hear, apart from the men at the table?'

'No, lord. Catula didn't hear any of it. I hid her in the orchard with my horse before I went to spy on them.'

'Do you understand what Eldof was talking about?'

'They want a new king,' Marc said. 'And they probably want it to be the Lord Vortimer.'

'Yes,' Kerin said. 'But you must promise me – you *must* promise me, on your life and your grandfather's life – that you'll tell no-one else about this. No-one at all.'

'I swear,' Marc said, hand on heart. He paused, as if wondering whether the question was admissible. 'Will you tell the Lord?'

'I don't know,' Kerin said truthfully. 'I have to think about it, and about what might happen if I do. Or if I don't,' he added, with a wry smile. He paused, sensing another question, as yet unasked. 'Marc, I can't take Catula. I couldn't take Edra for Padarn, and I can't take this girl for you.'

Marc looked back at him with his experienced eyes. 'I wouldn't have asked you,' he said.

The army struck camp as the glimmer of dawn became a general blue light. The town was heaving itself into bleary-eyed life. The innkeepers and the whores, if no-one else, must have been grateful for the night's business. Kerin sat on his young horse Blaidd and watched as wagons were loaded, animals harnessed and wounded men lifted aboard their transports. The birds singing deafeningly from the thickets beside the river sounded far more cheerful than anyone looked.

'I feel better for that,' said Macsen. 'You should have come with us.'

'I didn't feel like it,' Kerin said. Macsen looked perplexed.

'The ale or the women?'

'Either,' Kerin said. Macsen sighed.

'It's that girl in Glevum. You're really sweet on her, aren't you.'

'Yes,' Kerin said. There was no point in denying the obvious, and besides, he knew that his admission would save him from further scrutiny. Macsen shook his head and clicked to his horse.

'She'd never have known, you know,' he said, trotting away to join his father. Kerin watched them go, rather envying the qualities they shared; the ability to live for the moment, and a complete lack of curiosity about what might happen in the future.

'Here, drink this, Lord Kerin.' It was Malan. He had left his wagon and its precious cargo a couple of horse-lengths away, in the care of Edryd. Kerin had hardly spoken to the old man since they picked him up on the way to Kent. Astonishingly, he looked in better health than before. He was holding up a small leather-bound flask. Kerin reached down and took it. The contents smelled bitter and sweet all at once.

'What's this?'

'Something Marcellus *magister* mixed up. All those days and nights helping with the wounded, it gets you down in the end. You look as if you could do with it, if you don't mind me saying.' Kerin took a mouthful of the liquid and let it dribble down his throat, drop by fiery drop. He recognised it at once; the remedy Marcellus had fed to him in the praetor's courtyard, the day after Faria killed herself. 'Is it true that you and Lord Vortimer have been friends since you were nippers?' Malan asked.

'Yes,' Kerin said. 'We grew up together. I expect you've heard all about it on the march.'

'Religion turns men's heads,' Malan said. 'I don't mean decent men like the warriors' priest. But I heard Vortimer talking to your lads, that night when you saved us from Bertil Redknife's cut-throats. All he cared about was giving the bastards Christian burial, never mind that they'd tried to do away with me and my poor stupid granddaughter.'

'What's happened to her?' Kerin asked. 'I was afraid that she might try to follow us.'

'Edryd worked something,' Malan said. 'Come on, he can tell you.'

Kerin dismounted and followed Malan to the wagon. The smith had a heavily bandaged leg and a patch over one eye. He had fought fearlessly, armed with a terrifying spiked mace forged in his own workshop. He climbed down from the wagon, helped Malan up onto the driver's seat and slapped the black mule's rump to get him moving.

'How's that eye?' Kerin asked.

'On the mend,' Edryd said. 'Someone threw a rock at me. I can't see much out of it yet, but Morvid says it should be fine once the swelling goes down.'

Kerin passed him the flask. 'Malan says you did something with Flora, to stop her coming after us.'

'I did. After we spoke, I looked up a friend of mine. Another smith, a Glevum boy, but he spent a year or two in Calleva, working for a villa owner. His father's one of the bishop's guards, so he knows a few people in Eldof's household. They grabbed Flora at the market and locked her in someone's cellar for a couple of weeks. They weren't cruel, they saw to her needs, but they didn't let her go until we were well out of the way. One of the boys told Eldof's people that she'd caught a fever, we didn't want to make any more trouble for her than she's already got.'

'What will you do?' Kerin asked.

'About Flora? Keep as far away from her as I can. I came close to getting killed a few times in that battle. Seeing as I've still got a life, I want a good one. I know I'll never get that from Flora, but I still wouldn't trust myself if she was standing in front of me, so I'm keeping away from Glevum. Your warrior Hefin offered me work in Cambria – now there's a good, brave man – but I turned him down, in case Flora's stupid enough to go there after the king. I might stay in Londinium for a while. There's always work for smiths, and Publius Imperator said he'd put in a word for me.'

Kerin clapped Edryd on the shoulder. 'You're a good man too, Edryd. A good man and a brave one.'

Edryd grinned. 'Even if I did call you a fucking highborn the first time I saw you,' he said, and trotted off after Malan's cart.

Kerin mounted up, kicked Blaidd in the ribs and rode after the departing column. He soon caught up with the last of the heavy wagons. As he passed Cheldric's cart, with its cargo of sacks containing dried herbs and roots, something caught his eye. Poking out from beneath the covering of waxed blankets was the tip of a small white tail. Blaidd had seen it too. He whinnied and blew loudly through his nostrils. The tail wagged timidly before an unseen hand yanked it out of sight. I did not see that, Kerin thought, as he rode away.

36

'It's unfortunate about the prisoners,' Alberius said, shaking his head. 'A few chained captives make all the difference, you know.'

'Well, what would you like us to do?' Gwyndaf asked. 'Go back to the North and dig up some bodies?'

'No, no,' Alberius sighed. 'We'll make do with the beasts. In fact the selection of beasts is quite comprehensive, so I'm sure curiosity will be satisfied.'

Beyond the atrium, in the courtyard of the praetor's house, a procession was assembling. The whole household seemed to be down there, along with numerous musicians, jugglers and a stilt-walker. There was no sign of anyone who had seen action in the North.

'Lord Kerin Brightspear?' a timid voice enquired. It was Graecus, an olive-skinned lad promoted principal servant by Lupinus's demise. 'The praetor requests your attendance, lord. I'm sure I'll be in the most terrible trouble if I go back without you.'

Kerin followed the servant to the praetor's chambers and stood in the corridor outside, waiting to be invited in. Marcellus came out, holding a shallow box which contained some bottles and a beaker. 'It was less trouble dealing with the battle casualties,' he said. 'Have you been summoned?'

'Yes,' Kerin said. 'I've no idea why.'

The haruspex drew him aside to a quiet alcove. 'I entreat

you, whatever you plan to do next, don't leave the city until things are settled,' he said. 'I imagine your head is halfway to Glevum, in pursuit of your beloved. That's natural, I wouldn't presume to advise against it, but try to exercise some patience. I know it doesn't come easily at your age, but you must try. Please be aware of the power you hold, my young friend. Nothing has changed for the king in that respect, whatever he may have said. The peace is always the hard part, and he will need the strength of his right arm to deal with it.'

'Is this what you told me before we left for home?' Kerin asked. 'About having the most important task in the kingdom?'

'Yes,' Marcellus said. 'You could do worse than imagine a damaged branch on a tree. Only so many birds can land on it before something gives way. And we have had a few large birds of late. Don't leave until things are settled.'

'Someone at home told me this,' Kerin said. 'Our arch-druid, Caradog. He's wise and sees through people, like you do. He said that Vortigern was the best king we could have, but that the kingship would destroy him. Or words to that effect. Things were going well then, and I didn't know what he was talking about. But now I do.'

'Then the druid and I have probably reached the same conclusion, in our different ways,' Marcellus said. 'I'm not counselling anything dramatic, of course. Vortigern should be king indefinitely, in my view. But he can't do it alone. I doubt if any man could, but most men are not burdened with their people's blind faith. Don't leave here until things are settled. And then leave with some delicacy and care.' He smiled regretfully, patted Kerin's arm and shuffled off down the corridor.

Severus Maximus had not altered. His face was still grey, and anxiety preceded him like a miasma. Kerin was shown into the room where the praetor had received him, with Vortigern and Cheldric, after the beheading of Plicius. There was still a hole in the back of the chair where Vortigern's dagger lodged.

'Ah, Kerin!' Severus said, with patent relief. 'Please, take a seat. Some wine, perhaps?'

Kerin could smell Marcellus's medication on the praetor's breath. 'No, thank you. I need to keep a clear head.'

Severus seized his hands. 'You can't believe what a debt of gratitude we feel. I realise that you might consider the idea of a triumph rather foolish, but please understand that for some of us, it's the only way we can show our appreciation.'

'It's not me you should thank, Severus Maximus,' Kerin said. 'The king and Publius Luca deserve the credit.'

'And they shall receive it,' the praetor said rapturously. 'But nothing could have been achieved without the ordinary warriors. Everyone will get his reward today.' His eyes strayed to a nearby couch. A set of extravagant clothing was lying there; a deep purple cloak, a white silk tunic with gold embroidery around the hem and a pair of doe-skin boots, dyed purple to match the cloak. Kerin offered no comment.

'Is everything ready?' he asked. 'I know nothing about triumphs. I'm told it's a great honour to be granted one, in Rome.'

'Oh, indeed. I'm sure Alberius has everything under control. The main procession will assemble here; the beasts, of course, are in the castra and will fall in behind the marching musicians. It's unfortunate that there are no prisoners, but I suppose it can't be helped. The presence of the king is essential, though. You don't happen to know where he is, I suppose?'

'I don't,' Kerin said. 'Do you?'

'We met on your return, but after that, I have no idea. Gallus has been here looking for him too, and he wasn't at all keen to take no for an answer. Could you possibly – '

'No,' Kerin said. 'The king will be here soon enough, I'm sure. And perhaps I'll change my mind about the wine. It would be ungracious to refuse.'

Severus smiled and made a series of expansive gestures, prompting the arrival of an extremely large amphora. Some time later, there was a commotion at the door which Kerin was too drunk to interpret. Vortigern came in, followed by two anxious-looking praetorian guardsmen. 'It's time for this farce to begin, I take it?' he said.

Severus looked as affronted as he dared. 'Lord, it's hardly a farce. And if you don't mind, I'd like to present you with these clothes, as a token of our respect. A little more appropriate for such an occasion, perhaps?'

'Keep the clothes,' Vortigern said. 'If you want me to wear something more appropriate, I'll go and change.' Kerin followed him out. The passage was full of servants and anonymous minor officials in Roman dress.

'Where have you been?' Kerin asked.

'Drinking with Publius Luca. How else is this to be endured?'

Kerin remembered nothing after that, until he found himself being dragged out into the sunlight by Lucius. Marc had brought his horse. Lucius seized Kerin's foot and heaved him up onto the mare's back. 'Hold on tight. I've got to drive Publius Luca's chariot, and I don't think the wine he's had agrees with Marcellus's medication.'

Kerin thrust his hands into Eryr's mane and gripped with his legs. The mare looked round curiously, as if puzzled by the lack of direction.

'By the gods, boy, on the lash already!' It was Gorlois, in ordinary travelling clothes. 'Have you seen the horse? They've got Vortigern a horse. A beautiful big white horse, with jewels on its bridle and a mane like a woman's hair.'

Kerin was casting around for the animal when the water landed. It hit him full in the face and drenched his tunic from shoulders to waist. Gwyndaf was standing below him with a dripping bucket.

'Sober up and come with me, or I'll do it again,' he said.

Kerin followed Gwyndaf. Alberius was standing by the fountain, holding the reins of the white horse which Gorlois had described. The animal was beautiful in an almost unearthly fashion. Its huge dark eyes shone beneath white lashes, and its small neat hooves gleamed as though they had been polished.

'It's a horse of the imperial blood line, lord,' Alberius said, with a self-important sweep of his remaining hand. 'A direct descendant of the stallion Incitatus, who was declared a consul by the Emperor Caligula four hundred years ago.'

'Lord Kerin, please can you shed any light on the where-abouts of the king?' Severus Maximus asked, wringing his fine hands. 'We can't hold things up much longer. The horses are restless, and the beasts are becoming fractious.'

Gwyndaf shrugged, got up on his brown mare and removed the draco from its sling. The icy water had had a salutary effect. Kerin was now sober enough to identify the Cambrian warriors, waiting behind a row of chariots. They had all tidied themselves up, but there was no sign of ceremonial attire, although the Kentishmen to their right were dripping with it.

'Severus Maximus!' came a shrill voice, somewhere over by the gates. 'The king!'

The crowd parted to admit Vortigern. He came in from

the street on his black mare. He was wearing the shredded tunic and breeches he had worn on the day of the battle, the garments still encrusted with dried blood. The torn, bloody strip of the draco's banner was tied around his head. He rode straight up to the praetor's chariot and stopped. Severus Maximus stared at him, aghast.

'Lord King, I don't think – '

'Don't,' Vortigern said. 'Don't ever tell me that this is not appropriate, because this is how battles are won. This is what kept your city safe. Blood and death and pain. It's not beautiful. Your people should remember that, before they let it happen again.'

'Lord King,' Alberius faltered. Vortigern turned. 'Lord King, I don't know if you're aware, but it's customary for the victorious general to ride a fine white horse.'

'Oh,' Vortigern snapped. 'I believe it's also customary for the victorious general to ravish the city's virgins, and I'm not planning to do that, either.'

'Lord, the laurel crown, at least!' Alberius implored. Vortigern seized it and jammed it down on the head of the draco.

'There. The dragon can wear the laurel crown, for every warrior in my company and for every brave man who died in the North. Can we get this over with, please?'

Alberius raised his hand in a pre-ordained signal. The praetorian trumpeters let out a strident blast, and the veterans of the city garrison led the triumph out of the courtyard. The praetor's chariot followed, leading a string of lesser carriages full of nameless petty officials. Vortigern reached for Gwyndaf's rein.

'Let them go,' he said. 'Let them all go.'

A cheer resounded from the street. The chariots rumbled on, followed by jugglers and acrobats, a stilt-walker and several distinct troupes of musicians with pipes, drums and lyres. The gates of the castra swung open with a clang and the beasts fell in behind the musicians, if that was the word for it. There was a lion in an iron cage on a trundling ox-cart, and a sullen-looking bear on a chain. Another cage drawn by four straining mules contained a creature which was probably a leopard, if the frescoes of Bacchus's chariot were accurate. And then there was something which made Kerin wonder if Gwyndaf should have thrown the second pail of water. The beast was tall and sand-coloured, with a swan's neck and a solid mound of flesh in the centre of its back, upon which a small turbaned black boy perched precariously. A curious onlooker reached out to touch one of the long pacing legs, and the beast spat in his face.

The remainder of the procession came to attention as Vortigern rode a circle round the courtyard. Only those who had served in the North remained; the mounted warriors and the foot soldiers, the craftsmen and cooks who had sustained the army through it all, spilling out through the praetor's gates and far down the streets beyond. There were only two transports; a carriage bearing Marcellus, Morvid and Malan, and Publius Luca's modest chariot. Vortigern's eyes shone below the bloodstained headband, warm with affection and pride.

'Men are fools,' he said. 'They forget. They'll spit on us one day soon. But remember this. They may forget their debt to you, but I never shall. The victory is yours. Gwyndaf, raise the dragon!'

The great gilded head went up, the tattered banner floated out, and Gwyndaf led the procession out into the cheering, chanting din of the city. People lined the narrow streets, packed the alleys and hung from windows. Some sang, some wept; some waved laurel branches and others carried children on their shoulders for a glimpse of the king. One man lifted his little daughter up into Publius Luca's chariot with a laurel crown for the commander. Publius, wearing his ceremonial helmet and cape for perhaps the last time, could barely contain his emotion. Girls ran alongside with flowers, tankards or pitchers of wine, reaching up to touch the warriors or kiss them if they could. Vortigern seized a mug, emptied it down his throat and tossed it into the crowd. A howl went up as people fought and fell over each other, trying to get their hands on it. Behind them the street closed up as everyone fought to join the tail of the procession, until it seemed that the whole city was on the move. And so in the end they came to the curia, where it had all begun.

37

It was not at all like the day of Constans's coronation. The huge building was eerily quiet. Outside in the square, chaos prevailed. No-one wanted to go home, and enterprising tradesmen had set up stalls peddling ale, wine and sweet-meats. The musicians were still there, playing competing tunes, and the acrobats were forming a human pyramid in the spot where the Picts once dangled from the gallows. The beasts were encamped in front of the railings. The *camelus*, for that was its name, had been made to kneel by its small rider. Children were taunting it to make it spit. The garrison men were making a concerted effort to clear the square.

'We're trying to move everything down to the market-place,' one of them said as he opened the iron gate for Kerin. 'These things always come to a sticky end. They had one for Severus Maximus when he got to be praetor, and the lion ate one of the acrobats.'

Inside the curia they had removed the table from the dais and set it in the middle of the floor. Only a handful of men had been judged important enough to sit at it. On one side were Gorlois, Gallus, Eldof, and his brother Bishop Eldadus. On the other were Severus Maximus, Edlym and Kerin. A fair division of influence had been agreed before-hand. One representative of the capital's administration, one of the military and one of the Church; the master of the war fleet, and one man from each of the four regions which had contributed most warriors to the campaign. Lud had deferred to Kerin without question, whether by choice or order no-one knew. Gallus was wearing a look of desolation which Kerin could not interpret. He mouthed a silent question to the merchant, but no response came. The seat at the head of the table was reserved for the king, the one next to the praetor for Publius Luca. Both seats were empty. The praetor cleared his throat.

'Kerin, perhaps you could go to see – ' Kerin nodded and went outside, relieved to escape the prickling silence. He gave a ragged boy a silver coin to take him to Publius Luca's residence, and followed him down a side street to a large house with a walled courtyard, shaded by fig trees. Vortigern was at the gates, speaking to Titus Luca. He had shed his bloodstained rags and replaced them with his customary black. Kerin slipped into a doorway and waited. He did not wish to embarrass Titus, since they were not known to have met.

'Publius is unwell,' Vortigern said as he came out. 'Not in danger, but his wound has started to bleed, and Marcellus has rightly refused to let him leave his bed.'

'Have you spoken to Gallus?' Kerin asked.

'No. Have you?'

'No, but he's been looking for you. He's with the others in the curia. Something's happened, but I couldn't question him in front of them.' They walked briskly down the side street, keeping to the shadows under the wall. In front of the curia, Vortigern stopped.

'We are alone now. I had only one certain ally amongst the others. What do you think?'

'I think it'll be harder than crowning Constans,' Kerin

said, 'and God knows, that must have been hard enough.'

'Do we have a chance?'

'We've lost the only man, apart from you, who could make the case for a standing army. Severus is spineless. Eldof and Edlym will guard their own interests. I'd have put my horse on Gallus, but there's something wrong there, and I don't know what. Gorlois is a hero, but God knows if he's got the guts to face down the others.' Kerin looked out over the square as daylight faded. Sounds of merriment and anarchy were drifting from the marketplace beside the river. The praetor's slaves were shovelling dung into a cart, and a few beggars' children were ranging across the square, hunting for stray coins. One small girl picked up a crushed rose and a laurel twig with two or three bruised leaves. She twisted them into a bunch, hesitated, then approached and held them out shyly. Kerin smiled. 'A garland for the king,' he said. Vortigern accepted the gift with a solemn bow. The child's mother screeched at her and she fled.

'To the victor the consequences,' Vortigern said, threading the stalks through the shoulder-pin of his cloak.

'Lord King!' Severus Maximus exclaimed. 'We were anxious for your safety!'

Vortigern surveyed the assembled gathering with a sceptical smile. 'Let's proceed,' he said. 'Publius Luca cannot be with us; Marcellus *magister* has forbidden him to move. It is unfortunate, because the most vital decisions we must make are military, and no-one is better qualified to speak on these things.'

'Lord King,' the praetor said cautiously, 'I think most of us assumed that the decisions were, shall we say, monetary.'

Vortigern's eyebrows rose. 'It didn't take you long to get round to that, did it.'

Severus Maximus shifted in his chair. 'There was some opportunity for discussion whilst we were waiting, Lord King. I am merely reflecting the concerns of the meeting.'

'Ah,' Vortigern said. 'Who's going to come out with it, then?'

'I wouldn't put it quite like that, Lord King,' Severus said. 'The matter is complex, and requires discussion.'

Vortigern sat up straight, his patience evaporating already. Kerin knew that there had been a moment outside when he could have counselled restraint and a cool head, but some things were difficult to say to a man who had just led a harrowing campaign, and might soon face another against his own son.

'Oh no,' Vortigern said. 'The matter is not complex. The matter is blindingly simple. I have beaten off two invasions in the last few years, both of which threatened our peace and security. The kingdom can prosper now, but it won't, unless we prevent these things from happening again. I've lost hundreds of good, brave men, and I don't want to lose many more. We need to keep surveillance on the Wall and garrison our coastal defences, and we need a standing army large enough to deal with local trouble. It would be simple to arrange this now, because we already have good, battle-hardened troops. If we do nothing, they'll disband and drift away. We need to keep enough of them together to defend the kingdom.'

Gallus raised his large hand. 'We need to maintain our sea defences as well,' he said. 'Things are transformed since you became king. Even before the victory in the North, there was a return of confidence. No-one was prepared to spend money while the country was run by little jumped-up imitation emperors. Don't look at me like that, Severus, it's the truth. But now, wherever you look, men are planting corn and building workshops. I'm prepared to double the size of my fleet, but only if the safety of my ships at sea can be guaranteed.'

'We're getting away from the point here,' Eldof butted in.

'And what about those Saxon mercenaries?' Eldadus ventured. Vortigern looked from one man to another.

'Alright. To summarise, can we agree, in principle, on the need for defence forces and a standing army?'

'With respect, Lord King,' Edlym said, 'principles are all very well, but principles are expensive. Who's going to pay for them?'

'Everyone who can afford it, in proportion to his wealth,' Vortigern said. 'Essentially, this is no different from the fleet tax. For the love of God, Edlym, we're talking about one week's income for a man like you. Is that so much to ask, for a guarantee of peace?'

Edlym cleared his throat. 'With respect, Kent has already contributed the land.'

'The land? That worthless scrap of mud and bog?'

'There's corn growing on it now, lord king,' Edlym said. 'It can't be worthless.'

'Well,' Kerin said, 'if there's corn, it's thanks to the men who are farming it. Don't mistake me, Edlym, I'm no friend of the Saxons. But they're not afraid of anything, Picts or hard graft. Don't use their work as an excuse for not paying up. And before another word is said about Saxons and land, you all put your names to the agreement in Kent. It was written down word for word by Marcellus *magister*. As you know.'

Eldof's eyes glittered coldly. You'd kill me if you could, Kerin thought. 'They do well to call you Vortigern's right arm,' Eldof said, voice as tart as vinegar. 'You open your mouth and his voice comes out.'

Kerin smiled, doing his best to appear calm and unruffled. 'Not at all, Eldof. Vortigern's not the only man with common sense. I hope I have a rich fund, even if I am a robber's bastard.'

Eldof's jaw clenched. You were about to bring it up, Kerin thought, and now I have blunted your blade.

'Common sense?' Eldof blustered. 'Is that how you describe robbing a man to pay for something he'll never need? What good are Wall garrisons or coastal defences to the men of Glevum? We fought and bled in the North, knowing that the Picts would never threaten us. But it's done now. If the men of the North want a Wall garrison, let them pay for one. If the Kentishmen want to man the shore forts, let them do it. And if you Cambrians want to keep the Irish out, then all I can say is that it's up to you.'

It was nonsense, arrant nonsense; but most of the other men were listening and wondering and weighing things. Kerin had no idea where this was going.

'By the gods!' Gorlois roared, banging the table. 'I've heard more sense talked in an alehouse. We made this man king. Why? So that men like us wouldn't have to waste time arguing about things like this. For love of the gods, you've got a leader, so let him lead. Shut your mouths, pay up and sleep in peace at night.' He folded his arms. Vortigern restrained a smile.

'Thank you, Gorlois,' he said.

'Lord King,' Severus Maximus said, 'can I ask you to clarify precisely what it is that you want of us?'

'Yes,' Vortigern said. 'Enough money to pay for the defences I've described, including an expanded naval defence force for the merchant fleet, the contributions to be shared equally amongst all men of property or commerce, according to their worth. I'm sure your administration is stuffed with people who have nothing better to do than make the calculations. And whilst we're about it, we also need to pay the *annona* agreed between Publius Luca and the Saxon mercenaries. As you know, the agreement is for a combination of coinage and goods in kind. I shall be looking to each of you for a contribution according to your particular means.'

'Lord King, we have already contributed the land,' Edlym protested. 'And if I'm not much mistaken, were the mercenaries not also granted a piece of land on the eastern coast?'

Vortigern stared up at the painted ceiling. 'You know perfectly well they were, Edlym. You were one of the men who advised it. For everyone else's information, it was done in recognition of the Saxons' courage in the field, and as a defence against any future trouble from the Picts at sea. We were on the march, there was no facility for a written record, but it was agreed verbally by representatives of Glevum, Kent, Kernow, Cambria and the legionary army. Gallus, I'm sure you'll be in favour of a seaborne defence.'

'Of course,' Gallus said. 'And I'll contribute towards its upkeep. But Vortigern, I'm still awaiting payment for the ships requisitioned as war galleys. I know you can't be aware of this, or you'd have dealt with it.'

'What?' Vortigern said incredulously. Gallus shrugged.

'It's true. Ask the praetor. I've had a man round at his house every day since you marched, trying to wring the money out of the treasury. Don't ask me why, because I know that almost everyone paid the fleet tax, even if you had to wring it out of them.'

Vortigern looked at the praetor in disbelief. 'Severus?'

The praetor looked away, fiddling nervously with his rings. 'I'm sorry, Lord King. There were pressing matters – '

'What pressing matters?' Vortigern asked. Severus murmured something inaudible. 'What pressing matters?' Vortigern repeated, leaning across the table. Severus recoiled.

'The restoration of the administrative buildings, lord,' he whispered. 'And of course, the triumph.' Vortigern turned chalk-white. Eldof laughed out loud.

'You see? And you want me to pour all the money in Glevum down the same drain?'

'You can't blame us for that, Eldof!' Kerin protested. 'We were three hundred miles away fighting a battle, for God's sake.'

'Well, who else should I blame if the king can't control his own treasury?' Eldof said. Emboldened by his brother's outburst, Bishop Eldadus reared up in his seat and stretched his thin neck.

'A few words on behalf of the Church, gentlemen, if I may. The Church cannot condone the handing over of any more British land and goods to a band of heathen savages.'

'No?' Vortigern said. 'Even if they just helped us slaughter some other heathen savages, who murdered your brother in Christ?'

'No,' Eldadus said obdurately. Vortigern closed his eyes and steadied himself.

'Alright,' he said, looking from man to man. 'Now, you can listen to me. First of all, the *annona*. When we met in Kent, every one of you agreed to employ the Saxons and to pay them for their services. As Kerin reminded you, every detail was recorded by Marcellus *magister*. The agreement is in the hands of Titus Luca, and if you haven't had enough battles to last you a lifetime, you can try fighting it out with him in court because I intend to hold you to that agreement. Edlym, you are going to contribute the corn. If you won't give it freely, I'll go to Kent and take it. Gallus, I shall expect you and the company of merchants to provide weaponry to replace what was lost in battle. The rest of us will contribute the coinage in equal shares. Understand that there will be no argument about this. You may all be happy to dishonour your agreements, but there will be no dishonouring one made by Publius Luca.' He paused. No-one spoke. It seemed that everyone was considering his private memories and deciding that for a sum the size of the *annona*, the consequences were not worth risking. 'Good,' Vortigern said, with a brittle smile. 'I shall take that as settled. Now, to the other matter. Before you speak, think. Those of us who fought in the North know what the victory cost. The rest of you must be blind or stupid, if you can look at us and not see it. If you oppose me now, this city will burn. Not today or next week, but it will happen. The whole kingdom will burn. I am telling you now so that you can never say you were not warned. You know I can't enforce a levy without your consent, so I want an answer from you, and I want it now. Eldof?'

Eldof of Glevum stood up and cleared his throat. 'I have nothing to add, Vortigern,' he said. 'If you send men to Glevum and try to extract some hare-brained army levy, I'll close my gates and fight you. In my opinion, you only want an army so that you can use it for your own ends. You'll wait a long time for me to pay for that.' He rose, nodded to the meeting and walked out of the curia. Eldadus got up, looking nervously at the open door.

'I'm hardly qualified to speak about military matters, Lord King,' he said. 'But as for the heathens, I have already made myself clear. As has your son, I might remind everyone. I don't think we've heard the last of that.' He bowed, crossed himself and hurried after his brother. Vortigern looked from one to another of the men who remained.

'Well, then,' he said. 'Edlym. What about you?'

'Lord King, you must understand that I do not hold the true power in Kent.' Edlym adjusted his collar, which seemed to have grown suddenly tight. Vortigern smiled brilliantly.

'Perhaps not. But until your nephew crawls out from the stone he's hiding under, the decision is yours. I can garrison the shore forts for you tomorrow, but unless you contribute to the cost, it's impossible. Decide.'

'Lord King, there's nothing to decide,' Edlym said haughtily. 'You gave away our land, so why should I open the coffers of Kent to you? So that you can carry it all off to your hovel in the West? Not in this lifetime. We'll see to our own defences.'

He got up and stalked out of the curia. Vortigern laughed quietly. He and Kerin looked at each other, and at the three men who remained.

'Well,' Vortigern said, 'the hopeless cases have gone. I can carry this with half of you, if need be. What do you say, Gallus?'

The merchant did not reply. It was the first time Kerin had known him to be less than forthright. He looked stricken. We have lost this, Kerin thought.

'We should have spoken!' Gallus exclaimed. 'I looked everywhere for you before the triumph. Ask anyone.'

'Well, you have found me now,' Vortigern said. 'We are friends, or so I believed. Will you stand with me?'

'How can I?' Gallus shouted. 'How can I throw my money away for some witless incompetent to spend it on shabby buildings and mangy lions?' He breathed deeply and controlled himself. 'Think nothing of the *annona*. It will be paid tomorrow. But I've slaved my whole life, to be where I am. I can't contribute another denarius until I'm compensated for

351

my ships, and you find a way to extract a contribution from those miserable fuckers outside.' He glared, fists clenched, at Severus Maximus. The praetor shrank and fiddled with his rings.

'Get out,' Vortigern said under his breath. Gallus leapt from the table and seized him by the shoulders.

'This can't be. There'll be a way. We must find a way –'

'Get out,' Vortigern snarled, twisting free. With a bellow of rage, the merchant grabbed the praetor and threw him across the table. Severus staggered to his feet, clutching a bloody nose.

'By the gods!' Gorlois shouted as Gallus kicked the door open and marched out. 'The bastards. The rotten, unprincipled bastards. Vortigern, I know we've had our moments. But I would never, ever spit on you like those have done.'

'Would you pay, though?' Vortigern asked.

'Of course I'd pay! I'd pay, and I'd give my warriors to your army all over again. To the last man.' Gorlois paused, desperate. 'But to be honest, it won't do much good unless everybody else does it too, will it?'

'No,' Vortigern said. 'You have my respect and my eternal gratitude, Gorlois, but there's nothing to be gained. Take your boys home. Let them rest. You've all earned it, and this is no place for decent men.'

Gorlois looked on the point of tears. 'Send word the moment we're needed. The gates of Tintagel are open. They will always be open for you, Lord King.' He bowed deeply, gave Kerin a look of profound regret, and went out. Vortigern smiled at the praetor.

'Well, Severus Maximus. Do you know how much damage you've done?'

'Yes,' Severus said bleakly.

'No,' said Vortigern.

'If there's anything I could do –'

'There is. Of course there is. But you won't do anything with all those against you, will you. Will you?'

'No,' Severus whispered.

'No. I thought not.'

Severus got up, throwing his chair out of the way, and made for the door. They heard it close behind him.

'I could send for Marcellus,' Kerin said.

'No,' Vortigern said. 'I'm alright. And there'd be no point.' He folded his hands on the table and sat, staring down at them. Kerin heard a sound and turned. Severus Maximus had reappeared in the open doorway. He looked crucified with guilt.

'Our debt to you is beyond calculation,' he said shakily. 'It is a matter of shame and regret to me that I'm not man enough to honour it.'

Vortigern did not look up; whether he was unwilling or unable to, it was impossible to judge. Severus hesitated for a moment, a small, inconsequential figure dwarfed by the immensity of the building, then he turned and walked away. The sound of his footsteps grew fainter until it merged into the general murmur of the city, and then there was nothing; only the howling emptiness of the curia, and the bitter truth.

38

'How did you get in?' Eldof of Glevum asked. He looked worried, and there was every reason to be. He had guards on the gate of the vacant merchant's house which he had commandeered for his stay in Londinium; guards on the gate and lookouts posted in every upstairs window, and there weren't any other breaches in the glum grey walls, as far as Eldof knew. And yet here, sitting at the table in his private quarters, smiling like an angel, was the man now commonly known as the king's right arm; and beside him, to make matters worse, was Gwyndaf of Craig Goch.

'It wasn't difficult,' Kerin said. From a skiff on the river; up the steps to the door of the scullery behind the kitchen, where they gut the fish straight off the boat. Perhaps it was necessary to be low-born, to know about things like that. Gwyndaf had removed his sword from its scabbard and laid it on the polished table. Even Kerin did not know whether he had done this to signal his peaceful intentions, or to ensure that the weapon would be easily accessible if he decided to cut Eldof's throat.

'What do you want?' Eldof asked. A single bead of sweat appeared on his florid brow, gleaming like a pinhead in the light of the candles on the wall.

'Hengist's *annona*,' Kerin said. 'In coin, preferably. You know how much it is. Publius Luca notified everyone in Kent. There's a man sitting in Titus Luca's house with an abacus, waiting to count it when I get back.'

'I wouldn't cheat, you know,' Eldof said, scowling darkly.

'I hope not.' Kerin smiled. He supposed that Eldof had enough armed men at hand to kill him and Gwyndaf, however many of their assailants they managed to take with them; but Eldof would first have to get as far as the door.

'Where's Vortigern, anyway?' Eldof asked sullenly. 'Hasn't he got the stomach to do his own dirty work?'

'Healing all those battle wounds,' Kerin said. 'Marcellus's advice. And it isn't dirty work. It's a formal agreement, ratified by everyone. So do you have coin, or shall we take something else instead? Something of equal value, naturally.' He allowed his eyes to wander over the contents of the room. Some costly silver platters and drinking vessels; a small carved box, its lid open, revealing a coiled gold necklet studded with malachite. There was no need to watch Eldof. Gwyndaf was doing that.

'I have coin,' Eldof said sourly. 'And my own men will take it to Titus Luca's house. If you think I'm handing over a chest full of *aurei* to a horse thief's bastard, you can think again.'

The movement was so quick that Kerin did not see it, but he heard the hiss in the air and Eldof's yelp of shock as Gwyndaf's dagger skewered the sleeve of his tunic to the polished table.

'Don't say that again,' Gwyndaf said earnestly. 'And in case you're thinking of calling your guards, don't. I've got a hundred cut-throats waiting outside. If we don't come out by the time the moon gets above the roof of the curia, they'll burn the gate down and kill everything in here.' He jerked his dagger free, spat on the blade and ran his finger along the cutting edge.

'Get out,' Eldof breathed, rubbing his arm. 'Get out before I vomit. You'll have your *annona* tonight.'

They walked out through the front gate, raising courteous hands to the guards who opened it for them. No-one was going to question men coming from within. Outside in the deserted street they broke into a trot, and didn't stop until they reached the praetor's house, two long streets and a wide square away. Kerin leaned against the wall and stared up at the sky. The mist which had hung around all day was still there. There was no moon to see.

'You were lying, obviously,' he said.

'About the hundred cut-throats?' Gwyndaf said. 'Of course I was. But you were lying about Vortigern too, weren't you. You don't have an idea where he is.'

'No,' Kerin said. It was impossible to avoid the admission, but there was nothing he wished to add. He was growing to like Gwyndaf, and even if he had not, would have esteemed him as the most able warrior in their company. But there was so much history. Gwyndaf's loyalty had been beyond reproach in the North, but was that Vortigern's doing, or simply the considered action of a man putting aside old enmities to protect his family?

'I know you're not going to say any more, least of all to me,' Gwyndaf said. 'That's as it should be. I wouldn't expect less of you. He'll be back, of course. If the Romans couldn't kill him, this won't. But until then, it's up to you. No-one else can do it.'

'Up to me!' Kerin said. A malign presence was tapping his shoulder; the despair and downright fear which had stalked him since he woke from a fitful sleep after the night of the curia and realised that he was alone. He had fought it off, ignored its wheedling voice; but now here it was again, running its clammy fingers all over him. 'For God's sake, Gwyndaf,' he said softly. 'I'm –'

'What?' Gwyndaf retorted. 'A horse-thief's bastard?

What difference does that make? What was Vortigern's father? A rich, Roman-loving arse-licker. And I suppose that's why we all followed him into hell up at the Wall.'

'No!' Kerin exclaimed.

'No,' Gwyndaf said. 'So before I go off to get drunk, you'd better decide what we're doing next.'

Kerin took a steadying breath and looked up at the high wall beneath which they were standing.

'Well, we're here,' he said. 'It may as well be this.'

The servant Graecus stood in front of them, eyes wide with alarm. He had probably not believed the young guardsman who came to drag him away from whatever he was doing. The king's warriors, at this time of evening? And after all that had happened in the curia?

'Lords, I was hardly expecting you,' he quavered, his hands skimming a casual-looking white gown. 'Some wine, perhaps?'

'No, thank you,' Kerin said. 'We've come to see Severus Maximus.'

'But, lord! The praetor has retired to bed. He's not a well man. I can't possibly disturb him.'

'You can't?' Kerin said. 'Then think on this. If you don't go and get him, straight away, I'll go and get him myself. And however unwell he is, I can promise you he'll feel a lot worse once he's been dragged out of his bed by the balls.'

Graecus gulped, gathered his skirts and scuttled away down the passage. His voice echoed back from some distance, a rising yodel of panic, soon joined by others. It sounded as if a flock of squawking little birds had been let loose in the atrium. Gwyndaf nodded, his lips forming a compressed smile.

'That's better,' he said.

Graecus had been right about one thing. Severus Maximus was not a well man. A film of sweat glistened on his sunken grey face and on the skinny forearms protruding from the sleeves of his white bed gown. There was a beaker on the table which Graecus had brought.

'What on earth do you want?' Severus's voice was a hoarse rasp.

'Well, let's think,' Kerin said. 'Shall we start with the fleet monies?'

'What?' the praetor whispered, aghast.

'Why not?' Kerin said easily. 'We know that the money was collected, and we know where it went. But now it has to go to Master Gallus. Not the closest man to my heart at the moment, but a debt is a debt. Is there anything in the treasury?'

'Not much,' Severus said, staring down at the table.

'We'll start with the gold, then. You can't move for it in this house, can you? It's one of the first things I noticed. Plates. Drinking vessels. Your jewellery. Your wife's jewellery, I'm sure, although we don't see much of her, do we? Do you give gold to your boys when you screw them into the bed, or is it all part of a slave's duties?'

Tears sprang from the praetor's sunken eyes. 'You have no right to be doing this!' he shouted. Kerin sprang to his feet. His fist slammed the table.

'I have every right!' he bellowed. There was a hand on his arm, drawing him down. He sat, quivering with rage. The beaker had wobbled, spilling a little of its contents; beads of yellowish liquid on the polished table. It didn't look like wine.

'You have no choice, Severus,' said Gwyndaf, the calm one for the moment. 'If you don't comply, we'll come back with an army and empty the house. The praetorian guard aren't going to stop us, are they? But if you're reasonable, we might only take what we need to pay Gallus for his ships.'

'And of course Londinium's contribution to Hengist's *annona*,' Kerin said. He had mastered his anger now, but the shock of its overwhelming power remained. He had not felt it coming. It was like getting knocked off your feet by a freak wave. For a moment, the praetor's cry of indignation had flung him back to the curia. Vortigern had known what was coming for months, and yet in some recess of his being he must have clung to a hope that something could be salvaged from all that blood and grief. That someone might stand firm. Perhaps it was the scale of the betrayal that had floored him. Severus took a nervous sip from his beaker.

'Where is the king?' he asked.

'As far from you as he can get,' Kerin said. 'And anyway, I am empowered to act on his behalf.' He nodded to Gwyndaf and stood up. 'We'll be back in the morning. With a wagon.'

The mist had cleared. The moon was sailing up high, casting a pale golden light over the city roofs. The streets were quiet now; just a few knots of revellers stumbling home from the alehouses.

'That was a good night's work,' Gwyndaf said. They were standing outside the main gate of Marcus Arrius's courtyard; locked and barred at this time of night, but Kerin carried a key to the small side gate in the pouch at his belt. After the debacle in the curia it had been impossible to return to his quarters in the praetor's house; and Lucius, dependable as ever, had stepped forward with a large amphora and an offer of lodgings. The remainder of the king's company had de-camped to the castra; large enough to accommodate anyone's army now that the beasts had returned to wherever beasts lived when their ceremonial services were not required.

'I'm going to Kent tomorrow,' Kerin said. 'I don't think Edlym's going to offer us any corn without persuasion, do you?'

Gwyndaf snorted. 'Not a chance. Do you want me to make ready?'

'No, I need you here. Go back to the praetor's house in the morning. Marcus Arrius will give you an ox cart. Take Titus Luca's actuary with you, and a man who can value gold and statues and all the other stuff these people have. Titus is bound to know someone. We need a list of everything that's in there, and what it's worth. But I want to remove exactly what Gallus and Hengist are owed, not a jot more.'

'Why the list, then?' Gwyndaf asked.

'Because it might be useful later on,' Kerin said. 'We don't know what's coming, or what we'll have to deal with. When you're done, go round to Alberius's house. He should pay up too, he's had his hands in this all along.'

'His hand,' Gwyndaf corrected him. They leaned against the gate and laughed. 'Alright,' Gwyndaf said. 'I can do all that. But what the hell am I supposed to do with a cart full of gold and statues?'

'You may as well take Gallus's share straight to him. We haven't got time to waste on trying to sell it. And anyway, Gallus is a merchant. He's bound to be able to get a better price for it than we could. He might even make a profit.'

'You should be the merchant,' Gwyndaf said.

'God forbid,' Kerin said. 'It's bad enough being –' he hesitated, just for an instant. It was fractional, but it was there.

'What?' Gwyndaf said. 'The chief warrior? The king's right arm? Don't try denying it this time, Kerin Brightspear.' He winked and went off into the darkness.

39

'What do you want me to do, then, lord?' Dimos asked. He was standing outside the gate of Marcus Arrius's house, next to a small cart drawn by a placid brown donkey. 'I realise that you may not have time for reading lessons just yet, but it was difficult for me to remain in the praetor's house under the circumstances.'

'I understand,' Kerin said. 'And you're right, I have no time at all.' He surveyed the contents of the cart; two modest wooden chests, and the bag in which the scribe kept his writing materials. 'Is that everything you have?'

'Yes, lord. I've never gone in for possessions.'

Kerin took the pouch from his belt and tipped the coins it contained into Dimos's hand. 'We'll come to an agreement later, but this should do for now,' he said. 'I can't leave here until the mercenaries have been paid, but the rest of our company will be heading for Cambria soon. They're out on the Campus Martius. Go there and ask for Hefydd. He looks a bit wild, but he's friendly enough. Explain who you are, and ask him to take you to Morvid the healer. He lives in my house. He can explain why, if he wants to.'

Dimos grinned. 'Marcellus *magister* was right,' he said. 'When I told him you'd engaged me, he said that it would be an interesting journey.'

* * *

Kerin recognised the horse at once. It was standing in the pen alongside Marcus Arrius's stables, making nervous conversation with the fat chestnut pony belonging to Marcus's granddaughter by the son of his first marriage. The servant Petrus, who had brought Kerin to see the horse, stood by whistling cheerily as he awaited a comment.

'Alright,' Kerin said. 'How did it get here?'

'Lord Gwyndaf brought it, lord. When you were in Kent. I think it's the stallion that Alberius bought for the king. Lord Gwyndaf said it was the spoils of war.'

Kerin exhaled; a long sigh of resignation. 'Petrus, do you understand what Lord Gwyndaf and I have been doing?'

'Oh yes, lord,' said the servant, with undisguised admiration. 'You've been getting the money and stuff that's owed to those Saxon mercenaries. And of course the taxes that were collected to pay for the war fleet and the battle in the North, except that Severus Maximus and Alberius spent most of it on their bathrooms.'

'Who told you that?' Kerin asked.

'Graecus, lord. Yellow Numidian marble and best porphyry from Egypt, or so I'm told.'

Kerin regarded the horse. It stared back at him with its beautiful white-lashed eyes. He supposed that it must have been easier to remove a horse than to tear out a bath house. And the animal must surely have some value, if people were stupid enough to believe that its ancestor belonged to a Roman emperor.

'Alright, Petrus. I expect the horse is ours, but I'm invited to Publius Luca's house this afternoon, so you can look after it for now. Give it a good feed of oat bran and groom it. It looks quiet enough.'

'Oh yes, lord,' Petrus said, looking happy with his new responsibility. 'It's quieter than Mistress Julia's pony.'

Kerin walked away. He didn't want any of the tainted goods he had sequestrated, even the valuable horse. He remembered what Varro said, at the meeting which engaged Hengist and his Jutes; something about men of politics, who lined their pockets while the ordinary man starved. Kerin had not given it much thought, because it held no resonance for him. Now he was standing knee-deep in the cesspit and the reality was here, hitting him in the face and forcing its way down his throat until he almost retched; men like Severus and Alberius, squandering money that wasn't theirs to spend, while he and his friends floundered around in a morass of mud, blood and guts to keep them and their city safe. He wondered where Varro had gone, when he rode away from Brianus's estate in despair. Wherever it was, he wanted to reach out and shake the man's hand.

* * *

The wagon rattled under the echoing arch of the city's north gate and out onto the open road. The driver, a small, middle-aged man with short-cropped dark hair, had introduced himself as Cornelius, the principal servant of Publius Luca's household.

'Where are we going?' Kerin asked.

'The master has land outside the walls. Did you know that every man who serves in the legion is granted some land when he retires? There's a little orchard, lovely at this time of year, and we grow corn and fodder for the beasts, and vegetables for the kitchen. And there's some grazing land for the horses and the milking cows.'

Kerin half-closed his eyes, letting the warm air wash

over him in a healing stream. The people walking along the roadside; the riders, wagons, mules and donkeys on their way in or out of the city; all reduced to a blur, washed along as he was on a tide of trapping hooves and birdsong. It was easy to forget, for a moment, that the world was a dark and perilous place, and that he felt more alone in it than he had ever been. The Campus Martius looked busier than ever, with a scatter of chariot teams, drilling garrison men and people riding good horses for the sheer hell of it.

'I've never seen it like this,' Kerin said. 'What's going on?'

'It's the same everywhere, lord,' Cornelius said. 'It's the victory, isn't it? People are feeling good. The merchants are commissioning new ships, the craftsmen are building work-shops and training up youngsters, the farmers are bringing more land into cultivation. They know they're not going to get invaded, at least for a while. And if another lot of bad barbarians comes along, well, we've got a good, strong king to see them off, haven't we?'

'Yes,' Kerin said; not only because there was nothing else he could say, but because he believed it. Wherever Vortigern was, whatever had befallen, he believed what everyone else believed; that the king could burn himself alive, like the bird of legend, and leap from the ashes with a shake of his red and gold plumage, to protect their hearth and home and keep the kingdom safe while they and their children slept. But none of these people had been in the curia; not one of them had stood in Quintus Parvo's stinking hut, or in a moonlit clearing where a son drew a sword on his father. And so their faith was blinkered, and unqualified, and simply grateful; while Kerin's was raw with pity and dread.

'Here we are, then,' said Cornelius. Beyond the Campus, the land rose gently towards distant wooded hills; and here in front of them, down a well-made track, was an open gate.

Cornelius drove through, waving to a bald-headed old man who was chipping away at a large stone with a hammer and chisel. The wagon creaked to a halt beside a grove of trees, all in pink and white blossom. 'I'll leave you here then, lord. There's plenty of horses if you want one to get back to the city. And you'll find the master at the other end of the orchard, sitting on the old ox cart. Much stronger, thank the gods, but don't let him near his cavalry horse or I'll get the blame.'

Kerin stood quite still for moment and listened. The wheels of Cornelius's wagon grinding away up the track, a light wind scattering apple blossom, the almost deafening hum of bees, hoverflies and a myriad other tiny insects. The old man chiselling his stone; someone a little further away hammering something with a slow, steady rhythm. And now, almost under his feet, a gang of grubby children, chasing each other in and out of the trees, pelting each other with clods of earth. One went astray and smacked Kerin in the chest. Howls of panic, a headlong flight towards the gate. Laughing, Kerin picked up the clod and hurled it back.

Publius Luca was sitting up on the driver's seat of the ox cart. The colour had returned to his face, and he had gained weight. Kerin climbed up onto the seat and sat down. For a while, neither man spoke. After everything they had endured since last year's blossom time, it was good to enjoy this moment of peace.

'You've done good work,' Publius said. 'Titus sits on the ordo, and there wasn't much else discussed yesterday. The *annona* in hand, and Gallus paid out. Who'd have thought it? You're the talk of the city, young man.'

Kerin smiled awkwardly, feeling a faint flush of colour creep up his neck. 'It had to be done. And no-one else was in a position to do it. Eldof was the hardest, because he was the first. After that it was easy.'

'Good,' Publius said. 'Because of course, we haven't seen the worst of this. It's peaceful at the moment; people feel secure. Complacent. No-one suspects the treachery within. They think the kingdom's safe, and I suppose it is, for the time being.'

'It doesn't trouble them?' Kerin asked. 'That they haven't seen the king for a while?'

Publius shrugged. 'Why would it? The Christians don't see Jesus too often, but it doesn't stop them believing that he'll save them from all their sins.'

Kerin watched the way his gaze moved slowly back and forth. Publius Luca looked as if he was doing nothing, but of course he was not. There were at least twenty other living souls working or playing on the land, and Kerin had no doubt that Publius could have told him the life story of every one. Not for the first time, he found himself wondering about the way other men lived. Who would not be tempted by all this; a flourishing orchard with well-kept buildings alongside, a pasture with a slow-moving stream and bright young corn in the field beyond? All this, and a modest house where a lovely young woman would take up her lyre, and sing the song her mother had taught her.

'I didn't know you had this place,' Kerin said. 'I thought you spent all your time in your house, and the garrison headquarters.'

Publius chuckled. 'I grew up on an olive farm in the foothills of the Apennines. The soil's in my blood. The city drives me mad.'

'Why the military, then?' Kerin asked.

'I was the youngest of three brothers. The farm couldn't possibly support all of us, so I had to leave to make my way. My father had a cousin in the army, and they were recruiting, so it was an obvious choice. I don't regret it at all. Not many men have had the privilege of commanding a great legion. And I've seen the world, met my wife and lived to tell the tale.'

Kerin looked out over this benign place and thought, despite himself, of a small, shivering girl and a white dog. The people here were working hard, but they didn't look driven. Three lads and a girl pulling weeds in the corn; a thin, older man sweeping the yard; two stocky youngsters mucking out the byre; a well-built man, stripped to the waist in the warm sun, taking a sledgehammer to a pile of rocks on the far side of the cornfield. Two short, brown-haired boys carting the fragments up the track to the greybeard with his hammer and chisel. The wild children in the orchard. Kerin wondered what it would take to insinuate one small girl and one dog into this happy-looking company.

'Do all these belong to your household?' he asked.

'Most of them,' Publius said. 'The youngsters in the corn and the byre are all children of the household staff. The older man in the yard has been with me since he was ten, the mad children belong to the cooks, and the two lads carrying rocks are Cornelius's sons. The gentleman with the chisel, however, is a skilled stone mason; very much his own man. And you might want to take a good look at the fellow with the sledgehammer and ask yourself if you'd really want him living under your roof.'

Kerin shaded his eyes from the sun and looked. The man had put down his hammer and was taking a breather, looking out across the heath where a knot of wild goats had gathered. As Kerin watched, he turned and wiped the sweat from his brow with a forearm.

'My god,' Kerin said softly.

'Indeed,' Publius said. 'I can confidently claim that I am the only man in history to have had the King of all the Britons breaking rocks in his cornfield.'

Kerin breathed deeply as he fought the urge to leap off the ox cart and run headlong down the track. 'How long has he been here?'

'A week or so,' Publius said. 'I came down here one morning and found him. He asked if I had anything for him to do. I gave him the sledgehammer and told him to get on with it. With the benefit of some experience, I do believe that mindless physical toil is the best cure for a lot of things.'

'Has he said anything?' Kerin asked. 'About anything?'

'No,' Publius said. 'I've told him a few things. He hasn't been to the house. He sleeps in the byre with the cattle and horses. The servants leave food for him; much as you would do for a wild animal if you were trying to get near it. Perhaps that's what I'm doing.'

Kerin closed his eyes. The sound of the sledgehammer resumed; bang, bang, ring, ring, driving him to distraction. 'Should I go down there?'

'I have a suggestion,' Publius said. 'Dine with us tonight. I'll invite him. He may or may not come, but your company will be more than welcome. I need an excuse to open a good *fundanum*.'

40

Cornelius opened the iron gates and led Kerin into a court-yard shaded by ancient fig trees. Vines clothed the walls, bursting into bright new spring growth. Their leaves rustled in a warm, light breeze; doves murmured from the branches of the fig trees and the columbarium overhead. A carriage was standing outside the front door.

'Lord,' Cornelius said, 'Marcellus *magister* is here, attending the master. He craves a word with you before he leaves, if you have time.'

'Of course,' Kerin said. There would never come a day when he had no time for Marcellus. He sat on the low wall of the pool and closed his eyes, letting the soft sounds of the water and the doves calm him, and trying very hard not to think about what might be waiting for him inside the house.

'My lord chief warrior?' a voice enquired, after a while.

'Marcellus!' Kerin rose to embrace the old man. They sat down together on the wall.

'Good,' Marcellus said. 'There is to be no argument about the chief warrior business. It's time to put an end to the pretence, and for me to offer you my congratulations. That corn would not have found its way to Londinium without some help, I imagine.'

'Not a chance,' Kerin said. 'Edlym was shamefully reluctant to part with it.'

'But part with it he did,' Marcellus said. 'You've learnt

a trick or two, I'm sure. And now you are about to dine with Publius Luca and his family. The invitation did come from Publius, I take it, and not from his distinguished house guest?'

Kerin smiled ruefully. 'His distinguished house guest was never one for invitations, Marcellus.'

'No,' Marcellus agreed. 'More often the command or the twisted arm, I imagine. But then, he is clearly not in the mood for such stratagems, or Edlym's corn would have arrived long ago. What will you do?'

'I don't know.' Kerin paused. 'Was he there when you saw Publius Luca?'

'Indeed he was. Watching me like a large predatory bird, in case I gave Publius the wrong medicine.' Marcellus smiled as Kerin grimaced. 'Don't worry. Whatever it is, you will deal with it. You have worked things in these past few days that would have been thought impossible a year ago. Men would have laughed at the suggestion. Am I right?'

'You are. But this is different.'

'Yes,' Marcellus said, 'but you will deal with it. In fact you must deal with it, because whatever happened in the curia that night, Vortigern is still King of all the Britons, and the only man who can possibly hold the kingdom together when the next disaster comes along.'

'I know,' Kerin said, 'but the expectation is – ' he hesitated, hardly knowing how to put it.

'Unfair?' Marcellus said. 'Yes. I know.'

'How did you find him?'

'Courtesy itself,' Marcellus said. 'Always bad news, in my experience. Good luck.' He rose, patting Kerin's arm, and shuffled off towards the waiting carriage.

Cornelius came from the house, smelling faintly of spices

and roast meat, and led the way to a small inner courtyard, where he introduced Kerin to Publius Luca's wife. Gaia Fulvia was a tall, gracious woman, beautiful in late middle age, and despite having borne a son and two daughters. For God's sake, she looks like an empress, not a soldier's wife, Kerin thought. It was easy to see what had captivated Publius all those years ago.

'Kerin Brightspear!' she said. 'I have heard a great deal about you.'

Kerin smiled. 'All of it good, I hope, my lady.'

'Most of it very good,' Gaia Fulvia said. 'They say you can be a little impetuous. But there; if the young man is not impetuous, what hope is there for the old? Come, let us join the others.'

She took his hand and led him from the courtyard. His fingers enclosed by her light, perfumed clasp, Kerin was acutely aware that he had not known a woman's touch since he was in Gael's bed, months ago, in what seemed like another life. They passed down a dim corridor with frescos on each side. There was a statue of one of the emperors; a small shrine to Mithras. A deep red banner hung on the wall, bearing the strange image of a goat with a lobster's tail, in faded gold. Kerin recognised the insignia from Publius's shoulder-pin, and supposed that it must be an old battle standard of the Second Augusta. He could hear voices close by, one unmistakably Publius Luca's, the other a woman's. The corridor opened into a large, light space with cheerful yellow-gold walls and a central hearth.

'Our son Titus, whom you have met, and his family,' Gaia Fulvia explained. Publius Luca was sitting on a cushion-strewn couch beside the hearth. Titus was standing alongside. A dark-haired young woman, his wife, Kerin supposed, was sitting cross-legged on the floor, laughing as her two small daughters besieged the commander of the city garrison. 'Publius is far too indulgent with his grandchildren,' Gaia Fulvia said, in a tone which conveyed both mild disapproval and affection. Publius looked up. It seemed odd to see him in the white toga of a Roman gentleman.

'Kerin!' he said. 'Come, join us over here. You've met Titus, and here is his wife Clodia and their children.' Cordial greetings were exchanged, and Kerin was invited to sit on the couch.

'I'm glad you've come, Kerin,' Titus said. 'A sane opinion regarding the body-count amongst the Picts would be welcome; my father's estimate grows every day.'

'As you know, Titus is a lawyer,' Publius Luca sighed, as if that explained everything. 'They can talk, but they can't count.'

'Well, I'd say your estimate was on the low side,' Kerin said. 'You can't possibly have included the ones we fought after you were wounded.'

Titus raised his hands. 'I give up,' he said amiably. 'I might have known two warriors would stick together. And we lawyers may be able to talk, but we still need men like you and my father to keep the barbarians outside the gates.'

Publius Luca winked. 'I've told him it's an occupation for knaves and robbers. But I can't expect him to take much notice when he's worth more than I am at the age of thirty-five.'

Titus chuckled and picked up his daughters, one under each arm. 'Come on, Clodia,' he said, 'let's leave the military men to their dinner. Father, we'll meet tomorrow morning to decide what to do about Severus Maximus.'

Clodia kissed her father-in-law, gave Kerin a shy smile and followed her husband out. Gaia Fulvia went with them, fussing over her granddaughters.

'Don't take any notice of me,' Publius said. 'He's as good a son as a man could have, and he could jump over my head where brains are concerned. He'd be wasted in the military.'

'What did he mean? About Severus Maximus?'

'Well,' Publius said, 'we're going to tell Severus that unless he resigns his office, we'll prosecute him and his associates for misappropriating state monies. Titus is the best lawyer in Londinium, and much feared; that apart, I have an efficient army at my disposal at the moment, and Severus was always receptive to a little pressure. I never thought I would get involved in this sort of thing. It's my fervent belief that soldiers should stay out of politics. But when the men of power are this corrupt, and cause this much damage, there's not much choice. I've seen enough over the past few weeks. Severus will resign. Or we could just kill him, of course.'

And on that note, Cornelius came from the kitchen to say that the cooks could hold the food no longer, and it was time to go to table.

* * *

It all began normally enough. Publius Luca was seated at the head of the table, as became the *paterfamilias*. Kerin had been invited to sit at his left, next to the older daughter of the family, Larentia, who was staying with her parents whilst her husband was away on business. Gaia Fulvia was sitting to her husband's right, opposite her daughter. Next to her, facing Kerin, there was a vacant seat. Vortigern came in as the serving boys were bringing the first course of stuffed vine leaves. He spoke courteously to the family, sat down and greeted Kerin with a formal bow of the head.

'I trust you are well,' he said.

It was a patrician's greeting; the sort of thing Kerin had

heard him say a hundred times to members of ordines and petty officials. Polite, bloodless, non-committal; designed for men who were essentially a waste of his time.

'I'm well, thank you,' Kerin said stiffly. The boys served the vine leaves and poured the wine, a clear, pale *falernum*. 'And are you well, lord?' He could manage the restraint, if not the polish.

'Quite well,' Vortigern said.

Kerin picked up one of his vine leaves and tasted it cautiously. It was delicious, stuffed with a forcemeat of chicken and dried fruit. The wine was sweet and not too strong. He smiled at Gaia Fulvia.

'The food is excellent, my lady. You have a good cook.'

Gaia Fulvia appeared to restrain a smile. 'I stole him from Severus Maximus several years ago. So you see, you were not the first to rob the praetor's kitchen.'

Publius Luca raised an eyebrow. 'My wife is not the praetor's most fervent admirer. It was ever so, although things have gone downhill of late.'

'There's more stuffing in these vine leaves,' Gaia Fulvia said crisply. Kerin chuckled. He would have liked to laugh out loud, but he wasn't sure if it was seemly to laugh at or with Gaia Fulvia. Vortigern ate his food in silence, with neither relish nor complaint.

'How is your Saxon cook these days?' Publius asked.

'Keeping his head down since Hengist came ashore. But he's a good, honest man and a marvellous cook. Just don't ever make him lose his temper.'

'So,' Gaia Fulvia said. 'What will happen when you take a wife? Will she be happy to find a grumpy Saxon installed in her house?'

'My lady, I'm sure she'll be happy not to have to do the cooking,' Kerin said, then paused with a foolish smile, realising that he had spoken as if the event were already planned. Publius Luca twinkled at him.

'Wisely spoken, Kerin. There are far better things for a woman to do than spend her time stirring a pot. And besides, she must have delicate little hands if that's her ring.'

Kerin coloured to the roots of his hair. He realised, with terrible apprehension, that Vortigern was looking straight at him. He smiled weakly back. Vortigern shrugged.

'What of it?' he said. 'You'll leave whenever it pleases you.'

Like all the others, Kerin thought, although nothing was said. The boys collected the empty platters and brought a sucking pig surrounded by stuffed dates and baked apples. Kerin's patience was leaking away. He had neither wanted nor expected lavish praise, but some brief mention, some acknowledgement of his efforts did not seem too much to ask. 'I've got Hengist's corn,' he said. 'And the rest of the *annona*. And the fleet monies.'

'I had heard,' Vortigern said. Publius Luca made an almost imperceptible gesture of resignation. The serving boys carved the pig and passed the platters. The family ate with gusto, and there was a pleasant conversation about Larentia's children and their dogs.

'I'm staying at Lucius Arrius's house,' Kerin said. When this drew no response, he added, 'I didn't feel that I could stay on at the praetor's residence, under the circumstances.'

Vortigern looked up. 'Don't bleed on my behalf,' he said. 'That's a fool's pastime.'

Publius Luca must have seen the flash of anger, because he raised his hand as Kerin opened his mouth to speak. Kerin composed himself and mouthed a silent apology to Gaia Fulvia and her daughter. He knew that none of this should have been happening at their dining table, but he felt bitter and demeaned, and beyond keeping his mouth shut.

'I could have done nothing,' he said, his voice calm, flat with effort. 'I could have sat in some alehouse and got drunk. That's what most of the others have been doing.'

Vortigern's eyes flashed. 'I know what you've done,' he said. 'We are all in your debt.'

Kerin felt as if something had shifted within him; like some great dam of branches and debris, years and years of it, all the obligation and habit and pure love, shifting and admitting a slow trickle of resentment. He stared down at the table, fists clenched in front of him as he fought to steady the flow, knowing that if he let it overwhelm him, everything might be lost.

'Lord, you will never be in my debt,' he said. Larentia's chair squeaked anxiously on the flagstones. Kerin looked up just in time to catch Vortigern's eyes – so eloquent, on the rare occasions when the guard dropped. He flinched.

'You must excuse me.' Vortigern rose, bowing briefly to Publius Luca and his wife. He went out and closed the door behind him. His footsteps echoed away down the passage towards the courtyard. Kerin got up hurriedly.

'Forgive me, commander,' he said. 'Forgive me, my lady, Larentia. Your hospitality is wonderful, but I must deal with this.'

The outer gates were closed and locked. There was an archway on the far side of the courtyard leading to a small, formal garden of lavender and clipped bay trees, with a stone balustrade overlooking the lawn of some rich man's house and the gleam of the river beyond. Kerin marched straight up to Vortigern and grabbed his arm.

'How could you address me like that? Like some Roman functionary?'

Vortigern freed himself. 'Formality has its uses,' he said. 'It stops things getting out of hand.'

It would be some time before Kerin understood what he had been told. For the moment he simply felt aggrieved. He stared at the river, rippling under the moon. 'I didn't want thanks. But to have all that ignored – '

'I don't ignore it,' Vortigern said. 'Publius has made a point of telling me about it. In detail and with great relish. And what you did was beyond any expectation I ever had. I hoped you could hold things steady. But not that.'

Kerin shrugged. 'Someone had to do it. I'm still not sure it was my place.'

Vortigern returned to his examination of the river. 'It was my place, I know.'

'No, lord, that's not what I meant. It would have been Rufus's place, if things had fallen out differently. He should have been here, doing all those things without a second thought. But he wasn't, and in some ways I suppose that made things easier for me. Please don't think I wished it; I couldn't possibly wish it, for you or me, or for him. But while he was around there were things I couldn't do, simply because it was your oldest son's place to do them. Whether he was actually doing them or not wasn't the point. It wasn't my place.'

Vortigern looked round. 'You know, I never thought he'd go. Not like that, anyway. I don't think it surprised you at all, though, did it?'

'Not really,' Kerin said. 'When a man starts telling you that God's more important than bedding a willing girl, anything's possible.'

Vortigern smiled to himself; whether because he found the idea amusing or for some other reason Kerin neither knew nor cared. He was simply glad to see it. Slowly, almost imperceptibly, he could feel a few things beginning to slide back into place.

'We'll leave tomorrow with Hengist's *annona*, then,' Vortigern said. 'God knows, I'd sooner go straight home. But we have to do that first, and do it ourselves.'

'Yes,' Kerin said. 'But Hefydd and his boys should head for home with most of our army. We owe it to those men to see their families and heal their wounds. Apart from the warband, we don't need more than a hundred good warriors here, and we want all our men fit and ready for when we need them next.'

'Yes,' Vortigern said. There was no need for discussion at this point. Both men knew what the Cambrian army would be needed for; it was simply a matter of sequence, and even Kerin did not know that yet. 'We're going to do this properly,' Vortigern said. 'No sneaking out at first light, as if the *annona* were something to be ashamed of. We'll leave in the morning, by the north gate. The king's company, in battle trim.'

'I'll see to it,' Kerin said.

'Yes. Whatever you think, it's your place now. Not Rufus's, even if he comes back. It's your place.'

Kerin could find nothing to do but stare down at his boots, trying not to weep like a child.

'Thank you, lord,' he whispered. A silence enveloped them, clinging like fog. Kerin knew that he could not let it settle. 'I'd prefer not to raise this now,' he said. 'But our first concern should be whether Glevum and Kent make common cause with Rufus. I don't think it'll happen immediately, but we should be on guard for it.'

Vortigern looked away. 'Gorlois was right. They're a bunch of faithless bastards.'

'Well, of course they are,' Kerin said. 'But you always

knew that. You said it to Publius, the night I killed Quintus Parvo. There's nothing new in it, lord. The way it happened was unforgivable, but it was coming some time. And whatever was said in the curia, not one of them would have the nerve to stand up and say it in public. I expect things will stay as they are now, until they all find something else to be frightened of. Then they'll be back.'

'And Rufus?' Vortigern asked. 'What will he do, do you think?'

'I don't know. I'm not that good a prophet.'

'Get some sleep, then,' Vortigern said. 'I'll see you outside the castra at daybreak tomorrow.' As if nothing had happened. He strode off towards the stable. Kerin watched him go. It looked normal, but it was not. It was like the sudden light on a day of sunshine and violent showers; brilliant and fragile, impossible to predict. Kerin hoped that it would be enough.

'Well?'

Publius Luca had come from the house with a goblet of wine in one hand and a silver jug in the other. He handed the goblet to Kerin and took a draught from the jug. It was not the gentle wine they had drunk at table.

'Not entirely,' Kerin said. 'But perhaps well enough for now. Tomorrow we leave with Hengist's *annona*. And then home to Cambria for a while, if I have my way.' He paused. 'Thank you, commander.'

'Thank you?' Publius Luca looked perplexed.

'For this. For everything.'

'I want no thanks where he's concerned,' Publius said. 'Call it an unpaid debt, if you will.'

'I can't,' Kerin said. 'None of that was your doing.'

Publius sighed and raised his hands. 'I know. But I don't think I'll ever be rid of it. When evil is committed in your name, it leaves a taint. And then you spend the rest of your life trying to scrub it away.' A smile flickered. 'But by Jupiter, I'm glad you killed that old bastard.'

Kerin grinned. He was glad too, although it had not really solved anything.

'How long do we have?' Publius asked.

'How long is it until the twenty-second day of Junius?' Kerin asked. Publius Luca calculated.

'Six weeks,' he said. Kerin performed some calculations of his own.

'Well,' he said, 'in six weeks' time, Rufus will be on his knees, praying to St Alban that I'll walk into his chapel a changed man.'

'You are a changed man,' Publius Luca said. 'But not in the way Rufus might wish.'

'No,' Kerin said. 'He ought to know that it's pointless, but he'll keep on hoping. And praying, I suppose. Praying that I'll change my mind, and that God will tell him what to do next. If God tells him to fight his father, I'll have to start sharpening my spears.'

'Does he want the kingship?'

'Not for its own sake, I don't think. But as a means of doing God's will – yes, of course he does. And I've heard the way men like Eldof talk. They think Rufus is soft. A pushover. That they could use him to grab power for themselves. If we're lucky, once they get back to their home comforts they may not think it's worth the trouble. They've all been to war, they probably want peace as badly as we do. Abbot Paulinus would fight us in an eye's blink, but only if the others joined him. And I don't think they will, unless something happens to stir them up. Something I haven't foreseen. It would have to move the priests, the real fire-breathers, as well as men like Eldof and Bertil who just want the power.'

'Something like a massacre of Christians?'

'Yes, but not that. Who'd do it? If nothing happens, we'll probably have a year. It would take that long for Rufus and Paulinus to raise a real army. Or for the Saxons to grow strong enough to be a nuisance. Because we'll probably have to fight them too, in the end.'

There was more he could have said, but there was little point in saying it to Publius Luca; soldiers had no truck with the insubstantial, even soldiers as wise and perceptive as Publius. They wanted enemies they could see; threats they could counter with strategy or physical force. They didn't want premonitions. They didn't want feelings that defied explanation; even though Kerin's was so real, so vivid, that he could feel it thrusting its bony fingers into the back of his neck. Out there in the darkness, something was waiting for him. It was nothing he had divined, nothing he had foreseen; but perhaps his interpretation was at fault. He was a warrior, and he had made a warrior's forecast; a prospect of savagery, as much of his life had been, where men drank from golden cups then went out to kill and maim and burn each other to death. But there was more than one way to wield a knife. Perhaps he had simply not seen where it was coming from.

41

Vortigern was outside the castra at daybreak, just as he had said. He and the black mare looked ready for anything. Kerin rode out through the praetor's gateway and stopped alongside him. Gwyndaf was in the garrison's barren courtyard, marshalling his warband. Beneath the statue of Minerva, Lud was readying the warriors who would escort the transports. A door opened somewhere and the sound of voices echoed under the archway. A very young, uniformed soldier appeared. It was Kerin he had come to see.

'One of Marcus Arrius's lads for you, lord,' he said apologetically. 'Not Petrus; it's the skinny lad who cleans out the animals. Silvius, is it? He looks in a right pickle.'

It could have come at a better time. 'Alright, send him out,' Kerin said. The soldier trotted away. Silvius was soon standing where he had been; a pale, gangling lad, always hanging around the stable yard with a bucket, as Kerin recalled. But there was no hanging around this morning, the boy was panting, as if he had run all the way from Marcus Arrius's house.

'You'd better come, lord,' he gasped. 'Your horse has kicked Petrus's brother through the fence and broken his arm.'

Kerin chuckled. 'You've got the wrong horse, Silvius.'

'No, lord.' The lad looked desperate. 'The big white one. It kicked Mistress Julia's pony too, and bit it in the neck. I wouldn't make it up, lord. The praetor's servant Graecus is there, with the boy who used to look after the horse when Alberius had it. We thought he might know what to do.'

'Go and get them, then,' Kerin said. Silvius scuttled off down the street.

'What's this about?' Vortigern asked.

'That white stallion,' Kerin said. 'The descendant of Caligula's horse Incitatus. When I went to Kent, I sent Gwyndaf to collect valuables from the praetor and his cronies. The horse was part of the bargain.'

Vortigern gave a snort of derision. 'That lady's riding horse? It's broken somebody's arm?'

'I can't believe it has,' Kerin said. 'You saw the horse when Alberius brought it to the triumph. It was meek. It just stood there. I'd be less surprised if Marcellus *magister* had kicked someone through the fence.'

The boys were coming back. Graecus had with him a slight olive-skinned boy dressed in silken pantaloons and a loose green embroidered jacket. Short jet-black hair, eyes dark as pools. Fourteen or fifteen years old, Kerin supposed. He looked in terror of his life. Graecus made a hurried bow.

'Lord King,' he said. 'Lord Kerin. This is Ashur, Master Alberius's stable boy. Please to excuse him, he's from Egypt and they only bought him a few months ago, so he doesn't speak much British or Latin yet. I can help him out if you like. Some of my master the praetor's slaves speak his tongue.'

'Well, for God's sake tell him that we're not going to eat him,' Kerin said. Graecus translated. Ashur smiled nervously. He looked less than convinced. 'Did you look after the horse?' Kerin asked. 'The big white horse?'

'Yes, lord,' Ashur whispered.

'And was it a nice horse? A friendly horse?'

A grimace. 'No, lord. Not much.'

Graecus was twitching with impatience or nerves; perhaps both.

'You know what this is about, don't you,' Vortigern said. 'Come on, spit it out, or we'll be here all day.'

Graecus smiled half-heartedly. 'Well, Lord King, Master Alberius couldn't resist buying this horse for you to ride, because – well –' he floundered to a halt.

'Because everyone would think he was a man of stature and genius if he could provide this horse for the king?' Kerin suggested. 'This horse that's supposed to be descended from the emperor's beast?'

'Yes, lord. Exactly that. But I think he was expecting a well-behaved horse. One that would march nicely in the procession, like an emperor's horse is supposed to do.'

'And instead he got a bad-tempered bastard that kicks people through fences,' Kerin said. 'Alright, then, Ashur. It's your turn now.'

Ashur smiled hesitantly. 'I hope you not tell my master Alberius.'

'No. We won't tell him. What happened?'

'We feed the horse, lord,' the boy said. 'We buy in the market and we feed him.'

'You feed him? What do you feed him?'

'A man says seed-heads of the *papaver*, lord. I am sorry, I cannot say in British.'

Kerin could not say either, and there was going to be no assistance from Vortigern, who was helpless with laughter.

'Lord, can you explain?' Kerin asked. Vortigern recovered himself.

'Poppies,' he said. 'Those red things you see around the cornfields. But they grow a different kind in the south, and extract opium from the seed-heads. Marcellus uses it to knock people out before he cuts them open or chops their legs off. And some of the rich men take it because they can't bear their lives. I've never heard of anyone feeding it to a horse, though. Was that your idea, boy?'

Ashur stared at the ground. 'Yes, Lord King,' he whispered. 'In Egypt, I – ' he broke off and stared beseechingly at Graecus.

'His father's a horse master in Egypt,' Graecus said. 'Quite a rich man, with a big house and a garden with fountains and date palms. They came from Parthia or somewhere and settled there. It was pure bad luck that Ashur got caught by the slavers and ended up here. He's been with horses since he was born and he's got a way with them, so when they had trouble with the white one, Alberius asked if he knew how to make it quiet. And this is what happened.'

Vortigern looked the boy over. 'That's a strange set of clothes for a stable lad,' he said. 'Not much good for working in.'

Ashur's dark, almond eyes clouded over. He started fiddling with his fingers. Kerin noticed that his nails were bitten to the quick. 'I have to do other things too, Lord King,' he said, scuffing the dust with the toes of his sandals. 'Things for Master Alberius. I not want to say, I am sorry.'

'Ah,' Vortigern said. 'And would you prefer not to do these things?'

Ashur glanced up. 'Yes, Lord King.'

Vortigern nodded to Graecus. 'Alright. Take him to Publius Luca's house and give him to Cornelius. Say the boy belongs to me. Tell Cornelius to burn those clothes and dress him in something decent. Then tell Ashur that he's coming with us, to look after my horses. Tell him I'll work him like a dog, but I won't beat him and I won't screw him. That's all. Off you go.'

The boys set off for the house, their feet pattering on the damp flagstones. Graecus looked nervously over his shoulder.

'Lord King, what shall I say to Master Alberius?'

Vortigern's eyes rested on the Parthian boy. A small wrinkle of disgust, then nothing. 'Tell him I've got his piece of meat. That'll suffice, I'm sure.'

Kerin watched the boys vanish amongst the gathering horsemen. 'Lucky lad,' he said. Vortigern looked round.

'I went out to our camp at first light. I wanted to see Hefydd and his boys before they left. Morvid was there, pulling rotten teeth. Your lad Marc was with him. And a child I haven't been told about.'

Kerin stared up at the paling sky. 'I would have come to it.'

'There's no need now. Marc told me what happened.'

Kerin twitched uneasily. 'What did he tell you?'

'The truth, I'm sure,' Vortigern said. 'He told me he found the girl near the villa where Eldof and his crew went. He said she was running away because that brute Balin had raped one of the other children. That you'd forbidden him to bring her, but he hid her in one of the cooks' carts.'

'It's all true,' Kerin said. 'I refused to take Padarn's people, so I didn't think I should take the girl for Marc. I found out, but I hadn't the heart to send her back.'

'It doesn't matter,' Vortigern said. And probably it did not, amidst the slew of troubles confronting him; but somewhere in all this Kerin heard an echo of something older.

'What do you want me to do?' he asked.

'You can tell Marc to wait for the boy at Publius's house. Then send them all home with Hefydd and the army. Your hangers-on and the Parthian boy. That scribe of the praetor's, if you want him. And the descendant of the Consul Incitatus.'

* * *

Padarn sat high on the front of the horse-drawn wagon, twitched the reins and started whistling as the walls of Londinium receded. Kerin, who had hitched his horse to the tailboard, was sitting beside him. He knew the tune because Iustig used to sing it, years ago, when the abbot was trying to teach him; something to do with sun and rain and the creatures of the woods, and, of course, with God. Padarn looked like a cleric again. He had got someone in Londinium to shave his crown and was wearing a modest ivory crucifix, a gift from Abbot Giraldus. It was startlingly white, carved from a walrus's tusk. This was no ordinary cart, of course; it was the one which carried the triple-locked strongbox containing Hengist's money. Another substantial chest was stowed beside it, banded with iron and secured with a stout padlock. Malan, not to be done out of his responsibilities, was riding escort; but it was Padarn who had been entrusted with a key. Keeping his voice low, he explained what it contained.

'The little olive-wood box that the Lord Vortigern keeps his writing materials in,' he said. 'All the papyrus, some already written on. He's had some craftsman bind them inside a beautiful leather folder. Then there's all the unused papyrus, and some scrolls; I'm not sure what that's all about, one of them looks ancient, as if it might go right back to the Romans. The Lord's had a box made for it; he was putting the scroll inside when I met him in the praetor's library, and he was handling it really carefully, as if he thought it might fall apart. Then another scroll, much newer. I didn't ask. I was honoured to be trusted with the key, but what's in there is the Lord's business.'

'He's writing a history,' Kerin said. 'Like Julius Caesar did.

An account of our campaigns, the battles, the arrangements between leaders. He believes that it's the only way to keep a true record. That if it's not done, things will be twisted, and no-one will ever know the truth of what happened. And he's right. It's getting twisted already. You weren't there that night in the curia. I'll tell you when I can. But for now, make sure you guard that key. I've no idea what the scrolls are, but everything else is to do with the history. Guard it well.'

'I will,' Padarn said, holding up the key. It was hanging on a leather thong, next to the cross of walrus ivory. He took a deep breath of the clear air. 'It's good up here. Cities are no good for country boys. I'll be glad when we've got rid of this stuff and we can all go home. It's still alright for me to come along, is it?'

'Yes, of course it is,' Kerin thought of all the monk had done in the North, and how well he deserved a reward. 'What did you do with Edra and the children?'

'Sent them down to Eburacum with some other refugees. I told Edra to look for the horse-dealer I knew years ago; he was a good man.'

'I know you couldn't leave them,' Kerin said. 'And you were back when we needed you. The men won't forget that.'

'Nor I,' Padarn said; no doubt the vision of blood and agony which came to Kerin's mind had also come to his, as he remembered those days.

42

On a warm, cloudless morning, Kerin shook himself awake and went down to the nearest stream. They had camped in a thin birch wood, not far from the villa where Marc found Catula. The stream was wider than the Roman road, tumbling down over glistening black rocks into a deep pool where minnows darted in the shallows. Kerin threw off his clothes and plunged in. The clear, cold water closed over his head. He surfaced, gasping and blinking water from his eyes, and struck out for the far bank.

'Much better than the Roman baths,' a voice said, startlingly close. Vortigern was swimming alongside. They dived and swam underwater to the base of the rapids, surfacing beside the dark rocks. 'We'll be with Hengist by tomorrow, even at the wagons' pace.'

'Earlier,' Kerin said, pointing towards a low ridge. 'The sea's just over there.'

'Of course it's not. It's two hours' ride on a good horse.'

'No, lord. If we climb to the top of that ridge, we'll be able to see it.'

'How much do you wager?' Vortigern asked.

'Well, I don't know. What about the belt I had from Gallus? The one with the silver buckle?'

'Done,' Vortigern said. 'If you're right, you can have that flask of wine Publius gave me.'

They hauled themselves out onto the bank, shook

themselves dry in the warm wind and flung on their clothes. The ridge was steeper than it looked. By the time they reached the summit they were both panting, but Kerin at least was justified in wearing a self-satisfied smile. Not far to the east, glinting brightly under the sun, lay the sea. Vortigern sighed.

'Enjoy the wine,' he said, turning for the camp.

'Wait.' Kerin touched his arm. 'What's going on down there?'

A lazy curl of smoke was rising from a blackthorn thicket. They approached cautiously through the bracken. Two thin men were squatting beside a brushwood fire, watched by two scruffy ponies. The men's clothes were in rags, although one was sporting a jaunty brown hat with a pheasant's tail-feather. His dirty red cloak was hanging from a bush nearby. The other was wearing a faded blue tunic and had tied a strip of frayed brown cloth round his head. They were examining a collection of articles laid out on a torn cape beside the fire; two cheap daggers, a broken bridle, a belt without a buckle, an oil-lamp and three sesterces.

'Come on,' Vortigern murmured. 'Leave them to it.' They turned to go. A dry twig snapped under Kerin's boot. The robbers leapt up.

'Oy, come back here, you two!' the one in the hat shouted. Kerin glanced at Vortigern, who shrugged helplessly as the robbers advanced. The struggle was brief and one-sided. The ponies watched without apparent concern as their owners were knocked senseless and laid out on the ground.

'Well, what now?' Kerin said. 'We don't want any of that stuff.'

Vortigern's face, unsmiling for so long, assumed a conspiratorial grin. 'Come on,' he said. 'Let's have some fun.' He shook out the tattered cape and flung it round his shoulders.

Kerin threw on the dirty red cloak and the brown hat with the pheasant's feather. Vortigern looked down at the unconscious robber with his blue tunic and headband. He bent down, ripped a strip of cloth from the hem of the tunic and tied it round his own brow. Kerin laughed out loud.

'Lud wouldn't recognise us!'

Vortigern seized the reins of the robbers' ponies and handed one set to Kerin. 'Come on, then. Let's go and see what Hengist's up to.'

They rode up out of the hollow and off across open moorland towards the sea. Kerin didn't feel too comfortable bobbing around on the stocky pony, but his spirits lifted as the keen sea air rushed to meet them. He would have given anything at that moment to be the anonymous thief he was impersonating; riding for the sheer hell of it, as they had done once, in another world.

They drew rein at the rim of the valley. Below lay a scene of prodigious activity. Hengist's island was seething like an ants' nest. A big central building and several smaller ones looked finished, but others were in various stages of completion. Teams of men were toiling back and forth across the causeway carrying logs for the walls and bundles of reeds for the roofs. A fleet of galleys rode at anchor in the lagoon, drawn up in an orderly row with sails reefed. A wooden jetty had been constructed on the bank of the creek. Hengist's ship was tied up there, distinguished by the ornate blue and gold designs on its prow. Two figures were moving about on deck, cleaning up and coiling ropes. The whole spectacle reeked of industry and organisation.

'Come on,' Kerin said. 'Let's see what pickings there are for a couple of robbers.'

They kicked their reluctant ponies and cantered down

through the bracken. By the time they reached the jetty, one of the two people working on Hengist's boat was walking away with a rolled-up sail on his shoulder. As they came alongside the prow Kerin saw, to his complete surprise, that the person working on the fore-deck was a woman. She was wearing the usual rough brown tunic and cross-gartered breeches of the Saxon seafarers, and a grey woollen cap was jammed down anyhow on her head, but none of this could disguise the fact that she was an arrestingly good-looking girl. She noticed them and stood up straight, holding the rope which she had been coiling. She pulled off the woollen cap, liberating a mass of long corn-coloured hair. Her deep blue-green eyes regarded them curiously; or at least, they regarded Vortigern. It did not take Kerin long to realise that she was completely unaware of his presence. Vortigern looked straight back at her. The woman's eyes did not leave his as she spoke.

'What did she say?' Vortigern asked.

'She asks who you are, lord,' Kerin said grudgingly. He did his best not to sound indignant. Oath-bound or not, spoken for or not, it was galling to be ignored by a beautiful young woman in favour of a man almost twice his age on a robber's pony. Vortigern leaned on the front of his saddle.

'Tell her I'm a brigand chief,' he said. Kerin told the woman. She tossed her silky hair contemptuously as she replied. 'What did she say?' Vortigern asked.

'She says that there are already enough brigands in the ship's company,' Kerin said.

'Alright, then. Tell her I'm the King of all the Britons.'

Kerin grinned. 'She's not going to believe that, lord.'

'Tell her anyway,' Vortigern said. Kerin translated. The woman laughed out loud and let out a stream of invective which would have done credit to any of the ship's crew. Vortigern looked round enquiringly.

'She calls you a lying dog, lord,' Kerin said calmly. Vortigern chuckled.

'Tell her she's got a nerve to say that to the King of all the Britons,' he said. Kerin told the woman. She planted her hands on her hips and her sea-green eyes flashed.

'Well?' Vortigern asked. Kerin shrugged.

'She says that she spits on the Britons.'

Vortigern nodded. 'Tell her that I spit on them myself, most of the time,' he said. Kerin told the woman. She frowned, then flung down her rope, hurled her hat at them and stamped off towards the stern of the ship. Laughing to himself Vortigern slipped from the pony's back and untied the rope securing the galley to the jetty. He put his shoulder to the prow and heaved. The galley drifted gently out into the creek. The woman, sensing movement beneath her feet, spun round. Spitting fury, she seized a spear from the deck and raised it to her shoulder.

'Move!' Kerin said. 'If she can throw that thing as well as she can swear, we're in trouble.'

Vortigern jumped onto his pony and they rode for the causeway. The spear whistled between them and splashed into the lagoon. Vortigern dragged the pony to a standstill. He turned and bowed ceremoniously. The woman shrieked at him and threw her arms about as the galley drifted on, colliding with one of the boats moored in the middle of the lagoon.

'Come on,' Vortigern said, as all the boats began to knock into one another. 'Before she finds the oars.' At the village entrance their way was barred by a group of ferocious-looking youngsters. One bellowed a bloodcurdling challenge.

'He says we'll be fish food if we don't surrender,' Kerin said. 'I don't recognise any of these, do you?'

'No. Ask them where Hengist and Horsa are.'

Kerin enquired and listened carefully to the response. 'At sea, not far from here. Hengist has a new ship, and they're trying it out. I've told this one who we are. He doesn't believe me, but he's prepared to take us to Hengist.'

They dismounted and allowed themselves to be marched into the village. The warriors took them to a small boat. It looked strongly made and had two pairs of oars. Kerin and Vortigern were ushered aboard and made to sit on one of the crossbenches. Two of the Saxons sat opposite them, swords across their knees, whilst another two shoved the boat out, sprang aboard and seized the oars. The sea was much choppier than it appeared from the clifftop, and the boat bobbed and took on water as it met the waves. The Saxons all looked blithely unconcerned, and Kerin supposed that they must know what they were doing.

'There!' one of them shouted, pointing. 'Out there, do you see? Hengist's ship. Now we shall see who's telling the truth.'

The galley was bearing down on them with alarming speed. It was larger and faster by far than any Saxon ship Kerin had yet seen. He supposed that Hengist must be feeling confident in the arrival of his *annona*.

'Lord Hengist!' one of the oarsmen bellowed. 'Look what we've got here!' Horsa and Oswi appeared on the deck of the galley. They hauled the sail down and reefed it, and the ship drifted gently on the waves. Hengist came to the side. 'Look, lord!' the warrior shouted, hardly able to contain his glee. 'These scabby beggars say they're the King of all the Britons and his chief warrior. Shall I feed them to the fishes?'

Hengist exploded with mirth. Horsa and Oswi joined in.

'No!' Hengist roared. 'Hengist will do it himself!' As the rowing boat arrived below him he climbed up onto the side of the galley. Horsa and Oswi followed. Kerin and Vortigern exchanged uneasy glances. The three Saxons flung their arms in the air, roared some oath which even Kerin didn't understand and leapt from the side of the galley, landing with a force which nearly capsized the rowing boat. Water poured in as it rocked about, and the four Saxon warriors started bailing frantically with their hands. Kerin found himself wrestling with Horsa in the bottom of the boat. He was hoisted up the side of the galley and landed on the deck between Vortigern, who was gasping and spitting seawater, and a pile of freshly-caught fish. Hengist clambered over the side, laughing and shaking water from his hair.

'Well, you scabby beggars!' he said, 'I hope you've come with my *annona*.'

'Of course we have, Hengist,' Vortigern said. 'Did you doubt us?'

'Not for a minute, lord,' Hengist said, sitting down on the deck. 'You and your friend the Roman are men of your word. How far away are your people?'

'Half a day's march for the wagons,' Vortigern said. 'They'll be with you by tonight.'

'Then tomorrow night we feast!' Hengist exclaimed, clapping his hands. 'You have not lived until you have known a Jute feast. So much ale, so much meat!'

'You've got a new boat, then, Hengist,' Vortigern said, looking up at the tall mast.

'Oh yes, lord,' Hengist said proudly. 'The finest ship-builder I know has made this ship. I think the Picts will not trouble you while Hengist has a ship like this.'

Kerin studied the ship. There was no doubt at all that it had been built by a master. Every joint looked tight and firm, every surface beautifully finished. He knew next to nothing about ships, but two things were apparent; firstly, that building one like this was costly, and secondly, that it could not be done overnight.

'Do you like my ship, Kerin Brightspear?' Hengist asked.

'Yes,' Kerin said. 'I don't know much about ships, Hengist, but this looks like a good one to me. Have you paid for it?'

Hengist looked affronted. 'You think Hengist would take something without paying?'

'No, of course not,' Kerin said. 'But a ship like this must cost a great deal, and I know what a poor country you come from. I was wondering if perhaps you had made an arrange-ment – ' he waved his hands vaguely and gave Hengist a knowing wink, of the sort which he imagined might be exchanged by men of the world.

'Alright, I pay part,' Hengist said grudgingly. 'I pay the rest now you have brought my *annona*. You have brought my *annona*, yes?'

'Of course we have,' Kerin said. 'You'll have it this evening.' He wondered whether Hengist would have been confident enough to spend the money if he had known how hard it might be to extract it, and just what it was that had made him commission a ship like this all those months ago, before he even set foot on the beaches of Kent. Horsa and his lads had the sail up again now, and the wind swelled it as they secured the ropes, making the ship leap forward like an eager horse. They sped towards the lagoon, leaving two of the warriors labouring behind in the rowing boat. Oswi seized the steering oar at the stern and aimed the vessel to-wards the narrow passage into the lagoon. It was miraculous to Kerin that something so large and so much at the mercy of the wind could be guided with such accuracy. Hengist's blue-painted ship was tied up at the jetty where they first saw it. No-one was on board. The remaining galleys were spread out all over the lagoon; one was listing slightly, and another had beached itself on the shingle. Hengist frowned.

'Something has happened here, I think,' he said. Vortigern stifled a laugh. Hengist jumped ashore, leaving Horsa and Oswi to tie up, and marched off towards a couple of men who were standing on the bank, holding the two ponies. The men gesticulated and pointed at the old galley. Hengist turned, incredulous. 'Lord, these are your horses?'

'Those donkeys?' Vortigern said. 'Hardly. We'll borrow them to ride back to our camp, though. Unless your cooks want to use them, of course.'

'No, lord, take them, take them, we do not eat these beasts!' Hengist entreated. 'We already have meat and drink enough,' he added, eyes glinting. 'And for your brave young warriors, we have also many pretty girls, who have come over in the ships of their fathers and brothers. Battle is for the warriors, but when a man builds a village, it is not good if there are no women in it. That is the way to trouble, don't you think, if there are no women?'

Vortigern raised his eyebrows. 'It's trouble either way, if you ask me,' he said.

'Did you tell anyone where we were going?' Kerin asked as they mounted up.

'No,' Vortigern said. 'They probably think we've drowned. We could ride straight back to Henfelin, and nobody would be any the wiser.'

'On these?' Kerin chuckled.

'On anything,' Vortigern said. 'On a mule. On an ox-cart. We could walk. We're going to give Hengist his *annona* and go to his wretched feast, and then we're going home.'

They turned the ponies towards the head of the valley. A group of girls had gathered beside the river. Some were washing clothes in the water whilst the others sat in a huddle chirruping like a flock of sparrows, just as Kerin had seen Mabli and her friends do when they were discussing what they had done the night before, and with whom. As they rode away, a girl in the centre of the group started singing. Her voice was soft and clear, pitched higher than Gael's; the tune sweet, melancholy and instantly memorable.

'What's that about?' Vortigern asked.

'A girl's waiting on the shore for the man she loves,' Kerin said. 'She fears for his life, and asks the gods of the sea to speed his ship.'

Vortigern drew rein and listened until the haunting little melody ended. The songbird went back to chirruping with the sparrows. Vortigern smiled and kicked his pony into life. Up on the rim of the valley, two riders were coming towards them at a canter.

'Lord!' Lud exclaimed. 'Where have you been? And those clothes? And the ponies? This is dangerous country, for the gods' sake!'

Kerin and Macsen exchanged knowing grins. There would be time enough for explanations over that flask of best *fundanum*. Had Kerin known what was coming, he would have taken more care to savour the pleasures of their slow ride back to camp through the warm afternoon; the laughter, the bright sky full of wheeling gulls, and Lud on his towering warhorse, remonstrating with a smiling brigand chief who dismissed his advice before drifting off on a track of his own, humming a wordless song about ships and the sea.

43

Kerin awakened late in the afternoon. Something had hit him in the back. The empty amphora was lying beside him under the ox-cart.

'Sorry to kick you, Lord Kerin,' said Malan, 'but if you and your friend don't get up soon, you'll miss the feast.'

Kerin crawled out. Malan was holding a water-skin and trying hard not to laugh. 'Go and do the same to him,' he groaned, emptying the water over his head. He soon heard Macsen retching behind his tent; not the best precursor to a feast.

It must have rained heavily in the night. There were deep puddles everywhere and the slope down into Hengist's valley was slippery and soft, but a stiff breeze had blown the bad weather away eastwards. As they rode across the causeway into the village, the moon was up and stars were coming out. Padarn met them by the animal pens. He had declined the invitation to the feast, but had come along to look after the horses.

'You can't move in there,' he said, taking the reins. 'I didn't realise they'd got so many warriors here. How are your heads, then?'

'Not too good after Publius's wine,' Macsen said. 'But a few jars and some food will sort them out. Why don't you come in, then, Padarn? I expect the horses can manage.'

'Oh no,' Padarn said. 'There are already things going on

that a monk shouldn't see, and the feast hasn't even started yet.'

Oswi and Aelle were standing at the door of the hall. They greeted Kerin and Macsen cordially.

'That way, that way!' Oswi cried, propelling them forward. 'The ale it is here, and the food and the women, they come soon!'

Inside, benches and narrow tables had been set out along each side of the hall. Serving girls were bringing out jugs of ale and mead. A trestle had been erected in the centre of the floor, and kitchen slaves were piling food on it. Vortigern and Hengist had already occupied the place of honour, at the centre of a raised table at the far end of the building. There was a vacant seat at Vortigern's side.

'You're late,' Vortigern said, as Kerin arrived. 'But you've missed nothing, unless you want to watch some of our boys making fools of themselves.'

'Well, I'd call it having a good time,' Katigern chortled, from his seat to Kerin's left. A casual glance along the hall revealed only rows of warriors drinking, but then Bened's head popped up for air. There was a gap about the width of a man's body between the benches and the outer wall, and as Kerin looked more closely he saw that Bened's was only one of several bodies thrashing around down there. Some of the serving maids had got no further than delivering their first jug of ale. One, a tall girl with fair curls, smiled coyly as she presented Kerin with a tankard and a jug. She was wearing a low-cut brown dress with a loosely laced bodice, revealing more of her full white breasts than a man with another woman's ring around his neck might ever have wished to see. Kerin closed his eyes and took a deep breath. Katigern guffawed.

'Come on, man!' he said, clipping Kerin across the head.

'Your girl's never going to know. Make the most of it, for God's sake.'

The servants had finished bringing the food. There were cauldrons of stew, legs and ribs of pork, pigs' heads and four whole roasted sheep, carried in on spits. Horsa came loping across the hall, impaled a leg of mutton on his sword and presented it to Vortigern with a regal bow.

'Taste, Lord King! Does our meat taste as sweet as those Cambrian lambs your men keep talking about?'

Vortigern hacked a chunk of meat from the joint. 'The best I've tasted this side of the river,' he said. Horsa waved his arms and roared an invitation to the warriors. They all came leaping over the tables and threw themselves upon the food. Meat was devoured, ale flowed and the torches burned high on the wattle walls, casting a warm yellow light over the cheerful, rowdy gathering. Hengist surveyed the scene.

'It is a good feast,' he said softly, with a look of satisfaction and profound relief.

Evening slipped into night. The racket in the hall became deafening. The Jutes, who looked as if they had been drinking all day, finished gorging themselves and broke into raucous songs. The Britons joined in, making up a few uncomplimentary lines in their own language. A group of girls had arrived in the hall, far more richly dressed than the servants; daughters and sisters of the well-born, Kerin supposed. There were some beauties amongst them, tall and strong like their male relations, their long, luxuriant hair ornamented with jewelled combs and fine gold slides. The warriors on the packed benches, who had been elbowing each other out of the way all night, soon managed to make room for the girls. Hengist grinned.

'I think your warriors like our pretty girls, Lord King.'

Vortigern watched the performance. 'Do you know what the Christian priests would tell them, Hengist? That the devil will carry off their souls, if they lie with pagan women.'

Hengist chuckled. 'I have only one thing to say to that, Lord King. Odin be praised that our gods are more tolerant.'

As the songs petered out, Oswi strode forward into the middle of the hall, carrying a drinking horn. The servants, who seemed to know what was coming, hurriedly removed the trestle table. Oswi drained his drinking horn, planted his hands on his hips and launched into a tale of his prowess as a horseman. The Saxon warriors applauded as he flung his arms about, describing how he had once leapt his horse into a raging whirlpool to rescue his beloved from the sea-god. Kerin yawned, homesick for Henfelin and the bard's poems. Cynfawr was as big a liar as Oswi, but at least he only boasted on behalf of others. Oswi's story shifted from the whirlpool to the bedchamber. The well-born girls were being more than friendly towards the Cambrians, who seemed cheerfully unconcerned about the fate of their souls. Hengist leaned across and offered wine.

'It's a pity you don't understand much of our tongue, lord. Oswi tells a good tale.'

Vortigern grimaced, watching Oswi's explicit gestures and facial contortions. 'I don't need the Saxon tongue to know what he's talking about.'

Hengist began to look anxious again. 'Does our feast not please you, lord?'

'Forgive me, Hengist.' Vortigern patted his arm. 'Your hospitality is wonderful. And you have a fine place here; no-one could possibly have made more of it. But it's a while since we saw our home in Cambria. I need to be on the road to the West.'

'But, lord,' Hengist reasoned, 'surely if the meat is good and the company is good, the place does not matter?'

Vortigern shook his head vaguely. Hengist withdrew with a forced smile. Kerin sipped his drink uneasily. The Saxons outnumbered their guests by two to one. There could be alarming consequences if all that hospitality were suddenly to turn sour.

'Lord King!' Horsa bellowed. 'What do you think of these lovely girls? Are they as pretty as your little Cambrian lambs?'

Vortigern ran his eye over the Saxon women. 'Which one sings the songs?'

'She is not here,' Hengist said.

'Bring her,' Vortigern said, yawning and rubbing his eyes. 'Anything's better than listening to Oswi.'

Hengist gave his brother an odd look which Kerin could not interpret. Horsa winked at him and went out of the hall. Hengist shouted to his servants, who brought more ale for the warriors and wine for the high table. Soon Horsa reappeared in the doorway at the far end of the hall. Hengist got up and hammered a tankard on the table.

'Silence!' he roared. A sudden quiet descended, broken only by the occasional cough and creak of timbers. Hengist smiled. 'Silence for the singer of songs.'

The young woman came in through the door and stood quite still. Her long, silken hair gleamed in the torchlight. She had exchanged her rough seafarer's clothes for a leaf-green dress, the colour of her eyes. It was fastened modestly at the neck with a small gold brooch and fitted her like a second skin, flaring gently from the hips to float about her ankles as she walked. Katigern whistled softly.

'Have you ever seen anything as beautiful as that?' he murmured. The woman was holding a golden chalice, its bowl set with jewels. It was filled to the brim with wine, and the wine was the colour of blood. The woman acknowledged

Hengist with a smile, then her eyes met Vortigern's, and the smile faded.

'No,' Vortigern said softly. 'Not this.'

The woman came up the room as if drawn on an invisible beam. She knelt before the table, but there was no submissive bow of the head. Her eyes did not leave Vortigern's as she spoke. Hengist looked bemused. 'Lord?' he said curiously, reaching for Vortigern's arm.

Vortigern closed his eyes. 'To hell with it all. Kerin, what's she saying?'

It was as much as Kerin could do to reply. 'She would like to greet the King of all the Britons. But first, she has a score to settle with a brigand chief.'

Vortigern leaned forward, his eyes on the girl's. 'She can settle it later.'

The words seemed to require no explanation. A faint flush of colour rose to the girl's cheeks. Hengist looked nonplussed.

'Lord, this is my daughter, Rowenna.'

'Your daughter!' Vortigern said.

'My only daughter. She is as dear to me as my life.'

The girl rose to her feet and held out her golden chalice. '*Laverd cyning, washael!*' she said. Vortigern gripped Kerin's arm. 'What's she saying?'

Kerin looked mutely at the young woman and the brimming chalice. 'Lord, don't drink,' he said.

'What's she saying?' Vortigern repeated. 'What should I do?'

Kerin looked away, sick at heart. 'She calls you lord king and asks you to drink. Lord, don't drink. Please, don't drink.'

Hengist laughed. 'This is an old custom of our people,' he said merrily. 'The receiver of the wine should say *Drinkhael*. Then he should drink the wine, and kiss the giver.'

Kerin seized Vortigern by the shoulders. 'Lord, don't drink!' he shouted. Vortigern freed himself.

'*Drinkhael!*' he said, and smiled. The girl held out her chalice. Vortigern scrambled over the table, seized it and drained it dry. A rowdy cheer went up from the warriors. Oblivious to it, Vortigern took the girl's hand and pressed it gently to his lips. Kerin turned away. Hengist moved up to make room on the bench. Vortigern tried to make conversation, stumbling awkwardly over his few words of Saxon. Rowenna laughed, but entirely without mockery; it was the warm, good-natured laughter of an old friends' meeting. Hengist intervened, a willing translator. Kerin tried to close his ears. Katigern was getting distracted by one of the Saxon servants. She squeezed into the tiny gap between Lud and his son, whispering something in Kat's ear as she sat down. Before he had a chance to reply, she unbuckled his belt and slipped her hand inside his breeches.

'What do you think, Kerin?' he gasped. 'What do you think? What do you think?'

'It's the end of everything,' Kerin said. Katigern guffawed happily, too full of drink and too excited by what the woman was doing to care much about anything else.

'What on earth are you talking about?' he slurred.

'Well, Kat,' Kerin said, 'if I were you, I'd get my horse's saddle out and give it a good clean, because he's going to marry that girl.'

Katigern blinked and sat bolt upright. 'What?' he said, removing the woman's hand. 'Almost everyone's got a girl. It's for one night, for God's sake.'

'No,' Kerin said. 'Not that.'

'But he can't *marry* her!' Katigern exclaimed. 'She's no older than we are. And she's a pagan. It's impossible. It's forbidden. No priest would do it.'

'Did that stop him crowning Constans?' Kerin asked.

'Well, no,' Katigern said, 'but – ' the remark was stifled as the woman planted her open mouth over his. Katigern shoved her away, horrified. 'Kerin, do you mean this?'

'He'll marry her,' Kerin said. 'I see it all. He'll marry her, and Eldof and the Kentishmen will go running off to Rufus. And then they'll fight us.'

'Horsa!' Lud bellowed. 'What's Oswi up to?'

Oswi the Horseman was on his feet. He marched up the hall and stood glaring at Hengist and Vortigern. Horsa chuckled.

'Poor old Oswi. He's lusted after Rowenna for years. She'll have none of him, or any other man. Pure as the virgin snow, my niece. Gifts, pretty compliments; all no good. And now look what's happening, in the time it takes to down a cup of wine.'

Vortigern had noticed Oswi. He stood up. Kerin returned instinctively to his side as the singing and laughter died away. A brittle silence fell as the two men confronted each other. Kerin had forgotten how tall Oswi was until he saw them standing face to face. The Saxon looked straight across Vortigern's shoulder at Hengist.

'Your daughter's gone mad,' he said, speaking in British to ensure that all the right people understood him. 'She could have any of our young warriors. Now she wastes her time on a crazy Briton, who's almost past straddling a horse. Let alone a woman.'

Vortigern's eyes half-closed. 'I could better you on both counts.'

'A horse race!' someone bellowed. The warriors roared their agreement. Oswi grabbed Aelle and said something Kerin couldn't catch. The young warrior ran from the hall. A wave of laughter ran along the benches. The Saxons seemed to be sharing some private joke. There was a commotion outside. The blanket screening the doorway was torn aside and Aelle barged in, leading Oswi's horse. The Saxons jumped up and cheered. Oswi smiled proudly, taking the animal's reins. The stallion tossed its jet-black mane and gazed around the hall, stamping its forefeet and quivering.

'Merciful God,' Vortigern said. 'It's Garagon's racehorse.'

'This horse was a gift from the gods,' Oswi said, glaring defiantly. 'I was asleep after the battle in the North. I heard a sound and the horse was there, waiting for me. I think Odin sent him, to reward Oswi the Horseman for the way he fought the Picts.'

Vortigern smiled faintly. 'Well done, Odin,' he murmured. Kerin raised his hands.

'I couldn't possibly have known,' he protested. 'And you can't race that horse. It's the fastest thing I've ever seen.'

'I'm not going to race the horse,' Vortigern said. Oswi caught what he said and turned.

'You fear to race Oswi the Horseman!' he crowed.

'No,' Vortigern said. 'I don't fear it at all. But there'd be no point. I've already won.'

Oswi's brow creased. 'Now you mock me. There has been no race. No race, no prize, no winner.'

'There's only one prize I desire,' Vortigern said. His eyes moved to Rowenna, who was standing at her father's side. Hengist blinked. The warriors fell silent.

'Lord,' Hengist said, 'I do not think you should take Rowenna's little jest too seriously. This matter of the cup and the kissing, it's an old custom of ours, no more.'

Vortigern's eyes held the girl's. 'Ask her if it was a jest,' he said. Hengist frowned. He bent his head to speak to his daughter. Rowenna's head went back and her eyes flashed. She spoke quietly, but with a perfect clarity which enabled Kerin to understand every word.

I have always told you that this would happen. I have always told you that I would know him when he came to me. If you give me to Oswi now, I will sail your ship out to sea and drown myself.

Hengist cleared his throat and looked up. 'Lord, my daughter is a virtuous maiden, and a princess of our people. Hengist does not lend out his daughter for a night's sport. Even to the King of all the Britons.'

Vortigern's lip curled with disgust. 'I'm not looking for a night's sport,' he said. 'Unless that's all your daughter wants, of course. Ask her if it's all she wants.'

'Lord, that is not something a father can ask his daughter,' Hengist said stiffly. 'And as you already know, my daughter is a virtuous maiden. How could that possibly be all she wants?'

'It couldn't,' Vortigern said. 'So ask her what she does want.'

Hengist, looking increasingly anxious, took his daughter by the arm and led her outside. Vortigern watched the open doorway whilst his warriors milled about, muttering uneasily.

'Lord,' Kerin said, 'how can you do this? How can you even consider it? If you marry this girl, there'll be war within weeks. Leave it. Leave it now. I know Eldof and the others have turned, but we do have some friends left. We could go back to Cambria now.'

'And let it all happen again?' Vortigern said. 'What's left for me, Kerin? My son has tried to kill me. The other two will go to him when it suits them. The men we fought with have betrayed me, and broken every agreement we made.'

'And you're going to solve all that, by marrying this girl?'

'No,' Vortigern sighed. 'No, of course not.'

'No,' Kerin said. 'And what would happen in Cambria, if you arrived home with a pagan wife?'

Vortigern stared up at the sky. 'I think you know quite well. The ordinary people wouldn't give a damn. Then the priests would go mad, and try to persuade all those ordinary people to side with Rufus and the Sword of God.'

'Then don't do it, lord. Every man here would die for you if necessary. We can hold Cambria against Glevum and Kent, if they decide to come after us.'

'We could have stayed in Cambria in the first place, and let Garagon's cornfields burn,' Vortigern said.

'Well, of course we could,' Kerin said. 'But it's no good expecting him to remember that now, is it?'

'No,' Vortigern said resignedly. Hengist appeared in the doorway. Vortigern seized Kerin by the shoulders, his eyes glistening in the torchlight. 'Kerin, you cannot tell me what to do in this.'

Kerin shook his head. 'Lord, please. I know you want the woman, but –'

'Oh no,' Vortigern said, letting his hands fall. 'It's worse than that.'

Hengist came to them. He looked utterly perplexed. 'Lord, Rowenna tells me that you wish to marry her. I know for certain that you have not asked her, because I have been beside you all night, and you do not speak our tongue. Is she right, or has she gone mad?'

'She's right,' Vortigern said. 'And she's no more mad than I am. Some men might regard this as an honour for their daughter. I don't expect you to. She's not marrying the King of all the Britons. She's marrying a brigand chief.'

Hengist threw his hands up. 'Lord, I do not understand. But my daughter is saying the same thing. She does not care if you are a king or a criminal. Well, so be it. I shall not prevent this. But for me, you are the King of all the Britons. You are asking me for my dearest possession, and there must be some recompense.'

'Of course,' Vortigern said. 'I'd expect nothing less.'

Hengist bowed. 'Then I must speak with my brother Horsa.'

'Do it,' Vortigern said. 'I want this settled.'

'Lord, this is mad,' Kerin said as Hengist withdrew. 'Do you realise what you've said to him?'

'Yes. I realise what I've said to him. But in the end, unless he asks me for the West, which he will not do, what difference does it make? Let him ask.'

'Let him ask,' Kerin echoed. 'And what did you tell me when I asked? When I told you I loved Bertil Redknife's daughter, and couldn't give her up? You told me to forget about it, because it would split the kingdom in half and we'd end up with two thousand dead. A woman I'd loved for months. And now you're going to do the thing – the *one thing* – you forbade me to do, for a woman you don't even know. A pagan woman, when half the people opposing us are cleansed-in-the-blood Christians. Do it, then. Do what you like. But you can do it without me.'

He ran, between the huts and round the edge of the village to the horse-pens. His tack was hanging on the rail with all the rest. He fumbled through the tangle of reins and girths looking for his bridle. Padarn came out of the darkness.

'Kerin! What on earth's the matter, lad?'

Kerin realised that he was weeping. 'He's going to marry that girl. Hengist's daughter. He's going to marry her.'

'Oh, God the Father,' Padarn groaned. 'Why can't he just sleep with her and have done with it?'

'Don't ask me,' Kerin said, throwing the bridle over Eryr's head. 'Don't ask me anything. I'm going.'

'Where?' Padarn seized the reins. 'You can't just go, lad. What'll happen?'

'I don't know.' Kerin flung on his saddle. 'I'm going, Padarn. Please don't try to stop me.'

Padarn let the reins drop. Kerin galloped away across the causeway and up the valley. The men were singing about ale and whoring and fighting. The sound was punctuated by female squeals and laughter. Above it all Kerin could have sworn that he heard Vortigern's voice bellowing for him in the darkness, but it was probably the valley's echoes playing cruel tricks. He had no idea where he was going. He was aware of the ground rushing by beneath the mare's feet, of her breathing growing harsh as the miles wore on, of the blast of wind in his face. Nothing more.

It was dawn by the time he realised that flight was pointless. He reined in on a low hill and tried to get his bearings. The sky was still cloudless and the pole star was shining like a beacon. After resting the mare, he let her drink from a bog pool then set off across the empty moorland. Soon he struck a cart-track. Fresh ruts and piles of dung confirmed that it was frequently used. A man came in sight, driving six fat milking cows. He nodded to Kerin and stopped, leaning on his stick.

'Am I going the right way for the sea?' Kerin asked.

'You are, sir. Over that way, maybe ten Roman miles. Your horse looks tired. You've ridden a long way, I suppose.'

'Yes,' Kerin said.

'She's a fine horse, if I may say so. Are you one of the king's warriors?'

'Yes,' Kerin said. He didn't know what he was any more, but there was nothing else to tell the cowman.

'Well, when you see the king, make sure you tell him that this land's his to the last drop of blood. We'll never forget what he did for us in the North.'

Kerin nodded an acknowledgement and rode off before the cowman had time to ask any more questions. Ahead of him, a scattering of alders became a thin wood. It fringed the clearing where the wagons had halted before heading down into Hengist's village. He turned onto the Roman road and stopped. Two riders were approaching at a fast canter; the steady, ground-eating pace of men who had a long way to go. Katigern and Paschent drew rein as he rode to meet them. Kat looked white and haggard.

'We're going to look for Rufus,' he said.

'He did it, then.'

'Married the girl? Oh, yes. For the love of God, couldn't he have picked a British girl, or a Christian, or someone his own age? She's younger than you, for God's sake.'

'He's jealous,' Paschent said, with a sly grin. 'One look at her and he nearly burst out of his breeches.'

Katigern turned crimson. 'Shut your mouth, weasel-face.'

'All that's beside the point, anyway,' Paschent said. 'The point isn't that this goddess prefers my father to my brother, although she does.' He laughed at Kerin's blank look. 'At last, something he hasn't discussed with you. Well, let me inform you that in return for his daughter, Hengist decided that he would like to have another piece of Kent. I'm sure Garagon and Edlym will have different ideas when the Saxons arrive in their cornfields.'

'That's why we're going to look for Rufus,' Katigern said. 'Kent will go mad, and I suppose Rufus will join in. Or is it the other way round? I'm not sure any more.'

'No,' Kerin said. 'Neither am I.'

'Come with us, then!' Katigern grabbed his arm. 'Rufus is your friend, your blood-brother.'

Kerin said nothing, but just below the surface lay the bald statement which Vortigern himself had made, on the night when he could have ended his son's life. An echo of what Katigern had said, but so much more consequential; so much worse. *He's your friend. Your blood-brother. You could take his side – Eldof's side. They'd give you Bertil's daughter on a platter as a gift of thanks.* Kerin sat waiting for Kat or Paschent to say something, because that would save him from confronting this question which had no answer. He wanted nothing more, at that moment, than to turn tail and ride to Glevum. To snatch Gael from her father's hearth and take her to some deserted house, and lock the door, and lose himself in her.

'Don't waste your time, Kat,' Paschent said. 'You might as well have a conversation with that dead tree over there.'

They left him in the middle of the road and rode off towards the south. Kerin watched them go, then he slipped from Eryr's back and sank down on a boulder at the edge of the road. Nothing in his life had equipped him to understand what was happening. No-one had ever thrown him out of his home, or locked him up and tortured him to the edge of death. No-one had betrayed him. Even his love for Gael was only a foretaste of what promised if he could build a home with her, father children on her. But he could not begin to comprehend how he would feel if he won all that, only to lose it; far less how he would bear with it. As he sat in the still twilight, bereft of hope, he felt a thin hand clasp his arm. No-one was there, of course, but he could feel the pressure of those fine, bony fingers as surely as if their owner had been sitting beside him. Yes, said the steady, wise voice of the haruspex; we have come to it at last. How perverse, that it took a moment of rank madness to make you grasp the only sane solution.

For the first time, Kerin understood precisely what Marcellus had told him months ago, in his green garden

413

in Londinium. The most important task in the kingdom was not merely to anticipate, to predict, to use his fighting skills and speak the truths others feared to tell. It was to do the things Vortigern could not do. Kerin had missed the point because he grew up believing that the man was indestructible. Immortal, in some way. The people of the West had believed it for years, and in the truest sense, there was no illusion at all. Everything the people loved was real and enduring. No wonder they had faith. But their faith was blind, perhaps because it had to be, to save them from despair. It took no account of costs they would never have to pay, of consequences that could not harm them. They had bequeathed all those to a man who was not a god, whatever they thought; not indestructible, not impervious to fear, agony and doubt. Now, Kerin realised, it was for him to take this upon himself. To be measured when Vortigern could not be; steadfast when fate left him broken. To navigate through insanity like the past hour in Hengist's hall, and to do all these things with such sleight of hand that no-one would even notice. They would see only the peerless warrior who had saved them from their enemies; not the man standing beside him, quietly keeping things steady.

Kerin had no idea if he was equal to this task. It would demand the sacrifice of his own dearest hopes, at least for now. The perfect way to honour his debt, he supposed. A life for a life in almost every way. As frightened and daunted as he had ever been, he turned his horse towards the sea.

* * *

The sun was rising when Kerin reached the valley. He rode across the causeway and into the sleeping village. Snores and grunts came from some of the houses. Kerin dismounted, unsaddled Eryr and turned her in with the other animals. Against his expectations he found that he was hungry. One of the ox-carts had been drawn alongside the cooks' hut, its load of oak casks brimming with corn. Bread seemed unlikely at this hour, but the hut might hold a few leftovers, if the cooks were careless and the dogs not too enterprising. Kerin trudged along the shingle bank towards the hut, then stopped short. Vortigern was sitting on the tail of the wagon, watching the sun come up over the sea. He turned as he heard Kerin's footsteps crunching towards him.

'Lord,' Kerin said. Vortigern looked back at the sea. Kerin leaned against the end of the cart. Vortigern picked up a handful of corn and let it trickle back into the cask.

'You'll have heard,' he said.

'Yes,' Kerin said.

'Padarn married us. I thought you should know that before anyone tells you that some pagan priest did it.'

'Good,' Kerin said, wondering what might have been passing through Hengist's mind at the time, let alone the monk's. Vortigern took up the clipeum and let it spin.

'You'll have heard the rest too, then.'

'About Kent? Yes. I saw Kat and Paschent on the road.'

'I owe nothing to Garagon,' Vortigern said. 'Nothing at all.'

'No. That much I do agree with.'

A light breeze ruffled the sea. A flock of sandpipers rose from the mud-banks in the lagoon and flashed away along the beach. Vortigern turned. 'I thought you'd gone.'

'So did I,' Kerin said. 'But here I am.' He picked up a flat pebble and sent it skipping across the water.

'If you had any sense, you'd have kept on riding,' Vortigern said. A tense silence hung between them until he seemed unable to bear it any longer. 'Say it.'

'Why?' Kerin said. 'What for? What's the point?' Vortigern said nothing. His silence drove Kerin mad. 'For the love of God, give her back to her father! You've lost your sons, and after all you said about the men losing their souls –'

'Losing their souls?' Vortigern said. 'You don't believe that nonsense, do you?'

'I don't know what I believe any more, lord,' Kerin said. Vortigern picked up another handful of corn and let the little hard yellow grains run away through his fingers.

'What difference does it make?' he said. 'If it's drivel, nothing matters. And if it's true, my soul is damned to perdition as it is.'

44

The village was in chaos. Half of the Saxon warriors were loading their ships ready for the voyage round the coast to Kent, while the rest prepared wagons, oxen and horses for the long trek overland. Aelle would remain at the village, overseeing the building works. Hengist and Horsa themselves would lead the seaborne convoy, while Oswi the Horseman took charge of the wagon train. The corn supplied as part of the *annona* had already been unloaded into a sturdy grain store, leaving the transports available for the journey. It seemed ironic that all those oxen and carts were going to find their way back to Kent; although Kerin, for one, could not foresee them ever finding their way back to Edlym.

He helped himself to some bread and salt meat from the Saxons' kitchen and threaded his way through the wagons. Padarn was moving patiently amongst them, adjusting badly fitted harness and securing loads. Kerin found Lud outside Hengist's hall. He was standing alongside a cart to which he had harnessed two fine grey mules. The cart was full of cushions and blankets and looked comfortable enough for an empress to ride in, but Lud was red-faced and perplexed. He threw his hands in the air as Kerin arrived.

'She won't ride in it,' he said.

'Why not?' Kerin asked. 'It looks fine to me.'

'Oh yes. It's perfectly fine, but that's not the point. She

wants to ride a horse. Forget, if you can, that she's never sat on one in her life before.'

'It'll kill her,' Kerin said. 'Does she know how far it is?'

'Yes. She knows. Of course, I can't get to the bottom of it because we don't understand each other, but Horsa says there's no shifting her once her mind's made up.'

'I'll sort it out,' Kerin said. 'Where is she?'

'In the hall, arguing with her father. She says she can't ride a horse in a dress, but Hengist says it's not seemly for the king's bride to wear breeches, and it'll bring disgrace on his house.'

There was a crash inside the hall, like a piece of pottery shattering. Rowenna came out. She was wearing the clothes Kerin had first seen her in, on the deck of her father's galley. Her face was flushed, and her eyes were dangerous. She noticed that Kerin was smiling.

'You think it's funny?' she demanded, in her own language.

'Well,' Kerin said, 'when a man as powerful as your father can't tell his daughter what to do, then yes, I suppose it is.'

Rowenna gave him a disapproving glare. 'Do you have a wife?' she asked.

'Not yet,' Kerin said. 'Why do you ask?'

'If you did, would you let her ride a horse?'

Kerin raised his hands. 'Please, if you're having an argument with your father, don't ask me to take sides. Perhaps it's Vortigern you should ask.'

'But would you?' Rowenna persisted.

'Well, yes, I would,' Kerin conceded. 'In fact, my wife would have to ride a horse, because in Cambria all the warriors do, and I wouldn't expect her to walk behind me.'

'You see?' Rowenna shouted, and stormed back into the hall. Lud covered his eyes with his hands.

'I'd go before Hengist comes out, if I were you,' he

said. Kerin wandered off towards the horse-pens. Oswi the Horseman was there, checking the legs and feet of the Saxons' ponies. It was the first time Kerin had seen him since the feast. He felt sorry for Oswi, even though he was boastful and had insulted Vortigern. Not only had the man lost a girl he'd wanted for years, he had lost her publicly, in front of all his fellow-warriors.

'Hello, Oswi,' he said, leaning on the rail. The Saxon looked up, grunted and went back to picking a brown pony's foot. 'How's your horse?' Kerin asked. Oswi dropped the foot and stood up.

'You make fun of Oswi the Horseman?'

'Not at all,' Kerin said. 'Why should I do that?'

Oswi shrugged. 'No reason, perhaps,' he said, leaning beside Kerin. 'But you know how a man feels, in front of a girl, in front of the warriors –' he groaned aloud.

'You were unlucky, in a way,' Kerin said. 'Vortigern didn't need to take up your challenge. But if there had been a race, you'd have won it. Your horse is the fastest I've ever seen.'

Oswi frowned. 'You see him before, then?'

'Yes,' Kerin said, wondering how best to put it.

'But Odin –'

'Yes, I'm sure Odin guided the horse to you. But before that, he belonged to Garagon, the Lord of Kent. Garagon brought him on a ship from a hot country where they have lots of racehorses. He wanted to ride him in the North, but the horse knows nothing about fighting. He'd have got frightened, and someone would have killed him. So the night before the battle, I let him out. He must have wandered around for a while before Odin decided to lead him to someone who'd look after him.'

Oswi shook his head. 'I think you cannot make this up.'

'No, it's all true. I thought perhaps I should warn you.'

'Ah!' Oswi said. 'You think something happens, if I take the horse to Kent?'

'Well, I thought you should know about it,' Kerin said. 'I'm sure you're not too worried about Garagon.'

'The balls of a house mouse,' Oswi said darkly. 'You are right, Oswi the Horseman is not too worried.' He paused. 'Why do you tell me this? I call your Lord Vortigern a crazy old man.'

'I don't blame you for that,' Kerin said. Oswi grimaced and stalked back to the ponies. Kerin left him to it and strolled back towards the hall. Oswi was exactly the sort of warrior he liked to have on his side, but for now a lack of hostility was enough. Rowenna was not to be seen, but Hengist was standing beside the wagon having a tight-lipped conversation with Lud. As Kerin arrived, Vortigern emerged from the house alongside Hengist's hall, blinking and rubbing his eyes.

'Lord,' Hengist said, 'I have told my daughter that the wife of the King should not wear the breeches of a common seafarer. It is an insult to your house and mine. I hope that you will agree with me.'

Vortigern shook himself awake. 'What's this about?' he asked.

'Lord,' Lud said wearily, 'we've prepared this wagon for your wife, but she won't ride in it. She says she wants to ride a horse instead.'

'Where is she?' Vortigern asked.

'In my hall, lord,' Hengist said tartly. 'She refuses to come out.'

Vortigern shook his head. 'Come on,' he said to Kerin. 'I'll need you for this.'

Rowenna was standing in the middle of the hall. The light from the doorway revealed a streak of tears glistening on her cheek.

'Ask her what this is about,' Vortigern said.

'I think I've got a good idea, but I'll ask her anyway,' Kerin said. Rowenna clenched her fists as she replied. 'She believes that when a woman marries, she should live as her husband lives,' he said. 'You ride a horse; she'll ride a horse. And once we leave this village, she doesn't want me to speak Saxon to her. She understands a lot of British because she listened to Oswi teaching her father, but she wants to learn to speak it properly. That's all, really.'

'Tell her how far it is to Henfelin,' Vortigern said.

'Lud's already told her that, lord. She's insisting on the breeches because she says you can't ride a horse in a dress.'

Vortigern beckoned to Rowenna, stretched out his hand and tilted her chin.

'Tell her that if she wants to kill herself, it's her privilege,' he said. 'Tell her that we're taking the wagon anyway, to carry the body.'

Kerin translated. Rowenna laughed; a cold, brittle laugh like her father sometimes gave. She tossed her head as she replied and marched out of the hall.

'She says your body will be in the wagon before hers, lord,' Kerin said, stifling a smile. 'And that that was the last word of Saxon you'll ever hear from her.'

45

It was close to midnight. Vortigern had been writing. As Kerin drew the flap and went into the tent, he was holding the end of a wax stick to the candle flame. A red, circular blob dripped onto the raw edge of the linen sleeve which enclosed his writing tablet. Vortigern stamped it with his seal and set it aside to harden.

'You sent for me, lord, ' Kerin said, sitting down at the small table. He had no idea why he had been summoned. Scarcely a word had passed between them on the long journey south. He could not recall a time when he had had less idea of what Vortigern was thinking; and rightly or wrongly, he found it impossible not to blame Rowenna for this distance. She was sound asleep on the floor beside the table, the top of her golden head all that was visible outside her sheepskin blankets.

'I've written to Publius Luca,' Vortigern said. 'He needs to know what's happening.'

'How much have you told him?' Kerin asked.

'That I've granted the Saxons more land in Kent,' Vortigern said. 'Out on the eastern tip, beyond Durovernum, in case you were wondering. I think the Romans called it Tanatus. Simply an extension of what they already have. Garagon probably hasn't got the balls to fight them for it, but I've told Publius that if I'm wrong, he should send Lucius down there with enough of an armed force to deal with it.'

'You haven't told him about your marriage, then.'

'No. I'll tell him to his face; not like this. When you leave here, pick two good men with strong horses and send them off with the letter tonight. Tell them to wait for a reply from Publius. Once they've got it, they can come straight home.'

'Is that why you sent for me?' Kerin asked.

'No,' Vortigern said. There was enough of a pause for Kerin to realise that something unpalatable was coming. 'This is the last thing I want to do, but I'll have to send most of our company with Oswi. Two thirds at least. If the Saxons go alone, no-one will believe that they're entitled to the land I've granted them. They need an escort of my own warriors and something that Edlym or Garagon can read. Oswi won't be strong enough to oppose them until Hengist comes ashore, and he's got women and children to defend.'

Kerin thought about what he had been told. He knew that Oswi and his company faced a perilous journey to Kent; but possibly no worse than the prospect of trying to reach Cambria with a depleted force of thirty men and a woman who had never sat on a horse before.

'What are you thinking?' Vortigern asked.

'That I'm not sure which I'd prefer,' Kerin said. 'Trying to get to Kent with sixty-odd warriors. Or trying to get home with thirty-odd warriors, knowing that we have to pass Glevum to get there.'

Vortigern slipped the letter into a leather bag and closed the neck. 'As I told you,' he said. 'This isn't a choice I want to make. But we have to avoid fighting in Kent if we can. If Oswi goes alone, he'll be easy meat. But the Kentishmen won't want to confront our warriors after seeing them fight in the North. They'll probably hold back long enough for Oswi and Hengist to get established. Then, I hope, they'll all decide that growing corn and fooling around with boats and horses is better than butchering each other. I can't think of another way to do this.'

'There isn't another way,' Kerin said. 'At least we won't have bloodshed now. We'll have it later whatever we do, but by then our men and horses will have healed their battle wounds. I'm not at all sure who we'll have to fight first, but whoever it is, there's no point in losing.'

He helped himself from a pitcher of water. There was no sign of the chronicle. Kerin was not surprised. He suspected that, in Vortigern's position, he would have had trouble thinking clearly enough to write his own name. A large scroll, secured with a faded blue cord, was lying on the table. The papyrus had started to crumble slightly at the edges, betraying its age. A polished oak case sat beside it. Here, probably, was one of the documents Padarn had described on the way to Hengist's village.

'What's this?' Kerin asked, running a finger over it.

'The imperial list of British cities with functioning *ordines* in the time of Constantine the Great,' Vortigern said. 'I wanted something else to think about.' He leaned down and drew a second scroll from a leather bag lying at his feet. Unlike the imperial document it was slim as a wand and unblemished. 'And this is a list of the same, when I became king. I had Severus's people draw it up.'

Kerin looked at the two scrolls lying side by side on the table; the one so large and venerable, the other so slender, barely a tenth of its size. Suddenly, and without warning, he felt overwhelmed by a sadness so profound that it brought a lump to his throat.

'And you want to turn this – into this?' he asked. Vortigern nodded, with a rather wistful smile.

'What's the matter? Are you shocked, to see me following the Roman way?'

'No, no, it's not that,' Kerin said. 'But the size of the task, the cost to you – '

'I know,' Vortigern said. He slipped the new scroll into its leather bag. 'It may not even be possible, after what happened in Londinium. But we can have something like this – ' he patted the bag – 'or we can have a country full of men like Hefydd and Dull Bened, throwing rocks at each other from hill forts. I despise the Empire and all it stands for, but no-one's ever found a better way to order things.' He shook his head and placed the imperial record in its case, then gathered his writing materials and stowed them in the olive wood box which accompanied him everywhere. 'I'm sure there's something you want to say.'

Kerin leaned back in his chair and stared at the roof of the tent, swelling gently in the night breeze. 'Lord,' he said, 'when Rufus and Paulinus hear about your marriage, they're going to explode out of wherever they are like water coming over a dam. And then it won't matter at all whether or not Garagon wants to fight the Saxons, because the army of God is going to march off to Kent and do it for him. So I'd advise Oswi to build his villages near the sea, because he might need to reach his boats in a hurry. And I'd send at least two good leading men with this escort of his, because we need as much time as we can buy to prepare for a civil war.'

'You blame me for this,' Vortigern said.

'No. You're the King of all the Britons. You're entitled to marry anyone you like. And everything that's coming was coming anyway, but marrying this girl has hastened it. It may come before we're ready. That's the danger. I'll go to Kent with the escort, if you want.'

'No!' Vortigern said. Kerin heard the shock in his voice.

'Why not?' he asked. 'Most of the others have families

waiting at home for them. I don't have a family. And you don't need a prophet, or even a confidant.'

It sounded more brutal than Kerin had intended, but he had nursed his hurt for mile after lonely mile as the horses jogged south; the rejection of all he had foreseen and advised, the sudden dislocation – how could he have predicted it – of the companionship which had sustained him throughout his life. The denial of his own love, when Rowenna was here; a young woman who was little more than a stranger, sleeping on the floor of the king's tent. Vortigern stood up and put the olive wood box and scrolls in their chest. 'You're not going,' he said. 'Now, find Macsen and Hefin and send them to me.'

'You're sure? They're the best we've got, apart from ourselves and Lud and Gwyndaf.'

'I'm sure,' Vortigern said. 'Lud's a magnificent warrior, but his best days have gone. And Gwyndaf's given more than I had any right to expect. I can't ask this of him too.'

'I'll bring them, then,' Kerin said, and paused. 'I can tell them myself, if you like.'

'No,' Vortigern said. 'I wouldn't wish it on you. Lud's already missing one son, and Hefin's got a child on the way. It's the devil's own work, this sort of thing. It'll come to you one day. But it needn't come yet.'

He had spoken as if to a beloved successor. For a moment Kerin felt the distance between them lessen and vanish, as if it had never existed; but then Rowenna stirred beneath her blankets, whimpering softly in her sleep, burrowing down like a little animal hiding from a predator. Vortigern's eyes strayed to her. Kerin wondered if he knew this man at all.

'I'll get them,' he said, and went out into the night. It was pitch black, apart from a circle of warm light where the lads had lit a fire. Derfyn was sharing some hilarious tale with Macsen, Hefin and Dull Bened. A moment of happy, thoughtless fun, Kerin thought; and I am about to end it.

'Alright there?' It was Cenydd, on his way to inspect the wagons, as he did every evening.

'Yes,' Kerin said; but it was not. Standing here in the darkness, surrounded by friends and loyal comrades, he felt utterly alone. For longer than his own lifetime, Vortigern had held the West in a grip no-one presumed to challenge; and it had appeared effortless. Only now, as Kerin felt the weight bearing down upon him, did he realise that it could not have been. He supposed that Vortigern must have felt like this at times, when the odds seemed insurmountable and all the choices impossible to make. He had never understood it at all, and most of the people who now depended upon him never would.

46

'What's up, then, lad?' Padarn asked, as he pulled the harness off his oxen and turned them loose to graze. 'It's a fine afternoon, and we haven't had a decent rest for days. Make the most of it.'

Two-thirds of the way home, they had made camp in the gentle hills north-east of the city which the Romans named Corinium. It remained a Roman town in the way Londinium had, with fine houses, temples and administrative buildings. There was still an iron-fisted ordo, and its influence could be seen everywhere; the well-farmed villas, the groves of fruit trees and the immaculate state of the roads.

'It's not easy, this close to Glevum,' Kerin said. 'Eldof would as soon have cut my throat as give me Hengist's *annona*.' That was not the true reason for his agitation, of course. He tried to banish Gael from his head, and threw himself down on the warm grass bank overlooking the water meadow where they had pitched.

'I never thought she'd stick it, you know.' Padarn sat down beside Kerin and looked at the wagon containing three large wooden chests full of Rowenna's belongings, but as yet, no bodies.

'No,' Kerin said grudgingly. 'Neither did I.'

'Why be so hard on her, lad?' Padarn asked.

'She's doing her father's work,' Kerin said. 'And whilst we're about it, how could you possibly have married them?

She's a pagan, for God's sake. And it makes the whole thing seem –' he hesitated.

'Legitimate?' Padarn enquired.

'Yes, legitimate,' Kerin said. 'As if you approved of it, even.'

'Well, who am I to disapprove of it?'

'A monk!' Kerin exclaimed. 'A Christian. A man of God, for what it's worth. Wouldn't you have preferred him to marry a British woman?'

'Well, of course I would. But he's spent – what – twenty years, deliberately *not* marrying a British woman, or any other woman. Do you think it would have made any difference, if I'd refused to marry them? Of course not. He'd either have married her by her own rites or taken her without anyone's sanction. I thought it was better to ask God's blessing and hope for the best. And before you say anything else, don't tell me you wouldn't love that girl in Glevum if she worshipped a three-headed horse or something.'

'That's not the point!' Kerin retorted, colouring violently.

'It is the point,' Padarn said, roused to anger. 'It's exactly the point, but you're like all the other warriors. Blind as a fucking bat, when you want to be.' He got up and marched off across the water meadow. Kerin watched him go, profoundly shocked. Iustig would never have lost his temper like that; but there was a hard edge to Padarn that Iustig would never have, born of loss and bloodshed, and perhaps of other things too.

Kerin got up and wandered off in the same direction, hoping that the sunlit afternoon would inflict some of its peace upon him. The meadow ran down to a slow-flowing river fringed by reeds, and some of the boys were swimming in it, whilst others lay about on the banks, dozing or tickling trout in the clear pools. Beyond was a wood, interspersed

429

with broad clearings where the sun cast a dappled light. Kerin stood quite still amongst the trees and closed his eyes. He could hear nothing but birdsong and the quiet trickle of water, but quite suddenly the calming wash of sound was interrupted by a woman's laughter. It came from close by, beyond a screen of elder bushes. Kerin stepped cautiously forward and parted the leaves. Vortigern and the girl were sitting cross-legged on the ground in the middle of the sunlit clearing, a few feet distant from each other. Rowenna had exchanged her travelling clothes for a light summer dress and brushed her long pale hair out loose. The skirts of her green dress covered all but the tips of her bare toes. She was leaning slightly forward with hands held loosely in her lap, gazing at Vortigern with what Kerin, had he not known better, would have described as an enraptured smile. Vortigern was attempting to explain something to her. Rowenna laughed in an easy, good-natured way and reached out to caress his face. Vortigern caught her hand and held it where it was. Curiously, he looked as enchanted as she did. Kerin let the leaves close up and walked quickly back the way he had come, knowing that all he had seen was simply part of Hengist's chain of deceit.

Out in the meadow someone had lit a fire and was cooking trout on a spit. Kerin heard hoofbeats coming down the road as he emerged from the wood. The rider was Varro. Kerin ran to catch the reins as he dropped to the ground, caked in sweat and dust. Lud arrived running. Men started to come from the river and the woods.

'Send them back,' Varro croaked. 'I must speak to Vortigern first. You two can stay.'

Lud told the men and called Elir to care for the exhausted horse. Varro knelt beside the stream, drank thirstily and splashed water over his face. Lud and Kerin sat down and waited. Behind Varro's back, Kerin saw Vortigern and his wife come from the wood. Vortigern sent Rowenna to the wagons and came to them.

'Lord,' Varro said, starting to get up.

'Sit down, man.' Vortigern dropped to the ground beside him. Varro lowered his eyes, looking close to tears.

'I've left Eldof. I'm not a deserter, you know that, but I can't serve him any longer.' He coughed painfully. 'Eldof never wanted you to be king. He supported you because he knew we had to beat the Picts, and that no-one else could pull it off. I'm probably telling you nothing you haven't guessed. But I never expected things to fall out as they have.'

'None of this is new,' Vortigern said. 'Why now?'

'I'm dishonoured!' Varro cried. 'Eldof has made a pact with Garagon. There was a meeting at Calleva. They wouldn't risk Londinium, your support there is too solid. I couldn't put my name to it. I know they tried to get out of the *annona*, and I know they'll never pay for an army. It'll come back to bite them, but they're too stupid to see it. All they want is to bring you down.'

'So, where's Eldof now?' Lud asked.

'God knows. When he left for Calleva, I rode north to look for your company. I sent my son to take the family somewhere safe. It'll be death for them in Glevum now.'

Vortigern remained controlled, as if he were dealing with some minor dispute in his own citadel. 'What do you want from me, Varro?'

'To serve as your warrior, if you'll have me. I swear on my father's life that I'll be your man until death if you'll take me.'

'The honour is mine, Varro,' Vortigern said. He extended his hand and Varro grasped it, his eyes full of tears.

'Where are your wife and family?' Kerin asked.

'At Ganarew. You might know the place; it's just upriver from Blestium, only a day or two's ride from Glevum. There's a fortress there, deserted for years.'

'I know it,' Vortigern said. 'My grandfather took me there once. It looked like the sort of place a few men could hold against an army.' He got up, hauling Varro to his feet. 'Now, go and jump in the river and get the dust off. Kerin, tell Cheldric to prepare food for him.'

'You won't regret this, lord,' Varro croaked.

'I don't expect to,' Vortigern said. 'Do you bring men with you?'

'A warband of thirty. Good, solid boys; good swordsmen. They're at Ganarew presently with my son, but we'll fight anywhere you need us.'

'You can go for them as soon as we've crossed the river,' Vortigern said. 'But for now, I need your sword. After you've eaten, Lud will equip you. You're a Cambrian warrior now.'

* * *

It was the village beside the Via Legionis, which Kerin had first heard of when an old man and his granddaughter came blundering into him, running from Bertil Redknife's bunch of thugs. Malan's people had found their way back. Probably they had tagged along with Eldof's company on its way home from Londinium, just as they had done when it was going in the opposite direction. Kerin remembered Malan complaining that all his daughters had married fools and lazy bastards. Here was the evidence. Most of the wooden huts needed repair. There were sagging doors and rotting thatch. The livestock pens had missing rails. The vegetable patch looked well-tended, but it was probably the women and children who saw to that.

Vortigern's band dismounted in the centre of the village, outside the headman's house. Malan's daughter, Berget, came out.

'Lord King!' she exclaimed. 'Have you got him? My stupid father?'

'He's with the wagons,' Vortigern said. 'Not far behind us. And don't worry about him. He's tougher than most of my warriors, and he still can't keep his mouth shut. Now, do you have a place where my wife can rest? We've been travelling since first light.' Berget looked up at Rowenna, sitting motionless on her white pony, her long hair braided up. Her eyes took in the Saxon breeches, cloak and shoulder-pin. 'My wife is a princess of the Jutes,' Vortigern said. Berget swallowed.

'My own house, of course, Lord King!' she said hastily. 'It won't be what you're used to, but I know the roof doesn't leak, because I mended it myself.' She dived into the darkness within and rousted out some giggling women.

'Some sport for the youngsters,' Gwyndaf chuckled. Kerin nodded half-heartedly, unable to share Gwyndaf's good humour when every step took him nearer to Gael in Glevum. A smiling face peered from a dark doorway. Dunia, he thought, remembering the way she had fed him metheglin and torn her dress off for him in her stinking hut.

'Lord Kerin, a word,' Berget murmured as Vortigern lifted Rowenna from her pony. 'My idiot niece is here. Someone locked her up before our men left, or she'd have followed them somehow. Then there was an argument in Eldof's household and they threw her out. She should have married that good man Edryd, but of course she wouldn't, and now the king's here with his new wife. She doesn't know, this is the first we've heard of it. And a beautiful girl like that, my God! I've no idea what she'll do, but for pity's sake keep your eyes open.'

'Thank you, Berget,' Kerin said. 'And you should know that your men did you credit in the North. Your husband was one of the best, and he's alive, not too badly wounded. I hope they've all learned a few lessons, and that you won't have to go on mending your own roof.'

Berget grinned. 'Thank you, Lord Kerin. And I've kicked the arses of the lads who were too young to go, so we won't be having any more trouble with them.' She glanced around, to ensure that no-one was listening. 'There are things I have to tell the king. I trust you, of course, but I know my father would tell the king first. It's only right. It's what the head-man would do. And I suppose I'm the headman now, at least until he gets back.'

'You are,' Kerin said, shaking her hand. 'And if I were your father, I'd sit beside the fire and let you carry on with it.'

Vortigern and Rowenna were with the horses.

'Berget's got something to tell you, lord,' Kerin said. 'It could be important.'

Vortigern nodded. 'Go with Rowenna. See that she's got what she needs.'

Kerin unhitched Rowenna's saddlebag. They went into the smoky darkness of Berget's house. There was a pile of blankets beside the fire. Rowenna sank down amongst them and covered her face with her hands. It was the first time she had let her exhaustion show. Kerin felt a degree of sympathy, despite himself.

'You're tired out,' he said, in her own tongue.

'I am not tired!' Rowenna said defiantly, in British.

'You should tell Vortigern. We don't have to ride quite as hard as this.'

Rowenna looked down at her hands, raw and blistered by the reins. 'No. I will not hold him back.'

Kerin handed her the bag and sat down. 'Do you miss your home?'

'Of course,' Rowenna said, 'but we are not like you. I miss my father and my uncle, and my two brothers who are still at home. But with Vortigern it is a sickness. You Celts are all the same. You think your country is the home of the gods. And you think there are no other men who can ride or fight, or make love to a woman.'

Kerin grinned. 'Perhaps there are not,' he said. Rowenna looked up.

'We have fine young men too!'

'Then why didn't you marry one of them?'

Rowenna laughed. 'Vortigern was right,' she said.

'Why? What did he say?'

'That you speak always the terrible truth,' Rowenna said. She let down her braided hair and shook it loose, then took a whalebone comb from her bag and began to separate the long, fair strands. 'You do not like me. It is not fair. I have done nothing to you. It is my fault that I was born a Jute?'

'No, of course not,' Kerin said. 'But you could have stayed with the Jutes. Everyone knows you could have had any of the young warriors.'

'But I did not want them!' Rowenna protested.

'Perhaps not,' Kerin said. 'But this is about what your father wants, isn't it? He wanted a piece of Kent, and he saw a way to get it.'

'Of course he wanted Kent.' Rowenna flung her comb down. 'And you think that is all.'

'Yes,' Kerin said. 'I know that is all.'

'You think it is my fault that Vortigern's sons have gone.' Rowenna retrieved the comb and dragged it furiously through her hair. 'A son who leaves his father is worth nothing. Do you think my brothers would leave my father Hengist?'

'You know nothing about any of it,' Kerin said.

'I know what I think about a son who tries to kill his father!'

'He told you about that?'

Rowenna stared into the flickering yellow flames. 'I am Vortigern's woman. Should he not speak to me?'

'You've been with him four weeks,' Kerin snapped. 'Four weeks!'

'This is nothing,' Rowenna said scornfully. 'Four weeks, four years, it is the same. And I know now why you hate me. You are jealous, because Vortigern prefers to be with me.'

'Not so!' Kerin exclaimed. He turned away, feeling a warm flush rise to his face, and realised that she was right.

'It is so!' Rowenna said triumphantly.

'Alright.' Kerin squatted down and stared her in the face. 'It is so. And I'll tell you why it is so. I've served Vortigern all my life. I've killed for him, starved for him and shed my blood for him, and I've done it for love. And now you've come. He talks to you. He looks at you, and I see a man I do not even know. And are you here for love? No. You're here to do your father's work.' He gave a bitter smile. 'That is so too, isn't it.'

Rowenna stared past him at the dancing flames. 'I am Vortigern's woman,' she said. Kerin choked back his anger and walked out of the hut. He went over to the edge of the village where Gwyndaf was unsaddling the horses. He knew quite well that he should have handled things differently. There was no hope of keeping everyone else on an even keel, if he couldn't even control his own temper. 'I'll do this,' he said curtly. 'Can you go and see to the girl? She might want some food or something.'

Gwyndaf strode off towards Berget's house, whistling cheerily. Kerin moved along the line of horses, heaving off their saddles and flinging them onto the bank. By the time he had finished he was sweating, but in command of himself.

'He is married, then,' a voice said beside him. Kerin turned.

'Flora!' She was as beautiful as ever, with her faded blue dress and spiritual eyes. She looked, and had sounded, utterly forlorn. 'She's a princess of the Jutes,' Kerin said. 'Her father's the leader of his Saxon mercenaries.'

'Yes,' Flora said absently. 'I have just been told.'

Kerin hesitated, not knowing what to say. She had looked fragile before, but now there was a vacancy there, as if something within had broken, and made her mad.

'Flora, you can't have thought –'

'No,' she said, laughing softly. 'No, of course not. And the fault is mine. He saved me from something horrible, and I should have known that that was all he intended. It was a kindness, as you said, no more. I suppose you think he lay with me? All the girls do.'

'I don't know,' Kerin said. 'Most men would have done.'

Flora gave him a deprecating smile and drew the hood of her cloak up over her head, although the evening was warm.

'I have watched the road every day,' she said. 'Please, don't tell him we have spoken.'

She walked away as silently as she had come, turning aside at the first hut and vanishing amongst the trees. Kerin watched her go. In an odd way, although he would never have wished it on her, it was almost a comfort to know that someone else's desolation outweighed his own. The smell of roast boar was drifting across from the cooking-fire. Kerin walked back and sat down. Lud thrust a hunk of meat into his hands.

'Here, eat while you can. We'll be on the road again soon.'

'I thought we were spending the night here.'

'Something's happened.' Lud looked towards the other side of the fire, where Vortigern was still in conversation with Berget. 'He wants to cross the river before first light.'

Vortigern looked up and caught Kerin's eye. Kerin picked his way over the warriors' sprawling bodies.

'What's going on?' he asked, as Berget withdrew.

'A bunch of Eldof's warriors passed through here yesterday,' Vortigern said. 'Heading east, with a string of fifty fresh horses. Some of them had escorted Eldof to that meeting in Calleva. They weren't high-ranking enough to know what it was about, but Garagon and Edlym were there. And a man they described as "that pious son of Vortigern's".'

'Damn,' Kerin murmured.

'There's worse,' Vortigern said. 'After the meeting, Eldof sent two of them down to Caerwynt with a letter for Paulinus. When they arrived, Katigern was there, crying his eyes out. So Eldof and Paulinus know everything. There's one saving grace. They know we're riding home, but they think we're days back. They told Berget to look out for us. They said they'd hang her if she let us pass without sending word to Eldof's deputy in Glevum. You know what this means.'

'That we have to move tonight, and cross the river in the dark, before they start guarding the bridges,' Kerin said. He did not add what they both knew; that a fast, mobile warband could have swum its horses across the Hafren at any of the crossing points around Eldof's capital, but that there was no doing that with an exhausted woman and a wagon containing all the possessions of her young life. Vortigern turned to him.

'You know that I'd have had to give Hengist more land at some time. He can already call on enough men to make a fight of it, and fight he will, when he realises that there's no more *annona* coming to him.'

'I know that,' Kerin said. 'But some of them will make it mean whatever they need to, to make men listen to them.'

'You're right,' Vortigern said. 'But there's enough to think about between here and Henfelin. Now, go and sleep if you can. We're leaving here at sunset.'

Berget was stirring a pot of stew on the fire.

'The king has told me,' Kerin said. She looked up.

'You're leaving at sunset.'

'Yes. Give it until first light, then send word to Eldof's deputy. By the time one of your lads gets there, we'll be halfway home.'

'I could keep my mouth shut and risk it,' Berget said.

'No. You and your people have risked enough. It'll go better for you if Eldof thinks you're on his side, at least for now. If there's trouble later, you must bring everyone across the river. The king has set a place aside for you, far better than you have here, but for now he needs your eyes and ears. Please explain all this to your father when he gets home, and tell him to keep his mouth shut.'

Berget laughed aloud. 'You give me the best jobs, Lord Kerin. I'll have to crack him on the head with this pot and gag him. Can I tell him about the place, though?'

'No,' Kerin said. 'I think the king would like to do that.' And I would like time enough to tell the king and find the place, he thought. He walked across to the fringe of the woods and found himself a mossy bank at the foot of a tall elm. There was no prospect of sleep. If Eldof was somewhere near Calleva, he would have most of his best men with him. Bertil's citadel would be lightly guarded; there might never be a better time. But what then? He had no idea what Gael would make of the task he had taken upon himself.

A shout came from the village. A rider clattered in on a

dull-coated pony, scattering hens; a skinny youth who had been feeding the fires earlier.

'Berget, riders!' the boy gasped. 'Five of them, coming from the south.'

Kerin crossed the clearing in a few bounds. Vortigern came out of Berget's house.

'Five riders coming from the south,' Berget said.

'Yes, Lord King!' the boy said. 'One of them's a priest.'

'And the others?' Kerin asked.

'Warriors, lord, well mounted and well-armed. They've got big blue crosses on their tunics. Even the priest is armed, lord.'

The quiet thud of hoofbeats came slowly in the warm evening. Paulinus of Caerwynt was riding at the head of the group, wearing a mail shirt over his monk's habit. They reined in outside Berget's house. Paulinus jumped from his ugly roan gelding.

'Is it true?' he bellowed. Rowenna came from the house. 'Well, there is my answer,' Paulinus said, with a tight-lipped smile. Rowenna backed towards the house, the colour rising to her cheeks. 'You may well blush, you pagan whore,' Paulinus roared. 'Go back to your filthy kinsmen!'

Rowenna fled into the house. Gwyndaf came out. 'What's happening here?' he asked. Vortigern looked so pale, so still, that Kerin knew he was on the edge of murder. Gwyndaf gave Kerin a look. Slowly, quietly, Kerin's hand moved to the hilt of his sword.

'This is Paulinus, abbot of Venta Belgarum,' Vortigern said. 'He wants me to send my wife back to her father, and throw Hengist out of Kent.'

Gwyndaf's eyebrows rose. 'What's it to do with him?' he asked, drawing one of his daggers. Paulinus glowered at him.

'The cross of Christ is on our side. You won't frighten me with that thing. And you should save your strength, if you've bound yourself to this accomplice of Satan. There is a greater force behind us than your dwarf's mind can even comprehend.'

Gwyndaf laughed out loud. 'You mean the power of God?'

Now it was Paulinus's turn to laugh. 'The power of God is with us, have no doubt,' he said. 'But I was speaking of God's instruments. The men who have already pledged themselves to His service, and the ones who are answering His call as we speak. Our forces are gathering in Gallia. Our ships are ready to sail. And even if they are stricken with storms, Christ the Lord will calm the waves, as he calmed the Sea of Galilee. Our faith is the true faith, the sacred doctrine of the One True God!'

'Then damn your religion!' Vortigern bellowed. 'And damn you too, you malignant old bastard. If you're the best God can find to do his work, I'm better off with Caradog and his bonfires.'

'Burn in hell,' Paulinus spat. 'And take that idolatrous bitch with you. I have better things to do than breathe the same air.' He crossed himself and scrambled aboard his horse. Kerin walked straight up to the animal, seized bit and bridle and forced it backwards.

'Do not ever address the king and his wife like that again,' he said. Paulinus's little eyes opened wide.

'And who are you to forbid me?' he shouted. Kerin went on walking, forcing the horse backwards, ignoring the abbot's guards, who were already reaching for their swords.

'I am the king's right arm,' Kerin said, placing one hand over the horse's muzzle until it calmed and stood still. 'Not that he really needs one; his own right arm is perfectly serviceable, even though his son tried to cut it off. You'll be seeing him soon, I'm sure. The Lord Vortimer. You can tell him I burned his letter. All that wax made quite a good fire.' He released the horse, which stood twitching nervously, as if wondering what was coming next. 'You see? Your horse isn't as nasty as it looks. Be assured, with me, it's the other way round.'

He turned, ignoring the drawn swords and angry comments, and marched back to Berget's house. Paulinus led his band away at the gallop. Warriors and villagers stood, looking blankly at him, and at each other. Berget's lads began clearing the remains of the meal.

Kerin walked away into the wood. There was no-one he wished to speak to. He stood for a long time, leaning against a tree as the light faded. He knew that he had put down a marker. The consequences could not yet be calculated, but the mark had to be made, if he hoped to hold the line he had set for himself. A hoof clicked on stone. Vortigern was standing there with Blaidd and the black mare, both saddled and ready to go. Kerin looked at him in bewilderment.

'Well,' Vortigern said, 'do you want the woman or don't you?'

47

They rode through shadow and moonlight, keeping to the backwoods, avoiding the Roman road and the well-trodden forest tracks. After a few miles Vortigern stopped, getting his bearings. Far away to the north-west the river gleamed. Somewhere over there was Glevum, and somewhere between the city and the point where the horses now stood were Morvid's valley and Bertil Redknife's citadel.

'*Why?*' Kerin asked.

'Because you deserve it,' Vortigern said. 'And because I cannot deny you what I could not deny myself.'

They rode fast, without stopping, until they reached the summit of a high ridge. The moon was still brilliant, and the river looked very close.

'It's over there,' Vortigern said, pointing.

'How do you know?'

'When I was a lad my father spent half his time kissing the Roman arse in Glevum. We used to hunt these woods, and Bertil's father made feasts for us. He kept a terrible table.'

The beech forest gave way to scattered oaks interspersed with patches of tall grass. Kerin began to recognise familiar landmarks; an elm standing alone on a bare mound, a Roman orchard run wild, glimpsed in the distance as he rode with Septimus. Vortigern raised his hand. They dismounted and led their horses into the thick of the trees.

Kerin heard voices coming from beyond the orchard. A man shouted something, then there were howls of laughter, followed by a chorus of rowdy singing. They tied their horses and crept forward, daggers drawn. Bertil's gates were open and unguarded. They sprinted across the open ground and inched along the inside of the stockade. Sounds of revelry were coming from the large house next to Bertil's hall.

'Like the old rutting stag, boys, we roved through the town;
The skirts they went up, and the breeches came down,'

someone was bawling, while everyone else kept time, hammering on the benches with their tankards. Bertil's hall was quiet, but a light was burning inside.

'Go on,' Vortigern murmured. 'I'll keep watch.'

Kerin crept to the side entrance, eased the latch up and peered through the tiny crack between door and frame. The woman was kneeling beside the couch, the hood of her blue cloak drawn closely round her face.

'Like the old rutting stag, boys, we gave them our best,
We rode them all night till they begged for a rest –'

'Gael!' Kerin said softly. The woman spun round and the hood fell back. A stranger's face stared at him. The woman gasped and her eyes opened wide. Kerin grabbed her and clamped his hand over her mouth. 'Scream and I'll slit your throat,' he hissed. The woman struggled frantically, then her body became limp. Cautiously Kerin removed his hand. She stared up at him, trembling violently; a thin, dark-haired woman, plain to the point of ugliness, probably ten years older than Kerin himself. 'Who the hell are you? And where's Bertil's daughter?'

The woman turned away, wringing her hands distractedly. Vortigern appeared at the doorway.

'Come on, for the love of God. You'll have time to bed her at home.' The woman turned and his face dropped. 'On my mother's grave. Is this what we're risking our necks for?'

'No!' Kerin protested. 'This isn't Bertil's daughter.'

'Lords, I am Morwen,' the woman blurted. 'I'm a cousin to Balin, Lord Bertil's chief warrior, and I serve the Lady Gael.'

The expert who hasn't lived a nun's life, Kerin thought, seizing Morwen's arm. 'Where is she? What's happened here?'

The woman stared up at him. 'Lord! Are you Kerin Brightspear, the great lord of Henfelin in Cambria?'

Kerin glanced uncomfortably at Vortigern, who cast his eyes up to the ceiling. 'I'm Kerin Brightspear. What of it?'

'Gael knew you would come for her,' Morwen said. 'And her father knew it, too. That's why he put her away.'

'Her father? Bertil knows? Where is she?'

'Lord, I can't,' Morwen quavered. 'Bertil will kill me.'

Vortigern cupped her chin in his hand. 'Look,' he said, 'Bertil is miles away, and I am here. You can tell us now, and save yourself some pain, or I can tie you to that couch and flay the last inch of skin off you. Now, where is she?'

Morwen sank down on the couch. 'Lord Kerin, Bertil was told a few weeks ago in Calleva. He came straight back here and flogged Gael for a liar and a whore, then he sent her to his cousin Eldadus in Glevum. He told the bishop to instruct her in the faith. She's to take her vows, and spend the rest of her life in holy orders.'

'Over my body,' Kerin said. 'Who the hell told Bertil?'

'I don't know, lord. Bertil wouldn't tell me anything like that. He's on his way to Kent with Eldof. They say they're going to hang Vortigern and drive the Saxons into the sea.'

'Alright,' Kerin said, raising his hand. 'Where's Gael now?'

'Still in the bishop's house in Glevum, lord.'

Kerin looked round. 'Do you know the house?'

'Yes,' Vortigern said. 'I've never been in it, but it's like a fortress.'

'Lord, I can get in,' Morwen said. 'I'm allowed to visit Gael, to take her what she needs. I don't think bishops have much idea about that sort of thing.'

'Alright,' Kerin said, dragging her to her feet. 'We're coming with you, and if we're challenged, you'll say that we're men of Kent, bringing a message from Gael's father.'

Vortigern opened the door and looked around. 'Where are the horses?'

'At the other side of the village, lord. There's a pen over there, next to the smithy. There may be one man on guard, but no more.'

'Do you have a saddle and bridle?' Kerin asked.

'Yes, lord, in my own house. And I can show you the fastest horse.' Morwen smiled hopefully. She seemed to have decided to make the best of a bad bargain.

'Where's that cousin of yours?' Vortigern asked.

'Drinking with the rest of the men, lord. Most of the warriors have gone with Bertil, but he left Balin in charge. He's the one singing the shameless songs.'

They slipped out of the hall into the bright moonlight. Kerin pressed the point of his dagger lightly between Morwen's shoulder-blades, in case she changed her mind.

Like the old rutting stag, boys, we knew what to do;
We upped with our spears and we ran them straight through –'

Balin bellowed, half-drowned by a drunken chorus. They ran from hut to hut, from one protective pool of shadow to the next.

'Here's my house,' Morwen whispered. 'My mother's inside, but she's been at the mead, so she won't wake.'

Kerin followed her into the suffocating darkness. The

embers of a cooking fire cast the dimmest of lights. He could just distinguish a heaving mound huddled under a pile of skins, snoring rhythmically. Morwen threw on a heavy riding cloak and picked up a saddle and bridle from the earth floor.

'My father's,' she said. 'But he's been dead for a year, so he won't miss them.'

They caught up with Vortigern at the horse-pens. A brawny warrior was stretched on the ground at his feet with a dark stain spreading slowly across the back of his tunic.

'The grey mare with the white face,' Morwen whispered. 'She's Balin's hunting horse.' Kerin took the bridle and slipped into the pen. The horses moved about nervously. Kerin threw on saddle and bridle, dragged the gate open and drove the other horses out towards the gap in the stockade. Vortigern tossed Morwen onto the grey mare's back and ran after him. They crashed through the orchard and found their own animals, stamping and jerking at their reins as they heard the loose horses blundering about in the underbrush.

'Listen!' Kerin said. The singing had stopped, and shouts were echoing round the village. They mounted up and rode away through the orchard, low branches whipping their shoulders. After a headlong dash through thickets and clearings they emerged, scratched and breathless, on a deserted Roman road.

'We're safe now,' Vortigern said. 'By the time they catch the horses, we'll be in Glevum.' He and Kerin drew the hoods of their cloaks closely around their faces. Flanking Morwen, they set off towards the city at a purposeful trot.

'The house is next to the river,' Morwen said as they passed through the open gates. Tall buildings rose above them, their mellow gold stone stark and white in the moonlight. Lights glimmered here and there. A door opened suddenly, low in the wall beside them. Two figures appeared, black in the bright square of light.

'Who goes there?' one of them bellowed. Young and muscular, holding a short-handled spear with practised ease. Kerin nodded to the woman.

'I am Morwen, of the Lord Bertil Redknife's household,' she said in a clear voice. 'I serve his daughter, Gael. I'm going to visit her in the Bishop's house. These are men of Kent, bringing messages from her father.'

The second man hurried back into the house and re-emerged with a flaring torch. He squinted up at them, an elderly, wizened man with broken teeth, wearing a long robe in the style of a Roman toga.

'Marcus!' Morwen said, with relief. The old man smiled.

'Well, it is you, Morwen. But who are these? Men of Kent, did you say?'

'Yes, sir. Warriors of Lord Garagon's following.'

Marcus screwed up his failing eyes and peered at Kerin and Vortigern. 'Are you with this army of Eldof's, then?'

'Indeed we are,' Kerin said, in what he hoped might be a Kentish accent. The younger man pressed forward.

'Can I ride with you, when you go back?' he pleaded.

'Of course!' Kerin said heartily. 'We need your kind to beat that bastard Vortigern.'

Marcus sighed. 'I can't believe what he's come to. He was such an accomplished young lad. A master of literature and the pen. And his father a true Roman.'

'Fear not, old friend!' Kerin said. 'We'll hang the heathen dog and drive his friends out of Kent.'

'Yes,' the old man said. 'I fear you must, although it gives me no pleasure to say so.' He patted the woman's arm. 'Go, then, Morwen. Take these brave warriors to Lady Gael. And I hope their news will cheer her more than her devotions seem to do.' He saluted them and they rode away down the echoing street.

'I'll kill you,' Vortigern said, between clenched teeth. 'I'll hang you from the highest tree in Cambria.'

Kerin chuckled. 'Who's the old man?'

'A creature of Eldof's household. Half Roman. His father was in the Second Augusta, long before Publius's time. Marcus had a lame leg, so he couldn't fight. He lived in Eldof's father's villa and taught the children.'

'How do you know that, lord?' Morwen asked. Vortigern grimaced.

'The old goat used to teach me Latin.'

'Latin, lord?' Morwen said, smiling, as if she didn't believe a word of it. Vortigern raised his eyebrows.

'*O lente lente currite noctis equi,*' he said. 'You see? The Cambrian peasant has more learning than you, you unlettered bitch.'

Morwen shrank down inside her cloak as if she would have liked to dematerialise. Kerin prickled with apprehension.

'This is too quiet,' he said.

'Most of the fighting men have followed Eldof,' Morwen said. 'The trained warriors, that is. All the ordinary men are still here, and to be truthful, they're not all Eldof's men by any means.'

'Whose men are they, then?' Kerin asked.

'The king's – er, the Lord Vortigern's, probably,' Morwen said, with a nervous giggle. 'I'm sorry, Lord Kerin, you have to be careful what you say these days. And please take care when we get to the bishop's house. His guards are all still here, looking after his treasures. All kinds of silver and gold things, and precious stones from the lands of the sun. Balin says that Eldadus drinks from a cup set with so many jewels that the stars themselves could not outshine it.'

'Priests shouldn't be rich,' Vortigern said. 'They should stick to their vows of poverty. Don't you think so, Lord Kerin?'

'I couldn't care less,' Kerin said through gritted teeth, willing him to be quiet. He gave Vortigern a barbed look, and found that he was trying not to laugh. This is mad, he thought. We are both mad, and this may be the last day of my life, if this stupid, chattering woman can't charm the bishop's guards.

They came to it at last, a tall, square house presenting a windowless face to the street. Solid heavy gates, shut fast, were set in a high courtyard wall. It looked quite impenetrable.

'Well, great lord of Henfelin, what shall we do now?' Vortigern enquired. Kerin looked up at the towering wall.

'Will they let you in?' he asked Morwen.

'I expect so. I know the chief guard. He's a good friend of Balin's, and he'll probably let us all in. But they won't let Gael out. She's forbidden to leave this house until she goes to the holy sisters at the end of the summer.'

'Is there another way out?' Vortigern asked.

'I don't know, lord. The room where I meet Gael has no windows. All I know is that there's a fine terrace somewhere which overlooks the river. This street runs down to the wharf. Sometimes I go there to watch the boats, and I've seen Eldadus on his terrace, taking the sun.'

'A boat?' Kerin said dubiously. Vortigern pursed his lips.

'With a full moon and no wind? And a fine terrace for the guards to stand on throwing spears at us?'

'I know,' Kerin said. 'But if we take the horses inside, and they bar these gates –'

'And if we leave them outside? What fool rides all the way from Kent and leaves his horse outside in the street?'

'Alright,' Kerin said to Morwen. 'Get us in. The rest will come.' He drew his sword and hammered on the massive oak gate with the hilt. Vortigern pulled the hood of his cloak forward to conceal his face.

'Who's that?' a voice bawled from inside.

'Morwen, Balin's cousin,' Morwen called. 'I've brought messengers for Lady Gael, from her father. They've ridden all the way from Kent.'

From within came the sound of a heavy wooden bar being drawn. The gate opened a crack. A man peered cautiously out, bearded, wearing a leather helmet. 'Hello, Gwrth,' Morwen said. The guard's face relaxed into a smile.

'Morwen! I had to be sure. We were warned to be careful.' He swung the gate wide open. The three riders passed through and the gate closed behind them. Seven other men were on duty inside, dressed like Gwrth in leather helmets and brown woollen tunics. They carried spears, short Roman stabbing swords and white-painted shields bearing the sign of the cross. The courtyard was bare and lit by torches set at intervals along the walls. The main entrance to the house stood opposite the gate, fronted by a flight of steps and a row of tall columns; Severus's house in miniature.

'Wait here,' Gwrth said. 'I'll tell His Grace.' He ran up the steps and through an archway behind the colonnade. A door slammed somewhere.

'Shall I see to your horses, friends?' one of the guards called.

'No, thank you,' Kerin said, 'my servant will stay with them. We'll be gone, as soon as our message is delivered.'

Two of the guards left their posts on the steps and came to join them.

'So soon?' one of them said jovially. 'Glevum's full of good ale and pretty women.'

'Yes,' his mournful companion said. 'Though the holy bishop keeps us short of both.'

Kerin grinned. 'What about this Lady Gael, then?' he asked, with a knowing wink.

'You can forget about that,' the guard said. 'Eldadus keeps her shut up like a bird in a cage. You can hear her singing sometimes, but it doesn't sound very cheerful. They say her heart's given to some mad Cambrian. One of those young hot-heads who ride with Vortigern. They say she'll have no other, that's why Bertil locked her up here before he went off to Kent. Gwrth's told us to kill the rat if he turns up here.'

They turned, hearing Gwrth's footfall. Bishop Eldadus was with him. Kerin steeled his nerves, praying that the bishop was as short-sighted as everyone seemed to think.

'Your servant, Lord Eldadus,' he said, with a respectful bow.

'Greetings, young friend,' the bishop said. 'You have a message for my niece, I understand.'

'May I see her, sir?' Kerin asked, trying desperately not to sound impatient.

'Since you come from her father, I suppose it may be permitted,' the bishop said. 'But this young woman is preparing to take holy orders, and it would be quite improper for her to spend time alone with a warrior, although I'm sure that you're a man of honourable intent.'

Kerin stared at the bishop's haughty, beaked nose, trying vainly to obliterate a vision of Gael lying naked in his arms in Morvid's hut. 'As you wish, sir,' he said politely.

'Come, then,' Eldadus said. 'And you too, woman. Gael speaks of you with affection, and looks forward to your visits.'

They followed Eldadus up the steps, under the archway and across a small, echoing court floored with mosaic. Gwrth followed, spear on his shoulder. Morwen reached for Kerin's arm.

'You must take my horse for Gael,' she whispered.

'What about you?' Kerin asked. Morwen shook her head.

'Don't worry. I'll make my own way.'

'But you brought us here. We can't leave you.'

Morwen smiled dispassionately. 'When a woman is not beautiful, she learns to live by the talents she has. I will make my own way.'

They walked on under flickering yellow lamplight. Kerin counted three guards besides the ones they had left in the courtyard. Eldadus led them up a broad marble staircase and along a dim gallery. At the end was a door. Kerin's heart thudded. Beyond that door lay the resolution of all the longings which had tormented him through half a year's fighting and travelling. So close now, he was both eager and terrified. He pulled the hood down tight to his face. Eldadus tapped the door.

'Keep watch, Gwrth,' he said, and led Kerin and Morwen into a tiny dark room. A single candle burned on a side table. It cast a wavering light over the scant furnishings; a bare couch, a single wooden chair. A carved chest was laid out as a simple altar. Gael was kneeling before it, head bowed on folded hands. The candlelight glinted on her red-gold hair.

'Good evening, uncle,' she said, without looking round. 'This is a strange time of day for you to visit me.'

Her voice was dull and expressionless. Kerin felt a flood of anger surge within him.

'Rise up, Gael!' the bishop said. 'I've brought visitors for you.'

Gael turned sharply. Her face lit up. 'Morwen!' she cried.

'Yes,' Morwen said, smiling as she embraced her. 'And see, I've brought a warrior of Kent, with a message from your father.'

Gael looked up at the hooded figure. She frowned, as if at something half-remembered. Kerin stepped forward into the pool of light and threw back his hood. Gael's eyes opened wide and her hand flew to her mouth.

'What's the matter, my lady?' Kerin asked, as coldly as he could. 'Don't you want to hear your father's message?'

Gael composed herself rapidly. 'Forgive me, sir,' she said, lowering her eyes. 'I am preparing to take holy vows. It's months since I spoke with any man except my lord the bishop, and you are a warrior. Please excuse me if I am a little nervous.'

'The fault is mine, my lady,' Kerin said, with a reverence.

'Come on, then, young fellow,' Eldadus said, clapping his hands. 'Say what you've come to say, then the lady and I can return to our devotions.'

'Of course. My lady, as you know, your father is riding to Kent with his warriors. Near Durovernum they were set upon by Saxon warbands. There was a great slaughter, but a few heathen escaped, and they spread evil lies. They said that Lord Bertil had perished. I suppose they thought it would strike fear into us Britons, if so brave a warrior had been lost.' Kerin smiled. 'So that's why your father sent me. Such rumours spread like the plague. Please be assured that he is alive, and unharmed.'

Gael looked up. Her eyes held his. 'Thank you, sir. May God bless you for bringing me this news.'

'There is one more thing,' Kerin said, looking at her directly. 'I am to tell you that the gifts you gave as tokens of your affection have gone with him through every danger he has had to face. They have brought him joy from despair, and light out of darkness.'

Gael's eyes filled with tears. 'Then they have served their purpose, sir.'

'Good, good!' Eldadus said, clasping his hands together. 'A happy conclusion. That's all now, I take it?'

Gael turned to him. 'Uncle, please will you pray with me for my father's safe return?' she asked. The bishop smiled.

'Of course, my dear. Come, we'll kneel before the cross of our saviour. Please bear with us a moment, young sir.'

They knelt side by side before the little altar and bowed their heads. Kerin glanced around the room. Morwen nodded towards the side table. Standing beside the candle was a silver communion chalice, heavy and solidly forged. Seizing it with both hands, Kerin brought it down hard on the back of Eldadus's head. The bishop crumpled onto the floor with a grunt. Kerin seized Gael and crushed her in his arms, then drew his dagger and crept to the door. Gwrth was leaning on his spear, staring along the empty gallery. Kerin grabbed him round the neck and drove the dagger into his back. Gwrth's eyes rolled as he struggled and died. Kerin freed his dagger and let him fall. He would have preferred not to kill Gwrth, but Gael's life was in his hands, and he would have killed the whole of Glevum to save her if necessary. He seized Gwrth under the arms and dragged him inside the room. Gael and Morwen stared at the bloody corpse.

'I had to,' Kerin said. 'Now, quickly. Balin will be here before long.'

'My lyre!' Gael exclaimed. She dived under the couch, dragged out a bag with a long strap and slung it on her back. They ran along the echoing gallery. A guard was standing at the foot of the marble staircase. Kerin drew his sword.

'No,' Morwen whispered. 'I've known this one for a long time. Leave him to me.'

'Morwen!' Gael said. Morwen pressed her hand.

'Go, my lady. And love this man well. He's come far enough to find you.' She ran lightly down the stairs. The guard turned as she touched his shoulder. Morwen smiled coyly, murmured something inaudible and slipped her arms round his waist. The guard chuckled and leaned his spear against the wall. He grabbed Morwen and kissed her hungrily. Morwen freed herself, giggling, and disappeared round the corner. The guard followed her. A door slammed.

Kerin grabbed the abandoned spear and they walked quickly down the long dim corridor towards the main entrance. A pair of guards appeared in a side passage.

'Hey, wait!' one shouted. Kerin hurled the spear. He heard the familiar hiss as it travelled; the heavy thud as it found its mark. The other guard gave chase, bellowing for assistance. Kerin seized Gael's hand. Voices were shouting not far off. They ran for the main entrance. The mosaic court opened ahead of them.

'Look out!' Gael shrieked. Kerin ducked as a blade sliced the air above his head. He hurled Gael to one side as three guards fell on him. Hacking and slicing, they drove him backwards into the open. He dropped one with a sword through the heart. The dead man's sword spun in the air. Gael seized it in a two-handed grip and slashed the nearest guard across the thighs. Two more came pounding down the corridor, one a bearded giant with forearms like Lud's. A spear whistled past Kerin's ear and sank itself in the bearded man's chest. He pitched backwards, clutching at the shaft. Hooves rattled and Vortigern was on top of them. Another man fell, his neck spouting blood. Vortigern leaned down and swung Gael up onto his mare's quarters. Kerin ran after them as the remaining guards fled, howling for Gwrth.

'Guards!' a thin voice screeched from an upstairs window. 'Oh merciful God in heaven!'

Kerin cursed himself for not hitting the bishop harder. He reached the steps as Vortigern loosed the grey mare and tossed Gael onto her back. Eldadus was coming down the steps. He had found more guards. Kerin ran for the gate, heaved the bar aside and swung it wide open. Vortigern threw Blaidd's reins to Gael and whacked the grey mare's rump with the flat of his sword-blade. 'Ride!' he roared. Kerin seized Blaidd's mane as he flew past and vaulted onto his back. A spear grazed his thigh and bounced off the paving stones. They clattered through the gateway. A band of horsemen appeared, just visible at the far end of the street.

'Balin!' Gael gasped. Bertil's warriors bore down at the gallop. Above the racket of hooves Kerin heard swords clashing in the courtyard.

'Kill the bastard and his whore!' Balin bellowed, swinging an axe round his head. They raced down the street towards the river. At the corner Kerin glanced behind, in time to see Vortigern and his warhorse hurtle through the gateway under the noses of Bertil's warriors. Balin hurled his axe. It spun through the air before striking the wall and rebounding harmlessly onto the cobbles. Vortigern caught up with Kerin and Gael on the wharf, and they galloped for the fringe of the city, past houses where torches were being lit as the commotion brought people from their beds. A huge stack of empty casks was standing against the wall of a merchant's warehouse. Kerin leaned out and jerked one of the lower ones free, sending all the rest rolling into the road. Balin and his men roared with rage and dismay as they encountered the unexpected obstacle. The crossing was less than half a mile upriver, and no warrior of Glevum had dared to cross it in anger for years.

'We've done it,' Kerin breathed. 'Oh God, we've done it!'

He reached out to touch Gael's fingers, laughing aloud with joy and relief. The road veered towards the crossing. They drove their horses into the shallows. The sky was turning from black to deep blue over the hills behind Corinium, shooting a pale, cold gleam across the gliding water. The horses swam steadily through the deep central channel, pulling against the current. The river bed rose beneath their feet again, then banks of mud and shingle, and then the soil of Cambria. The riders reined in and looked back. Balin and his warriors were watching impotently from the far bank. Vortigern looked Gael up and down. His black cloak was cut to shreds and his face and forearms were liberally smeared with blood. She looked back with an apprehensive smile.

'Well,' Vortigern said, 'at least you picked one who can ride.'

48

Kerin knew the place; they had stopped there before, on their journeys around Cambria. There was a row of shallow caves, just below the brow of a steep hillside whose bare crest rose above a hanging oak wood. A spring bubbled from the rocks, broadening into a swift-flowing stream as it tumbled downhill on its way to the river. The caves were always dry, and there was plenty of timber and brushwood for cooking fires. They reached the place just before dawn. The smell of wood smoke and roasting venison came to meet them. Lud and the others crowded round, laughing, cheering and slapping their backs as they dismounted. Kerin lifted Gael from her horse and held her tightly while the merry crowd jostled around them.

'He told me what you were up to, lad,' Lud said, gripping his shoulders. 'No less than you deserve. And look, you've brought home a beauty!' He flung his arms around Gael, almost suffocating her. 'There's a fire for you in that little cave behind the bent alder. I daresay you can do without the meat just now.'

The cave was warm, and Lud had spread his own blanket on the floor beside the fire. Kerin unfastened his sword-belt and let it fall.

'Are you alright?' he asked. 'Are you cold?'

Gael smiled. 'I'm alright,' she said. 'And I shan't be cold for long.' Kerin laughed and pulled her tightly to him. A shadow fell across them. Vortigern appeared at the mouth of the cave, a figure all black except for the wink of the firelight in his eyes and on the golden clipeum. Gael ran to him and clasped his hands. 'I don't know who you are, sir, but you saved our lives tonight. We can never repay you.'

'Payment is not in question,' Vortigern said. 'Kerin's quarrels are mine, as mine have always been his.'

'Are you his warrior, then?' Gael asked. Vortigern chuckled.

'No, child, it's the other way round,' he said gently. 'I'm Vortigern of Glywysing.'

Gael's eyes widened in dismay. 'Forgive me, lord!' she exclaimed. 'But to risk your own life for your warrior, and a blood-enemy's daughter –'

'Enough of that,' Vortigern said. 'If a man can't face the dangers he expects his warriors to face, he's no man at all. But then a man who has to beat obedience into his daughters is no man at all, so perhaps I shouldn't expect you to know better.'

Gael lowered her eyes. 'Lord, my father is no coward,' she said.

'No?' Vortigern asked. 'What is he, then? What terrible thing has he done, to make you run away from his house for this young nobody?'

'Lord, he married me to an evil man, old enough to be my father,' Gael said indignantly. Vortigern raised his eyebrows.

'A fate worse than burning,' he said. Gael's brow creased. She seemed aware of having said something inappropriate, although she could not possibly have known why.

'Lord, I love your warrior Kerin Brightspear, and if I can't have him, you can burn me whenever you like,' she said. Vortigern regarded her curiously.

'You're not afraid of me, are you,' he said. Gael gave a confident smile.

'No, lord, I am not.'

'Why not?' Vortigern asked, with a trace of indignation. 'Most people are. And you must have heard what your bishop has to say about me.'

'Oh yes, lord. He says you're a murderer and a heretic, and a friend of the heathens. And that you've lost your soul, of course.'

'Well, then?' Vortigern enquired.

'Lord, Kerin has told me what you did,' Gael said. 'It couldn't have profited you to save him. He was a poor man's child, an orphan, with nothing to give you. Any man who would save a child like that cannot quite have lost his soul.'

Vortigern took her by the shoulders and kissed the top of her head. 'There's someone here you should see,' he said. They turned. Brother Padarn was standing just outside the cave.

'Good evening, lad,' he said. 'I wasn't too polite to you, the last time we spoke. Am I forgiven?'

'There's nothing to forgive,' Kerin said. Padarn cleared his throat.

''In that case I could do you a service, if you want,' he said. 'I've already married the Lord, here. I've got a cross and some wine, and you've been wearing that ring round your neck for months, so you may as well put it where it belongs. On the marriage finger, I hope.'

Gael gave a little gasp and seized Kerin's hand. 'Brother!' she exclaimed. 'Can you do this? Here? Without my father's permission?'

'I can,' Padarn said. 'I've got God's permission, and your father's a bastard. So if you're minded to marry this young lunatic, let's go down to the fireside. There's a crowd of witnesses there waiting for us. Pagan girls, enemies' daughters, I don't think it's here or there for them.' He gave Kerin and

461

Vortigern a look. 'You two might want to wash the blood off first, though, and give the lady a moment to tidy up.'

Padarn had placed his cross on a fallen tree trunk, which someone had covered with his horse blanket. A little amphora stood beside the cross, with two of the battered pewter mugs the boys used for herbal brew when the warband was on the march. Torches burned to each side. Kerin stood in front of the makeshift altar with Vortigern on one hand and Lud on the other, petrified with nerves.

'What can be taking her so long?' he murmured. Lud snorted.

'Get used to it, boy,' he said. 'It takes Mora half the day to get dressed.'

There was a movement at the mouth of the cave. Gael and Rowenna emerged together and processed, arms linked, down the steep path towards the fireside. Gael was wearing an exquisite deep blue gown which, Kerin supposed, must have come from one of Rowenna's travelling chests. It was a little too long for her, and her free hand was holding its skirts clear of the ground. The fluid drapes shimmered in the torchlight. Her hair was pinned up with silver slides, and an amber necklace glowed at her throat. Saxon ornaments, but Kerin didn't care. He would hold this picture, this moment, in his heart for the rest of his days. As the two women reached the fireside, Rowenna placed her hands on Gael's waist and propelled her gently to Kerin's side.

'Brothers and sister,' said Brother Padarn, 'we come here to join this man and this woman in marriage. If any of you know a reason why they shouldn't marry, speak up now.' There were some stifled chuckles before seriousness took over. The reasons were real, but not one of the men beside the fire would have given voice to them. After all they had endured together the devotion was too deep, the bonds of brotherhood too strong. An argument with Glevum was only one of many things which might kill them before the year was out, and they were prepared for it. They would uphold the king, their infallible light. Perhaps only Gwyndaf of Craig Goch, watching silently from the shadows, understood that there was now more than one hand on the reins of the kingdom.

Brother Padarn joined the hands of the betrothed, and guided them gently through their vows. Kerin stumbled over his, but yes, he would love, honour and be faithful. Padarn left out Gael's vow of obedience. Perhaps he had already deduced that that was a waste of time. As the ring was blessed and slipped onto Gael's finger, the warriors erupted in shouts and applause; then, quite suddenly, they were gone.

'Come on,' Kerin said, kissing his wife. 'Go to what passes for our marriage bed, and take that dress off. There's only one thing I want to think about tonight.'

He went to the mouth of the cave, drew down the lower branches of the alder until they formed a makeshift screen and weighted the tips of the pliant twigs with rocks. Something moved in the darkness beyond. Rowenna had come from the cave next to his. Vortigern shook his head silently, then took off his tattered cloak and wrapped it around her shoulders before gathering her up and carrying her to the shelter of the cave. A sleeping image stirred somewhere deep in Kerin's memory, of a man who lifted a child in his arms on the high moors of Henfelin, and set him on the back of a chestnut mare.

*　*　*

They made love and slept, more than once; but some time later, Kerin awakened to the sound of shouting, horses whinnying, the crash of breaking branches. Brilliant sunlight was filtering in through the alder screen. Gael sat up with startled eyes.

'Lord, they've crossed the river!' Bened bellowed from beyond the camp. Kerin could hear it already. Hoofbeats, the chink of bridle rings and weaponry. Fast horses. Armed men.

'Stay here,' he said, flinging on his clothes. 'And keep Rowenna with you.' He grabbed his sword-belt and ran out into the sunlight. Vortigern was standing in the clearing beside the smoking remnants of the cooking fire. Gwyndaf was there with sword, spear and daggers. Rufus came out of the trees with five of his followers and leapt from his horse. Barking an order to his men, who stayed where they were, he marched across the clearing.

'Why?' he shouted. 'Why, when you could have had any woman in the kingdom?'

'I can kill him now, if you like,' Gwyndaf said calmly.

Look at me, Kerin thought. The force of his gaze drew Rufus's eyes. There was nothing there but unshakeable certainty. Rufus turned to his father.

'Send that woman back to her people, and tell them all to get out.'

Vortigern stared back. 'And if I don't?'

'If you don't, we'll do it without your help. I know you've sent men to Kent to protect Hengist's settlements. I think you should send word to them this moment, and bring them back to Cambria where they belong.'

'You think?' Vortigern said incredulously. '*You* think?'

'Yes, I do,' Rufus said. 'Because if you don't remove them, we'll have to fight them.'

Vortigern looked at him in disbelief. 'You'd fight your own kinsmen? Cambrians? Your own countrymen? For the sake of Garagon's pestilent cornfields?'

'No!' Rufus exclaimed. He seized his gold crucifix and thrust it out. 'For this! Eldof and Garagon are sworn to me, and there will be others. We already have a bigger army than you could raise if you turned Cambria upside down and shook it until it was empty.'

Vortigern's hands clenched. 'My army. Publius Luca's army! How many of them have you poisoned already?'

'One or two,' Rufus said, without a blink. 'But that's not where our strength lies. What do you think I was doing in Gallia, riding around on a beach and listening to old men spout poetry, like you do at home? We have men, thousands of men, and weapons you've never even dreamed of.'

Vortigern's face bore the dumb shock of a man stabbed by an unsuspected knife. 'All those months ago? Before we'd even set eyes on the Saxons? When I was risking my neck to raise arms against the Picts?'

Rufus ignored the question. 'Go on,' he said. 'Go home. Stand on top of the highest mountain in Cambria, and tell everyone that you're the King of all the Britons. It means nothing. You may as well hand the crown to me now, because if you fight us, we'll crush you. I won't fight you here, but cross the river and you're a dead man.'

Gwyndaf moved so quickly that Kerin saw nothing more than a flash of grey and a metallic glint. Vortigern grabbed his wrist and the blade sliced the breast of Rufus's tunic. Gwyndaf dropped the dagger with a growl and stalked away. Rufus gaped, his hand moving to the rent in his tunic. Vortigern picked up the dagger. The blade was thin but lethal, easily long enough to have pierced a man's heart. There was blood on its fine tip.

'I'm glad that my mother's at peace,' Rufus said, backing away. 'If she could see you, defiling yourself with that –'

'Shut up,' Vortigern breathed. 'And don't mention that girl in the same breath as your sainted mother.'

Rufus's eyes blazed. 'Why not?' he shouted. 'You take her to the same bed.'

The blade flashed in the air. Kerin lunged forward, but as he moved, Vortigern flung the dagger away. Kerin seized Rufus by the shoulders.

'That's your third life gone. Get out while you can.'

Rufus twisted free. One of the white-clad warriors brought up his horse and he scrambled onto its back. 'Paulinus met us on the road,' he said, voice shaking. 'He told me what you said to him. And about the letter. You burned my letter.'

'The letter from the Lord Vortimer?' Kerin gave him a withering look. Rufus flinched.

'I didn't know how to address you. You're not the man I knew.'

'I'm exactly the man you knew,' Kerin said, keeping his voice low and steady. 'Not Lord anyone. A horse-thief's bastard, who keeps his word and pays his debts. I don't want to hurt you; it's the last thing I want. But lift a finger against your father, and I swear I'll drop you where you stand.'

Rufus reined back. 'You even sound like him now.'

'All the better if it works,' Kerin said, following the retreating horse. 'And we should speak with one voice. Your father will be king for as long as we both live. Accept it, or kill me. It's that simple.'

'I cannot possibly accept it!' Rufus shouted. 'And you can't prevent this. I have thousands to call on.'

'Bring them, then,' Kerin said. 'But as someone just told your father, cross the river and you're a dead man.'

'Do you think we should leave, Lord Vortimer?' one of the warriors asked, a little uneasily. Rufus leaned down and seized Kerin by the shoulder.

'I pray we don't meet in battle!'

'It's in your hands,' Kerin said. 'We won't be the ones to start it.' Rufus made no reply. Kerin turned aside. Something wet hit his cheek; tears, horse sweat? God knew, but it tasted of salt. The riders crashed away through the wood. Kerin watched them go.

'I heard it all,' a voice said at his shoulder. 'You've burned your bridges now.' Kerin turned. He had not realised that Vortigern was standing behind him.

'I burned them a while ago,' he said. 'And anyway, Rufus gave me the torch.'

'I know. But it was your choice to use it. And he was right. I could almost hear myself speaking.'

Kerin bent to pick up the dagger. He had no doubt that Gwyndaf would be needing it. 'After Hengist's feast, you thought I'd gone for good,' he said. 'So did I. But months ago, I was told that I had a task to do. By a much wiser man than I'll ever be. At the time I had no idea what he was talking about, but that night I understood. When you became king, Father Giraldus said that it would be a crown of thorns. I can't wear it for you. But I'll blunt the thorns, if I can.'

Vortigern's eyes held a silent acknowledgement. He flung an arm around Kerin's shoulders and they walked slowly back to the fireside.

'Was that your son?' a tearful voice asked. Rowenna had come from the caves with Gael, and they were standing at the foot of the bank with their arms around each other. What could they possibly have been thinking; these two women who had left family and all they had ever loved, to marry men they hardly knew?

'Yes,' Vortigern said, watching the gap in the trees. 'He was my son, once.'

Gael moved to Kerin's side and took his hand, as if to confirm that, whatever terrors the future held, they were now hers to share. Above the harsh calling of disturbed birds, Kerin could hear the horses plunging into the river. He thought of Rufus lying defenceless in the dirt with the point of Vortigern's sword at his throat, and thought, 'You should have killed him then.'

Author's Note

In approaching *Under The Dragon*, I should begin where I began in my note to The West Rises. My retelling of Vortigern's story is fiction, not serious history; or at least, a fictionalised account of what we know, intertwined with events which may have happened. As the story progresses this becomes more apparent, as the High King's fictional associates acquire lives, loves and preoccupations of their own. But throughout the writing, I have tried to stick to two principles. Firstly, to ground a story which is known largely through legend in enough knowledge of the age to make it credible. Secondly, not to write about anything which would have been frankly impossible. Unforeseen archaeological discoveries may yet catch me out here, but in the meantime, my aim is to turn a story worth telling into one which is worth reading.

Quite a few readers have asked me if it would be possible to provide a map. Vortigern and his people do move around a lot in this second book, and I hope that the map will help to keep track of them – not always easy, in an age when most places had more than one name. Places which had their own names before the Romans arrived were given Latin names by the occupiers. Over time, these names were sometimes conflated. Educated Romano-Britons would probably have used Latin or Latinised names, while the old Brythonic names clung on in rural, less Romanised areas. As in *The West*

Rises, this story has a mixture of Latin and British names. I don't claim consistency or historical accuracy. I've used the ancient Kernow for Cornwall, but I've stuck with Kent, not too far removed from the Latin Cantium or Welsh Ceint. In all cases, as with the map and glossary of place names, my aim has been to make clear what is happening, and where.

Having mentioned the art of the possible, I should mention that I've given my Welsh warriors a formidable asset – the fighting horse. A state-of-the-art weapon which their enemies don't have. Fighting war dogs have always been well known; the Romans were famed for the molossus, ancestor of today's mastiff. It was largely a matter of encouraging the dog's natural fighting instincts, more prevalent in some breeds than others. But horses; who knows? Vortigern touches on it in *The West Rises*, when his warhorse attacks a man who attempts to take her reins from him. I've never heard of them being trained to do more than carry warriors into battle, but anyone who has ever watched horses fighting will know what a brutal, vicious business it is. Could all that destructive power be channelled? I've spent a lot of time on horseback, so I have an idea of the potential limitations. For the rider, the greatest challenge would probably be to stay on whilst not getting injured or killed themselves. For the horses, there could hardly be more risk of injury or death than they already faced every time they went to war. It's an interesting question, but the caveat 'don't try this at home' could rarely have been more appropriate.

As you may know, the dragon of the title isn't the mythical beast of legend, but a battle standard based on one used by the Romans. It was known as a draco, and the man who carried it was called a draconarius. It consisted of a dragon's head on a pole, with a long sleeve or tube of fabric attached to the neck, which hung limp when the rider was at rest but streamed out in the wind when the horse galloped. It is thought to have originated with the cavalry peoples of the steppes – the Sarmatians, Alans, Parthians and Sassanid Persians – and was probably adopted by the Romans some time in the 2nd Century AD, when Sarmatian cavalry were incorporated into the Roman army. The dragon's head was probably constructed by hammering copper alloy over a carved original. It's thought that the draco made a noise, probably a hissing or shrieking sound, and that this was loud and eerie enough to frighten the daylights out of the enemy. In 2005, Channel 4's Time Team constructed a draco and, after much trial and error, concluded that this noise was probably made by a number of fine wind flutes (as in the Chinese kite-making tradition) and that they were probably mounted just below the dragon's head rather than within. They managed to build a draco whose whistle/shriek was audible 200 metres away, above the sound of the charging horse.

It's quite feasible that Vortigern's cavalry would have used a battle standard like this. The Roman army was a daily reality in Britain for 400 years. Older people would remember the mounted units – some of them only too well. They would have passed their stories on, just as we have learned about World War II from listening to parents and grandparents talk about their experiences. In Wales, it's widely believed that the red dragon of the Welsh flag, Y Ddraig Goch, may be a descendant of the draco.

If you follow me on social media, you will know that *The West Rises* was shortlisted for the adult fiction prize at this year's Selfies Awards, which were founded to recognise the best independently published books of the year in the UK. Even though my book didn't win, I was both shocked and delighted even to be on the shortlist with a first novel – it was so encouraging.

Acknowledgements

The people who have helped me bring this book to life are, with few exceptions, the same as those who contributed so much to *The West Rises*. Rebecca Horsfall, for her constructive criticism, and for seeing all the faults which I am too close to the work to see. Jane Dixon Smith, for her terrific covers, elegant interiors and – on this occasion – a lovely clear map, which several readers have requested to help them navigate around Dark Age Britain. Debbie Young, whose advice and encouragement continue to help me, long after the end of her Simply Self-Publish course.

Under The Dragon takes its title from the draco, the ferocious-looking battle standard of the Roman cavalry. Many thanks to Robert Vermaat and the members of Fectio Late Roman Re-enactment Group, for allowing me to use the photographs of their magnificent draco, who can be seen in action on the front cover of this book. Special thanks to Robert for the phenomenal amount of research into early British history which he has made available online for many years – a treasure trove of information.

Finally, and as always, thank you to my family and friends for your constant support, patience, faith and love.

About the Author

Photography by Raul Rucarean (www.raphotography.org.uk)

Born in South Wales, S.M. Davies read English at Cambridge, specialising in medieval literature and exploring the history which underlies the spellbinding legends of Early Britain. After graduating she worked as a professional indexer for leading publishers, usually on historical texts – everything from Ancient Babylon to World War Two. Since then she has spent her working life on the Gower Peninsula, first as a farmer, then a hotelier, and finally as a pub and nightclub owner. During these years she continued her research and wrote the first draft of the High King series, much of it based amidst the Welsh landscapes she knows and loves. She still lives on the edge of Gower, close to her children and their families, and shares her home with her sheepdog.

See where it all began …

Thank you for reading *Under The Dragon*.

If you have enjoyed it, and would like to know more about some of the characters you have met, go to smdaviesauthor. com/the-foundling to join the High King Readers' Club and receive your free copy of *The Foundling*. This eBook is a free, no-obligation download, available exclusively to members of the Readers' Club, and will not be available elsewhere.

The Foundling is a short story about the night, many years earlier, when Vortigern saved the infant Kerin from certain death. Only the barest outline can be deduced from *The West Rises* and its sequels. Vortigern's story is seen through Kerin's eyes, and the young warrior was a newborn baby when these events took place – the foundling of the title.

Members of my Readers' Club will receive an occasional email about forthcoming books, my research for the series and the locations where it is set. You'll have first access to any free offers, including another short eBook later this year. I care about your privacy, and it'll be easy for you to unsubscribe from the list should you ever wish to. All downloads are yours to keep regardless.

Once again, thank you for reading my books. If you have enjoyed them, and would like to tell others what you thought about them – whether by leaving a review on Amazon, Goodreads or any e-store, or on your social media – that would be great. Word of mouth matters more than anything to a writer, and any effort you make will be much appreciated.

SMD

Coming Next –
High King 3

A fragile peace is shattered on Midsummer's Eve when Rufus's allies strike a cruel blow, forcing Vortigern's hand. Conflict breaks out in Kent as Hengist's Jutes fight to keep the land granted to them. Kerin, the High King's indispensable companion, must rally the battle-weary armies of the West and seek new allies to confront Vortigern's power-hungry rivals, as they proclaim Rufus king and bring reinforcements from overseas. Amidst the chaos and brutal conflict in Kent, Rowenna and Hengist both show their true colours. Desperate to protect his homeland and Gael, his new wife, Kerin will risk everything to hold the river as Rufus's armies sweep towards Glevum. When Gael's beloved friend Father Septimus brings news of a plot to assassinate Vortigern and the Cambrian leadership, Kerin and Father Iustig make a dangerous journey to Glevum, to try to pre-empt it. Rufus denies all knowledge of the plot, but is still set upon invading Cambria in the spring.

At Midwinter, Rowenna's attempt to win over Rufus puts her own life in peril. Gael welds the women of Henfelin into a formidable resistance force as Vortigern and Kerin prepare their defences; but shocking news from Glevum will threaten to destroy everything they are fighting to preserve.

For more about High King 3, visit my website www.smda-viesauthor.com where I will post more news as publication approaches.

Get in Touch!

Thank you for reading my books. I hope that you have enjoyed *The West Rises* and *Under The Dragon*, the first two books in the High King series. If you would like to know more about the historical background, my research, future books or my writing life, it would be great to hear from you. Visit my website, smdaviesauthor.com, where you can contact me – or why not join the High King Readers Club? You will be the first to hear news about forthcoming books, and you'll get exclusive free downloads, as well as interesting stuff about the books, their background and how I write.

Or follow me on social media –
https://www.facebook.com/smdaviesauthor
https://twitter.com/SmdWelshAuthor
https://www.instagram.com/smdaviesauthor
Buy my books from Amazon, or The Great British Bookshop.